"The Squeaki

and

"The Evil Gnome"

TWO CLASSIC ADVENTURES OF

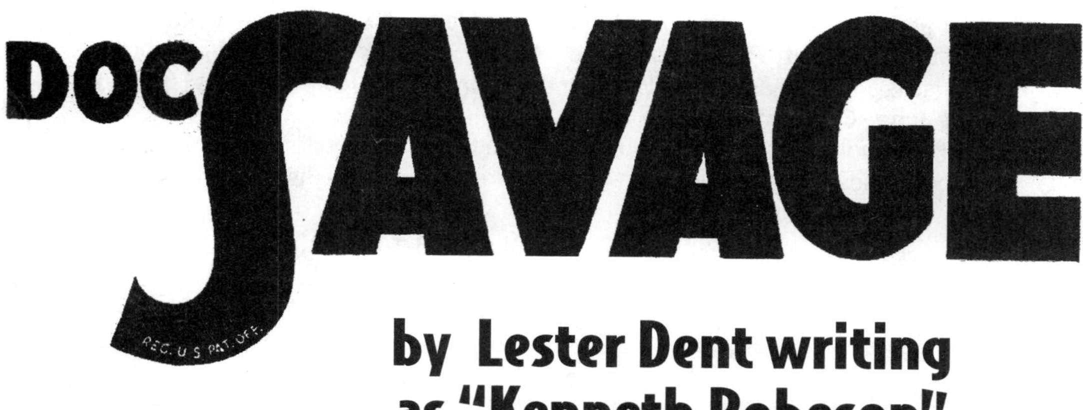

by Lester Dent writing
as "Kenneth Robeson"

with new historical essays by Will Murray

Published by Sanctum Productions for
NOSTALGIA VENTURES, INC.
P.O. Box 231183; Encinitas, CA 92023-1183

This Nostalgia Ventures edition is an unabridged republication of the text and illustrations of two stories from *Doc Savage Magazine,* as originally published by Street & Smith Publications, Inc., N.Y.: *The Squeaking Goblin* from the August 1934 issue, and *The Evil Gnome* from the April 1940 issue. This is a work of its time. Consequently, the text is reprinted intact in its original historical form, including occasional out-of-date ethnic and cultural stereotyping. Typographical errors have been tacitly corrected in this edition.

ISBN: 1-932806-85-7 13 Digit: 978-1-932806-85-4

First printing: November 2007

Series editor: Anthony Tollin
P.O. Box 761474
San Antonio, TX 78245-1474
sanctumotr@earthlink.net

Consulting editor: Will Murray

Copy editor: Joseph Wrzos

Proofreader: Carl Gafford

Cover restoration: Michael Piper

The editors gratefully acknowledge the contributions of Tom Stephens, Jack Juka and the Lester Dent Estate in the preparation of this volume, and William T. Stolz of the Western Historical Manuscript Collection of the University of Missouri at Columbia for research assistance with the Lester Dent Collection. *The Evil Gnome* restorations by Will Murray and Scott Cranford.

Nostalgia Ventures, Inc.
P.O. Box 231183; Encinitas, CA 92023-1183

Visit Doc Savage at www.nostalgiatown.com and www.shadowsanctum.com.

Thrilling Tales and Features

THE SQUEAKING GOBLIN by Lester Dent (writing as "Kenneth Robeson") 4

INTERMISSION by Will Murray 72

THE EVIL GNOME by Lester Dent (writing as "Kenneth Robeson") 75

PULPSMITH 126

Cover art by Emery Clarke and Walter Baumhofer
Interior illustrations by Paul Orban

Dead a hundred years or more, yet so great is its terror among feuding mountaineers that Doc Savage takes up the trail of

The Squeaking Goblin

A Complete Book-length Novel

By KENNETH ROBESON

Chapter I
THE COONSKIN CAP GHOST

THE cream-colored yacht was anchored fully a mile from the nearest shore habitation. That in itself was vaguely suspicious.

It was night and a moon hung high, spilling a silver flood of brilliant light. By that luminance, a close watcher might have perceived two men on the yacht deck, crouched in the shadow of an upper deck awning. Both held rifles, and their attitude was one of a strained waiting and watching.

Other and better coves were to be found nearer Bar Harbor, the Maine summer rendezvous of yachtsmen, but these held anchored pleasure craft of varying size. The inlet where the cream yacht lay was otherwise untenanted. It was as if those aboard wanted solitude.

The watching men maintained silence, keeping their eyes on the shore and occasionally cupping their hands behind ears. One used binoculars.

"See it, Tige?" asked a man with a rifle.

"Ain't sartin," said the one with the binoculars. "Calculate I'll know in a minute."

Tige continued to peer through his glasses at the shore, often lowering them as if he distrusted their prisms, and using his naked blue eyes that were like the snouts of two rifles seen from directly in front.

He was a lean, brindled man with something of the hawk in his face. His slab of a jaw moved regularly and the tobacco it masticated occasionally made a squishing sound.

Sumptuous, luxurious, flamboyant and befitting a king, were descriptives applying to the yacht. The craft hardly exceeded a hundred feet in length, yet she had obviously cost as much as a less pretentious vessel three or four times as long. The woodwork was of mahogany; upholstery was genuine and rich, and there was a profusion of built-in trinkets—bars, indirect lights, radio speakers and the like.

Rugged, rocky, misshapen, a place where anything might happen, described the cove. It was a harsh crack where the stony shore had been gouged by nature, and there were no trees and little vegetation to garnish the place. Boulders were present in profusion, ranging upward to the proportions of a railroad locomotive.

The silver light sprayed by the moon made black, awesome, shapeless shadows behind the boulders, shadows that somehow were like monsters asleep.

"That be it!" Tige breathed abruptly, "I be plumb sartin!"

"Better give the signal, huh?" asked the other man.

Tige hesitated, seemed to consider while his teeth mashed at the tobacco quid; then he shrugged.

"Yeah," he muttered. "But lemme do it."

A moment later, Tige walked out on a wing of the bridge and lighted a cigarette, letting the match flame up like a torch in his fingers for a moment before he twirled it over the rail. The gesture was casual, a natural one—but the match flame could have been seen from shore.

Tige strode back out of sight, dropped the cigarette on the deck and extinguished its tip with a lance of tobacco juice sent expertly through the darkness.

Perspiration droplets, not unlike spattered grease, had come out and covered Tige's forehead while he stood in plain view on the bridge. He scraped some of the sweat off with a forefinger, eyed the moist and slightly glistening digit and shuddered violently.

"Suppose they saw the signal?" asked the other.

"Damn well better have seen it, or reckon as how they'll get fired," Tige growled.

THE cream yacht might have been a floating sepulcher, so dead was the silence which held it. Tige and his companion waited, rifles nursed close to cheeks, eyes on the shore.

"How many times has it tried to get Chelton Raymond?" Tige asked quietly.

"Twice." The other stirred and the moonlight glistened faintly on brass uniform buttons and the shiny visor of a yachtsman's cap. "Thought Chelton Raymond told you?"

"He did." Tige expectorated, and did it so that there was only the noise of the liquid hitting the deck. "You better keep down. That shiny cap bill would make a tolerable shootin' mark."

The yacht officer ducked lower. "Thanks."

"Chelton Raymond gab much?" Tige inquired.

"Gab? You mean talk?"

"Yep. About this thing gettin' after 'im, I mean."

The other hesitated, as if thinking. "No-o-o. He did not talk, exactly. He just said two attempts had been made on his life, and that he was going to send to the Kentucky mountains for what he called 'a real fighting man'."

Tige's chuckle was as emotionless as paper crackling. "Us Raymonds be all fightin' men."

"Chelton Raymond sent for you, and you came," concluded the other. "That's all I know about it."

Silent for a time, Tige scrutinized the shore; the shadows were too much for him, and he shook his head disgustedly.

It would have taken sharper eyes than the gaunt mountaineer possessed to follow the exact course of the skulker ashore—if there was really a skulker, for a close watcher would have doubted at times that the marauder was a flesh-and-blood reality.

There was something of the phantom about the figure, a touch of the supernatural, since the form merged with the dark shadows in uncanny fashion, making no sound appreciable to the ear. An apparition might have been a-prowl.

In the lee of a great boulder the ghostly presence came to a halt, and all of its attention seemed bent upon the yacht.

The yacht portholes—those along the upper decks, were squarish and almost as large as windows, and several were whitened by lights ablaze in the cabins behind. Framed against a port was a head and shoulders, the lines of which indicated the presence of a man in a chair inside the cabin.

On this shadowy outline the attention of the phantom figure seemed to concentrate, and there was a dead silence, stirred only occasionally by the mushy slop of a wave piling onto the stony beach.

Then, out of the black shadow jumped a tongue of flame which could only come from a rifle fired by the ghostly prowler.

Instead of the usual rifle blast, there was only a squeak. It was shrill, almost ear-splitting, a sound such as might be made by a titanic mouse.

The figure behind the yacht porthole upset, vanishing from sight.

THE shore of the rocky cove blasted into life. The boulder shadows spewed men who had been in hiding, men who gripped guns, waved flashlights and yelled.

A flash beam sprouted a glaring wedge which waved and sought the spot where the rifle flame had licked. It came to rest upon a remarkable figure.

There was a ghostly quality about the form outlined by the flash, coming, perhaps, from the dead, immobile grayness of the face. The sunken holes where the eyes should have been, the rigidity of the mouth, gave it a corpselike aspect.

Most striking was the garb of the figure, for the clothing was that of a frontiersman of another century. Moccasins were of beaded deerskin; the trousers were buckskin, the blouse of doe, beaded and fringed. A powder horn was slung over a shoulder. A belt supported a bullet pouch and a sheath containing a long-bladed knife.

Standing high like the headgear of a Cossack, lending an unnatural height to the strange apparition, was a coonskin cap, the tail dangling down behind.

Notable also was the rifle the figure carried. A muzzle-loader, it had an extraordinary barrel length, the barrel being thick, heavy. The weapon was obviously handmade, a rare piece.

Hardly had the flashlight outlined this fantastic form when the rifleman gave a great leap and vanished behind the boulder with a speed which defied the eye.

Half a dozen pistol and rifle slugs screamed through the space he had vacated, the lead being fired by the two men on the yacht and by the other men around the cove edge.

"Git that thar cuss!" Tige bawled from the yacht deck.

More flashlights sprayed radiance. The beams darted, searching. With its confusion of lights, the rugged cove shore became eerie in aspect. Weapons ready, the men advanced.

The rock masses through which they worked made it difficult to light every recess, so they went slowly and kept the white funnels of luminance prowling. The first excited shouts subsided, and their manners became grim, determined, deadly.

"Hit's a crafty critter!" Tige howled from the yacht. "Take a heap a' care!"

One of the men, advancing on the spot where the weird figure in ancient frontiersman's garb had been seen, swore softly.

"Listen to that hillbilly!" he grunted. "He's talkin' like that guy in the fur cap ain't human."

A circle of glaring flash beams, the men closed upon the spot where the deerskin-clad figure had stood. They fanned their lights, staring, and a few hands quivered with tension that arose from expected action. But after a few seconds the searchers swore softly in a low-voiced and dazed manner.

There was no trace of the weird figure in the coonskin cap.

WHAT'S a-happenin'?" Tige yelled. "Did that thar thing git away?"

Every man on the shore noticed that Tige was not speaking of the deerskin-garbed figure as if it were human, and that fact obviously impressed them, especially in view of the uncanny way in which the quarry had escaped.

"Looks like the guy give us the slip," called one of the group on shore, answering Tige.

After shouting, the man brushed back his coat to hook a thumb in a suspender, and a small badge was disclosed, pinned to his vest. The shield marked him as an operative for the Coastal Private Detective Agency. From time to time, badges were visible on the other men, an indication that they were all private detectives of the Coastal Agency.

"Mought as well give up a-lookin'!" Tige bellowed. "You all won't find nothin'."

"Hell!" said one of the detectives. "That bird must've left some tracks in this sand."

"You ain't agoin' t'find nary a one," forecast Tige.

The sleuths began to search, confidently at first, then with an almost stunned carefulness. There were no footprints to be found, although the sand was soft enough to allow them to sink in to their ankles.

"You-all find any?" Tige demanded.

"He must've jumped from one rock to another!" snapped a detective.

"Ya-h-h-h!" jeered Tige. "Ain't no use scratchin' around thur for the varmint. Come a-runnin'. We got tur see if the fisty cuss hit Chelton Raymond with thot thur bullet."

The sleuths hesitated, puzzled. One remarked that he had seen the shadow behind the yacht porthole upset after the loud squeak which had accompanied the flash of the coonskin-capped one's rifle. Tige overheard this statement.

"Come a-runnin'!" Tige howled urgently.

"We'd better do that," grunted a Coastal Agency man. "After all, that hillbilly and Chelton Raymond hired us to take orders."

"We were to be bodyguards, too," interjected another. "A swell job we did of that, lettin' this spook in the coonskin cap come up and take a shot at the porthole of Chelton Raymond's cabin, even after the hillbilly warns us, by lightin' that cigarette, that the thing is prowling around here."

"Horsefeathers! Now you're talking as if the thing wasn't human." The other sleuth was frankly skeptical.

"Well, it got around like a ghost, didn't it?"

They ran down to the water's edge and dragged out a small boat concealed among the boulders. Floating it, they got aboard and paddled out to the yacht.

Tige was not on deck, but the newly arrived detectives could hear loud blows from below, accompanied by an occasional expletive.

The sleuths ran below and found Tige with a fire ax, battering at the door of a stateroom. The blows had a metallic sound.

"Carn-sarned door's locked!" snapped the gaunt Tige. "'Pears like she's made a' iron."

The mountaineer delivered a great smash with the ax, with the result that the blade penetrated the sheet metal. He wrenched it free and struck again, opening a triangular aperture at which he chopped vigorously.

"'Low I kin git a hand in thar directly!" puffed Tige. "Mought be able to unlock the door."

He struck, chopped, wrenched—and the metal squealed and bent; then he thrust a hand through the hole he had made, groping for the knob of the spring lock.

"Here, Tige!" called a new voice. "Let me go in there first."

Tige wrenched his hand out of the hole as if he had taken a hold on something hot. He wheeled, his eyes protruding a little and his mouth sagged far open so that the little lake of tobacco juice within was revealed.

"Chelton Raymond!" he gulped. "You wasn't in this hure cabin!"

"No," said Chelton Raymond. "Damned lucky for me, eh?"

CHELTON RAYMOND was a long, thin man who looked as if he bathed frequently in peroxide. He was very blond. His hair, eyebrows, and waxed and upturned mustache were almost white, and contrasted with his tanned skin. His tan, however, did not have a weathered look, but more the velvety aspect of one who had gone deliberately and carefully about the business of having the sun darken his skin.

The man's clothes were rich of fabric, expert of cut. The frames of the spectacles perched on his sharp hook of a nose were obviously of platinum. He had an air of wealth about him.

He advanced quietly on rubber-soled shoes and reached through the rent Tige had made in the stateroom door.

"I was up forward, watching through a porthole with these." He drew a pair of binoculars from a pocket, then let them slide back. "I kept an eye on the shore after the detectives put off."

"Kaitch sight a' anythin'?" asked Tige.

"Nothing." Chelton Raymond's voice had a drawl which marked him as having spent some time in the mountains, possibly his youth, but it was seldom that he slipped into the abused English which was Tige's vocabulary.

The stateroom door swung open. Chelton Raymond entered, drew Tige inside, then motioned the private detectives and members of the yacht crew back, closing the door after them.

"So you-all fixed a jigger in the cheer to fool the fisty cuss," Tige mumbled, eyeing the chair before the porthole.

Chelton Raymond went over and examined the cleverly constructed dummy of pillows and bed-clothing, coat and a yachting cap, which the chair held. Particularly, he gave attention to the head.

"Look, Tige," he suggested. "See where the bullet struck."

Tige examined the head. "Plumb swack a-tween the eyes."

"Amazing shooting."

"Right peart," Tige agreed. "'Tain't nohow unusual fer thot varmint, though."

Chelton Raymond ran the tip of his tongue under his waxed, blond mustache, keeping his eyes fixed unblinkingly on the gaunt, knobby mountaineer.

"You ever see *it* before, Tige?" he asked abruptly.

Tige moved over to the porthole, stood to one side of it and expectorated a noisy, slanting stream of brown fluid through the port, which was open.

"Kain't say as I have," he muttered. "Thot ain't to say as how I'm a stranger to the varmint, 'cause I been a-seein' a lot a' his work back in my mountains."

"I saw something about it in the newspapers," Chelton Raymond said, nodding slowly.

"Them thar level-land newspapers hain't been a-hearin' the half a' it."

"Tige," the other said slowly, "I want your honest opinion."

"You be my cousin. I wouldn't go fer tellin' you no lies."

Chelton Raymond made a grim mouth. "Do you think this fellow in the coonskin cap is actually a ghost? Do you really think he is the Squeaking Goblin?"

"Squeakin' Goblin been dead nigh eighty years or thar'bouts," Tige said slowly.

"I know."

Tige pulled a sigh from deep in his chest. "Tige Raymond Eller ain't never been one to believe in hants, anyhow not a hant of a cuss that's been a-layin' in the grave fer eighty year."

"Don't beat around the bush, Tige," Chelton Raymond said dryly. "Do you think the man in the coonskin cap was human?"

Tige was silent a moment, then took a deep breath and spoke loudly and rapidly, as if desperately resolved to get the words out.

"Thot varmint wur a hant!" he exclaimed. "I'm a-tellin' you it wur a spook, 'cause I shot right at it and thar warn't no sign a' the bullet hittin' nothin'."

SOME moments of silence followed Tige's earnest declaration, both men keeping faces long and sober, as if engaged with thoughts that were gloomy.

"It's silly, of course," Chelton Raymond said at last.

"Yop," agreed Tige. He poked a bony finger thoughtfully into the hole the bullet had made in the head of the chair dummy. "This here ain't so silly, though."

"No." Chelton Raymond, hardening his lips together, was suddenly harsh and wolfish of feature. "Listen, Tige; I'm thinking this is more than you and I can handle."

"A Raymond ain't 'feared a' no man," muttered Tige.

"Hell, no, but this Squeaking Goblin isn't a man. He's been dead more than eighty years, and he was almost a hundred years old when he died, if there's anything to the story about him that my granddad told me."

"We ain't spook fighters, fur a fact," Tige agreed.

"That's the idea. Did you ever hear of Doc Savage, Tige?"

"Who?"

"Doc Savage."

Tige puckered his brows. "Kain't say as I have."

"Your education has been badly neglected, Tige," said Chelton Raymond, and there was no levity in his tone.

Chapter II
THE SAVAGE SUMMONS

CHELTON RAYMOND opened the stateroom door, swung outside and moved along the corridor, the silent and staring detectives making a path for his passage.

The sleuths were curious, but when the tall, expensively dressed blond man made no suggestion that they accompany him, they did not move to do so.

Tige trailed Chelton Raymond. They stepped through bulkhead doors, mounted a companionway and entered a cubicle walled with instrument panels—the radio room. A rather meek young man was handling the instruments.

"I want a shore line," said Chelton Raymond briskly. "Get the Aquatania Hotel in Bar Harbor, hooking up by telephone."

The radio man flicked switches; generators began to hum. After some moments of low-voiced speaking, the operator spun in his swivel chair.

"Your connection, Mr. Raymond," he said. "Radio-land line hookup."

Tige looked on, as his blond and more sophisticated cousin lifted a mouthpiece-receiver set, and there was an almost open-mouthed wonder in the gangling mountaineer's expression. The look told plainly that Tige was awed by the fact that one could converse from the boat to shore with such ease. Radio transmitters were evidently foreign to Tige's environment.

"Aquatania Hotel?" Chelton Raymond asked over the radio-land line hookup. "It is. . . . Has Doc Savage registered there yet? . . . When he does, tell him Chelton Raymond desires his presence at once aboard the yacht."

With a few words, the blond man gave the location of the cove where the yacht was anchored. Then he hung up, nodding at the radio man to break down the connection.

Tige blinked. "You already sent fur this hure feller?"

"I radioed for him this afternoon," Chelton Raymond admitted.

"You 'lowed as how we'd need 'im?"

"Don't we?" the other demanded dryly.

"Yop. We be needin' somebody." Tige knobbed a fist and looked at its flinty hardness. "Mought take a pow'ful lot a' man to put the fritz on this hure Squeakin' Goblin spook."

"This Doc Savage is a 'powerful lot of man,' as you call him."

"How d'you know?"

"I've heard talk, Tige."

"I ain't never heard a' him."

"Talk don't get around the mountains much, Tige."

"Yop, thot's so. This hure Doc Savage—whut mought be the trade thot he makes his livin' with?"

"His profession is helping other people out of trouble, Tige."

Tige drew out a twist of native "long green," then extracted a knife from a holster inside his shirt. As indicated by certain small marks, the long and razor-sharp blade had been hand-hammered from a file. He cut himself a fresh chew.

"Doc Savage be a hired fighter?" he asked. "Thot it?"

"No!" Chelton Raymond shook a vehement negative. "This man never takes money for his services."

That seemed to bewilder Tige. "He don't go fur to take no pay?" he asked incredulously.

"Doc Savage is an unusual character—a very

famous individual," declared the other. "They tell many stories of his great strength and his remarkable knowledge. If we have time, Tige, I'll repeat some of the yarns before he arrives."

"Be he a lowlander?" Tige demanded.

Chelton Raymond shrugged. "I don't know."

"You ain't called in a furriner, be you?" Tige asked sourly. "Kain't no feller from the low country be man enough to help us."

Chelton Raymond smiled faintly at that. He had been away from the mountains and their people for many years, and contact with the wild scramble of the cities had caused the foibles and pet hates of the mountain folk to become small and trivial in his mind. It struck him as funny that the mountaineers should consider anybody not of their mountains as not worth associating with. Another time, he would have laughed.

ONE of the detectives came running toward the radio room. He was excited; he breathed rapidly as he popped through the door.

"Did you take the bullet?" he demanded.

"What bullet?" questioned Chelton Raymond, not comprehending.

"Slug that was fired at you, of course. The one that went through the dummy you fixed up in front of the porthole."

"No," said the blond man. "I didn't get it."

"We been huntin'." The sleuth threw out his hands, palms upward, to indicate defeat. "We can't find it."

"What?"

"There is a hole in the bulkhead, Mr. Raymond, where the bullet must have hit. It's a small hole, as if the slug wasn't much bigger'n a twenty-two. But there ain't no lead in the hole."

Chelton Raymond came forward suddenly and grasped a handful of the detective's coat front. "Are you sure?" he gasped.

"As sure as I stand here," the detective said earnestly.

Chelton Raymond released his grip and stepped back. He gazed thoughtfully at the floor, at his rubber-soled shoes, then roamed his glance up until he and Tige were exchanging steady, blank looks.

"Hell!" he said. "Not so good."

"'Pears like this spook shoots spook bullets," grunted Tige.

"Spook?" said the detective. "There ain't no such animal."

"So I always thought," Chelton Raymond agreed.

"Mought be," corrected Tige. "If thot be the Squeakin' Goblin, he's sure enough a spook, 'cause my great-grand-daddy shot the Squeakin' Goblin plumb dead comin' on eighty year ago."

The sleuth clapped fists on his hips, arms akimbo. "Say, what're you guys givin' me?"

"Did you," Chelton Raymond asked dryly, "get a good look at that figure in the coonskin cap?"

"Did I? You said it. I was holdin' the flashlight that first picked him out."

"How did he strike you?"

"Well—" The detective reached up absently and loosened his collar. "I didn't care much for him. If he didn't have the face of a corpse, I never saw one."

Chelton Raymond nodded vehemently, as if he had seen as much watching from the boat with his binoculars. "You don't watch the newspapers very close, do you?" he asked.

"I read the big stuff," retorted the sleuth.

"This wouldn't be big stuff," the blond man told him slowly. "It would be a small story on an inside page, about a mountain feud in Kentucky. There wouldn't be much. You see, the mountaineers do not talk to outsiders, to lowland men, as they call them. They regard such as foreigners. Many mountain feud killings never come to the attention of the local sheriff, much less to the newspapers outside."

"So what?" grunted the detective.

"So you haven't read those short newspapers items, and that explains why you don't know that a phantomlike figure such as we saw tonight, clad in deerskins and a coonskin cap and with a long rifle, has killed several mountaineers in Kentucky within the last two months."

"Several!" Tige snorted. "More'n thot!"

Chelton Raymond eyed Tige. "How many people has the Squeaking Goblin killed in the last few weeks, Tige?"

"Ain't sure a' the exact number," said Tige, "but hit's more'n twenty."

"WELL for—" The detective gulped, swallowed. "Twenty!"

Tige nodded soberly. "Ain't be no less'n thot."

"Twenty! Hell's bells! And *that* hasn't been in the newspapers?"

"Why should we-all 'uns peddle our troubles to lowlanders?" Tige growled.

Chelton Raymond put in dryly to the detective, "So you see why Tige and myself called in the Coastal Detective Agency."

"Yeah—for protection."

"Exactly. This Squeaking Goblin—this phantom, appeared and on two different occasions took shots at me. Once, the bulletproof window of my car saved me. The second time, the shot was directed at a mirror in my home, the sniper evidently being fooled by my reflection. I sent for Tige."

Tige nodded. "Raymonds stick by Raymonds, so I come a-runnin'."

"You sure it was the same guy who fired the first two shots as let that one go tonight?" asked the Coastal operative.

"The same rifle, at least. There was no sound of a shot in each case—only that loud squeak."

The sleuth rubbed his nose, pulled at an ear, the gestures indicating an upset mind and much puzzlement.

"But why's this Squeakin' Goblin after you, Mr. Raymond?" he questioned.

Raymond spread his hands. "You guess!"

"Meanin' you don't know?"

"I mean that very thing. I haven't the slightest idea why this Squeaking Goblin wishes to kill me."

The detective turned on Tige. "Well, why's the Goblin shootin' guys back in your mountains?"

"Kain't say," said Tige.

"I hope he ain't doin' it without a reason!" snapped the sleuth.

"Fur as folks kin tell, thar ain't no reason fur his shootin' nobody," Tige muttered.

The operative of the Coastal Detective Agency thought it over deeply, his heavy features wearing a profound expression, then ridded himself of an emphatic opinion.

"Damned if it makes sense," he said.

"Have you heard of Doc Savage?" asked Chelton Raymond.

"Who hasn't," grunted the sleuth.

"I have radioed Savage for help," said Raymond. "I hope there will be no professional jealousy on the part of you or your men when he arrives."

"Jealousy—hell!" The private detective grinned widely. "Say, I'd give my good right arm to see that guy Doc Savage work, just once. They say he's a ring-tailed wizard."

"What do you mean—wizard?" Raymond asked curiously.

"Savage can do anything," asserted the Coastal operative earnestly. "Or so I've heard. And that's no kidding, brother."

SHORTLY after this discussion, the yacht became silent and the lights went out. Chelton Raymond had suggested that the sleuths and the crew retire—with the exception of two guards posted on the upper deck, and three alert detectives, who took up positions on shore.

The cove walls were high and precipitous, and the moon had now descended in the night sky so that it was concealed from view, with the result that long, very black shadows had crept across the cove surface and enwrapped the yacht.

The private detectives on shore were extremely alert and kept close to the shelter of boulders. In truth, their hair felt an absurd inclination to stand on end when they thought of the spectral figure in the wilderness garb of the last century.

"Wonder what that egg who looked like Daniel Boone wanted?" pondered one in a whisper. "I mean—why's he tryin' to croak Raymond?"

"Search me," breathed the second. "It's a goofy business."

"Ain't it," added the third watcher.

A few seconds after this conversation, which could be heard farther away than those who took part in it imagined, there occurred a faint commotion in the cove waters. This was very subdued, and the cause of it approached shore cautiously, coming from the direction of the yacht.

On the beach some distance from where the three detectives conversed, the sound ended. It might have been someone swimming ashore from the yacht. Whatever the presence was, it landed with a minimum of disturbance; after which there was an interval of nearly absolute quiet.

The prowler in the night could move with the stealth of a ghost; the next sound it made was nearly a hundred yards distant, that space having been traversed with the utmost quiet. And it was not noise of physical movement of the skulker that became audible even then, but a product of pure accident, for a night bird took sudden, wild fright at the presence and fled with terrified cries.

By rare fortune, it chanced that one of the detectives had moved along the beach and now stood near enough to be greatly startled by the scared bird. The man held a flashlight. He nearly dropped it in his first shock, then recovered and thumbed the scalding white beam among the boulders. His eyes popped.

Before him stood the apparition in deerskins and coonskin cap, carrying the remarkably long rifle. The features of the figure looked more dead than ever, masklike, cadaverously pale. The eyes were cavities of black shadow that might have been the empty sockets of a skull.

The detective had half suspected to see just this; yet so surprised was he that he could only stand, gaping. In this moment of advantage, the form in deerskins whipped behind a boulder.

Wrenching out a revolver, the detective ran forward. He yelled for his two companions, then dashed his flash beam over the rocky protuberance behind which the figure had leaped. He found nothing. Racing to the rear of the upthrust, he still saw no sign of the ghostly vision.

He looked for tracks. There were none, although the sand was soft.

The other two sleuths ran up. They also

searched, and found nothing. They swapped blank looks.

"Say, I thought I heard somethin' in the water a while ago," muttered one man. "I wonder if that spook could have been on the yacht."

"Yeah!" rasped the second. "If he was, he might've learned Doc Savage has been called, and is gonna show up at the Aquatania Hotel. He might lay for Savage."

"His leather clothes was dry," insisted the one who had glimpsed the eerie figure.

"He could've pulled 'em off an' left 'em ashore 'thout much trouble," snorted another.

"Aw, the spook was just prowlin' and scared a bird an' I heard it," the other said decisively.

Chapter III
SQUEAKING DEATH

THE Aquatania Hotel, a summer resort establishment, stood high above the Atlantic Ocean, on a cliff, down which a sandy, zigzagging path led to the beach.

Immediately offshore at this point were numerous rocks and reefs, some visible only at low tide, against which the waves shattered themselves with an impressive display of white spray.

Southward along the shore some two hundred yards, the rocks disappeared, and there was open access to the beach. Here fishing craft and canoes and motorboats of summer visitors were beached, while offshore were moored yachts and motor vessels of all description and size.

At this late night hour there was little activity along the beach, although on one large yacht a noisy dance was in progress. The blare of brasses, the jangle of strings and the raucous bawl of the hi-de-ho singer made uproar that somehow illy befitted the natural rugged beauty of the shore.

So slowly as to be at first unnoticeable, a faint whining sound came into being and increased in volume. It emanated from the sky, growing loud enough to be heard plainly above the dance jazz.

A dancer on the yacht ran out from under an awning and looked up, then ducked as a great black shape all but blotted the moon for an instant.

A huge, dark plane had appeared. It flashed out to sea, the whine of air past its wings receding, then banked and came back. Besides being large, the aërial newcomer was streamlined until its every curve cried out of speed. It was an amphibian, tri-motored. It was painted a solid bronze color.

The ship landed, taxied close inshore and a grapple anchor was lowered by a concealed bow winch, the anchor cable making a faint noise.

It was while this sound was still echoing that movement might have been discerned on the trail leading down the cliff face. Since the moon was low, the path was lighted at only one point. Past this spot a figure wafted, becoming visible for a moment.

It was the eerie form in deerskins and the coonskin cap. The incredibly long rifle was tucked under an arm.

This ghostly prowler did not descend the full length of the path, but took up a position perhaps halfway down. There, standing in black gloom, the marauder waited. The muzzle-loading rifle was sighted on the plane an instant, as if testing the range, then the weapon lowered and waited.

Out on the water, the plane swung about and rode its mooring like a boat. A hatchlike door opened. A hand of tremendous size gripped the edge of the aperture, and a man hauled himself into view.

The fellow would have weighed in excess of two hundred and fifty pounds, yet so huge were his hands in proportion to the rest of his body, that he seemed small. An expression of profound gloom rode the man's features, which were long and angular.

Half out of the plane door, the big-fisted man peered sourly about. Judging by the acrimonious set of his visage, he held a low opinion of the world in general and of the Maine coast in particular.

Strangely enough, this meant the worthy of the huge hands was well pleased; he had the perverse trait of looking the most gloomy when he was happiest.

This was one peculiar trait of "Renny"—Colonel John Renwick, engineering genius extraordinary.

"Renny!" came a low-pitched voice from inside the plane cabin.

"Yeah?" The long-faced man had a voice so huge that he had difficulty keeping it low. "What's eatin' you, Long Tom?"

"Doc says not to climb outside yet," advised "Long Tom."

"Why not?"

"Man on the cliff with a rifle, Doc says," Long Tom imparted.

Renny did not change expression at the advice, nor did he duck from view so wildly as to arouse suspicion; neither did he linger outside overlong. Once back in the plane cabin, he eyed Long Tom gloomily.

LONG TOM was not "long". His head failed to reach Renny's shoulder. Nor did he offer a picture of robust health, his complexion being sallow, closely akin to that of a mushroom, and his frame in general was marked by a preponderance of bones and a scarcity of flesh. Long Tom looked as if he were a stranger to sunlight. His full name was Major Thomas J. Roberts.

"Holy cow!" Renny thumped. "I didn't see any guy with a rifle."

A number of boxes and cases were racked to the sides of the cabin compartment. Forward, the pilot's compartment was shut off with a bulkhead, which was pierced by a door, and this bulkhead door now opened.

An arm appeared, thrusting through the aperture. There was something incredible about that arm—Renny and Long Tom had seen it countless times, yet sight of the arm now brought faint wonder to their eyes, an expression of awe which long association had not alleviated. The shirt sleeve was rolled back to the elbow.

It was the arm of Doc Savage.

Two things were striking about it: the bronze hue of the fine-textured skin, and the gigantic sinews which cabled the back and wrist, some of the ligaments being almost as large as the fingers themselves. The hand conveyed an expression of incredible strength.

A device which resembled a misshapen pair of binoculars was extended by the hand.

"Have a look," said a voice from beyond the compartment door. The tones were as remarkable as the arm; they held power and a controlled quality of resonance.

Long Tom took the device which looked like grotesque binoculars.

"You got the infra-red searchlight turned on, Doc?" he asked.

"It's pointed at the cliff," said the unusual voice.

Long Tom carried the binocular contrivance back to a cabin window. Before lifting it to his eyes, he glanced outside. Complete darkness swathed the cliff face, except for a spot or two where the moonlight touched, nor were any lights showing aboard the big seaplane.

No surprise appeared on Long Tom's pallid features at the lack of visible light. Long Tom understood fully what was going on, for the pale, slender man was an electrical wizard whose name was known almost everywhere that electrical experts gathered.

In a streamlined mounting on the plane was a searchlight of an unusual type. Its filament was a device which produced a profusion of rays in the infra-red wave bands; the lens was a filter which shut off all visible light, but which had the property of passing infra rays that did not register on the naked eye, these therefore being invisible.

The searchlight was simply one which threw invisible light.

Long Tom knew that Doc had used the infra-searchlight purely as a precautionary move to ascertain the presence of possible danger. Doc overlooked no bets, which was one reason why he had a worldwide reputation.

Clamping the clumsy, binocularlike contrivance to his eyes, Long Tom peered at the cliff face. Use of the device made a striking difference in what could be seen, for the vista of the precipice could now be viewed almost as distinctly as in full daylight.

The oversize eye-glass was an apparatus constructed by Doc Savage—a device that was a product of infinite scientific skill. It made visible such of the infra rays as were refracted. The process by which this was done was an intricate one, probably fully understood only by Doc Savage himself.

Under the invisible light, the cliff had a harsh aspect, and distances were deceptive; there were no colors, the whole being in starkly contrasting black and white, like the negative of a camera film.

"For cryin' out loud!" Long Tom breathed—and passed the glass to Renny.

Renny stared, then emitted the ejaculation which he always employed when startled. "Holy cow! A guy dressed like Daniel Boone!"

LOW orders came from the pilot's compartment, Doc's voice being pitched so that it could not by any chance be heard ashore.

Complying with the commands, Renny and Long Tom lifted a collapsible fabric boat from a locker. This was folded open, the joints locked, the craft deposited in the water, then a light outboard motor attached.

Renny and Long Tom exposed themselves freely and did not indulge in unnecessary staring at the cliff where the weird figure in deerskins crouched. They knew Doc Savage was keeping a watch on the strange rifleman and would give warning if the fellow made a hostile move. They got the boat ready.

"Careful," Doc Savage's voice warned in a low tone. "Our friend in the coonskin cap is due for a little party. We do not want to spoil it. When somebody waits for us with a rifle, he'll bear inspection."

Renny clambered down into the boat; Long Tom followed. They started the outboard. Then Renny lifted his voice.

"Think you'll go ashore before we get back, Doc?" he asked, and his whooping tones carried over to the marauder on the cliff.

"I may," Doc called with equal loudness. "If so, I'll land at the base of the cliff here."

Renny and Long Tom departed at the head of a sudsy ribbon of wake. Their course paralleled the shore, and the low, muffled moan of the small outboard was soon lost to ear. Then there was silence, except for the clamor of the dance orchestra on the yacht, that uproar not having been interrupted by the arrival of the plane.

In the dragging minutes that followed, a night bird spiraled over the beach; waves lathered themselves on the reefs and half-submerged boulders. The dance music pulsed savagely.

The unusual figure in wilderness garb had not moved from the cliff path. The play of words before Doc's two men had departed was holding him there.

Renny and Long Tom appeared at the top of the cliff. They had landed down the shore and circled to flank the skulker.

Doc went into action, for he had been awaiting his two men. The plane motors whooped into life. Mechanism whined and the anchor was lifted more rapidly than it could have been done by hand. Blue flame and smoke spouted from exhaust stacks.

The seaplane darted beachward. From the top of the craft, two expanding rods of glaring white light protruded, waved, found the rifleman in the coonskin cap.

The death-mask face of the figure in deerskins was altogether hideous, even at that distance.

RENNY leaped over the cliff edge and followed the path downward. A glance had shown him there was no other way up, although several ledges did run, shelflike, along the precipice face.

Long Tom waited at the top. In his hand was a gun remindful of an oversize automatic pistol.

The coonskin-capped one had not moved, but stood in the beam of the searchlight while the plane neared the beach. All three motors were fitted with reversing propellers. These now reversed, headway was cut sharply, and the craft grounded gently on the sand. The cabin hatch flew open.

Doc Savage appeared.

The arm of this unusual individual had been something to command attention. His full figure was infinitely more striking. He was a giant in size, yet so perfectly proportioned, each muscle developed with such equality, that his size was evident only when compared with the dimensions of the cabin hatch.

Every line of the great frame advertised an almost incalculable strength. This aspect was made the more noticeable by the unique bronze color of his skin; it was remindful of a bronze paint coating muscles that were great metal hawsers.

The figure in the coonskin cap threw up the long muzzle-loading rifle, took deliberate aim and fired. The gun lipped small flame. There was no sound of a shot—only a loud, gruesome squeak.

Doc Savage was leaping ashore as the long weapon discharged. In midair he twisted; landing, he leaped far to one side. Smooth speed and enormous agility marked this dodging.

The bullet missed him, hit near the shore where the water was less than six inches deep, and dug up a tall geyser of brine. The slug did not glance, being fired at too steep an angle.

On the cliff top, Long Tom yelled angrily. He aimed—his big pistol whacked twice.

The electrical wizard distinctly saw both slugs hit the deerskin blouse of the rifleman—the hide flattened, and a little dust gushed. Yet the man in the ancient garments gave no sign of having been harmed.

"Careful!" Doc Savage called, and the whole beach volleyed with his great voice.

"Shootin' mercy bullets!" Long Tom shouted back. "Won't hurt 'im bad! Make 'im unconscious in a minute."

But the electrical wizard was too optimistic. The figure in deerskins cradled the long muzzle-loader under an arm. A leap of surprising length took him off the trail and to a ledge. He scuttled along this. Boulders shielded him some of the time.

"Watch him!" Doc Savage rapped. "He hasn't time to reload his rifle. Probably he's wearing a bulletproof vest."

The giant bronze man was coming up the cliff face. He made surprising speed, his vast leaps carrying him from ledge to ledge, a hand searchlight which he held boring steadily upon the rifleman.

High above, Long Tom discharged more mercy bullets, slugs which were mere shells containing a drug that brought unconsciousness. But the skin-clad target was a fleeting one, and now sheltered by rocks.

Long Tom, Renny and Doc converged on the quarry. They operated in concert, with no superfluous shouting.

Long Tom and Renny had worked with the big bronze man for a long time. They were two of a group of five assistants who went to the ends of the earth with Doc Savage, helping him in his strange career of assisting those in danger, of aiding the weak and punishing those whom civilized laws did not seem to be able to reach.

The gaunt figure with the long rifle fled wildly. The ledge which he traversed became narrower, the cliff above and below more steep. At the foot of the precipice the beach disappeared, and waves beat into white spume against the naked rock.

"He's gone about as far as he can," Renny boomed. "He'll have to stop in a minute. The ledge plays out!"

But the apparition in wilderness garb did not stop. Still gripping the long rifle, he sailed outward in a great leap, hit the sea and disappeared beneath the surface.

DOC and his two aides kept a sharp watch on the spot where the strange figure had vanished. Bubbles came up for a time, then ceased to rise.

From an inner pocket, Doc Savage drew what looked like a chopped-off candle. He twisted at the top of this and it began to blaze, spraying an eye-hurting glare of light. The bronze man planted the fusee atop a boulder, illuminating the sea for hundreds of feet in all directions. Then they waited.

One minute, two, then a third passed. The rifleman did not appear in the sea.

Doc Savage peeled off coat and vest, kicked free of his shoes, then arched into the water. His entrance into the brine was executed with little splash.

Some time elapsed without Doc reappearing, such a long time that Renny and Long Tom exchanged uneasy glances in the fusee glitter.

"Holy cow!" Renny rumbled gloomily. "Doc should be back on the surface by now."

Long Tom pulled at a colorless jaw. "Say, did you see the face of that bird with the rifle?"

Renny nodded. "Yeah. Looked as if he were dead." He began to tug at his coat. "I'm gonnna see what's keepin' Doc."

"Wait," Long Tom suggested. "I've seen Doc stay under the water longer than you'd think any man could hold his breath."

The unhealthy-looking electrical wizard was a prophet, for there was a turmoil in the green brine, and Doc appeared, trod water for a few seconds, breathing deeply, then glanced up at his two assistants.

"Any sign of him?" he called.

"Not a one," rumbled Renny. "He never came up."

Doc Savage charged his lungs with air, sank, was down for another almost interminable interval, and finally came up. He repeated this. Then he clambered out.

"Water about fifteen feet deep, with a sandy bottom," he advised. "Went all over it. There was no sign of the fellow."

"He must be part fish to vanish like that," Renny growled.

"Here's something else worth thinking about," Doc said thoughtfully. "Remember his rifle? Very long and heavy. A man could not swim easily with that weapon. But there was no sign of it on the bottom."

For some minutes longer they stood on the ledge, scrutinizing the sea, and the certainty came to them that no man could swim underwater a sufficient distance to get beyond the glow of the fusee, for the light was shed over a radius of fully a hundred yards.

"Drowned," Long Tom said emphatically.

Doc led the way back to the plane to get into dry clothing.

Near the craft he paused, then waded out until he stood where the brine was a foot deep, and, crouching, searched with his hands on the bottom. Using the hand searchlight, he located a pocket in the smooth underwater surface of sand. He explored this.

He ... opened his mouth as if to speak, then his eyes flew wide, fixed on the cliff top ...

"The bullet from the muzzle-loading rifle hit here," he said. "I'll get it. The thing might come in handy."

He searched deeper in the sand, using the light often, and finally he stood erect.

"Strange," he said. "It seems to have vanished."

A FRACTIONAL moment after Doc Savage spoke, a strange sound came into being—a weird, exotic trilling note which had the fantastic quality of seeming to come from everywhere, yet from no definite spot. The exotic trilling ran up and down the musical scale, pursuing no tune, defying description, almost unreal, and yet very definitely a concrete sound.

Renny and Long Tom looked at Doc Savage. The bronze man's lips were not moving; there was nothing to show that he was making the sound. Yet they knew Doc was its source.

The note was a vague, unconscious thing which the giant man of metal made in moments of excitement and stress, or when he was moved greatly by surprise. The fact that the trilling came into being now, Renny and Long Tom knew, meant that the bronze man was profoundly stirred.

"The bullet undoubtedly hit here, and it did not richochet," Doc said slowly. "Yet it is gone."

Renny hardened his huge fists. They made vast knobs of gristle, and he knocked them together, creating a noise as brittle as concrete blocks colliding.

"A ghost bullet, eh?" he muttered.

Long Tom frowned palely. "You meant that for a wisecrack, but d'you remember that guy's face?"

"I won't forget it for a long time," Renny rumbled.

"It was the kind of a mug I'd expect to see on a ghost," Long Tom advised dryly.

Chapter IV
MOUNTAIN MEN

ON the yacht, the dance orchestra still made melody of a kind, although a number of individuals lined the rail, staring shoreward, an indication that some of them had glimpsed the excitement, and were curious. One shouted a question, was ignored, and did not press the matter.

The plane lockers held extra garments, and Doc hurriedly exchanged some of these for his water-soaked clothing. Then they shoved the plane off the beach, taxied a little distance out and anchored.

A second collapsible boat—the plane carried three, all told—was rigged for the water and carried them to the beach again, where they stood for a time studying the spot where the rifleman had vanished.

"When he shot at you, Doc, did you catch the sound?" Long Tom queried.

"A squeak," Doc agreed.

The electrical expert sucked at a front tooth. "Queer, eh?"

"The whole thing was a bit strange."

"Any idea what's behind it?"

"Since he was waiting for us, it was obvious he was in a hurry to stop us. Our present mission is to aid this man Chelton Raymond, so it is probable that our friend in the coonskin cap didn't want us mixing in the Raymond affair, whatever it is."

They began to mount the cliff—and Renny, playing a flashlight beam, discerned a small sign in the shape of a pointing hand.

AQUATANIA HOTEL

"This Chelton Raymond was to meet us at that hotel, wasn't he?" the big-fisted man queried.

"Yes—according to the long-distance telephone conversation I had with him in New York," Doc agreed.

"What did he tell you on the phone, Doc?" Long Tom asked.

"He seemed excited," Doc said slowly. "His story was disconnected, although he did make it clear that his life was in danger. On that point, his story was quite coherent. And the menace hanging over him had already accounted for nearly a score of murders, he declared."

"A score!" Renny gulped.

"At least twenty, he put it," Doc replied. "It was that last statement which brought us up here in such a hurry."

Long Tom sucked at a front tooth again; it was a gold tooth.

"Did Chelton Raymond give any particulars on this menace?" he asked.

"Said he'd tell us the whole yarn when we arrived."

"He didn't hint anything about—a ghost in deerskins?"

"No."

They topped the cliff, the coarse sand of the path grinding a little underfoot, and found themselves in a forest of boulders and weathered stone through which the trail led in a rather trying fashion, traversing narrow walks and flights of rustic steps. The place was a gloomy labyrinth.

"Wait!" Doc Savage said softly.

Renny and Long Tom stopped. Renny opened his mouth to ask a question, but voiced no inquiry, however, for their giant bronze chief had faded into the shadows amid the boulders, vanishing as silently as wind-drifted smoke.

"Blazes!" Renny breathed. "Doc doesn't do tricks like that for nothing. Something's up!"

Like the stealth of a great cat, the passage of Doc Savage was marked through the maze of rugged stone. He seemed never to leave the shadow, and after he had traversed a number of yards, he slowed his pace and used even more caution, his gaze fixed upon the trail immediately ahead where an upthrust ledge of stone slanted over it.

Two men crouched there, obviously waiting.

IT was no gadget of science, such as had disclosed the skulker in deerskins, which had shown Doc these two. The bronze man's senses—hearing, sight, olfactory organs—were almost inhumanly keen, thanks to a ritual of exercises developing them, which he had taken each day since childhood. He had distinguished faint movement on the path where the two men waited, the motion caused by their shrinking back at the sound of Doc and his two men approaching.

Very close to the pair now, Doc jutted a flashlight out and put weight on the button. The two men started wildly as light sprayed upon them.

One was young; the other old. The young man was tall, red-headed, a rangy, heavily muscled sorrel colt of a fellow. He squinted tawny eyes in the flash glare, lifted red, lumpy hands in a half gesture of defense, and showed white teeth in a fighting snarl. Somehow he was like a healthy, cornered animal.

The old man had gnarled hands, faded eyes, a sparsely bearded chin, and no hair at all on his shiny head. He was small in stature, would have had to jump up to see over the younger red-headed man's shoulder. He peered into the flash glare with eyes very wide.

"Waiting for something?" Doc asked dryly.

The two continued to stare steadily into the light, trying to distinguish the bronze man behind it.

"Who in tarnation are you?" growled the red-head.

The very bald old man blinked. "Moughtn't you be a-minded to take thot light out'n our eyes."

Doc did not budge the light. "You two had better do some fast talking," he said. "Why were you skulking along the path?"

They were not good actors. The eyes of both shifted simultaneously as they sought to exchange glances. They hesitated. It was the elderly man who spoke.

"We-e-e-l, we'uns heer somethin' thot we figger as how mought be somebody a-shootin'." He paused to stroke his shiny pate. "We was a-comin' to have a look. Ain't no harm in that, be there?"

"That noise you heard was some time ago," Doc pointed out.

"Reckon as how we musta talked hit over a spell," said the elderly man.

The red-headed man put in angrily, "Who're you to be askin' folks a passell a' questions?"

Doc ignored that. "You two live around here?" he queried.

They hesitated about answering; then the old man, who seemed to have the most agile brain, said, "Reckon as how you mought call us visitors."

"Who be you?" asked the redhead for the third time.

"Doc Savage," said Doc, and turned the light briefly on himself.

If the pair had ever heard of the bronze man, they gave no sign of that fact.

"Figger we'uns'll go on 'bout our lookin'," the red-thatched one grunted.

They stepped past Doc and continued down the path toward the cliff edge, walking close together, not looking back. They passed the spot where Doc had left Renny and Long Tom, but did not encounter Doc's two aides, for they had cannily left the path and crept up to listen to what was being discussed.

Renny and Long Tom stepped out of the gloom a few feet from Doc, after the two strangers had gone on.

"Did you hear what was said?" Doc asked them.

"Yep," said Long Tom.

"Follow those two," Doc directed. "Report to me at the Aquatania Hotel. I'm going there to talk with this Chelton Raymond."

THE word exchange was couched in whispers so that the two who spoke in mountaineer dialect would not hear. Renny and Long Tom were careful to make no noise as they set out after the pair.

"That was a fishy yarn they told Doc," Long Tom breathed.

Renny agreed. "They were punk liars," he said.

The two quickened their pace so as to catch sight of the quarry, who had become lost in the darkness. Footsteps of the two ahead, however, were audible, and Renny, listening intently, was sure he could distinguish the clumping of four feet, which meant both of the men were descending the path down the sheer cliff.

"C'mon," Renny whispered. "Hear 'em both on the path?"

Long Tom listened. "Yes, both of them, undoubtedly. They're going down."

Renny leading, Long Tom close at his heels, the two ran forward. They neared the brink. Boulders were profuse about them, very high.

No warning prefaced what occurred next. A long arm clubbed down out of the murk behind a stone mass. The hand on the arm gripped a rock somewhat smaller than a football. The rock and Renny's head, coming together, made a clanking sound. Renny dropped as if poleaxed.

Long Tom gasped, spun around. The mysterious hand snapped the rock at his head. He ducked—and the missile sailed on and over the cliff and downward, after a time sinking with a faintly audible *chung* in the ocean.

Out of the rock shadow came the red-haired mountaineer. It was he who had wielded the rock. He sprang upon Long Tom.

The undersized, pallid electrical wizard did not look as if he were a match for his assailant. The gaunt mountaineer grinned confidently and reached out to gather in his smaller foe. He got a surprise.

Came a dull smack. The sorrel-headed man's mouth flew open, air roared out, and he folded like a limp ribbon about the fist which Long Tom had driven into his middle. With an uppercut, Long Tom straightened him. He hit the fellow again.

The older man appeared, bounding up the trail from the cliff face. In his hands he carried the younger man's heavy shoes.

Seeing the shoes the old man held, it dawned on Long Tom what had happened. The bald fellow had merely gone down the cliff path on all fours, the extra footgear on his hands giving the impression of two men walking which had deceived Renny and Long Tom.

The fight ended shortly after the bald gentleman joined the scrap, swinging the brogans. One heavy shoe descended on the top of Long Tom's head. That stunned him. A blow to the jaw toppled him over, unconscious.

"Tarnation!" puffed the younger man. "Lil' scamp kin scrap!"

His bald companion surveyed the senseless Renny and Long Tom.

"Kinder lucky we thought a' usin' thot there extra shoe trick to see if anybody be a-follerin' us," he grinned.

"What ought we better do with 'em?" asked the other.

The older one did not answer directly, and for a moment there was silence. Then, as if the two understood each other's desires perfectly, they stooped over, the red-thatched fellow picking up Renny's great bulk without undue trouble, and the other handling Long Tom's limp, slighter frame.

They faded quietly into the black shadows with their burdens.

Chapter V
MOUNTAIN GIRL

DOC SAVAGE did not hear such faint sounds as accompanied the reverse which overtook Renny and Long Tom. The bronze man had gone on rapidly toward the Aquatania Hotel immediately after leaving his two aides, and was out of earshot when they met catastrophe.

The Aquatania was a huge, vast lump of native stone, mortar, gables and green roof which could be seen far out to sea. Unlike most resort hotels, it was open the year around.

The cliff path led to a side entrance, so Doc left it and moved across the lawn, ascending steps which led to the veranda.

The lobby was huge, rather cleverly done in native stone and rustic work, and dimly lighted by bulbs behind seashell shades. Doc swung toward the desk.

The lobby had at first appeared deserted, but there was a stir in a corner—a young woman arising from a chair. She came forward rapidly, stopped, and stared at the giant bronze man.

"You-all are Doc Savage?" she asked. In her voice was the smoothness of velvet and the lazy drawl of the mountains.

She had height, and a slender, graceful roundness of figure. Her hair was the yellow of cornsilk, her skin was sun-bronzed nearly the hue of Doc Savage himself, and there were tiny wrinkles at the corners of her blue eyes, a squint that might have come from going bareheaded a great deal in the sun.

"I am Doc Savage," Doc admitted, and studied the girl.

Her age was twenty or less. Her clothing, while neat enough, was certainly nowhere near the current style in cut, and looked as if she had made it herself, although the general effect was nice enough.

"I want to talk to you powerful bad," the young woman said rapidly. "Let's go outside where we can do our talkin' without nobody overhearin'."

Mountain bred—from her voice. She advanced, and it was evident that she was exquisitely pretty.

"I'm Frosta Raymond," she said, "but you ain't never heard of me."

"Any connection with Chelton Raymond?" Doc asked her.

She seemed to grope in her memory, then shook her head slowly.

"No-o-o. Kain't say that I ever heard of one in the Raymond tribe called Chelton."

"What do you want to see me about?" Doc questioned.

The girl drew in breath slowly, then let it out, and there was a faint quaver, a trace of a shudder, with the exhalation.

"I've been a-hearin' that you and your five assistants make a business of helpin' folks out of trouble," she said.

"You are in trouble?"

"Not me, exactly. But I want you to look into somethin'—a somethin' that has killed nigh onto twenty people."

Doc Savage did not change expression, but it was almost these identical words that Chelton Raymond had addressed to him over the long-distance telephone.

"We'll go outside and talk," he agreed.

The screen door of the lobby was fitted with a closing device, and made little noise as they passed through. The girl led Doc to the left, where the veranda jutted out into the shrubbery and boulders of the cliff top, forming a roofless sun porch. The young woman indicated a chair.

"This will do," she said quietly.

As if the words were a signal, there came a wild commotion from the nearby shrubbery. Doc whirled.

Men had appeared, almost a dozen of them. A grimly purposeful swarm, they charged Doc Savage.

DOC glided to one side to get on a part of the veranda which was uncluttered by chairs. He waited quietly.

Most of the strangers were tall, wiry men. There was one exception—a hulking fellow who led the rush. That man was a monster. He was almost as tall as Doc, and the heavier by thirty or forty pounds. His body was tremendous, his head small in proportion; arms and legs were thick and powerful. For all of his bulk, he came in lightly as a dancer. He wore light buckskin moccasins.

"Git 'im, fellers!" he said in a deep, bullfrog voice.

"Hit'll be easy, Jug," one of his followers grunted.

Doc let "Jug" come within a double arm's length, then advanced, doing so slowly, fists up in a clumsy, sluggish fighting position.

Jug showed big white teeth in his small face. He was confident. He sent out thick, clutching fingers, setting himself in his moccasins.

There was a loud report, like a tremendous handclap. Jug slowly lowered his paws, and a pained grimace overspread his features. He wavered, his knees buckled, and he came down heavily on all fours. Then he shook his head and reared up dizzily.

"W-w-what—" His tongue tangled thickly with the words.

"He popped you, Jug," a man growled. "Crimminy! He's mought nigh greased lightnin'! You never even seed him hit!"

They circled warily, surrounding the giant bronze man. Doc stood perfectly still, waiting. Once he glanced around to see how the girl was faring.

She was gone.

"Gang up on 'im!" Jug snarled.

The men rushed. Their hands were empty of weapons, but they seemed supremely confident.

It was a misplaced confidence, for the first two combatants went spinning back before blows from the same fist which had hit Jug with such eye-defying speed. Jug himself was again upset, falling so that the soles of his moccasins showed. A hole was visible in one.

There was something unearthly about the speed with which the bronze giant struck, drew aside, and struck again. Men saw him several feet distant; the next instant they collapsed, and how the big fellow had gotten to them so swiftly, they could not comprehend.

Jug saw the fight was going against his men, superior though his odds were. He was no fool.

"Git yur blamed rifles!" he howled from the hard veranda floor. "Pop 'im with a bullet!"

Men backed away from the fray, dashed into the shrubbery and reappeared with rifles. These were modern, efficient pieces.

"Puttin' out his light is next best to grabbin' 'im!" Jug grated. "Kain't make much difference neither way. Let 'im have it."

Rifles came up.

Doc Savage might have many remarkable qualities, but he was not bulletproof. He flattened below the low veranda rail, traveled lizard fashion to the right—and slammed into the senseless form of one of the men he had dropped with an earlier blow.

Doc shoved the unconscious one ahead, picked him up, and carried him as he leaped into the shrubbery.

Jug swore round mountain oaths in a choked voice. With his followers, he rushed in pursuit of Doc. But the bronze giant had merged with the night in magical fashion, carrying his burden.

The mountaineers—they were all of mountain stock, it was apparent—searched industriously and futilely, then drew together for a few comments.

"He's plumb shook us," a man muttered.

"Let's git out'n here," advised Jug.

They moved off.

"Way thot feller got away makes a body think a' thot spook in the coonskin cap," a mountaineer grumbled.

DOC SAVAGE chanced to be near enough to hear that last remark, and it furnished enough of a surprise that the strange trilling note which was the bronze man's exclusive property came into existence for a moment, roamed the musical scale without definite tune, and sank away into nothingness.

The Aquatania Hotel was in an uproar. The clerk—only the clerk would be wearing a green eyeshade at this time of night—popped outdoors and stared about. Guests appeared in pajamas and dressing gowns. The fight had aroused them.

Doc, his senseless prize cradled in his arms, angled back toward the battle scene, noted that Jug and his party had helped away those unable to walk, and left the vicinity.

Some moments later Doc was moving along the path, approaching the cliff lip, still carrying the unconscious mountaineer. He stopped suddenly, eyeing the white sand and gray stone underfoot. There was a wet, red smear faintly visible on the rocks.

He lowered his captive and began to investigate. Some two minutes afterward, he found Renny and Long Tom. Both men were very much alive and both lay in the forest of boulders, hands and ankles bound, jaws distended by gags.

Doc freed them.

"Holy cow!" Renny thumped. "Did those two hillbillies make suckers of us!" Then he told the exact nature of their misfortune.

"Overhear anything to shed a light on this?" Doc asked.

Long Tom answered that: "Not a thing. They just tied us up and left us. Say, what've you got over there on the path?"

Doc told them what had happened on the hotel veranda.

"Maybe the girl led me into a trap and maybe she didn't," he finished. "I'd like to know something more about her. Suppose you two go ask the hotel clerk about her. I'll be down at the plane, reviving our boy friend here, who may be able to answer some questions. Ask at the hotel about Chelton Raymond, while you're at it."

Renny and Long Tom departed in the direction of the Aquatania Hotel.

Doc scooped the captive from the path, noted the fellow was still profoundly unconscious, and moved to the cliff and down it to the beach.

Leaving the prisoner on the sand, Doc paddled out to the moored plane in the collapsible boat, got restoratives from the medical kit, and rowed back. As he landed, he could hear Renny and Long Tom clattering down the cliff path.

They reappeared shortly.

"The girl wasn't registered at the hotel," rumbled Renny. "She'd only been hanging around a few minutes. Came in all steamed up and asked for you. They told her you weren't there, but were expected. She said she'd wait."

"That all?"

"Far from it!" Renny boomed. "Chelton Raymond left a message for you. He ain't at the hotel. And this Jug guy who jumped you with his gang, ran into the hotel and grabbed the message."

"Jug knew the message was there?"

"I don't think so. He just asked if there was anything for Doc Savage, and the dopey clerk handed Chelton Raymond's message over."

"Did the hotel clerk recall the text of the missive?"

"It was unusual enough that he did," Renny chuckled. "That's a break for us. Here it is. This is the copy he wrote out as he remembered it."

Renny extended a small envelope.

DOC SAVAGE opened the missive. It was the telephone message which had come from Chelton Raymond by radio-land line hookup, and it informed Doc that Raymond wanted the bronze man's presence at the yacht. The note contained the location of the yacht.

"Blazes!" Renny boomed. "Jug got that dope!"

"The yacht isn't many miles from here," Long Tom put in. "But what's Raymond doin' on his yacht when he told us he'd meet us at the hotel?"

"Possibly he was afraid to come to the hotel," Doc suggested dryly.

"That's an idea." Renny eyed the prisoner, who was showing some faint signs of reviving. "Know anything about that man Raymond, Doc?"

"Very little, except that Chelton Raymond is a Wall Street plunger."

"Gambles in stocks, eh?"

"That is what it amounts to. He's quite a wolf along the Street, I understand. Noted as a man who takes long chances."

The gaunt mountaineer groaned weakly, lifted an arm in a feeble gesture and dropped it across his eyes as if to shut out the moonlight. After a while he hoisted the arm slightly and peered, blinking, from under it.

Doc thumbed on a flashlight and planted it in the sand so that the beam bore steadily upon the captive's angular features. Not only would the glare make the fellow uncomfortable, but it would show them small expression changes, which would possibly indicate when he was lying.

"What was the idea of trying to seize me?" Doc demanded.

The prisoner only glared, weasel-like.

"Better loosen up," Doc advised. "Was that girl one of your gang?"

The other snarled into the light, "You-all kain't git nothin' out'n us Snows. We ain't talkers, us Snows."

"You're a Snow?" Doc asked, although the name meant nothing.

Pride glittered in the man's eyes. "Sure am!" he cried.

"Was Jug a Snow, too?" Doc persisted.

"Thot whole shebang was Snows," the man said proudly. "Some of 'em moughtn't carry thot name, but they all be blood kin, anyhow."

Doc was silent a moment. "Was the girl a Snow? She told me her name was Raymond—Frosta Raymond. But was she a Snow?"

As the captive muddled this query about in his mind, deep puckers came between his brows, and finally he fell to peering suspiciously at Doc.

"Be you a-stringin' me, feller?" he demanded. "Ain't you be a-helpin' them thar throat-cuttin' Raymond skunks?"

"If you mean that girl, I never saw her or heard of her before tonight," Doc said quietly.

Once more, expression played on the mountain man's face; he seemed to come to a conclusion, to decide to talk freely, for he put both hands behind his hips and propped himself up on the sand.

He leaned his head back, opened his mouth as if to speak, then his eyes flew wide, fixed on the cliff top, and his mouth fell wider open, simultaneous with a loud *thuck* noise.

FROM the distance, in the direction of the cliff brink, there came a short, ugly squeak of a sound.

The mountain man shut his mouth suddenly and fell back. His lips pinched tightly together, and his eyes closed. He began to squirm. The squirming became a threshing so violent that he was turned over, and by that time, red fluid had started stringing from his nostrils and squeezing past his tightly pressed lips.

When he was lying face-down, a little fountain of scarlet played above the nape of his neck.

He had been shot in the mouth, the slug going entirely through.

Renny leaped erect, whirled, eyed the cliff top, yelled, "Look!"

On the precipice brink stood a tall, gaunt, death-faced figure in deerskins. A long, muzzle-loading rifle was just lowering.

"THE spook!" Long Tom squawled.

He drove a hand for the spot where he usually carried the pistol which discharged the mercy bullets. But that weapon had been taken by the red-headed fellow and the elderly man.

The gaunt phantom in skin garments whipped back from view, the tall coonskin cap being last to vanish.

Doc pitched for the path. He ran up with great leaps. His hands were empty, but he seemed to give that no consideration.

No trait was more unusual about this giant bronze man than the fact that he did not carry firearms, although he was an expert in their use. He had a reason for that, a reason based in psychology. Should he carry a gun habitually he reasoned that, if it were taken from him, the loss of the weapon would leave him with a helpless feeling that would be a great handicap in itself.

Such was his amazing physical condition that his breathing was hardly quickened as he reached the top. He flashed toward where the form in deerskin had stood. Gaining the spot, he began a rapid, grim hunt.

He found nothing.

True, his ascent of the cliff had taken some moments, for all of its speed, and a good runner could have made his escape, but that did not detract from the eerie nature of the disappearance.

"I failed to even scent the burned powder from his rifle," Doc said when he had returned, empty-handed, to the beach. "Of course, there might have been a slight gust of wind to carry it away, which I failed to notice."

Renny kneaded his huge fists together. "Doc, you think that could have been the same cuss that we chased into the water?"

"It certainly looked like the same one," Doc replied.

Long Tom indicated the mountaineer. "He died instantly."

"Strange that mug with the squeaking gun didn't shoot at you, Doc," said Renny.

"That is simply explained," Doc told him. "Remember—we were in the darkness, while a flashlight was trained on the face of our prisoner. The man above could only shoot at a target so brilliantly lighted that his rifle sights would be outlined against it."

"Unless he was a ghost," Long Tom grunted.

"Rats!" snorted Renny.

"I know it's a nutty idea," agreed Long Tom. "But suppose you suggest a more sensible one. That egg in the coonskin cap jumped into the ocean and didn't come up. We saw him. I'd swear on a stack of tombstones that he drowned. Yet—there he was, a minute ago."

Doc Savage, saying nothing more, bent over the slain mountaineer, moved him slightly, and began to probe in the sand, where the death bullet had struck.

Renny, an eye on the cliff brink lest there be another murderous visitation, pondered, "I wonder if the pair who grabbed us—the bird with the red hair and the old geezer—are part of the gang who grabbed Doc—the Snows, if that's what they call themselves."

Doc stood up. "Here's something more puzzling for you to think about," he said.

"What?"

"The bullet that killed this man."

"What about it?"

"Gone."

Renny swallowed with an effort. "It couldn't be!"

"It is, though."

"But we were standing right here all of the time!" Renny waved his great hands. "I give up!"

Doc said grimly, "We'd better get hold of Chelton Raymond and find out what this is all about."

Chapter VI
DERELICT

DOC SAVAGE and his two men were delayed slightly in their take-off to fly the few miles to Chelton Raymond's yacht, for their fuel supply was almost exhausted and it was necessary to replenish it. That necessitated rousing the proprietor of a floating gasoline pump out of bed.

Altogether, however, not more than half an hour was lost, and part of that was expended in telephoning the nearest State Police post concerning the body of the slain man at the foot of the cliff.

There was some shouting on the police end of the wire at first—demands that Doc Savage stay on the scene, and threats that unpleasant things would happen if he did not. That talk was before Doc had disclosed his identity. When he gave his name, the voice of the officer underwent a marked change.

The policeman seemed aware that Doc Savage held a commission, honorary but none the less very real, as a high officer on the State force. This commission was in line with the bronze man's habit of acquiring such posts whenever it was possible, for it had the effect of making him one of the lawmen, and they, not looking upon him as an outsider, would coöperate to a much greater degree. The cops were only human.

The big plane took the air, motors not making a great deal of noise, for they were silenced to such a point that their only sound was a great hissing. Even this note did not penetrate into the cabin, once all of the windows were closed, as the walls were thick and lined with a soundproofing material of choice quality.

Renny flew. He was a pilot of ability, as were

Doc's other four aides. All had received instruction from Doc Savage, and the giant bronze man had the power to transmit some of his own incalculable skill to those whom he taught.

Doc was back in the cabin, working over the radio apparatus.

"Who you tryin' to raise, Doc?" Long Tom questioned.

"Chelton Raymond's yacht."

"Any luck?"

"No."

Long Tom watched Doc Savage try for a moment longer and get no response from the radio, then the bronze man adjusted knobs and dials, and the electrical expert, observing, knew that he had shifted wavelength and was seeking to contact another station.

"Who now?" Long Tom asked.

"Monk, Ham and Johnny," Doc advised.

Long Tom moistened his colorless lips with a tongue. "Monk," "Ham" and "Johnny" were the other three members of Doc's group of five aides, who had been left behind in New York. The three—as were all of Doc's assistants, for that matter—were professional men who stood high in their respective lines.

Monk was a chemist, Ham a lawyer and Johnny an archaeologist. They worked at their professions when not adventuring with Doc Savage.

Doc had left New York in such a hurry that there had been no time to assemble the other three members of his group.

"Think this thing is big enough that we're gonna need their help?" Long Tom asked curiously.

"Looks like it," Doc said thoughtfully.

After a time Doc raised Monk, the chemist, who had a radio station in his laboratory atop a skyscraper in the downtown sector of New York City. A few seconds were expended in advising Monk to get Ham and Johnny and set out for Maine in a fast plane. Doc furnished the location of the cove where Chelton Raymond's yacht lay.

"Be up there before you know it, Doc," said Monk, who had a ridiculously tiny and childlike voice.

Doc listened, transmitted, listened again for a time in another effort to raise the yacht.

"No luck," he said finally.

Renny leveled an arm. "We're here, anyway. There it is."

THE yacht was barely discernible, a grayish blur on the cove surface. The moon was low enough now that it shed little light, so the cove was enwrapped in murk, while the waves, breaking on the nodular shore, made an irregular line like a smudged chalk mark.

"Sour-looking place," Long Tom offered.

Renny flew twice over the cove, at Doc's suggestion, while the bronze man used the infra-light projector and the binocularlike eyeglasses to survey the vicinity.

"No sign of life," Doc vouchsafed.

Renny turned a solemn face. "Eh?"

"Not a soul stirring on yacht or shore," Doc elaborated. "Land, will you."

The big plane heaved over on a wing and sank whistling for the sea until its altitude was less than a hundred feet; then it leveled, skidded sidewise through the night air, a maneuver that killed much of its air speed so that the landing, executed at last, was smooth, without undue shock or splash.

Whooping blasts of the motors taxied the plane close to the yacht, the anchor went down, and the motors were silenced.

"Ahoy the yacht!" Doc called.

Echoes of his great voice cracked back from the cove shore, but there was no other response.

"This is the place and this is the yacht," Renny rumbled gloomily. "But where is everybody?"

Long Tom snapped a collapsible boat open and planted it in the water, then added telescoping oars.

"Ahoy Chelton Raymond!" Doc tried again. "Ahoy the yacht!"

Silence replied.

They clambered into the bobbing boat, laid heavy on the oars, and were soon alongside the yacht. From the port side of the craft projected a boat boom, and from the end of this dangled a line which no doubt had been used to moor a launch. Doc grasped the line and went up.

The bronze giant climbed the rope easily, employing only the grip of sinewed hands and the lift of corded arms. Once atop the boom, he maintained the balance of a tight-rope walker in running to the rail. He stopped, hands resting on the rail, and stood looking at the yacht deck.

Behind Doc, Renny surmounted the rope; then Long Tom. Neither experienced much difficulty, a fact indicating each of the two had physical strength beyond that of an ordinary man.

When they joined Doc, they did as he was doing—stopped, stood very still, and stared fixedly over the rail.

"Holy cow!" Renny rumbled deep in his chest.

A corpse was spread-eagled on the deck. It was a man. He had been shot.

The man was a lengthy fellow with the face of a horse. The position of his body indicated he had been shot while running, a trail of brick-colored drops on the deck strengthening that supposition. He wore corduroys, blue shirt, a hat much used, and coarse, unpolished work shoes. Nearby, where it must have fallen from his hand, lay a modern high-powered rifle.

Doc Savage sank beside the slain man and his fingers turned down the cuffed bottoms of the corduroy trousers. A few weed seeds and dry leaves fell out. The fellow's pockets were empty, except for a small quantity of money, mostly in silver, and a tin of snuff, the label on the latter indicating it had been made in a small town deep in the Kentucky mountains.

"Seeds and leaves in his trousers cuff are those of mountain plants," Doc said slowly. "Snuff made in a remote mountain town. That indicates the fellow is a Kentucky mountaineer."

Long Tom and Renny showed no surprise at the identification of seeds and leaf particles; they knew the amazing knowledge of botany which Doc possessed.

Renny ran forward and looked into the deck house, then stepped inside, but came out almost instantly with his solemn face blank, his tongue traveling slowly over his lips.

"More dead ones inside," he boomed.

THE slain inside the deck house numbered two. One was stocky and clad in the natty uniform of a yacht officer, a circumstance indicating he was one of Chelton Raymond's crew. He had been shot to death, as had the mountaineer outside.

On the officer's wrist was a watch which had been smashed by his death fall. Doc eyed the time at which the hands had stopped.

"Look," he suggested.

Renny and Long Tom came over and squinted.

"Blazes!" Long Tom barked. "He wasn't killed more than fifteen minutes ago!"

The second dead man was another mountaineer, who likewise had been shot.

Doc went out on deck and listened for a time. Since the fight had occurred only a few moments before they hove in sight, it was possible some of the combatants might be close enough to make audible sound. But he heard nothing.

Renny and Long Tom, below, pushed a rapid search of the yacht, then came on deck with the results of their scrutiny.

"Nobody else aboard," Renny said, "dead or alive."

Balancing out on the boom, Doc slid down the rope into the collapsible boat, then paddled ashore. With his flashlight—it had no battery, but got its power from a spring-operated generator mounted in the tubular handle—he examined the beach. He found tracks—and these told a story.

One set of the tracks had been made by huge feet in moccasins, one of the moccasins having a hole in the sole.

Jug's tracks, undoubtedly. The giant leader of the mountaineers who had attacked Doc at the Aquatania Hotel had worn such moccasins, and during the fight Doc had noted a hole in the bottom of one.

A few yards inside the forest of boulders, Doc found a fourth slain man. This one was burly, wore a dark blue suit, and pinned to his vest was a badge of the Coastal Private Detective Agency. The knife with which he had been dispatched still protruded from his chest.

He had been knifed from the front during a hand-to-hand fight, judging from the disheveled condition of his clothing. Doc made a careful scrutiny of the tracks about the body, noting that the slayer had worn moccasins with a hole in one sole.

Jug had killed the private detective, it would seem.

Doc now followed the beach for some distance, observing that Jug and his party of raiders, after having gone to the yacht—probably by swimming—had not returned to shore.

"They must have left in the yacht launch, taking their prisoners," Doc stated when he rejoined his two aides on the yacht.

"Sure it was Jug and his gang who attacked the boat?" Long Tom asked.

"It seems fairly apparent."

"Jug and his crew of Snows, eh," Renny ruminated noisily. "One sure thing—they mean business."

"Raymond, his yacht crew and private detectives, if the latter were working for Raymond, put up a fight, losing two of their own party, but killing two of Jug's raiders," Doc concluded.

"But why all this hell-raisin'?" Renny pondered.

"Let's see if we can find the answer to that," Doc suggested.

THE big bronze man went below and examined staterooms until he found a suite which radiated the most luxury. Raymond's quarters, obviously. Doc pushed a search.

Many places yielded conventional things. Then a writing desk gave up a bundle of new currency, bills of large denomination, the ends of which were smeared with black.

"Ink's been spilled on them," Doc decided aloud.

There was an automatic pistol—a very distinctive gun, because of the thin, long barrel and the careful workmanship.

There were check books, bank deposit slips, and bank books showing deposits and withdrawals.

"Chelton Raymond seems to be slightly less wealthy than Wall Street supposes," Doc said slowly. "But he is not exactly broke, as yet, if the stubs of these check books are any guide."

"Hm-m-m," said Renny. "Anything else?"

"Chelton Raymond has been withdrawing much money from the bank within the last few weeks," Doc said, eyeing the check books.

"Anything to show what he's been doing with it?"

Doc examined more of the papers.

"Yes. Here's the explanation." He passed the papers to Renny. "What do you make of that?"

The big-fisted engineer took the documents, riffled them, then glanced up sharply.

"Stock market *calls!"* he exclaimed.

"Exactly," Doc agreed. "Options to buy stocks at certain prices at any time within the next few months. Stock brokers term the agreements 'calls'. If the market goes up, as it seems certain to do, Raymond stands to make considerable money through these calls."

Doc now passed several larger paper slips to Renny.

The engineer studied them. "Options to buy business property and even a couple of small factories," he muttered.

"Which looks like what?" Doc queried.

Renny considered. "Chelton Raymond must have been expecting to get hold of a considerable sum of money within the next few months."

"Exactly."

"Chelton Raymond—get money in few months," Long Tom put in slowly. "What's that got to do with this spook that carries the squeaking rifle, and the rest of this mystery?"

"Hard to say," Doc replied. He replaced the stuff in the desk.

"I'm goin' outside and stand guard," said Long Tom. He mounted the companion that led to the deck.

"IT'S just possible there is a hidden safe aboard," Doc said, after the electrical expert had gone. "Wealthy men like such things."

The bronze man began going over the suite with more care. It had a tiled bath of ample size, befitting a sumptuous city apartment. Being without portholes, it was a logical spot for a concealed safe. No one could observe the owner concealing valuables.

A few minutes later Doc located a panel of tiling blocks which could be made to swing outward by pressure properly applied. This disclosed a steel door with a regulation dial.

Doc examined the safe closely, gave the dial a few slow whirls, then put an ear against the metal door, shut his eyes so that visual distractions would not interfere with the concentration of listening to the vague tumbler clicks.

Five minutes later he gave it up.

"No cheap safe," he said. "It's the latest thing in small strong boxes. May take hours to open it. We can't waste the time, but we'll make a stab at finding what is in it, anyway."

He went outside, strode out on the boat boom, lowered himself into the boat and paddled to the plane. A few seconds afterward, he paddled back. In the boat was a metal case which bore an identification number.

Renny eyed the case, then asked, "What's the idea?"

"Watch," Doc advised.

Doc went to the secret safe. From the case, he took first a flat slab which looked as if it were made of aluminum a quarter of an inch or so thick, and perhaps a foot and a half square. He propped this up in front of the safe.

The case disgorged other mechanism including a spring-operated generator of small size, but which was capable of generating a powerful current for a short interval. Doc hooked up the generator with the other apparatus.

He carried the contrivance around to the opposite side of the wall which harbored the safe. A switch was thrown. The apparatus buzzed.

Doc substituted a second aluminum panel for the first, buzzed the apparatus again, this time pointing it at a different angle. He did this three times, changing panels in each instance.

Renny looked on, interested but saying nothing.

Doc took his mechanism to the plane, remained there in the darkened craft perhaps five minutes, then came back to the yacht. In his hand he carried large photographic negatives. He handed these to Renny.

"Holy cow!" exploded Renny. "You got X-ray pictures through that safe!"

Doc nodded. "Fortunately, there was no metal absolutely opaque to X rays. Take a look at what's in the safe."

Renny used a flashlight and squinted at the negatives, turning them to various angles, and at length gave a verdict.

"Looks as if there was a paper in there with a rectangle about four by six inches drawn on it, and with some lettering inside the rectangle."

"The rectangle is the ornamental design on the cover of a book," Doc said. "Or so it appears. The lettering is the title of the book. The design and lettering is done in genuine gold leaf, I surmise. Gold is more resistant to the passage of X rays than iron."

Renny studied the lettering.

THE LIFE AND HORRIBLE DEEDS
OF THAT ADOPTED MOOR,
BLACK RAYMOND

"It's a book, all right," rumbled the engineer.

"See that name?" Doc pointed, using the tip of a metallic finger.

"Black Raymond—sure. But what's it mean?"

"That," Doc said, "is the question."

OUT on deck, Long Tom suddenly cried out.

A rifle banged, its echoes slamming noisily back and forth across the cove.

"Somebody took a shot at Long Tom!" Renny yelled, and lumbered for the deck companion.

Doc followed.

Long Tom was crouched near the bridge companion, growling, balancing one of the overgrown weapons which resembled automatic pistols. He did not stir when Doc and Renny approached, bending double to keep in the shadows.

"Keep down," Long Tom advised.

"You hurt?" Doc demanded.

"Naw. Slug missed me six or eight feet. Funny, too."

"Blamed if I see anything funny about getting shot at," Renny snorted.

"It was a rifle—from the sound of it. They shot from shore. At this range, even a kid should come closer than six or eight feet."

"You mean—"

"Looks as if they *tried* to miss me."

Doc moved over to the pallid electrical wizard. "Got the gunman spotted?" he asked.

Long Tom pointed. "There. Think there's two of 'em."

The spot Long Tom indicated was in the brush and boulders along the shore. Doc Savage moved to the bridge, located a large searchlight and sighted it at the shore, then clicked the switch.

A great column of glittering white leaped across the water and slapped against two men. They stood embedded in the glitter like surprised animals.

One was tall, husky, red-headed. An aged stoop and a bald head characterized the other.

"Them's the two lugs who grabbed us back at the hotel!" Renny howled.

The rusty-haired young man carried a rifle. He flipped it up.

Doc flattened.

The rifle whacked. The searchlight went out, and glass from the broken lens sprayed over Doc.

"Guess it was him shot at me!" Long Tom growled. "He ain't shootin' ghost bullets, neither. Here's his slug. It flattened against some of this brasswork. It's a softnose, about a thirty-thirty."

Doc Savage replied nothing. He crossed to the opposite side of the yacht. Hidden from the view of the pair ashore, he ran out on the boat boom, slid down the dangling line and dropped into the water. He sank quickly, and swam under the surface.

The yacht did not draw a great deal of water, and Doc stroked downward under the keel and on toward shore, traversing a surprising distance before he came up and, projecting only his nostrils, replenished the air supply in his lungs.

The bronze man had spent a lifetime of careful exercise and intensive study in perfecting his amazing physical ability, and he had learned diving and swimming from those who were masters—the pearl divers of the South Seas.

It was dark enough that he was not observed in the few moments that his nostrils protruded. He swam on beneath the surface. Once he heard faint noise, it sounded as if someone were shouting. He came up, allowing his head to project.

A voice was calling. It was young and robust and must be the red-headed fellow, addressing Renny and Long Tom on the yacht.

"Pin yur ears back!" he yelled. "I be a-tellin' you news!"

"SHOOT!" Renny's great rumble directed from the yacht.

"Chelton Raymond ain't thar, be he?" asked the redheaded man.

"He's not."

"Reckon I mought tell you where he was took'd. Them damn good-fur-nothin' Snows carried 'im and the rest a' 'em off to some place they called Raymond's Island."

"How do you know that?" Renny demanded.

"We-uns was a-hidin' heer and heerd 'em yappin' at each other."

"Who're you?"

There was low conversation between the two mountaineers at that, the words too vague to carry to the yacht, but not so nebulous but that Doc Savage, positioned quite near the beach, could hear enough to get the trend of the discussion.

"Ain't wise to tell 'em nothin' more," said the elderly man.

"But maybe we could help—" started the redhead.

"They're lowlanders, and not fittin' to be trusted. 'Sides, we ain't been able to figure where they fit in this here thing."

The younger man was doubtful. "I dunno—"

"I do. C'mon. Mought be best if'n we dragged it outa here. You 'member what we saw thot big bronze feller do to Jug an' the rest a' them damn good-fur-nothin' Snows? Thot lad ain't one to be fooled around none."

The two promptly left the beach, running.

Doc Savage hurriedly swam for the shore. Fast though his stroking was, it did not match the running pace of the two mountaineers, with the result that they were some little distance ahead before he reached the sand. His garments stringing water, he set out after them.

The pair had sharp ears. They heard him.

"Tarnation!" yelled the old man. "Run fur it!"

They sprinted. With the advantage of some knowledge of the wilderness of boulders, evidently gained by prowling earlier in the night, they almost held their own with the giant bronze man. A hundred yards were covered. Another. Doc gained now.

Ahead, the starter mechanism of a car whined out. A motor burst into cannonading. With a great clashing of gears, the machine got under way, and its tail light was a bobbing red spot a hundred feet down a road when Doc reached the thoroughfare.

The two mountaineers must have had the machine waiting.

Investigating, Doc found two other cars down the road a bit, both large tourings which bore the identifying plaques of a car rental agency. These were evidently the machines in which Jug and his gang of Snows had arrived, for the telltale prints of Jug's hole-in-the-sole mocassin were discernible in the road dust which had settled thickly on the floorboards of one.

The machines yielded nothing of interest, and Doc returned to the yacht. He told how the pair had escaped.

DOC SAVAGE'S next act was to recover the X-ray photographic films from a spot where he had dropped them when the excitement of the shooting started.

"Think those things are gonna be valuable in solving this?" Renny asked him curiously.

"What do you think?" Doc countered.

Renny shrugged. "It's got me up in the air. It don't make sense. First, that spook with the squeaking rifle, then the girl, those two you just chased, Jug and his crowd—aw-w! What's it all mean?"

"It means that those two a minute ago went to some trouble and took a chance to let us know where they thought Jug and his Snows have taken Chelton Raymond and the other prisoners."

Renny got back to his first question. "What do you make of the book in the safe?"

Doc fell to examining the negatives again.

"Look here," he said. "We missed this—down in the corner of the book cover."

Renny squinted. "A date! Must be the publication date of the book."

"Can you make it out?"

"Sure." Renny peered again. "Eighteen hundred and thirty-four."

"One hundred years ago."

"Huh!"

"That book seems to have been published one hundred years ago."

Long Tom came up.

"The Life and Horrible Deeds of That Adopted Moor, Black Raymond," he read. "Say, d'you suppose Black Raymond was any kin to Chelton Raymond?"

Doc handed him the negatives and moved in the direction of the bridge. There was an excellent array of charts, and he stripped these open on the map table and scrutinized them, giving particular attention to the coast in the vicinity of their present location.

His finger settled on an island. It was very close to the shore, but some miles distant.

"Here's that island of Raymond's," he called.

Renny rushed up. "Certain?"

"The name is marked on the chart."

"How far?"

"Only a few miles." Doc began bundling up the charts, preparatory to taking them along.

"Are we going to that island?" Renny asked.

"We are."

Chapter VII
THE SNOWS

THE three motors of the big plane were fitted with efficient silencers, but these were now uncoupled, so that the exhaust stacks whooped and moaned and spewed clouds of frightened red sparks. Long Tom flew.

Doc fiddled with the radio equipment, alternately transmitting and receiving.

"I'm in touch with Monk, Ham and Johnny," he explained for Renny's benefit. "They're on their way up."

"By plane?"

"Yes. The fastest ship."

Renny nodded and thought of Doc Savage's remarkable airplane hangar on the Hudson River waterfront, which was disguised as a commonplace warehouse and which held a number of planes, ranging from gyros that Doc himself had perfected and which could arise and descend almost vertically, to trim, streamlined speed ships able to do better than three hundred miles an hour.

If the other three members of Doc's organization of five assistants—Monk, Ham and Johnny—were in the fastest ship, they would not take long in coming, for the intervening states—Connecticut, Massachusetts and New Hampshire—were small. The three were coming, of course, from New York.

Forward in the cockpit, Long Tom knocked at a lever. The motors seemed to stop, although the propellers still spun. He had cut in the exhaust silencers.

"Be there in a minute," he said, without turning his head.

The ship, now a great and silent metal bat in the night, erected its tail and slid downward through the sky lanes, its passage fleet and ghostly, not even the sparks spilling from the silencer cans.

Snapping off radio switches, Doc got powerful binoculars, nursed back a sliding window, let in a great roar of air, braced against the gale, and looked downward through the lenses.

One of the Maine coast's innumerable rocky islands lay below. It was small—a dab of naked rock, a shred or two of vegetation—or so it appeared from this height. There was no moon, but neither was there clouds or fog, visibility being excellent.

The isle was a dark splotch on a platter of gloomy blue, and it was veined here and there with even darker smears which meant thickets of brush and small trees.

"Over the island, Long Tom and come straight down," Doc directed. "We might get in close enough to see something before they duck—if they're there."

The electrical wizard complied with the suggestion, and the ship suddenly stood on its streamlined snout.

Doc thumbed switches that threw current into the big bulletlike searchlight with a sepia lens—the infra-ray searchlight. He used the bulky eyepieces.

Wind squawled past the sleek plane, for they were dropping at some miles a minute, and the island swelled, bloated, took on detail, becoming larger than had at first appeared. What had seemed a vaguely regular shoreline became rugged, snagged with indentations.

At length, when a crash seemed impending, Long Tom hauled on the control wheel, there was a low whine of straining struts, and they flew level.

"See anything?" Long Tom called.

"Nothing but rocks and trees," Doc told him.

RENNY, seeming to think some word was necessary, put a great finger down on the chart he had brought from the yacht. The finger was so large that it not only covered the ringed isle on the map, but much of the Maine coast as well.

"This is the place that's marked," he defended.

"They may be there," Doc assured him. "Lots of rock crannies they could hide the launch in."

"They had time to get here?"

"Easily—if they had a fast launch."

Long Tom called back, "I'll circle the blasted island."

The big plane dipped a wing at the sea, the motors revved up, and the big ship scudded along the rocky shore. The coast of the little island were contrasting, for at one end—toward the sea—there were high cliffs and frowning reefs and no beach at all, while on the landward end there was low ground, almost a marsh, and wide beach.

They saw no habitation, no sign of living presence.

"Shall I land?" Long Tom questioned.

"Better," Doc advised. "We'll taxi around the island, using the searchlight, and see what we can find."

The sea was slightly rough; the plane hull slammed against wave crests as it came down, and shoveled aside great sheets of spray. The craft was staunch of construction, however, and withstood the buffeting. With moaning spurts of the big motors, the electrical wizard sent the ship jouncing across the surface.

Doc and Renny used searchlights.

They paralleled the beach for a time, noting that beyond the strip of wave-stroked sand—the beach was mud in spots—lay low marsh ground, out of which grew a coarse kind of grass indigenous to coastal swamp land, and a few ugly shrubs.

Then the island surface became higher, the beach narrowed, dwindled entirely, and they were soon swinging along a palisade of beetling stone. The craggy wall was perforated at irregular intervals by wave-worn pocks and even small inlets.

Doc Savage, watching the shore, called suddenly, "Long Tom, cut your motors!"

The engines died; the plane slackened speed. Under Doc's steady hand the searchlight beam sought a crag which projected above the surface, quite near shore.

Across the rock lay the girl. The rocky upthrust was no more than a yard wide, so that her slender legs dangled down one side, her hair, like a yellow cloth, down the other. She lay perfectly motionless, not moving when the searchlight glitter found her, and there was something unpleasant about her immobility.

"Look—running down the side of the rock!" Long Tom growled.

It was a thread of red liquid, still wet enough that it glistened in the brilliant light. Like scarlet yarns attached to the girl's throat!

"Been a razor used on her, looks like," Renny rumbled.

The engineer drifted an oversize hand into an armpit and brought out one of the weapons which resembled automatics, then drew from a cabin pocket several curled magazines which were daubed with varying colors, and substituted one of these for the ammo drum in the gun.

"Don't use anything but mercy bullets," Doc warned.

"I ain't," Renny muttered. "Just put in an ammo drum that's filled with tracer mercy slugs. They're marked with blue paint."

Doc Savage and his five aides had one policy to which they adhered, no matter how tough the going became or how great the provocation to forget—and that policy was never to take a human life directly, even when engaged in deadly combat.

They watched the girl. She did not stir.

"We'll pick her up," Doc said. "Swing between the rock and the shore, Long Tom."

Long Tom touched throttles, booted the rudder, and the great plane nosed inward, rocking a little, lack of speed making her sluggish. The craft depended on the regular control surfaces for turning, and those needed air speed to function.

Doc kept the searchlight trained on the girl, but did not lean outside the cabin to do so. The searchlight could be operated from inside with a device similar to a through-the-windshield automobile spotlight.

The plane angled over, swung parallel to the shore, and nosed into the space between the rocky beach and the rock jutting above the water on which the girl lay.

"We'll have her in a minute," Renny muttered. "I'll open the door—Well, for—Doc! Look!"

Big, barrel-bodied Jug had leaped into view on shore. He held a rifle. At least eight others appeared. They also gripped rifles.

They threw up the guns and fired a point-blank volley at the plane.

THE clattering roar of the rifles was terrific, for the muffled plane motors were making little competitive noise. The guns were modern pieces, lever and bolt action arms, with two semiautomatics which fired as rapidly as the trigger could be pulled.

Jug and his Snows discharged more slugs as fast as they could. The rocky shore winked with red muzzle flame. Echoes slammed in salvos. Lead screamed.

They were good shots—this Jug and his Snows. They fired with cold, impassioned precision. Brass empties flipped from ejectors in machine precision. And not a bullet missed the cabin of the big plane.

Doc Savage watched for an instant, unperturbed, except that his eyes were like pools of fine flake-gold stirred by an angry, but tiny, gale.

On the cabin windows before the bronze man's eyes, rifle bullets flattened with loud smacks, becoming shapeless lead blobs that fell back into the sea. The glass acquired tiny cracks, like condensed spider webs, but did not break or let any bullets through. It was bulletproof.

"Ain't doin' no good!" Jug screeched. "Tarnation! Shoot somewhere's besides at them thar winders!"

Jacketed lead was directed against the plane cabin. But that, too, was bullet-proofed. The slugs did not get through.

"Trap!" Renny thumped in the plane. "The darn girl was the bait!"

Doc Savage said nothing, but swung to the opposite side of the cabin. He opened the door on that side. The plane was barely moving. Ten feet or so away was the rock on which the young woman lay.

The yellow-haired girl had not stirred.

For use in picking up mooring lines and such, there was a long boat hook racked inside the cabin. It was fashioned of an alloy that embodied strength and lightness. Doc used it to reach out and tangle the girl's frock. The plane cabin protected him from the Snows.

A slight jerk toppled her into the water. He drew her toward the plane. She remained limp.

When he got her very near the plane, her head went beneath the surface for a moment and bubbles arose from her mouth and nostrils. She was alive.

Leaning down, grasping her arm, and lifting her into the cabin did not entail much difficulty. Her head hung back limply. Water dripped from her garments.

Doc glanced at her throat. There was no mark on it. Instead, there was a welt on her head where she had been knocked out.

"Get us out of here," Doc called to Long Tom.

The electrical expert nodded, struck the throttles.

Bullets were still battering the hull, coming more slowly now, and with precision, as Jug and his Snows sought some vulnerable spot. They had already tried to perforate the gas tanks, but without luck, for these were also bulletproof in construction.

Jug seemed to be yelling in rage, but his words were inaudible inside the plane because of the uproar of shots and striking bullets.

"I'm gonna give these lads a forget-me-not!" Renny boomed.

He snapped a window open a crack, jutted his oversize automatic weapon through, tightened on the trigger. An astounding noise came from the gun. It was deafening, very like a moan from a gigantic bullfiddle.

The weapon was really a machine gun with an incredible rate of fire. It could be latched into single-fire position. Doc Savage, whose remarkable mind embodied much inventive genius, had created the weapon for the use of his men exclusively.

Jug jumped to cover with a wild leap. Three of the Snows were not so fortunate. They staggered about, slapping at the spots where the mercy slugs had penetrated slightly under the skin. They tried to run; and finally they sagged down sleepily, becoming unconscious in the course of a little time.

The other Snows sought shelter. The bawling uproar of Renny's superfirer, the quick overcoming of three of their number, was something to make them cautious.

Exhaust stacks whistling, the big plane swayed away from the jutting rock. It was sluggish. There were other fanglike reefs protruding around about, and getting clear would take some slow, careful maneuvering.

"Hey!" Renny boomed. "Lookit!"

Around a headland, a motor launch popped. The craft was no more than a hundred yards distant. The bows were up, and its propellers scoured up a great wake.

Motor squawling, it headed straight for the plane.

"It's gonna ram us!" Long Tom barked.

ONE man occupied the launch—a long mahogany arrow—and he was hunkered low behind the wheel, a lean, grim man made bulky about the chest by a canvas-covered life preserver. With lengths of slender rope, he was doing a quick job of lashing the wheel.

When the tiller was secured, the launch pilot hurriedly struck several matches. The wind whipped the first few out, but at length one blazed long enough to ignite something on the launch floorboards—gasoline-soaked waste, judging from the way it flamed up.

The launch driver wrapped hands about his face and pitched into the sea. He bounced like a ball, legs gyrating in a cloud of sudsy spray, he went down, but was drawn back to the surface by his life preserver. He struck out for the shore.

The launch scudded straight for the plane, cockpit aflame.

Long Tom tramped rudders, hammered throttles, fought the wheel, but there is no vehicle more unwieldy than a seaplane out of the air. The craft lurched about loggily, too slow to escape.

The launch hit with a crunching and screeching of metal. Like a great ax, the sharp bows cut into the cabin.

Doc got clear with an agile leap. He carried the girl. Renny was knocked sprawling, but unhurt.

The fuel tanks were ruptured. Gasoline flooded, *whooshed!* as it took fire. Heat gave off in smoking billows.

From the shore, Jug and his Snows continued shooting. Bullets cracked against the plane. Their sound was that of buckshot dropped on a tin can, greatly magnified.

"We don't dare get out!" Renny rumbled. "They'll plug us, sure!"

"Long Tom!" Doc shouted. "See if you can't haul her inshore before we get roasted out."

The electrical wizard jacked the throttles wide. The props slashed over at top speed. The slipstream picked up burning gasoline and carried it away, the stuff blazing through the air like some magic flame. Heat increased intensely.

The plane sloughed completely around. The rudder control cables were jammed.

Doc dived back into the fuselage, forcing himself through a tiny door, and hauled and jerked at the cables. Thanks to his effort, the plane straightened out and wallowed for the beach. It grounded.

Renny used his superfirer through a cabin window, squinting in the heat and glare of burning gasoline. His gun spoke in short moans. Forward, Long Tom also released storms of mercy slugs.

Jug ran to cover. One of his men went down, then the others sought refuge with their chief. For a moment, their rifle fire was stilled.

Doc and his two men dived out of the plane and plunged into the forest of boulders. The bronze man carried the girl whose hair was like corn silk.

Behind them, fire finished the ruin of their plane.

Chapter VIII
THE SCARED RAYMOND

JUG and his Snows recovered themselves in time to fire a few shots, but these were tardy and only gouged stone particles off the boulders or ricochetted, screaming. No slug did damage.

Doc Savage doubled low, the girl's slack form cradled in his arms, and worked for more substantial shelter. Renny and Long Tom brought up the rear. No words were exchanged.

The rush and coarse grass made some noise underfoot. The grass seemed to be extremely dry for this season of the year. Some plant affliction had killed much of the brush within the last year or two so that many dry, dead stubs were underfoot.

"They be agoin' over thar!" Jug roared, hearing the sounds.

A rifle jarred. The slug *whack-zinged* through brush and rocks.

Renny promptly replied with his machine pistol. One of the Snows cursed. There was no more shooting.

"Damn thim Raymonds!" howled Jug.

Renny told Doc Savage, "Them guys seem to think we're named Raymond."

"So it seems," Doc said quietly. Then he lifted his voice to a shout which Jug could not help but hear.

"You fellows must be making a mistake. None of us are named Raymond."

"Ain't makin' no mistake," Jug disclaimed.

"But we are not named Raymond."

"Ain't keerin' what your name be," Jug bawled back. "You be a-holpin' thim Raymonds. Fer as we're concerned, thot makes you a low-down Raymond polecat."

"The light dawns," Renny said softly. "Those fellows are the Snows, and they hate us because they think we're with the Raymonds."

"Well, they ain't far wrong," Long Tom grumbled. "It was Chelton Raymond that called us up here."

Renny stumbled over a dry stick which crackled loudly, and drew a bullet. When they had gone on a few yards, he whispered, "That reminds me—what's become of Chelton Raymond and the others off the yacht?"

"Must be on the island somewhere," Doc hazarded.

They shuffled through very dry grass which came almost to their belts. The enemy did not seem to be following.

"These machine pistols got their goats," Renny snorted.

"I've been thinkin'," Long Tom offered. "You know what this thing looks like?"

"What?"

"A mountain feud!"

"Rats!" grunted Renny. "You'd better go back to your coils and vacuum tubes and sparks."

"All of these are mountain people," Long Tom pointed out. "There are two families who hate each other. If that don't smell of feud, I'd like to know what does."

"But we're up here on the highly civilized Maine coast where Bostonians and New Yorkers go for summer vacations. They don't have feuds here, except on the golf courses and over the bridge tables."

"I still say it's a feud."

"Who ever heard of a feud being carried out of the Kentucky mountains, or wherever it was going on?"

"Wait and see!"

DOC SAVAGE lowered the golden-haired girl in the lee of a rocky spire.

"We'll be safe here for a few minutes," he said. "Let's see if we can revive this girl, Frosta Raymond, or whatever her name is. She may be able to tell us what is behind all this."

Resuscitation, it developed, was simple, for the young woman was already on the point of recovering consciousness. A slight wrist chafing and cheek slapping revived her to the point where she opened her eyes, squirmed a little, tried to sit up, then grimaced and lay back, holding her head. When she spoke, her voice was fairly firm.

"Their trick—didn't work!"

Doc's strange golden eyes remained expressionless. "It seemed for a time that you were working with Jug. It *did* look as if you drew me into a trap back at the hotel."

"I didn't!" Her eyes flew wide. "When Jug and the rest of them good-for-nothin' Snows jumped you, I ran to get my old pappy's army pistol out of my grip-sack in the hotel. But Jug had a Snow a-watchin' the hotel door, and the no-good knocked me down, and, 'fore I could do anything, carried me off."

Long Tom, possibly to settle his argument with the big-fisted Renny, put in a question.

"Is this a feud?"

"Yes," the girl nodded.

Long Tom jabbed Renny with a thumb. "See!"

"'Tain't no ordinary feud, though," Frosta Raymond put in.

"What do you mean?" Doc asked curiously.

"There's somethin' big and horrible behind it. 'Tain't just one lineup a' mountain folks a-hatin' another lineup, although Raymonds have hated Snows as far back as anybody can remember. There's more to it than that."

"I still don't get you," the bronze man told her.

"I'm talkin' about the Squeakin' Goblin."

An intense silence followed the pretty mountaineer's words, for all three men instantly grasped to what she referred when she spoke of the Squeaking Goblin. It could be none other than the phantom in deerskins and coonskin cap who wrought death with a long muzzle-loader that squeaked, and the bullets of which vanished mysteriously.

"Squeakin' Goblin!" Renny thumped. "That name sure fits the guy!"

Frosta Raymond sat up. "You-all have seen him?" she cried.

Renny grunted, "You said it!"

"Did he—try anything?" the girl demanded hesitatingly.

"Well, he took a pot-shot at Doc, here, and then he up and killed one of Jug's pals whom we were trying to question."

Frosta Raymond gasped, sprang erect. "The Squeakin' Goblin killed a Snow? You saw it?"

Doc nodded.

"That proves what I have suspected," the girl said rapidly. "The Squeakin' Goblin is only supposed to kill Raymonds. The Raymonds have been a-claimin' he is a Snow who goes around disguised in buckskin clothes and a coonskin cap. Now he's killed a Snow. Don't that prove he's not a Snow?"

Renny pulled at a long jaw. "Well, from the way he vanished when we tried to corner him, I wouldn't swear that he was anything human."

The girl was silent for some moments.

"I was hopin' you wouldn't say that," she murmured at last.

"Why?"

"'Cause the mountain people claim the Squeakin' Goblin is a spook," said Frosta Raymond. "The spook of old Columbus Snow, who was killed a-feudin' more than eighty years ago."

THE night breeze, sweeping in from the sea, made fluttering sounds in the dry grass and an occasional crackle in the equally arid brush, while in the distance, toward the oceanward end of the island, there was an occasional murmur of conversation the text indistinguishable, as Jug and his Snows held consultation.

"Tell us about this original Squeaking Goblin," Doc suggested.

The girl complied promptly. "Old Columbus Snow lived back in the days when the Raymond-Snow feud was hottest. He carried a long muzzle-loadin' rifle that he had made himself, and when it went off it made a loud squeak, instead of a bang like another gun. Nobody ever did rightful know why that was. Old Columbus had sneakin' ways, and got around right spooky, so that he was called the Squeakin' Goblin."

"And he was killed eighty years ago?" Doc asked.

"About that long ago," agreed Frosta Raymond. "He killed a passell of people in his feudin', did old Columbus Snow, but one day he got kotched. My own granddaddy Raymond shot him right 'twixt the eyes."

"I see," Doc said—then was silent, his keen ears picking up sounds from the other end of the island. "What started this present feud? Or has it been going on since the original Squeaking Goblin's day?"

"It died down for years. It started up this last time less than six months ago."

"Why?"

"Squeakin' Goblin."

"Eh?"

The girl's voice turned grim. "The Squeakin' Goblin started bushwhackin' Raymonds. Then some Snows was killed and their houses burned."

"The Squeaking Goblin did that to the Snows?"

"Not accordin' to the Snows. They claimed it was Raymonds that did it. The Raymonds got mad and claimed as how the Squeakin' Goblin was some good-for-nothin' Snow dressed up in buckskins, who was a-killin' Raymonds."

"One word led to another, eh?"

"And words led to shots," Frosta Raymond said slowly. "And it wasn't long until the old Raymond-Snow feud was goin' full blast."

"All of this happened within the last six months?"

"Yes."

Renny, who had been dividing his attention between the girl's story and listening to the distant Jug and his men, put in a low rumble.

"Think Jug is fixin' up some devilment, Doc," said the engineer.

Doc gave ear to the suspicious quiet from the vicinity of the Snow clan and their bulky leader.

"You're probably right, Renny," he admitted. "I'll ask Frosta another question or two, then look into it."

Frosta Raymond seemed to read the query he intended putting.

"I've heard of you," she said. "Read some about you in a magazine. It said you made a business of helpin' others out of trouble, and that no job was too big for you. It told how you once stopped a revolution in some European country."

"That wasn't so long ago," Doc admitted.

"I got to thinkin' that you might be able to stop this feud and all of its killin'," the girl went on. "But the Raymonds, my folks, only laughed at me and made fun of the idea of callin' in a furriner when I put it up to them. I-I didn't know what to do.

"Then, the other day, a family of our neighbors was feuded—man, his wife and their kid. After I saw that, and helped bury them, I took a dab of money I had and came to get you, in spite of what my folks said."

"That explains your presence here," Doc told her. "One more thing. Why is Chelton Raymond so important that Jug and his Snows would come all the way from Kentucky to get him?"

The girl said, "I never heard of no Chelton Raymond until tonight."

"Eh?"

"Never set eyes on Chelton Raymond until the Snows got him tonight."

"Where is he being held?"

"The other end of the island."

"Others with him?"

"Yes. Some hands off his boat and some private detectives that he hired to protect himself. That sounds strange. A Raymond don't usually hire nobody to do his fightin'."

Doc considered. "Ever hear of a man known as 'That Adopted Moor, Black Raymond'?"

"What?"

"He lived a long time ago—a hundred years or more, possibly," Doc said. "We found a book about him on Chelton Raymond's yacht, in the safe—or so an X-ray picture seemed to show. Ever hear of him?"

Frosta Raymond thought that over. "Seems like I recall my granddaddy telling about a Black Raymond who once got to be king of a Moorish city, and who was an ancestor of ours. Do you reckon that's him?"

"Might be," Doc admitted. "But we'll go into it later."

He moved away, and the night suddenly swallowed him.

DOC SAVAGE was a man who possessed strength that, when measured by the comparative standards of an ordinary man's muscular ability, was almost incredible. Many an individual had come in contact with the remarkable bronze man, seen or felt his fabulous power, and thereafter had been stunned, unable to comprehend how a human frame could harbor such sinews.

Any mystery connected with Doc Savage's physical ability would have vanished had those who were puzzled been present at the two-hour routine of exercises which he had taken each day since childhood.

Those exercises were amazing. Strenuous, complete, they were calculated to develop each muscle, as well as the senses of sight, hearing, taste, scent, touch.

The bronze giant's great muscular ability had never been more evident than it was now as he went forward through the darkness, for his tread was as light as that attained by sinews of a great jungle cat.

Too, he seemed possessed of the eye of a feline, able to see in the dark, for he disturbed the dead noisy brush not at all, and avoided the dry grass in uncanny fashion.

Jug, muttering to a group of his men near shore, did not hear the bronze phantom draw near, and the darkness concealed him.

"Hit's a-givin' me a pain under my hat," Jug was growling. "Them detective fellers be scared too bad to do any plain and fancy lyin'. Thot's why I kain't savvy it."

"Figger yer right, Jug," agreed a follower. "Hit's a mystery."

"Reckon they ain't lyin' when they say as how this Chelton Raymond hired 'em to guard 'im from the Squeakin' Goblin." Jug went on. "Hell! Moughtn't thot friz yer hair!"

"Plumb' puzzlin', Jug. Who d'you figger this Squeakin' Goblin mought be?"

"Tarnation! I dunno."

"Jug, you calculate the Squeakin' Goblin might be a real ghost?" another man put in.

"Ain't believin' in no sech things!" Jug disclaimed.

"Mought be thot Tige rascallion," said a third Snow. "If thar was ever a scamp, thot Tige is it."

"He's a scrappin' son of a gun," Jug grunted. "Wonder what he was a-doin' with thot Chelton Raymond? Did thot scared detective say?"

"Said Chelton Raymond saint plumb to Kentucky fer 'im," the other relied. "Don't believe thot, nohow. Maybe Tige *is* that Squeakin' Goblin."

"Well, he ain't gonna squeak much longer," Jug said grimly. "Soon's we figger out how to git them fellers thot come in the sky-wagon, we'll massacre the whole passell a' 'em."

"Ain't no Raymond flttin' to live, nohow," agreed the second Snow.

Doc Savage moved away—and there was no sound, no visible stir in the darkness, to show that he had been present and had overheard.

DOC made for the seaward end of the island, where Frosta Raymond had said the prisoners were held, and as he moved, the bronze man considered. He was unable to place Tige, and concluded the fellow must be a mountaineer, a Raymond, whom Chelton Raymond had called in for assistance. Doc had not yet met tobacco-chewing Tige.

The breeze from the sea rustled the brush and whispered in the dry grass; waves slopped softly on the beach. No sound the bronze man made was audible above these.

Cigarette smoke showed Doc his objective. His sensitive nostrils detected the tobacco tang in the breeze. Movements wary, he traced the source of the burning weed, and soon found it.

A man lounged in the murk beside a rock, rifle across his knees, hand-rolled cigarette clinging to a lip. The cigarette end, glowing red at intervals, cast a faint aura on brush, grass and stone.

A few seconds later, when he had finished smoking, he expectorated on the glowing fag to extinguish it, a habitual precaution which came as second nature to a man who had spent his life where forest fires were a perpetual menace. He cast the fag away, yawning.

The yawn ended in a froglike noise, an unnatural croak. The man's arms jerked spasmodically. His rifle was flung away by the movement and fell into the undergrowth. He made a clutching gesture at the back of his neck; then air ran noisily from his lungs. His arms and legs stiffened and shook as if in contact with a strange electric current, and he seemed to go to sleep.

Doc Savage removed his right hand from the back of the man's neck. Doc had studied many subjects intensively, but above all other things, he knew human anatomy. With the hand, he had applied pressure which had paralyzed certain nerve centers, bringing senselessness as effectively as by the knockout route. The man had never heard his bronze nemesis approach.

Doc advanced swiftly. The stony island split apart suddenly in a gully. The sandy bottom of this carpeted his footsteps, so that, when he rounded a corner, those beyond had no warning of his approach.

Had they heard him, they could have done little about it, for they were bound and gagged. Doc moved among them, using his flashlight.

In closest proximity lay a lean, brindled man with the face of a hawk. He had gun-blue eyes, and a slab of a jaw over which tobacco juice was smeared and dried, as if he had been chewing the weed when taken violently by surprise.

Doc untied him.

"Who are you?" he asked.

"Tige," said the gaunt mountaineer. "Reckon you mought be Doc Savage, huh?"

Doc nodded, his metallic features showing in the backglow of the flashlight. Then he untied the other prisoners. Some wore the type of uniforms commonly affected by yacht sailors, while others bore badges marking them as private detectives of the Coastal Agency.

"Which one of you is Chelton Raymond?" Doc asked.

Tige cursed softly, violently. No one else made any answer.

"Which is Chelton Raymond!" Doc demanded more sharply.

"Chelton ain't here," said Tige.

Doc rapped, "The girl said he was among the prisoners."

"He was." Tige scrubbed at his soiled chin with the back of one hand, then the other. "Chelton up and got loose."

"How long ago?"

"Five minutes ago, reckon."

"Didn't he make an effort to free you?" Doc asked curiously.

Tige cursed again, still softly, but more violently than before; he managed to get utter disgust in his swearing without raising his drawl appreciably.

"Chelton jist skedaddled 'thout makin' a stab at untyin' us," he said. "And that war'nt no way fur a Raymond to act."

DOC noted tracks, evidently Chelton Raymond's, leading up the gully. Following them, he found a gag and lengths of rope where they had been cast aside.

The trail went toward the seaward end of the isle, and even the bronze man's highly developed faculties were unequal to following it without using the flashlight, which would betray him to Jug and his Snows.

Doc went back to the freed captives.

"Does Chelton Raymond own this island, Tige?" he asked.

"Yop," said Tige. "He told me 'bout hit. He's got himself a leetle cabin somewhere's on the place. Says he'd figured on fixin' up a right pert summer house here one day."

"Know where the cabin is?" Doc asked. "It must be located under a large tree or a rock overhang, because we failed to spot it from the air."

"Dunno whar it be," disclaimed Tige.

Doc led them back toward the spot where Renny, Long Tom and the girl waited. They walked Indian file, one behind the other, and took great care not to be heard.

"Blazes!" Renny thumped softly when they appeared. "You came up as spooky as a string of those Squeaking Goblins."

"Squeakin' Goblin!" Tige growled. "What you-all know 'bout him?"

"Not nearly as much as we would like to know, Tige," Doc replied. "Can you tell us anything?"

"Squeakin' Goblin is a durn good-fur-nothin' Snow a-wearin' a outfit a' buckskin duds and a-carryin' a muzzle-loader," grated Tige.

"You are wrong," Doc said.

"How you figger thot?"

"I overheard the Snows talking," Doc replied. "The identity of the Squeaking Goblin is as great a mystery to them as to us. They even think you are the Goblin, Tige."

"Tarnation!" Tige said wonderingly.

Renny suddenly emitted a bawling roar, then bounded atop a boulder.

"Look here, Doc!" he howled.

"Fired the brush, haven't they, Renny?" Doc asked quietly.

Renny wheeled and peered downward wonderingly. "You already knew it?"

"Caught the smoke odor a moment before you yelled," Doc told him.

A flamboyant sun seemed to be coming up over the eastern end of the island, a spreading glow which suffused the sky with harsh, red flush. Yet the hour was nowhere near dawn.

"Gonna burn us out!" Renny said, and his great voice was worried.

Chapter IX
THREE SKYMEN

DRYNESS of the grass and brush which furred the island, and the violence of the breeze which scurried in from the open sea, made a grisly combination.

Renny thumbed his flashlight on, the beam disclosing faint wisps of smoke, these increasing to great streamers, then clouds, so that Doc's group was nauseated, being forced, hacking and coughing, to sink close to the ground.

Bullets made a racket nearby. Renny doused his light.

Tige, who had been lurking in the background, ventured timidly forward and confronted the girl, Frosta Raymond.

"Tige!" the girl gasped, and there was delight in her tone.

"Kinda nice you war'nt hurt none to speak of," Tige said with the uneasiness of a man to whom smooth words are foreign.

Doc came over. "You know each other?"

"We be cousins," said Tige.

The girl nodded. "Both Raymonds."

"My name's Tige Raymond Eller," said Tige. "My mammy was one a' the Raymonds."

Doc said nothing, but his remarkable flake-gold eyes watched the pair closely as Frosta Raymond stared intently at Tige, seemed to consider, then abruptly put a question.

"You left the mountains mysteriously, two weeks ago, Tige," she said. "Why?"

"'Body kain't turn down his relations," Tige muttered.

"You mean that Chelton Raymond called on you for help?"

"Yop."

"How come you didn't tell anybody you were coming East?"

Tige squirmed, seemed more gaunt and hard-bitten than ever.

"Letter I got from Chelton Raymond 'lowed as how mought be best if'n nobody was told," he mumbled finally. "He 'lowed the Squeakin' Goblin might hear."

"Was Chelton Raymond scared of the Squeakin' Goblin?"

"Yop. The durn spook has tried to nail 'im three times, all told."

"Where is Chelton Raymond now?"

"Tarnation! I dunno."

That terminated the conversation. Tige hauled out a twist of long green which his late captors had not taken from him and, biting into it, wrenched and gnashed with his teeth until he had detached an enormous quid. Satisfaction sat his angular face as he began to masticate, and he watched the billowing smoke, the showering clouds of sparks, without visible concern.

"That guy's got nerve," Renny told Long Tom quietly.

"He may be deeper than his dumb actions indicate," Long Tom pointed out pessimistically. "Paste that thought in your fire helmet."

While the conversation went on the party had not stood still, but had moved backward, seeking some spot where the fire was not likely to burn, and where they could find safety.

They were having little luck. Even the rank grass on the low end of the island was dry. In places it was already flaming, having caught afire from the sparks which swirled overhead like clouds of glittering winged jewels.

"We can always wade into the drink," Renny grumbled.

A moment later, his optimism was punctured.

"Listen," invited Doc Savage.

Everyone halted and cupped hands to ears. Their features at first registered curiosity, then this faded and blank uneasiness came, and they exchanged strange looks in the fire glow.

A purring sound—it had a watery quality—had become audible. It could have only one meaning.

"Motor boat!" Renny rumbled. "Comin' from the other end of the island!"

Doc confronted Tige. "When you were brought to the island, how many boats did they use?"

"War'nt but one," said Tige. "They burned the plane with it."

"Then this one must be from a boathouse that Chelton Raymond had on the island," Doc decided aloud.

"We never saw no boathouse from the air," Renny reminded.

"Nor did we see a cabin. But Tige says there is one—or so Chelton Raymond told him."

They saw the launch they had heard a moment before. It was cruising the shoreline. The boat was filled with men, Jug occupying the bow.

Jug had a rifle, which he lifted; his men did likewise with their guns. They all fired almost together, launching bullets which came in a screeching storm, and forced Doc and his party to take cover.

"Dang 'em!" roared Renny. "They're sure gonna give us some trouble!"

IN a voice that vibrated power, in tones which carried over the increasing noise of the fire, Doc Savage directed his group to seek such substantial shelter as rocks offered, and remain there.

Renny and Long Tom obeyed, although Doc's lack of activity puzzled them. Their position was becoming more perilous by the instant, and Doc was taking it much too easily.

The yacht crew and the detectives commented among themselves on the bronze man's inactivity.

"I always heard there was no jam that bronze

guy couldn't get out of," growled a detective in a low voice.

"Balony!" snorted another.

"That's what I think," agreed the first.

"He got you away from Jug and the Snows, didn't he?" pretty Frosta Raymond put in caustically.

The men of the Coastal Agency looked uncomfortable, for they had not realized the girl was overhearing.

Tige got up and went over to Doc Savage. The tall mountaineer was scowling, his slab of a jaw out. He drove brown tobacco juice in the direction of the fire.

"Ain't yer gonna do nothin' 'bout things?" he demanded of Doc.

"Sit down," the bronze man invited.

Tige scowled. "If'n you ain't figgered out nothin', hit's time somebody with ideas took hold. We ain't a-wantin' to be burned up."

"Meaning?"

"I'm gonna start givin' orders. We'uns kin build a backfire and maybe stop the—"

Doc Savage reached up and clasped Tige's bony wrist. The move was executed so swiftly that Tige did not have time to jerk his hand away. The bony mountaineer did not comprehend fully until he was hauled down to all fours, yanked with a strength such as he had never expected to encounter in any man.

Tige opened his mouth to curse. His fists balled to strike blows.

The bullets stormed the space where he had stood. They screamed into nearby rocks and climbed, howling, into the boiling smoke above. Had Tige been erect, he might well have been hit.

Tige said nothing, but it was evident he realized the bronze man had saved him. After a bit, he grinned sheepishly and moved away, saying nothing more about taking charge of things.

"Hey!" Long Tom howled abruptly. "Upstairs!"

Eyes went skyward. A great glare of light was dropping out of the sky. Smoke made it vague, but did little to hamper its dazzling brillaince.

"So *that's* what you were waiting on!" Renny told Doc.

"They were about due," Doc said dryly.

THE glare in the sky was the landing light of a plane. They soon heard the motors over the cackling uproar of burning brush and grass. The ship swooped overhead, the lights scudding whitely through the smoke pall, then banked off in the direction of the launch which bore Jug and his Snows.

In the night sky, red with a hell-froth from the fire, giant snare drums seemed to beat a great cadenza.

Pips of water jumped up in the sea around Jug and his Snows. It was as if there had come a rain of hard tiny, invisible drops. And that deadly shower struck terror into the launchload of mountaineers, for they had no trouble realizing the droplets were of lead—machine gun bullets.

The plane, embodied with tremendous speed, whipped past, climbed high in the sky, heeled over and around and came swinging back like a great pendulum to the attack.

Jug took advantage of the respite. He jumped up and down in the launch, bawling orders.

The launch heeled around, the propellers threw up green water and ash-colored foam from the stern, and the craft gathered speed. It headed for the mainland, a mile or so distant.

The plane whooped overhead. Along its wings tongues of red flame flickered from the muzzles of machine guns mounted in the streamlined wing structure.

In the launch, men upset. Hard hailstones seemed to belabor the thwarts and flooring.

Jug cursed and wielded his rifle. Had he taken the time to examine his men, or some of the bullets which were barely embedded in the wood, he would have realized, possibly, that the slugs were hollow shells filled with a drug which merely produced unconsciousness. Or maybe he would not have realized. Jug was not possessed of much scientific learning.

Again and again Jug fired at the plane searchlights, but failed to put them out, much to his disgust. It did not occur to him that the lenses were bulletproof.

Good fortune rode with Jug, at that, for he reached the shore of the mainland with the launch. Unhit, he scrambled out, snarling at those of his followers who were still conscious, and helped haul the mercy bullet victims to cover.

Overhead, the plane buzzed like an angry wasp. Apparently those aboard concluded they would have difficulty corralling Jug and his gang if they did land, so they swept back out to the island.

The ship was an amphibian, as thoroughly at home upon the water as on land. It came down lightly on the sea, smashed spray off the tops of a few waves, then sank its hull in the water and swung to the beach.

The craft halted not far from where Doc Savage and his party were standing in the water, trying to avoid the fire ashore. The cabin hatch exploded open.

IN the sea up to his neck, Tige Eller eyed the first man to clamber out of the plane. He blinked.

"I'll swar!" he muttered. "Always figgered Jug Snow was the homeliest human critter livin'. But yonder be his beat."

Eyes went skyward. A great glare of light was dropping out of the sky.

The man getting out of the plane would weigh near two hundred and fifty pounds, and seemed bigger because he was not fat. The fellow was nearly as broad as high; his head was small; great beams of arms swung below his knees, and coarse red hair covered most of his visible hide. A casual observer might have thought a great gorilla was swinging out of the amphibian.

The apish one peered around out of small eyes. "O.K., Doc?"

"O.K., Monk," Doc told him.

Monk—he rarely heard his full name of Lieutenant Colonel Andrew Blodgett Mayfair—was a gentleman whose simian looks were misleading, for he was one of the world's leading chemists, a man whose name and accomplishments were mentioned with awe wherever knights of the test tubes gathered in conclave.

Monk jumped into the water, careless of an expensive suit of clothes. Then he swiveled and eyed the plane door.

"Ham!" he bawled at someone within the

plane. "Leggo that hog! What in the blazes—"

A loud squeal piped from the plane. Out of the door sailed a grotesque object of reddish hue—Monk's pet pig, Habeas Corpus.

Habeas vaguely resembled a flying bird—until he hit the water, for his ears were tremendous, his body scrawny, his legs long and thin. Habeas belonged to the same class as Monk, his master. Both were freaks.

"Dang you, Ham!" Monk squawled. "I'll tie that sword cane around your neck!"

An exceedingly dapper gentleman appeared in the plane door, scowled at Monk, eyed the water distastefully, then climbed atop the cabin where he would not be in danger of getting wet. He was thin-waisted, sharp of features, with the large mouth of an orator. He carried a slender black cane.

Glowering at Monk, the carefully dressed man slipped his dark cane apart a few inches, showing the thin blade within it.

"The next time that hog tries to bite me his tail is going to be amputated—right behind his ears," he promised.

The gentleman with the sword cane was

Ham—Brigadier General Theodore Marley Brooks. In the halls of Harvard hung a plaque honoring the man who was considered the most astute lawyer that institution of learning had ever turned out. It bore Ham's name.

A third man clambered out of the amphibian. He was a human granddaddy longlegs. It seemed that no man could be as thin as he, and live. His trousers whipped about his bony shanks as about wooden laths, and his coat hung as on a wire hangar. From his lapel dangled a monocle on a ribbon.

"The perpetual brawling of you two is an unmitigated annoyance," he said, scowling at Monk and Ham.

Johnny—the field of archaeology knew him as William Harper Littlejohn—liked big words. He never used a small word where he could think of a larger one.

These three men, Monk and Ham with their unending squabbling, and the bony Johnny, were, besides being the other three members of Doc Savage's group of five aides, each a leader in his particular profession. Each was moderately wealthy, or capable of making handsome fees when working.

All five of Doc's aides had one thing in common—a love of excitement and adventure. That was the thing which held them to the giant bronze man. Doc, by the very nature of his strange life's work of helping others out of their troubles, led a punch-packed life. Where he went, excitement was usually to be found.

Renny rumbled at the three newcomers, "For once, I'm glad to see your ugly faces!"

"Did we chase away the bad boys who were molesting you?" the sharp-tongued Ham asked.

"MONK," Doc called.

"Yeah?" The homely chemist looked up, having seized the swimming pig, Habeas Corpus, by one enormous ear.

"Did you get a look at the inside of the launch?"

"Yep," Monk replied. "Saw everybody in the boat."

Doc hurriedly described Chelton Raymond, giving a word picture of the man which was supplied by the bony Tige.

"There was nobody like that in the launch," said Monk.

"Come on," Doc rapped. "We'll find him, then get after Jug Snow and his outfit."

In order to get behind the fire it was necessary to board the plane, the ship in turn taxiing a few hundred feet out to sea, clear of flying sparks, then heading for the other end of the island.

The fire still burned with sufficient violence to cast an aureate brilliance over most of the isle and the sea. Bathed by this red light, the sea had a gory, sinister aspect.

Doc Savage stood on the hull of the plane, a little back from the whistling steel discs of the propellers, and scrutinized the rocky shore of the isle. Unexpectedly, he leveled an arm.

"Look," he said.

Chapter X
THE GOBLIN KILLS

OUTLINED in the early light of the dawn, a canoe had appeared around a sheer outjutting of stone. It traveled swiftly, a tiny shell that rode as light as a cork atop the unending procession of waves. A paddle dipped frantically, throwing green water in a manner which showed the wielder of the blade was not an expert.

One man occupied the canoe, a man who was very tall, very blond—his hair, eyebrows, mustache, being almost white.

"Chelton Raymond!" Renny exploded.

"Ahoy the plane!" called the man in the canoe. "Are you Doc Savage?"

Doc's powerful voice advised him his guess was correct. "Are you Chelton Raymond?" he asked.

"Right," called the canoeman.

"Where have you been?" Doc shouted.

"Hiding close to my shack at the other end of the island," Chelton Raymond said. "This canoe was lying in the brush there."

A Coastal Agency detective muttered, "That's Chelton Raymond, all right," then yelled in a louder voice, "You all O.K., Mr. Raymond?"

"Except for a few bruises, yes," called Chelton Raymond.

The canoe was still some distance down the shoreline, riding the waves, but coming closer.

Renny failed to contain his curiosity.

"What's this all about, Mr. Raymond?" he called.

The man in the canoe stopped paddling, cupped his hands about his lips and yelled, "Up until an hour ago, I had no idea. Then, what may be the explanation came to me. I'll tell you in a moment."

He began paddling again.

Renny shouted, "Say, are you any kin to Frosta Raymond?"

Chelton Raymond, they could see even from that distance, started violently and held the paddle close to his chest.

"What do you know about Frosta Raymond?" he demanded.

"Only that she's here with us," Renny retorted, the power of his bellowing voice making it a simple matter to carry on a conversation over that distance.

"There with you!" Chelton Raymond's voice was almost a scream. He sprang erect in the canoe.

"Sure," Renny replied. "Say, why the excitement?"

Chelton Raymond seemed about to answer, but

did not. His head dropped, eyes seeking the paddle in his hand vaguely, then his head turned slowly, and he seemed to be looking about while engaged in deep thought. Suddenly he emitted a piercing yell.

He leveled the paddle at the rocky shore, pointing.

"The Squeaking Goblin!" he screeched.

RENNY peered at the spot Chelton Raymond was indicating. "Holy cow! Danged if I see the spook!"

"Behind that square rock!" Chelton Raymond howled. "He's aiming his damned rifle at me!"

The square rock in question was easily distinguished in the early morning sunlight. It was very large, and its opposite side offered much shelter.

Doc and his men ran for the rock.

From the canoe, Chelton Raymond wailed, "The Goblin is going to shoot!"

Raymond then went through all of the gestures of a man who sees death as his lot in the immediate future. The blond man waved his arms, covered his eyes, then uncovered them hastily as if fearing to meet fate blindfolded.

"Dive overboard!" Doc called.

Chelton Raymond either did not hear or else was too terrified to take heed, for he did not dive into the sea, but covered his eyes again instead and flopped down into the canoe, apparently under the impression that its thin canvas-and-spruce sides would offer some shelter.

The Squeaking Goblin had not become visible on shore.

There came a squeak—short, hideous, very real.

Chelton Raymond stood up in the canoe, screaming. He had transferred his arms to his chest, where they were crossed, tightly clutching. Face contorted, eyes staring, he reeled, could not keep his balance, and toppled slowly.

A smear of crimson fluid had already covered the hands which were clenched against his chest.

The man hit the water—there was some splashing, and he sank almost at once.

"Hunt the Squeaking Goblin!" Doc rapped. Then he veered to the water, plunged in, and swam toward the overturned canoe with tremendous strokes.

Speedy as was the swimming of the bronze man, however, some seconds were required in reaching the canoe. Once there, he dived. He was down a long time. Coming up, his hands were empty.

He dived again, repeating this time after time, until at last he had explored the bottom of the sea for many yards in every direction, and especially in the direction of the tide, for there was a strong current toward the open sea.

He did not find Chelton Raymond, or his body.

"Tide must have carried it away before you got there, Doc," said the small-voiced Monk.

"Possibly," Doc admitted.

"Come over here. We want you to look at what we found."

Doc went over to the square rock behind which Chelton Raymond had screamed that the Squeaking Goblin stood. Nowhere to be seen was the gaunt figure in deerskins. Indeed, there was nothing but ashes where the grass of the island had been burned away.

"Get it?" Monk queried.

"No tracks," Doc said.

Monk wrinkled his homely face. "It just ain't possible, Doc. If this Squeaking Goblin was here, he'd have left tracks."

"So you say!" Renny jeered. "I tell you, this Squeaking Goblin has all the traits of a real big-shot spook."

THEY conducted a further search in the next few minutes, but the net result was exactly nothing. There were no tracks to show that a physical presence had haunted the island and fired the strange, squeaking rifle.

"I am going after Jug Snow," Doc said abruptly. "Johnny, you and Long Tom stay here with these private detectives and the crew of Chelton Raymond's yacht and see what you can find."

With Monk, Ham and Renny of his own little group of five, and Frosta and Tige, Doc put off in the plane. They headed for the spot where it was reasonable to believe Jug Snow and his party would have landed on the mainland.

Chapter XI
THE SAFE SURPRISE

JUG SNOW'S launch was found almost at once, abandoned on the beach of the distant mainland. Doc pushed a search for tracks. These were not difficult to find, since Jug and his followers had, at the time of their landing, evidently considered haste the better part of caution.

The trail led to a farmhouse, and there they encountered an enraged farmer who had just lost his automobile. The car, it developed, had been taken by Jug Snow at the point of a gun. The farmer's telephone wire had been cut to prevent an alarm being spread.

One interesting bit of information was disgorged by the irate tiller of the soil. Jug Snow, the farmer explained vehemently, had asked many questions about roads to the southward, toward a certain cove above Bar Harbor.

"That's where Chelton Raymond's yacht is lying," Renny boomed. "Looks like Jug was heading back there."

"We can beat him to the boat," Doc said, and led the race for their plane.

When they were in the air, bony Tige ambled up slowly and seated himself beside Doc Savage, produced his tobacco twist and began gnawing at a portion. When he had his jaws satisfactorily lubricated, he spoke.

"Raickon I got her figgered out why thot good-fur-nothin' Jug Snow an' his litter turned up in this here neck a' the woods," he offered.

"That point has been puzzling me," Doc admitted.

"Figger as how Jug and his Snows must've follered Frosta here from Kaintucky," said Tige. "Things they said when they was a-holdin' me makes me think that."

Frosta Raymond joined the discussion. "I think Tige is right. Several times, on my way here from Kentucky to see you, Mr. Savage, I thought I saw men following me."

Doc's flake-gold eyes rested on the young woman. "How did you know I was at the Aquatania Hotel, instead of my New York office?"

Homely Monk, in a seat nearby, started violently and exclaimed, "Gosh, Doc! I forgot to tell you!"

"Tell me what?" Doc asked.

"Some woman called the New York office and wanted to know where you were, and we told her."

"It was I who called," Frosta Raymond supplied.

The plane leaped violently as it encountered an air bump, and Tige gulped, then looked very surprised—and it was evident he had swallowed his tobacco quid. He bit a fresh supply off his twist of home-cured long green.

"This Jug Snow is a bad 'un," he offered. "Jug drapped his first man when he was less'n ten year' old. Hit 'im right 'twixt the eyes, Jug did."

"Kinda on the style of the Squeaking Goblin, eh?" Monk offered.

"Say, that's an idea," Renny put in. "Maybe Jug got back to the island some way and shot Chelton Raymond. Maybe Jug is the Squeaking Goblin."

They did not discuss that possibility further, for the yacht of Chelton Raymond appeared below and Ham, who was flying the plane, sent the big ship down in a steep dive. The others searched the cove with binoculars.

"There ain't no sign of Jug Snow and his gang," Monk grunted. "We beat 'em here."

"But why do you reckon Jug was coming back here?" Renny boomed.

DOC SAVAGE did not answer immediately, and when he did speak, he voiced an alternate possibility.

"Jug might not have been coming to the yacht," he pointed out. "By inquiring where the cove lay, he might have intended only to get an idea of where he was."

"We gonna wait here for him?" Renny wanted to know.

Doc unfolded a collapsible canvas boat which could be used to row to the yacht.

"Right now, we are going to look the yacht over a second time and see if we can find anything that might explain what is behind all of this," he declared.

"I'm curious about that book, *The Life and Horrible Deeds of That Adopted Moor, Black Raymond,"* Monk offered.

The repetition of the name of the book seemed to stir pretty Frosta Raymond's memory. She started slightly.

"Why, Old Jude Snow had a book by that title," she exclaimed.

"Who is Old Jude Snow?" Doc asked.

"Jug Snow's half sister," Frosta explained. "Jug's father married Old Jude's mother. Old Jude is older than Jug."

"How do you know about the book?" Doc wondered.

"Old Jude was always awfully nice to me." A faraway look came into Frosta's eyes. "It was strange, too. Snows and Raymonds never did mix much, yet Old Jude was always so friendly to me. When I was a little girl, she used to buy me things, and Dad would whip me for taking them. I never could understand it. She said I looked like she did when she was a girl, and I used to visit her. I saw this book one time, years ago. She was mad when I saw it, and her face got red and she put it away."

"You have no idea of what is in the book?"

"Oh, no. I never read it." Frosta shook her head.

They entered the yacht cabin. There, they got a surprise.

The desk had been opened since their last visit.

The money with the ink stains, the spike-nosed automatic, were both gone. Also missing were the call slips for stock purchases in the future at a predetermined price, the options on business property, and the other papers.

"But who in blazes got the junk?" Renny pondered.

"Someone has been here," Doc said grimly. "Except for the currency, those papers have no real cash value. And that makes the fact that they are missing, important."

"Why important?" Renny wanted to know.

"Whoever took them must have had a purpose," Doc pointed out.

With tools from the plane, an experience that had come from many hours spent studying all types of locks and strong-boxes, Doc Savage went to work on the safe in the bathroom of Chelton Raymond's private suite.

"I hope the book tells us something," Renny rumbled, standing by and watching the safe-cracking with much interest.

"It may be of no value whatever," Doc reminded.

The bronze man continued to work, listening with a special electrical device to the click of the tumblers. The contrivance he was using magnified each sound several thousandfold, and it was only a question of time until he got the box open.

But before the necessary time needed to open the safe elapsed, there came an interruption. Out on deck, Monk set up a great roar. Monk's voice was usually mild, but now it had tremendous volume.

"The Squeaking Goblin!" Monk squawled.

The shock of those unexpected words was sufficient to send Doc Savage and the others charging in the direction of Monk's voice.

THE apish chemist was bouncing up and down, beating on a cabin door.

"He went in here!" he howled. "I saw the cuss, coonskin cap and all!"

The door had resisted Monk, in whose long simian arms lay tremendous strength, but the panels cracked, the stringers splintered, and the whole went down at the first smashing charge which the big bronze man threw against it.

Beyond was a stateroom, empty. Another door gave access to the deck, and this gaped open.

"Blast it!" Monk gritted. "I didn't know about that door."

They proceeded to push a hurried search, but it was unfruitful. Doc dispatched two men to the masts as lookouts. Then they examined the yacht again.

They peered into bins in the galley, opened the fuel tanks, even probed the water reservoirs with bits of spars. No square inch of the boat escaped their scrutiny.

No Squeaking Goblin did they find.

Renny threw up his oversize hands in disgust.

"I'll give it up!" he growled. "That Squeakin' Goblin ain't human, and nobody can tell me he is."

"He could've gotten overboard without being seen," Monk pointed out.

"Sure, and then what?" Renny blew on rocky knuckles. "He turned into a fish, I suppose? We've been watching the water and the shore for half a mile in each direction. Tell me how he could get away?"

"Blessed if I know," Monk had to admit.

They returned to the bathroom where the secret safe lay. Doc Savage stopped suddenly in the doorway.

There came into being the tiny, fantastic trilling sound which was the characteristic of the bronze man, the thing he did in moments of surprise or stress. It trailed in uncanny fashion up and down the musical scale, its unearthly cadence penetrating to the far corners of the yacht. Then it ebbed away.

"What is it, Doc?" Renny thumped.

"The safe."

"What about—!" Renny let the rest go, his jaw sagging.

The safe gaped wide open—and it was empty!

THAT the strong-box had been opened during Doc's absence from the cabin in pursuit of the Squeaking Goblin, there was no doubt. That the safe was empty was also a fact.

They proved that by rigging up an X-ray apparatus and taking a picture through the safe. The purpose was to make sure there were no hidden recesses.

The X-ray negative showed no trace of the book, *The Life and Horrible Deeds of That Adopted Moor, Black Raymond.*

Tige, standing near, said, "Chelton Raymond be t'only one thot had the figgers to get in thot iron box. I heered him say so once't."

"Chelton Raymond is dead," Monk snapped.

Tige shrugged. "I was just a-tellin' you."

Monk scowled. "My guess is Jug Snow. He's the Goblin! He came back here and managed to get aboard the yacht."

"But where did he go, mastermind?" Ham snapped.

The question remained very much of a mystery.

Later, Doc had Renny use the plane to ferry Long Tom, Johnny, the Coastal Agency detectives and the crew of the Raymond yacht from the island. They had, they declared, searched the little island again and again, but had found no trace of the Squeaking Goblin.

With the coming of the noon hour, they received fresh information from a copy of a Bar Harbor newspaper.

The paper stated that several men of evil appearance and violent manner had appeared at the local airport, seized a large plane and a pilot, and forced the flyer to take the air, after inquiring whether he knew the route to Kentucky. The evil-looking men had been aboard the plane when it departed.

"That was Jug Snow and his crew," Monk declared, after reading the story. "What do we do now, Doc?"

"We follow them," the bronze man declared.

Preparations for the trip Kentuckyward went forward at once. In the course of the work, Renny approached Doc.

"Doc, you never have told the girl and Tige about the other two birds," the engineer pointed out.

"You mean the red-headed fellow and the elderly man?" Doc asked.

"That's them," agreed Renny. "When we last saw them, they shot at us to attract our attention and tell us that Chelton Raymond had been taken to the island."

Doc Savage considered. "We will not mention that for a while," he said finally.

"Listen," Renny gulped. "You don't suspect Tige or the girl?"

Doc's answer was hardly to the point.

"We want to have a look at that book of Old Jude Snow's," he said.

Chapter XII
MOUNTAIN TRICKERY

IT was hot in the Kentucky Mountains. The man perspired as he worked. The perspiration really simplified the strange task he was performing, for it mingled with the blackberry juice, thinning it, making it run.

The blackberry juice looked very like blood. Handful after handful of berries did the fellow pick, squeeze in his hands, and let the juice saturate his neck, shoulder and rough homespun shirt over his heart. His bands were rough from much hard labor.

The fellow worked furtively, pausing now and then to listen, an attentive expression on his stupid face. Birds made casual noise on the valley slopes to either side, but there was no other sound.

"Mought nigh due here," the mountaineer mumbled, and worked more rapidly at juicing the berries.

Once he pulled a roll of bills from a pocket of his patched overalls, eyed it, then replaced it and carefully fastened the pocket shut with a thorn which served him as a pin.

"Kain't kick 'bout the pay I'm gettin' fur this," he chuckled evilly.

His shirt saturated to his satisfaction with berry juice, he moved a few yards through the brush and came to a crude, ungraded road.

An automatic pistol came out of his clothing. He examined this to make sure it was loaded, then lay down in the middle of the road, so that he resembled a man badly wounded. The gun, however, was held out of sight beneath him.

The silence of a great death overlay the mountains. A farmer would have noted one peculiar thing about all the fields—they had not been tended properly. Some did not appear to have been cultivated at all.

Nowhere was anybody to be seen in the fields, although the tobacco needed hoeing and weeds were killing the beans and potatoes and the corn.

Many of the cabins near the untended fields were empty. Behind some were tiny family burial grounds, and in more than a few of these stood fresh, roughly fashioned crosses. Here and there, a smear of blackened ashes and a flame-reddened cook stove or bedstead marked where a cabin had been. Hogs ran wild; chickens and ducks and guineas roosted where they could, prey for raccoons, skunks, weasels. Milk cows, long gone dry, roamed the hills without attention.

The feud was in the mountains. Terror, death and violence was like a black blanket over the Kentucky Cumberlands.

The deserted cabins meant families had doubled up for safety. Women and children did not venture out. The men stirred abroad only for food, or to wage guerrilla warfare.

Snow stalked Raymond, and Raymond fought Snow with killing purpose, with nobody neutral. Most of the families in the mountains were related by blood or by marriage, or their sympathies were with one clan or the other, and those who wanted to walk the middle ground found themselves out of luck.

To a feudist, brain aflame with hate, humanity was divided into two classes—friends and enemies. The lowlanders, who weren't worth counting, had not dared to venture into the mountains for many a month, anyway.

The man who was pretending to be wounded lay in the road, waiting, the automatic pistol held out of sight beneath him. He was a good actor. He looked as if he might be dead. Then suddenly, from down the valley, he heard footsteps.

Around an angle in the road appeared a walking party. They numbered five; four were men, the fifth an extremely pretty young woman.

Swinging in the lead was a giant who looked as if he might be wrought of bronze metal, yet who was proportioned so perfectly that his great size was apparent only when contrasted with those accompanying him.

The group sighted the man in the road. They stopped.

"Know him, Frosta?" asked the big bronze man, indicating the figure sprawled ahead.

The attractive girl stared.

"Oh!" she gasped. "That is a Raymond, Mr. Savage! He is Tabor Raymond, a distant relative of mine!"

"He's been feuded by some durn Snow!" growled gaunt Tige Eller.

They ran forward. They had not seen Tabor Raymond's automatic.

WITH Doc Savage now were only two of his men—big-fisted Renny, the engineer, and sickly-looking Long Tom, the electrical genius.

The other three of Doc's aides—Monk, Ham

and Johnny—were working on what Doc had described simply as "a different angle." Strangely enough, Renny and Long Tom knew no more than that concerning the present whereabouts of their three pals.

Doc Savage had an unusual policy which he frequently put in effect when setting his little organization upon some task. The bronze man did not tell one group of his assistants what the others were doing, or where they could be found. This was a precaution. Should one of the five be unlucky enough to fall into the hands of an enemy, and be questioned by forcible methods, they could not divulge the whereabouts of their fellows.

Renny, a great tower of a man, drew out in the lead in the race for Tabor Raymond. Long Tom and Tige trod his heels. The girl was close behind. Hence none noticed that Doc Savage was no longer with them.

Doc had plunged into the thick brush beside the trail. Once out of sight, he ran parallel to the trail. He made tremendous speed, for the noise of the runners on the road made it unnecessary for him to exercise full stealth.

On the road, Renny reached Tabor Raymond. He sank to a knee, thinking to find how seriously the fellow was wounded. But Renny had sharp eyes. He perceived almost instantly that there was no wound.

"Hey!" he rumbled. "What the blazes! This bird isn't—"

He got no farther. Tabor Raymond came to life. Like a clock spring breaking out of its container, he twisted, heaving erect. The automatic pistol came into view. It swung up.

"I was ter git the big feller!" he gritted. "But reckon one a' you'll do!"

He seemed destined to shoot Renny point-blank.

But out of the brush beside the road slammed a great nemesis of bronze, a huge man of metal who moved with a speed that was hair-lifting to watch. One of his hands lashed out. The gun was knocked down—and it exploded. Bark leaped off a nearby tree, the only damage inflicted by the bullet.

Evil-faced Tabor Raymond wailed out in awful pain. Grinding sounds, soft and ugly, came from his gun hand, which had been enwrapped by the giant bronze man's fingers. Bawling softly, Tabor Raymond released the gun, surrendering completely.

Doc Savage searched him. The bronze man did not show by as much as quickened breathing the violent action through which he had just gone.

The roll of money came to light. Doc scrutinized it. On the corners of the bills were black smears, as if a dark liquid had been spilled upon them.

Doc tossed money and gun to Renny, asking, "Recognize these?"

Renny eyed the articles. A blank, startled look came over his features. He pointed at the ink spots on the bills, then tapped the automatic.

"Holy cow!" he rumbled. "This gun and money seems to be—"

"The same that we found in the desk aboard Chelton Raymond's yacht, and which were later removed," Doc affirmed.

VILLAINOUS-FEATURED Tabor Raymond got up and tried to run, but Doc caught him and slapped him back to earth with considerable force.

By that time, Renny had recovered from the shock of the discovery that the automatic and currency had come from Chelton Raymond's yacht on the Maine coast.

"After the Squeaking Goblin killed Chelton Raymond, somebody beat us to the yacht and stole the gun and the money," Renny boomed thoughtfully. "I wonder if it could have been this egg?" He glowered at the prisoner.

Small lights came and went in Doc's flake-gold eyes. "It is hardly likely," he said. "This fellow does not seem intelligent enough to be a great schemer."

"Hain't dumb neither, if thot's what you be a-sayn'!" snarled Tabor Raymond.

"No?" Doc said dryly. "Let us say that you make mistakes, then. It was a mistake to think blackberry juice would look like blood."

"To an eye as sharp as Doc's, anyway," Renny added.

Tabor Raymond subsided, glaring murderously.

"Reckon he's dumb, right enough," Tige Eller muttered. "Tabor allers did have skunk ways, too."

"Obviously, he was hired to kill me," Doc agreed.

Frosta Raymond had been in the background, but now she took a part in the conversation, her voice jerky, and her words somewhat nearer the illiterate speech of the mountaineers than usual.

"But I kain't—understand this!" she exclaimed. "This here man is a Raymond. Doc Savage, you are helpin' us Raymonds. Why should he try to kill you?"

"Kain't savvy thot, neither," Tige put in. "If'n it had a-been a good-fur-nothin' Snow, it'd be easy to see through."

"We'll learn the answer to that," Doc said slowly.

He looked at ugly Tabor as he spoke, and there was something in his flake-gold eyes, some power of threat and promise of terrors to come, that caused the would-be killer to squirm and show his teeth in a grimace of fright. The teeth were dark from tobacco chewing.

"Whut yer agoin' ter do?" he squealed.

Doc Savage replied nothing, but crouched down before the captive. Jacking the slide of the automatic, Doc removed a cartridge. He placed this between his strong white teeth, shiny brass end outermost. He held it there, and was motionless.

Tabor stared at the cartridge end. His eyes became fixed.

Doc did not stir. After a few seconds his corded, metallic hands began to make slow, straying motions through the air.

Tabor followed the hands with his eyes for a time, but his gaze finally went back to the cartridge, as if pondering what its purpose could be. Tabor seemed to have no idea as to the purpose of the weird procedure.

Renny and Long Tom, in the background, knew. Doc was putting the mountaineer under a hypnotic spell. That would make it much simpler to question Tabor.

But the spell was never completed. Came a loud squeak of a noise. Its echoes caromed from one side of the valley to the other.

Tabor Raymond let out a loud sigh, jerked violently, and lay back in the road. Red fluid began to ooze down this face from a spot in his forehead, and it was not blackberry juice this time.

"The Squeakin' Goblin killed him!" Renny thundered.

DOC SAVAGE was already racing from the vicinity. The echoes still piped shrilly back from the slopes. But the bronze man had caught the first squeak, and had an idea of its source. The point lay to the left, toward the stream which ran down the valley.

Doc Savage traveled swiftly, but used caution, keeping under cover as much as possible. Having traversed two-score yards, he paused to listen.

Muzzle-loading rifles such as the Squeaking Goblin carried had to be charged after each shot, and Doc was hoping to hear the tamping sound of the ramrod driving home another bullet. But there was no such noise.

Moving more cautiously, Doc went on. His sharp gaze searched for bent grass stems. Once he caught a faint tang which might have been the odor of burned gunpowder. Again, birds flew up ahead, and they might have been frightened by the passing of the Squeaking Goblin.

Doc reached the creek, however, without sighting his quarry. The water was slow-running, deep. If there had been any turtles and frogs along the banks in the immediate vicinity, they had been frightened to cover by the noise of the rifle shot.

With increasing intensity, Doc searched. He probed treetops, even climbing into the aërial lanes himself. He scrutinized the ground for crushed leaves, disturbed plants, and even noted the plentifulness of insects at one spot as compared with another, trying to ascertain if the passing of some concrete embodiment had frightened them away.

Ten minutes later, he was back with his companions.

"Got away," he reported.

Renny seemed stunned. "But Doc, how can—"

"I know it seems impossible," Doc told him. "Much experience with good woodsmen, men able to travel noiselessly, has come my way, but this is the first one that actually seemed to have all the qualities of a phantom."

Frosta Raymond put in grimly, "Somebody hired this Tabor to kill you, Mr. Savage, and the Squeakin' Goblin shot Tabor to keep him from tellin' who it was."

"My idea, too," Doc agreed.

Renny seemed to have something else on his mind. He squirmed, opened and closed his enormous hands.

"Doc," he said.

"Yes."

"The bullet the Squeaking Goblin killed Tabor with—"

"What about it?"

"It's gone."

"Gone!"

"Simply vanished. That's what it did—if there *was* a real bullet."

DOC SAVAGE made an examination himself, endeavoring to ascertain just what had become of the bullet, for it had certainly disappeared and was not to be found, although he conducted an extensive hunt.

Just what opinion the bronze man held, he did not state after he had completed his scrutiny. His lack of communicativeness plainly disappointed Renny and Long Tom, but they did not ask questions, knowing it would be useless in view of Doc's habit of keeping certain of his opinions to himself.

They moved the corpse of Tabor Raymond to one side of the road and covered it with coats, leaving it there. Later, some of the Raymond clan would come for the body and give it burial.

Then they resumed their journey into the mountains.

Long Tom drew Doc aside before they had gone more than a quarter of a mile. The electrical expert had something to import.

"Doc, that Tige guy was monkeying around the body before Renny started to hunt for the bullet,"

Long Tom whispered, after making certain the others were not looking. "Tige might have sniped the bullet. That was while you were off hunting the Squeaking Goblin."

"You suspect Tige?"

"Blast it, I dunno. He could have shot Chelton Raymond; he might have robbed the desk on the yacht of that money and automatic, and he could have hired this bird to waylay us."

"But he did not kill the 'bird', as you call him, or Tabor."

Long Tom sighed. "There might be more than one Squeaking Goblin."

Little more was said as they moved ahead. Frosta Raymond soon dropped back, evincing a liking for the companionship of Doc Savage. This was understandable, since the bronze man was not only a striking physical specimen, but he had a rare quality of personality.

Fabulous as was his knowledge—there were few subjects upon which he could not hold his own with the most learned and specialized of living men—Doc Savage did not conduct himself on an intellectual level. He had a remarkable faculty of making himself seem one of whatever group in which he might find himself.

A famous teacher once said that the mark of an educated man is the ease with which he makes himself at home everywhere—with learned statesmen, with factory laborers. Doc had that mark.

Frosta Raymond obviously liked the bronze giant, and did not feel uncomfortable in the face of his tremendous mental development.

Not that Frosta was a hillbilly. She was, as Doc had learned, a graduate of the best mountain schools and the state university. Except when she was excited, her speech was almost devoid of the mountain dialect.

No doubt it was Frosta's education outside the domain of the mountaineers which had caused her to seek Doc Savage's aid in stopping the feud that was striking such terror.

A true hillbilly would never think of calling on a "lowlander" for aid, and they classed everyone outside their mountains as lowlanders. Frosta, highly intelligent, had realized the uselessness of all the fighting.

Moreover, it was her clever brain which had first seen through what on the surface seemed a plain feud. She had realized there was something sinister, some vile and consummate force of evil behind the whole thing.

That there was something profound and mysterious behind the mountain trouble, they all felt sure, although the only proof as yet was the weird machinations of the Squeaking Goblin, and the disappearance of the book *The Life and Horrible Deeds of That Adopted Moor, Black Raymond* from the strong-box on the yacht of unfortunate Chelton Raymond.

The little cavalcade moved forward. The sun was hot above. Birds created noise with their cries, and grasshoppers clattered. A crow *caw-cawed* in the distance. Their footsteps on the road were dull.

Twenty feet to one side of the road, a man popped out of a ditch. He held a rifle in his hands. The gun leaped in Doc's direction with an expert speed.

"Durn lowlander!" gritted the rifleman.

"Red!" screamed Frosta Raymond.

Then the young woman leaped forward, deliberately throwing herself between the big bronze man and the rifle of the man who had appeared so suddenly.

Chapter XIII
THE TRAP

FOR a strained ten seconds or so, the tableau held. Frosta Raymond stood between Doc Savage and the rifle. Anger blazed in her eyes.

Behind Doc, Renny rumbled, "Hey! That redhead is the guy we saw with the old man—back in Maine."

"Right," Long Tom breathed. "He helped the old man grab us, and later he and the old man told us where Chelton Raymond had been taken."

Frosta Raymond bent a wrathful look upon the flame-haired young man with the rifle.

"Put that gun down, Red!" she snapped.

"Red" scowled uncomfortably over the rifle, and finally lowered the weapon.

"Blast it!" he growled. "Git out'n the way, Frosta. I ain't aimin' to do 'em no bad hurt!"

Doc Savage settled the immediate problem by stepping from behind the girl, although she shifted quickly in an effort to keep in front of him.

The rifleman, true to his grumbled word, did not fire.

"Reach them arms up in the air!" he invited sourly.

Doc addressed the young woman. "Who is he, Frosta?"

"Ralph McNew," said the girl. "Everybody calls him Red."

"Is he a Snow?"

"No-o-o." A trace of red color came into Frosta's cheeks. "He comes nearer being a Raymond, I guess."

In the background, gaunt Tige Eller laughed shortly.

"Red and Frosta be a-figgerin' on gettin' theirselves married," he said. "Reckon thot 'bout makes Red a Raymond."

Frosta colored even more prettily at that.

"Reach them there arms up!" Red repeated violently. "We all don't want no durn lowlanders 'round 'bout. I'm gonna take your guns and send you skedaddlin' back where you come from."

"Thinks he'll run us out of the mountains, eh?" Renny thumped and blocked and unblocked his great fists.

Tige Eller eyed Red and the rifle and laughed again, jeeringly.

"Red figgers he's some man," he chuckled. "But that's 'cause he ain't run up agin' Doc Savage a-fore."

Red and Tige Eller did not seem to be on the best of terms. Red glowered contemptuously at the bony Tige. Red did look like a very competent young man with his corded muscles, his big-boned brawniness.

"A fine Raymond you be!" he gibed at Tige—then indicated Doc, Renny and Long Tom with a gesture of his rifle. "No good Raymond would throw in with these lowlanders, Tige!"

"Ain't me a-bringin' 'em into the mountains," Tige disclaimed, then pointed at Frosta. "Hit's this hussy you been a-figgerin' on makin' yur woman."

"You leave the women folks out'n this!" Red grated.

Doc Savage interrupted the word exchange by moving forward. This caused Red to forget all about his quarrel with Tige. He shifted his rifle until he was staring at Doc over the sights.

"That's the idea, big fella," he said grimly. "You come a bit closer, then stop and I'll get yur gun."

A slight quaver was noticeable in Red's voice, and it was to be suspected that he was overawed by the impressive proportions of the bronze man, this being the first time he had glimpsed Doc at close range in the full light of day.

"That's far enough!" he added.

Doc halted. Red stepped forward. Doc's arms were in the air, and Red was confident. Standing well back, he began to search the bronze man.

A strange thing happened. Doc had not moved. But Red suddenly dropped his rifle. He swayed on his feet, sat down heavily, shook his head, then stretched out on his back and began to snore as if in a heavy sleep.

"Tarnation!" muttered the stunned Tige.

BOTH Tige and Frosta Raymond were startled at what had happened to Red McNew, for it smacked of black magic, Doc Savage apparently, having made no move, having done nothing to cause the sorrel-haired young man to collapse and start snoring.

Big-fisted Renny cleared up the mystery.

Doc had long ago perfected an odorless and colorless gas which produced swift unconsciousness, and the presence of which could not be detected without special apparatus. This vapor produced a senselessness which lasted lengths of time varying from a few minutes to many hours, depending on its strength.

Doc carried it in thin-walled glass balls, some spheres holding weak solutions, others strong ones. Perhaps the most amazing quality of the gas was that it became ineffective after mingling with the air for a few seconds. The nitrogen and oxygen in the air mixed with the anaesthetic vapor and nullified its effects. The nullification did not take more than a minute, and Doc could hold his breath that long, thus escaping the effects of the vapor.

Doc carried some of the balls in secret pockets in his clothing, where they could be broken by expanding muscles. As a rule, no one ever noticed the act of breaking the glass spheres. The thin glass could hardly be heard as it shattered.

Frosta Raymond eyed Doc with undisguised admiration, while Tige stood back and scowled as if he found the story about the anaesthetic gas hard to believe.

"So Red is your fiancé," Doc asked Frosta.

Frosta colored a little. "Red is a nice boy," she defended.

Red awakened after a while, sat up, peered about, then registered profound disgust. He was humiliated, but physically unharmed.

"What in blazes happened?" he pondered aloud.

No one enlightened him.

"What was the idea of holding us up?" Doc demanded.

"I told you!" Red mumbled promptly. "I was agoin' to chase you out a' the mountains. We hill folks ain't got much use for outsiders. And 'special, we don't like 'em mixin' in our troubles."

The small lights in the bronze man's flake-gold eyes seemed possessed of an understanding quality, for it had been a part of his fabulous training to become versed in the psychology of all peoples.

These mountain folk would fight to the death among themselves, but let an outsider, a "furriner," try to interfere, and the interpolating party was considered fair game for everybody and an enemy to all.

"Why were you and the elderly man in Maine?" Doc asked quietly.

Doc was watching Frosta Raymond as he spoke, and the violent start of the young woman told him that she had not known Red was in the East.

Red nodded at Frosta, after hesitating, and said, "We followed her."

"Why?"

"Figured we'd kinda look out for her." Red again nodded at Frosta. "We didn't have no sympathy for what she was adoin', but we didn't want none a' them blasted Snows a-harmin' her."

"Red!" Frosta gasped. "You followed me all the way to Maine? And I never knew it!"

"We was right keerful not to be seen," said Red.

"Who was the elderly man with you, Red?" Doc asked.

"Thought you knew." Red seemed surprised. "Thot was Frosta's pappy."

"My father!" the girl cried out in surprise.

RED MCNEW proved to be an uncommunicative gentleman. He knew nothing about the Tabor Raymond who had manifestly been hired to kill Doc Savage, except to opine that, "Tabor allers was a no-good scut."

"How did you know we were coming to the mountains," Doc asked.

"Didn't know. Just happened to be out a-huntin' Snows and seen you all a-comin' down the road," Red declared.

Doc Savage, watching the rather clean-cut features of the burly young mountain man, seemed satisfied with the answer.

"We'd better be moving," he said. "I want to get to Old Jude Snow as soon as possible."

"Old Jude?" Red was puzzled. "Why her?"

Doc answered with silence instead of elaborating about the mysterious book, *The Life and Horrible Deeds of That Adopted Moor, Black Raymond,* a copy of which was supposed to be in the possession of Old Jude Snow, half sister of Jug Snow, killing leader of the Snow clan of mountaineers.

Red was plainly piqued by the bronze man's act in ignoring his question about Old Jude, but as they set out along the mountain road, his feeling of injury subsided and he offered another bit of information without urging.

"Frosta's pap and me come back to the mountains by airplane after we learned Frosta was safe," he said.

"We was a-watchin' the yacht and we seed you come back with her and could tell she was safe enough with you."

"Watchin' the yacht, huh?" Renny boomed. "Say, did you see anything of that Squeakin' Goblin spook, or whatever he is?"

"Nary a see," Red disclaimed.

The heat of the sun increased, and what breeze there had been subsided, so that the sultriness was increased unpleasantly. The more sluggish of the birds fell silent, although an occasional woodpecker rattled on a tree and mocking birds made varied cries.

Renny moved up and strode alongside Doc Savage. Doc, noting that Renny had something on his mind, increased his pace and they drew far enough ahead of the others that they could talk freely without being overheard.

"Whatcha think of Red's story?" the engineer queried. "Thin, if you ask me."

"How do you mean?" Doc countered.

"Him just happening to meet us," Renny snorted. "Maybe he did. It's possible."

"But you think other things are possible, too?" Doc queried.

"It's possible this Red or the old man are the Squeakin' Goblin."

"The girl's father?" Doc asked.

Renny shrugged and swung his big fists as he walked. "Can't overlook no bets, Doc."

"You said something," Doc agreed grimly.

SOME miles remained yet to be traversed, and they went ahead without slackening speed. Frosta Raymond kept abreast easily, the lithe ease of her gait showing that she had tramped much over these mountains.

Red moved alongside her and spoke, his voice low, so that Doc Savage and Renny did not catch his words. But the young fellow's manner showed that he was trying to make his peace with Frosta. She cut him off shortly.

"That," chuckled Long Tom, "is like a woman. That guy has gone to a lot of trouble, following her back East to look out for her safety."

"That's *his* story," Renny said skeptically.

They sighted a column of black smoke, climbing straight into the still, hot air like a sepia genii. It had, somehow, a sombre hideous quality—and they broke into a run, anxious to reach it.

The smoke came from a burning cabin. Rafters and roof had already fallen in. Door casings were consumed, the glass was melted or broken from the windows, and the log walls were beginning to topple.

A pitiful twisted figure, an old man with white hair and a seamed, peaceful face, sprawled near the flames. He was poorly clad in overalls, homemade shirt of dotted percale, and was barefooted.

He had been shot through the brain.

"That's Uncle Obe," Tige said thickly. "He was warned them Snows mought get 'im if'n he stayed here by hisself."

Doc Savage circled swiftly and picked up the trail of the killers. They had set fire to the cabin, it seemed, and bushwhacked the elderly member of the Raymond clan as he dashed out of the flaming structure.

Doc located a moccasin print which had a hole in the middle. It was Jug Snow's track. Four men had been with him.

The slayers had mounted horses and ridden away, after slashing sets of harness in the shed of a barn, chopping through the tongue and running gears of a buggy, and committing other vandalisms aimed at the heirs of the man they had killed.

"Dang it!" Renny thumped from deep in his chest. "Ain't there a law to stop this killing? What's the matter with the sheriff? And don't they have state police?"

"Outsiders have never had much luck mixing in our troubles here in the mountains," Red McNew grunted. "Our own sheriff can't do nothin' and knows it. He keeps tryin', but he don't get nowhere. Take Uncle Obe, there. If'n he had been alive and the sheriff had come on 'im, Uncle Obe wouldn't a' told who it was fired on him. We fight our own battles."

Renny pondered. "How many have been killed, altogether?"

Red McNew felt stubbornly silent.

"More than forty," Frosta Raymond put in grimly.

"What?" Renny exploded. "And the governor hasn't sent the militia in to stop it?"

"People out of the mountains do not know how bad the feud is," the girl explained. "And if the soldiers did come, I don't think they could do much. The fighting would just die down while they were here, then start again when they left."

"Then how *can* it be stopped?"

"I don't know," the girl said hopelessly, and looked at Doc Savage.

There was profound silence as they went on, heading toward the cabin of Frosta's father, where Doc intended to leave the others, then penetrate alone into the Snow territory to interview Old Jude Snow.

The murder scene had affected them all—from the big bronze man whose emotions were schooled until they did not show, to Frosta, who sobbed a little, silently. Uncle Obe had been one of her best friends.

They came to a wide, fertile valley which had evidently been farmed in businesslike fashion until the feud came and put a stop to all agricultural pursuits. On high ground in the center stood a substantial neat cottage, an excellent barn. A tractor, threshing machine and other modern implements were in view. Men in overalls, carrying rifles, loafed about the farm.

"My place," said Red McNew. "Them's my hired hands on guard."

Tige, noting the surprise of the others, said, "Oh, Red is 'bout the most go-gettin'est young feller in these parts. He's quite a catch, ain't he, Frosta?"

Frosta only reddened.

THEY did not go to Red McNew's farm, but angled left, only waving at the farm hands on guard, and their way soon began to climb the side of a mountain. Brush thickened about them. They left the road.

"Short cut," Frosta explained.

Shrubbery pressed in. Frequently, they had to shove branches aside or crowd through an occasional curtain of wild grapevines, the fruit of which was beginning to ripen, an attraction that drew swarms of jays and blackbirds.

Tige and Red strode along close beside Doc for a time, then dropped back—a circumstance that the bronze man was shortly to recall. The girl dropped back also, another point Doc was to remember later.

Doc walked in the lead. He came to a spot where gray spider webs spanned the path. Other webs had crossed the trail, and he had brushed them aside; they were plentiful at this season in the mountains.

But this time Doc halted abruptly. He bent close to the webs. A folding magnifying glass came out of his pocket and was used to examine the extremely fine strands.

"Get back!" he warned the others quietly.

"Humph!" Tige jeered. "Plain spider webs ain't never hurt nobody!"

Doc slowly closed the magnifier and returned it to his pocket. He kept well away from the webs.

"You say in the neighborhood of forty people have been killed in this feud?" he asked Frosta Raymond.

She nodded.

"How many were Raymonds?" Doc continued.

"Over thirty," she said.

"Three Raymonds killed for every Snow," Doc repeated, as if he considered that point important.

The girl pointed at the spider web. "Why are you so interested in that?"

Doc did not answer. Instead, he got a stick and carefully broke the web down, rolled it up and, without touching it, managed to stuff a portion in a tiny bottle which he produced from his vest. Then he stamped the remainder of the web into the trail dirt.

They went on again. But now Doc carried a large bough ahead of him in such a manner that it would wipe aside any more spider webs.

Tige and Red seemed a little awed by the grimness of the bronze man's mysterious actions.

They came to a rather pleasant little log bungalow, neat and comfortable-looking, situated a short distance from a noisy, extremely clear brook.

"My father's house," said Frosta.

THE house of the elder Raymond was empty.

"That's strange," muttered Red. "I was past here this mornin', and Pap Raymond said he was gonna be here all day."

Doc Savage roamed through the cabin, moving slowly, his unusual eyes in motion ceaselessly, scrutinizing everywhere, missing no details.

He opened drawers, examined closets. An array of old test tubes, a retort, bottles, caught his eye. With the stuff was a book, undoubtedly old. He lifted this, dusted it off and read the title.

CHEMICAL MANUAL

"Would you mind explaining this?" Doc requested of Frosta.

"Father used to be interested in chemistry," said the young woman. "That's some of his stuff. Why do you ask?"

Doc's only reply to her query was silence. He continued his scrutiny of the cabin. There was a screened-in porch at the rear, with a screen door leading to the yard. The door was very low, so low in fact that a tall man such as Doc had to stoop slightly to avoid a head bump.

The top of the door was rough, splinter-covered. Doc reached up and from the top of the door plucked a grayish hair, light-tipped, something near an inch in length.

Renny, at the bronze man's side, tapped his big fists together. His long features were startled.

"Say, Doc, that looks like coon hair!" he whispered.

"It does," Doc admitted.

"It could've been scraped off a coonskin cap," Renny continued. "The Squeakin' Goblin wears a cap like that."

"The Squeaking Goblin is also a chemist," Doc said dryly. "Or he has an associate who is a chemist."

Renny whistled softly. "Then Frosta's father is—"

"Never jump at conclusions," Doc warned. "The Squeaking Goblin might merely have visited this cabin. Or that hair could have gotten there in some other fashion."

Renny nodded soberly. "Maybe so. But if the old man shows up, I'm keeping an eye on him. I'm keeping an eye on Tige and Red, too."

"How about the girl?"

"It *could* be her," Renny admitted reluctantly.

"The motive behind this is the thing we want to concentrate on finding," Doc told him. "When that is discovered, the field of suspects will be narrowed down."

Renny's oversize paws made a baffled gesture. "But how're we gonna find the motive?"

"Old Jude Snow and her book may help." Doc replied.

The bronze man departed almost immediately for the domain of the Snows, his purpose being to interview Old Jude Snow. He went alone, for it was without company that he worked best.

Before Doc was out of calling distance, he had a final word of advice to give.

"Be very careful not to touch any cobwebs," he warned.

Chapter XIV
OLD JUDE

THE buggy made very little noise on the woods road, for it was well greased and was, moreover, being driven slowly.

The tall mountaineer hunched alertly in the seat, his eyes fixed, not on the surrounding brush and timber, but on three dogs which ranged ahead and on the sides. They were fox hounds, redbones, with velvet ears and keen noses.

The fox hounds would scent out any Snows lurking in ambush, and that was why the man in the buggy watched them. The man was a Raymond. A Snow would kill him on sight. And he would kill a Snow.

Two mealy-nosed mules pulled the buggy which turned, in the course of time, into a rain-gullied driveway. There was a house beyond, but nearer ran a hog-tight fence with a gate through which the driveway progressed.

A hole between gate and gatepost had been much used by the hounds, and all three dogs now squeezed through while the man was getting out of the buggy to open the gate.

Immediately after wedging through the hole, sniffing the ground the while, the hounds began to sneeze. They sneezed violently, almost falling down, and galloped toward the cabin.

The mountaineer noted the sneezing but did not attach the true significance to it. There was ordinary pepper strewed on the ground at the gate hole, and that was making the dogs sneeze. The hounds now could not smell effectively. But the man was unaware of that.

The man pulled up before his little barn, walking and driving the buggy since opening and closing the gate, then began unhitching. He unhooked link tugs from single trees, clipped them atop the breechings, walked around freeing check reins, and dropped the neck yoke.

A bush fluttered beyond a hog lot which lay next to the barn. There came into view a rifle barrel. This shifted slightly, then steadied, it had centered on the man unharnessing the mules.

Behind the gun, a Snow aimed carefully. He

had his tongue thrust through his teeth and under his upper lip, and that made him look particularly vicious. He bit down on his tongue; his finger prepared to stroke the trigger. It was he who had spread the pepper.

There was a blurred movement of a small object traveling through the air. A clank followed. The Snow dropped his rifle; hands flew to his head.

He swayed there. A few feet away, he saw a round rock fall to the earth and roll to a stop. That, he knew, had struck his head. He peered around foolishly, could see no one, then stooped and got his rifle.

The Snow did not again glance at the Raymond whom he had been about to bushwhack. The thrown rock had shocked him beyond measure. He was bewildered.

He could discern nobody as he stared about. That turned his puzzlement to fear. His mind visioned a Raymond as having thrown the stone, and it was not long before he was in a mental state where the surrounding brush seemed full of enemy Raymonds.

The Snow fled. He looked back often, but there was no one to be seen, and the only sounds were his hard breathing and the flutterings of such mountain birds as were frightened by his precipitate passing.

The puzzle of the mysterious rock preyed on the Snow's mind, and he began to tremble appreciably when it occurred to him that the stone might be a hint from a Divine source. He decided to consult his leader and chief of the Snow clan, burly and loud-mouthed Jug Snow.

"I musta met a hant!" cried the man aloud, and began to run down a woods trail.

Suddenly, he flung up his hands and brushed at cobwebs into which he had run. His face contorted and he cried out as if there was something painful about the touch of the cobwebs. Then he endeavored to run on. His face grew mottled.

"I'm 'witched!" he screamed.

He fell down, then slowly struggled upward. Falling again, however, he did not have the strength to rise, but lay there with arms and legs squirming like live strings, eyes like white eggs half outside his skull, rattling noises pouring from his throat.

There was a stir beside the trail and the giant, metallic figure of Doc Savage appeared.

DOC SAVAGE had chanced to come upon the rifleman when the man was sprinkling the pepper to get rid of the menace of the hound dogs—and Doc had lurked nearby, preventing the murder of a Raymond by a thrown rock. Doc had hoped to follow this Snow to Jug.

Careful not to touch the stricken Snow, Doc made an examination. Even his superb medical skill could not save the fellow.

The man's squirming stilled, his rattling sounds subsided, even as Doc bent over him. He had died.

Across his face, and over his hands where they had torn at the cobwebs, were tiny, hairlike purple lines. They resembled raw burns, as if red-hot wires of infinite fineness had touched the skin.

Doc scrutinized the cobwebs. They, of course, had brought death, for they were actually not cobwebs, but hair-thin wires coated with some chemical compound.

Without a chemical analysis the bronze man could not tell with certainty the exact nature of the coating on the wires. Possibly it was some solution of cyanide or other violent toxic in combination with an acid which burned the flesh and thus caused introduction of the lethal potion into the human system.

It was clever, that poison—whatever its nature. It was the work of an experienced chemist.

Doc Savage went on, moving slowly and keeping watch for cobwebs which looked unnaturally stiff. It was this feature which had caused him first to become suspicious of them. But he saw no more.

This might be significant and might not, for in the two instances in which the deadly webs had appeared, they had been in the neighborhood of Raymond cabins. The webs were not the weapon of feuding mountaineers, therefore they must have been planted by the Squeaking Goblin, whoever that mysterious being was.

Over an hour later, Doc sighted smoke above the scrub oaks, a thin curl that came from a chimney. He went forward more slowly—and sighted a cabin.

Large and rambling, it had been erected in the last few weeks and was constructed like a fortress. Heavy log panels were hinged over the windows. An outer fence, which was more like a stockade, surrounded it.

Men stood about. Some were Snow clansmen who had been members of Jug's party in Maine. They talked earnestly. Their movements portrayed a tension and uneasiness.

The Snows were excited over something.

Doc Savage positioned himself behind a bush, drew small but powerful binoculars from a pocket, and watched the Snows. He hoped to get some clue that would show where Old Jude might be found.

Among the accomplishments which Doc Savage had mastered was that of lip reading. He managed to follow pretty well what was said among the Snows.

Jug Snow popped out of the cabin, waving his

arms. His voice, a great yell of anger, made Doc's lip-reading abilities unnecessary.

"Old Jude has been carried off!" Jug shouted. "Ain't a durn doubt a' it! Her room is all tore up!"

FOR some seconds following Jug's proclamation, silence lay over the clearing.

"Ain't nothin' else missin'?" asked a mountaineer.

Jug scowled. His words were inaudible, but Doc read his lips.

"Old Jude had a leetle tin box," he muttered. "Thot's gone, too."

"Whot'd the old gal keep in the box, Jug?"

"Some kind of a durn book and some other papers," said Jug. "Dunno what the papers was, but the book was some durn thing 'bout a Raymond by the first name a' Black. I seed the name a' the book once't."

Again those in the clearing about the cabin were silent, and for the briefest instant, the quiet was broken by an eerie note, a faint, nebulous trilling that seemed, because of the manner in which it appeared, to emanate from everywhere and yet from no definite spot, possessed of an essence of ventriloquism.

The Snows heard it. They were puzzled.

"Didja hear thot thar?" a man muttered.

But the fantastic sound was gone now, and the Snows dismissed it as something imagined, not associating the trilling with the presence of Doc Savage.

"How'd Old Jude get ketched?" someone asked Jug.

"The varmint shot Willie, here," Jug grunted. "Then they musta popped Old Jude over the head with somethin' an' packed her away."

Doc was momentarily puzzled over the mention of the unexpected Willie, but that became clear when Jug Snow moved to the right a few paces and lifted the body of a man. That would be Willie. He had been a guard, and the raider had killed him.

"Quare we never heerd no shot," a man suggested. "We all be down the crick a piece all mornin'."

"Hit's the work a' Raymonds!" Jug Snow snapped. "I'm gonna gouge out the bullet. Some a' them Raymonds use different size rifles than t'others. Bullet might show us which'n done it."

With his pocketknife and a manner which showed no squeamishness whatever, Jug performed a gory makeshift autopsy. He cut and probed for some time. Then he began to curse.

"There ain't no bullet!" he yelled.

"Hell's foire!" gasped a Snow. "'Twas the Squeakin' Goblin that's up an' carried off Old Jude!"

Chapter XV
THE UNEXPECTED DEAD

DOC SAVAGE did not remain where he was for long after hearing—seeing, rather—the words. He doubled down, seemed to merge with the tall mountain grass, and scuttled forward.

The Snows were congregated on one side of the cabin. Doc approached on the other. He slid over the low log wall. There were dogs near the cabin, but, fortunately, at the moment, on the other side.

Doc ran to a window. It was sashless, but covered with a mosquito bar. Stroking gestures of a sharp knife opened the netting soundlessly, and Doc made practically no noise climbing inside.

He had little trouble finding Old Jude's room. It was poorly furnished, most of the fittings homemade. Evidences of a search were profuse. A bureau of wooden boxes had been upset, and a family photograph album lay on the floor.

Doc's intent gaze found nothing of particular importance, and he picked up the album and riffled through its pages, noting that the name of each subject had been scrawled below the pictures.

Outside, the Snows talked.

"Jug, did you know Old Jude was gone all the time you and the boys was back East?" a man asked.

"What's thot?" Jug demanded. "The old rip warn't here?"

"A-course, Old Jude said she was up t' the farm she heired from her grand-pap on Calf Crick," the informant said hastily. "She mought have been, and her bein' gone mought not mean anything."

"And it mought, too," Jug pointed out.

About that time, Doc Savage came upon a picture in the album which interested him. A name was written below.

JUDALIA

That would be "Old Jude." The picture was of a girl about eighteen, and Doc, who had expected something of a hag, was surprised, for the photograph showed a person of rare beauty. There was something striking about it in another way, also.

The bronze man studied the picture from various angles. Then he got it! Old Jude at eighteen or so had borne a remarkable resemblance to entrancingly pretty Frosta Raymond as she was today.

Other pictures followed. They showed an unusual decline in beauty, starting at about the age of twenty. Lines had come into Judalia's face, her hair had become gray and stringy and her exquisite features had become ridden with an expression of misery. It was striking—that visible record of pretty Judalia turning into Old Jude, the crone.

Doc gave attention to what Jug Snow was saying outside.

"There's somethin' wham-slammed quare 'bout this whole shootin' match," said Jug. "Who in blazes is a-helpin' us, without lettin' us know who he be?"

Doc would have liked to put a question to that. Fortunately, one of the less informed Snows asked almost the exact interrogative which Doc desired answered.

"Help?" the man grunted. "Whatcha mean, Jug?"

"Don't you know what sent us back East?" Jug demanded.

"Nope."

"'Twas a note thot somebody up and throwed into the cabin," Jug explained. "We never seed who throwed it, 'cause a' the dark."

"What'd the writin' say?"

"Said thot Frosta Raymond was a-headin fur the East to get this Doc Savage feller to help her fight us Snows. Told us we could grab the gal and Doc Savage at thot Aquatania Hotel on the Maine coast."

"You be a-forgettin' part, Jug," another man put in slowly.

Jug scowled. "I ain't a-forgettin'. There was a passell a' money tied to that note, money fur us to chase East after Frosta Raymond and Doc Savage."

Doc was a very, very interested listener by now.

"THOT feller, whoever he be, sure knows his stuff," Jug continued. "We run into Frosta Raymond and Doc Savage right whar he said in his writin'."

A voice from the outskirts of the crowd asked, "What other help has this here mysterious person give you, Jug?"

"'Nother time, more money was throwed into the cabin," said Jug. "There was sure some spondulicks in thot roll."

"Was there a note with it?" asked the voice from the edge of the group.

Two men near where the words came from glanced about curiously.

"Sure there was a note," said Jug.

"What'd it say?" asked the voice.

The two men who had looked around stiffened slightly.

"Thot's a secret I'm keepin'," Jug said darkly. "But this here feller has sure got some good ideas."

"How do you know it is a 'feller'?" queried the voice. "Maybe it's a woman."

Attracted by the first two who had stared, two more men looked around. They started, staring around at their neighbors.

"Hell!" said Jug.

"Where are the notes now?" asked the voice.

All four men who were staring at the voice source became somewhat popeyed.

"Them notes up and disappeared," Jug said reluctantly. "Dunno how I could've, but I must've lost 'em."

"Could they have been stolen from you?" asked the interrogator.

But that question was never answered.

"Jug! Jug!" shrieked the men who were staring. *"There ain't nobody talkin' to you!"*

"Hell!" snorted Jug. "You're batty!"

"That voice has been comin' out of thin air!" screeched the informants. "We been watchin'! Kain't see a soul!"

"Tarnation!" Jug gulped.

"Durn place is 'witched!" wailed another Snow.

Inside the cabin, there was practically no sound as Doc Savage moved to the back window, slipped through and set out for the woods at a light run.

Doc was a skilled ventriloquist and voice mimic, thanks to his habit of practicing countless hours to master all accomplishments. He had simply put a few questions to Jug, standing unobserved just inside the front door, throwing his voice.

The Snows were baffled. Some of the more ignorant were near terror.

When a dog saw Doc Savage and sent up a great turmoil of barking as it charged in pursuit, Doc was forced to make the animal unconscious with one of his anaesthetic balls.

By the time the Snows had rounded the cabin Doc Savage was gone, and only the sleeping dog remained. When the dog revived some time later, entirely unharmed by its slumber, the most worldly of the Snows was shaken.

"Cur got a witchin'!" a man mumbled in very real horror.

DOC SAVAGE did not depart immediately from the vicinity of the Snow headquarters but swung in a circle, trained eyes studying the ground, seeking the trail of Old Jude Snow and her abductor, the Squeaking Goblin—if it were he.

The visit to the Snow cabin had been informative. It had cleared up many points.

Some sinister mastermind was urging the feud, actually directing it without the knowledge of the mountaineers who were killing each other. The first killings had been by the Squeaking Goblin—and they had set Raymonds upon Snows, because old Columbus Snow, the original Squeaking Goblin, who had been killed eighty years or more ago, had been a Snow clansman, and the Raymonds suspected a Snow of using the disguise of old Columbus.

The Squeaking Goblin had started the feud, then. The note thrown to Jug, intended to prevent Doc Savage from mingling in the affair, might well have been hurled by the Squeaking Goblin.

The other note about which Jug had been secretive would bear looking into.

The big fact was the certain knowledge that the evil and mysterious killer, the Squeaking Goblin, was promoting the feud for some obscure reason of his own.

That reason, coupled with the identity of the Squeaking Goblin, were the two mysteries to be solved.

Doc found the trail. He knew it was the correct trail because of the furtive manner in which it wound among the bushes and trees. Moreover, the footprints of the man were heavy, as if he carried a burden, and the feet had been wrapped with fabric, possibly gunny sacking, to prevent the tracks having any real identity of their own.

Doc followed the strange trail. It was not difficult, for the weight of the woman had precluded the Squeaking Goblin using much caution.

That it was the Squeaking Goblin soon became certain when Doc found, attached to a rough outthrust of bark on the level of his own head, a few strands of hair that certainly had come from a coonskin.

Further on, deadly cobwebs—hairlike wires coated with the lethal mixture—barred the path.

Doc circled these warily, pausing on the far side to get a stick and knock them down and crowd them under the soft loam where they would not trap another wayfarer.

The Squeaking Goblin had guarded against pursuit.

The trail took a westerly direction toward a region which, Doc knew from what Frosta Raymond had told him of this mountain district, was more desolate and thinly settled than any of the surroundings.

Doc topped a ridge and stood looking down into a valley through which a rather large stream ran.

Suddenly, crows gathered in the air at a point far below. A moment later—it took a little time for sound to travel up the valley slope—there came the noise which had frightened the crows. The time differential was small; the appearance of the crows and the noise of the sound reached Doc little short of simultaneously.

The noise was a squeak that might have been made by a gigantic mouse. The Squeaking Goblin's eerie muzzle-loader!

Doc Savage broke into a flashing run down the mountainside toward the sound.

OLD JUDE SNOW sat in the middle of the path, held her head in her hands and rocked from side to side, making low, inarticulate sounds the while. Between the fingers clasped to her head sluggish strings of red crawled, mingled together in one flow down her sleeves and the front of her homespun dress.

Doc came upon her—but not unexpectedly. He was somewhere near where the crows had flown up, and was going warily. He grasped her hands and pulled them away from her head.

The cut was not serious. The Squeaking Goblin must have cast her aside forcibly, so that she collided with a stub of a dead scrub oak. She was dazed.

"What happened?" Doc rapped. "Where did he go?"

Old Jude blinked, her lips writhed—but no words came. She was still too stunned to speak.

The photographs in the Snow family album had been good likenesses of Old Jude, although perhaps, now that she was only half conscious, she looked less cynical, less the crone.

"Where did the Squeaking Goblin go?" Doc demanded.

Old Jude revived a bit, tried to speak again, failed, then reverted to gestures. She pointed weakly down the trail.

Doc lifted erect.

Old Jude found her voice, mumbling, "The Squeakin' Goblin—Frosta's pappy."

"What?" Doc sank beside her.

"Frosta's pappy and the Squeakin' Goblin," Old Jude said slowly, painstakingly and clearly.

Doc came to his feet again and ran in the direction indicated by Old Jude as the one taken by the Squeaking Goblin. He ran with long strides and did not skulk behind trees, a procedure that to one not knowing the bronze man's capabilities would have seemed extremely reckless.

But Doc knew from long experience that he had a fifty-fifty chance of sighting any attacker and getting safely to cover, or countering with an attack of his own.

He covered a hundred yards—and knew the river was near. He could smell the mud, the waterlogged driftwood. The water appeared through the trees, still and deep.

Then Doc yanked to a stop.

A man lay in the rather dry weeds beside the trail. The weeds were crushed down for some feet around him, as if the man had been running at great speed when he went down, and had rolled, due to momentum. Some of the weeds were still straightening, so recently had they been mashed down.

Doc advanced, noting the man's gnarled

stature. The man lay face-down. His head had no hair on top. It was a very wet and red head, as if freshly painted with scarlet. When Doc lifted him to turn him over, a small fountain of crimson came to life in the back of his bald head.

Doc looked at the face. It was the elderly man who had been with Red McNew in Maine. Red had identified him as Frosta Raymond's father.

Frosta Raymond's father! He had died very suddenly.

Doc Savage conducted a brief search, eyes alert. He soon found where the bullet had struck in a tree, making a tiny hole. The bronze man used his penknife to dig in.

There was, mysteriously, no bullet. And that proved a point. Instead of Frosta's father being the Squeaking Goblin, he had been killed by the Squeaking Goblin.

Doc ran back to where he had left Old Jude.

Old Jude was gone!

DOC SAVAGE stood very still for some moments, and there was faintly audible the trilling sound which was his refuge in moments of mental shock, of surprise, of sudden excitement, although this time the note was scarcely appreciable to the ear and of very brief duration.

He slammed violently to the earth.

Ee-e-e-k! The squeak followed Doc's swift move by a fraction of a second. There was the *zonging* sound of a bullet overhead, an ensuing clatter of falling twigs cut off in its passage, and *zing-zow* as it ricochetted, then climbed away into skyward inaudibility.

Doc had seen the rifleman a split-second before he fired. That was what a lifetime of careful eye-training accomplished.

The rifle was a long muzzle-loader with a strangely large barrel, and the rifleman was a tall figure with a face of death and the deerskin and coonskin garments of another century.

The Squeaking Goblin! He lowered the long rifle and began the lengthy business of ramming home another charge.

Doc flashed forward. The Squeaking Goblin was perhaps a hundred and fifty yards distant. It was just possible the distance might be negotiated before the fellow reloaded the long rifle.

The weird apparition in deerskins looked up. The macabre quality of his features was starkly apparent, even at that distance. He sprang suddenly behind a sumac thicket. And with that, he seemed to vanish utterly.

When Doc reached the sumac, there was no one to be found, which did not surprise him greatly, for the timber was very thick. But when he searched for some time and still located no sign of the phantom rifleman, small, weird lights were discernible in his flake-gold eyes.

The bronze man ended his hunt near where the body of Frosta Raymond's father lay on the river bank. He gave it up, then, and went back along the trail.

He found one thing more of interest. It was a small, battered sheet-iron box which lay beside the trail. In falling, it had crushed some weeds, and the green juice of these was still wet on the metal.

It must be Old Jude's box which had held her copy of the elusive volume, *The Life and Horrible Deeds of That Adopted Moor, Black Raymond.* But there was no book in it. The box was empty.

There was no sign, not a vestige of tracks, to show what had become of Old Jude. As far as outward appearances went, the crone might well have vanished into the warm mountain air.

And as Doc Savage swung through the mountains, back toward the cabin of Frosta Raymond's unfortunate father, he gave some thought to what Jug Snow had been told about Old Jude being mysteriously absent from the Snow ranks during the time that Jug was in the East.

Chapter XVI
THE ENTERTAINER

TWO days passed.

A Raymond was shot from ambush while milking; a Snow and a Raymond came face to face on a mountain road, and when the smoke of battle cleared, both combatants lay dead.

Women kept their children in the house, and stayed in themselves. The men did not venture out, except when their families were in dire need of food, then they shot a chicken or a hog from a window, and dashed out only long enough to drag the carcass inside.

A few of the more reckless and blood-thirsty roamed the hills, rifles at full cock, their manners furtive. Through these, news spread, news that was eagerly sought—the name of the latest victim, were the enemy families "a-movin' out yit?"

It was the hope of the Snows to drive the Raymonds from the mountains, if they all could not be killed, and the Raymonds entertained the same sentiments regarding the Snows.

The feud was bloody. Even the old-timers—men eighty, ninety and a hundred years old, agreed on this. And that meant something.

Usually, to the old-timers, nothing was quite like the "good old days." The snow was not as deep in the winter, the young boys were not as full of devilment, the girls were not as nice, people did not work as hard—or so the gray-beards claimed.

But the feud was different.

"Ain't never been a feud bloodier'n this'n," was the consensus.

The miracle was that the governor had not sent soldiers in weeks ago. Only the close-mouthed nature of the mountaineers, their trait of fighting their own battles, was responsible for that. The outer world did not know the full horror of the feud.

Jug Snow was abroad much. Jug was a devil in many respects, in most respects, in fact, but he was not afraid of anybody. He was not reckless, though, and he always took a squad of his Snows along, if not for protection, then for aid should a party of Raymonds be encountered.

Jug was hunting Old Jude, who had never been found. He inquired everywhere, but no one had seen Old Jude. It was a mystery.

On the evening of the second day after Old Jude had vanished, Jug and his party rounded a turn in a road. They stopped, staring.

"Whut's thot?" Jug growled.

GLIDING along the road toward them was a strange figure. In height, it came hardly up to Jug's ample waistline. The figure was burly, ragged, and its movement along the road was rapid, accompanied by a rattling and squeaking.

"A feller 'thout any legs!" Jug muttered.

The individual under discussion came closer, and it was apparent he was not without legs. These latter limbs, however, were crossed in grotesque fashion under him, as if they might be stricken.

He rode a small platform on castor-mounted wheels, this being strapped to his lower body by a harness, so that it would not drop off on the rough road. In each hand was a short, stout, pointed stick, and he used these to pole himself forward.

The stranger came forward on his platform, seeming unaware that men were in front of him. Less than ten feet away, he pulled up suddenly, as if he had just seen Jug and his party.

"Who'n hell're you?" Jug growled.

If the man on the wheeled platform heard, he gave no sign, but peered near-sightedly, blinking. His shoulders and torso were enormous; his head small, his cheeks bulging.

Most striking, though, was the smooth hairlessness of his skin. He was without even eyebrows or eyelashes, and his head was bare of hair. He resembled a deformed, hairless monster. There was an accordion slung across his back.

"Answer me!" Jug bawled.

The monster on the rolling platform grinned, showing a hideous array of blackened teeth. He pointed at his mouth, his ears, then shook his head violently.

"He kain't heer nor talk, Jug," said a Snow. "He be a dummy."

The ugly one leered. Then, great muscles writhing under his clothing, he unslung his accordion, gave it a squeeze, and out poured melody that had volume if not quality.

"Stop hit, damn you!" Jug yelled. "Every Raymond in the woods'll be a-hearin' thot racket!"

The deformed man seemed not to hear. If anything, his music became the louder.

"He kain't heer you," said a Snow.

"He'll heer *this!"* Jug gritted.

With that, the burly chief of the Snows sprang forward, drove a big foot violently and kicked the musician head over heels.

What ensued was startling. The cripple maintained his clutch on the two sticks with which he propelled himself. He writhed like an upset spider, regained his balance on the wheeled platform and, with astounding speed, hurtled at Jug.

The sticks were as effective as a cop's nightstick, and they cracked against Jug's shins, his hands, and finally his head.

Jug and his assailant came to grips. Around and around they went, and a small cloud of dust arose and enveloped them.

After a moment Jug came crawling out of this, looking dazed. He had lost his rifle.

"Thot thing ain't human!" Jug grated, pointing at the deformed one, who was materializing in the cloud of dust.

Jug seized a rifle from another Snow. He cocked it, pointed it at his nemesis. It was obvious he intended to do murder.

There was a loud report—the crack of a rifle. The noise dived along the shallow canyon which the road made through the woods.

But the monstrosity on the wheeled platform did not upset.

Instead, Jug Snow squawled. The rifle flew out of his hands. The fore grip was splintered, and on the barrel was the shiny smear where a leaden bullet had struck.

AT the side of the road stood a man. He had appeared there so furtively that the Snows, interested in the deformed one, had been unaware of his presence. He held a rifle at his shoulder, and from the muzzle curled a faint haze of freshly burned powder.

"This be a repeatin' gun," he reminded in the lazy mountain dialect. He pointed a thumb at his own chest. "I be Fatty Irvin from down the mountains a piece."

"Whut's the idea a-shootin' my gun away?" Jug snarled.

"Fatty Irvin don't go in fur shootin' them thot kain't do no harm," advised the other.

"Kain't do no harm!" Jug rubbed numerous bruises aclministered by the deformed one's short, pointed sticks. "He durned near ruin't me!"

"You up an' popped 'im with your foot, first," "Fatty" Irvin advised.

This Fatty Irvin was a victim of the sly mountain humor which causes short men to be called "Slim" and tall men by correspondingly deceiving nomenclature. Fatty was extremely tall and freckled. His nose bulged, and a great quid of chewing tobacco pulled his face out of shape.

His skin was marked in various places with scars, as if he had indulged frequently in violent combat. His garb was ragged.

A brittle tension settled over the Snows. Rifles shifted suggestively, but not too much, for the thin stranger in the shabby clothes was alert, his own gun cocked.

Old Jude ... pointed weakly down the trail.

"What're you doin' in these parts?" Jug growled.

"Come to fit with the Snows," said the other.

Jug went over and got his rifle. His great bulk moved with extreme ease. He grunted with pleasure when he found the rifle not greatly damaged.

"Whut right you all got to fit with Snows?" he asked.

"Figger if a feller's mammy's sister married a Snow, hit makes 'im a Snow, don't it?" asked Fatty Irvin.

Jug scowled, wrinkling his small forehead. One of the other Snows advised him there *had* been an Irvin woman welded into the clan by wedlock many years ago, and that she had come from "down the mountains a piece."

"I was told to hunt up Jug Snow," thin Fatty Irvin put in. "Kin you fellers tell me whar he kin be found?"

"I'm Jug," said Jug Snow.

The slim man gave every indication of being dumbfounded. His lean jaw sagged. His mouse-colored eyes popped. He seemed actually to tremble.

"Not the g-g-great f-f-fighter, Jug Snow!" he stuttered. "G-g-gosh! I wouldn't a-shot a while ago f-for anythin' if'n I'd a-knowed t-t-that!"

Jug Snow expanded appreciably at this evidence that his name carried terror, and promptly began to snort and roar threats. When he felt that his dignity was properly regained he relented, perhaps moved a little by the fact that the Snows needed every fighting man.

"You can fit with the Snows," he granted.

Some discussion ensued about the disposal to be made of the deformed one who was deaf and dumb and carried an accordion. Jug was still in favor of shooting him.

"I got a leetle money whut we can use to throw a party tonight," Fatty Irvin put in. "Why not keep this twisted-up cuss to make the music for the doin's."

It was finally agreed to do that.

THE remainder of the evening was without incident of note. The Snows returned to their cabin stronghold for supper.

The new recruit, Fatty Irvin, proved to be something of a mixer. Not only did he fraternize with the Snows in the clipped, strange mountain manner, but he attached himself to Jug in a most admiring and flattering manner, a policy which put him in strong with Jug, who liked to be the subject of hero worship.

The man who sat always with his legs twisted under him played a little on his accordion. He ignored all questions put to him in a manner which indicated plainly that he could not hear.

Even frightful threats, voiced by straight-faced Snows, failed to put a flicker of emotion on his face, and the Snows burst into roars of laughter at this.

"He shore is deef," a man chuckled.

"Wonder whut's become a' Old Jude?" another pondered a little later.

"Squeakin' Goblin got her, a-course," muttered one of the group.

A short silence followed that.

"Then I'm a-feared Old Jude be dead," said the first speaker. "The Squeakin' Goblin is death on us Snows."

"Who you figger he be?"

"Squeakin' Goblin is a durn Raymond."

"Raymonds claim he's a Snow," the other reminded. "The Raymonds say the Squeakin' Goblin has been a-killin' a lot more a' them than he's killed a' us."

"Raymonds is all liars," dismissed the first.

Positioned nearby on his wheeled platform, the bald dummy gave no sign of knowing a conversation was under way. He was carefully polishing his accordion.

"Wonder whut Jug done with the money thot was throwed into the cabin a while back?" a Snow muttered thoughtfully after a time.

"There was a note tied to it," reminded the man next to him. "The note probably told Jug whut to do."

"Funny 'bout the two times money an' notes wus throwed into the cabin. This first one sent us to the East to stop thot Frosta Raymond gal from gettin' holp from Doc Savage, you know. Wonder who throwed 'em?"

"Somebody who's a-holpin' us again' them Raymonds, a-course."

"But who?"

"Dunno. Whoever he be, he knows 'bout everythin' thot goes on."

A few minutes after this conversation, the fellow on the wheeled platform found occasion to roll himself behind some bushes while no one was looking. There, grimacing, he hastily freed himself from the platform and sprang erect on legs which were perfectly intact and efficient, but which were cramped by the distorted position they had been occupying.

Now that the supposed deformed man was on his feet and moving about, it was apparent that he was Monk, the renowned chemist, member of Doc Savage's group of five aides.

MONK resumed his disguise after a time and rejoined the Snows. As a crippled dummy, he was in an excellent position to obtain information. The Snows talked freely, not thinking he could hear.

That Jug Snow had received money thrown mysteriously into his cabin, Monk had learned, and he intended to find out just what disposition Jug had made of the funds. The latter information, it developed, was not long in being divulged.

Shortly after dusk, there was a noise on the ridge to the westward. A man halloed. Jug answered, and thereafter began to grin widely.

A pack horse appeared, and was followed by others, coming from the direction of the ridge. There were mules and ponies, burdened with substantial wood packing boxes.

"Whut's this?" asked a Snow.

"This," Jug grinned, "is whut I bought with the money thot was throwed through the cabin winder."

They fell to unloading the packing cases, which were carried into the cabin and carefully stacked. Jug produced a rusty hammer from somewhere and knocked at a box lid.

Tall, thin Fatty Irvin stood just inside the cabin, leaning against the door jamb as if not greatly interested.

Jug got his box open and lifted out dozens of ribbed metallic objects nearly the size of baseballs.

"Hand grenades!" gasped a Snow who had evidently served in the War.

Jug leered, nodded, and opened another box. He casually removed oiled paper from one of the articles inside, held it up.

The object was a very modern automatic rifle.

There was case after case of ammunition, more rifles and machine guns, rifle grenades and, most deadly of all, cannisters of poison gas and a number of protective masks.

"Stuff enough to fit a war!" somebody muttered.

"Ain't thot whut we be a-doin'?" Jug chuckled evilly. "Thot note said as how I could buy this stuff with the money, and the note give the address where the guns could be bought outside, and the other stuff like this gas and all."

"You mean we're agoin' to use these killin' tools on Raymonds?"

"We be," Jug agreed. "We're gonna organize this here thing on a big scale—like we was an army a-moppin' up on the enemy. Tomorrow we'll get together all Snows, and the next day we'll be a-startin' our campaign."

"Did thot note give you the idea fur this, Jug?" a man queried.

"Whut if it did?" Jug growled. "Hit's a good idea, ain't hit?"

Messengers were dispatched through the growing dusk to spread the word among the Snows. All able-bodied men of the clan were to assemble at Jug's cabin as soon as possible.

"And tell them thot's finicky not to come," Jug advised the couriers. "We be agoin' to rid creation a' all Raymonds. Ain't no work fur nobody with a weak gut."

Chapter XVII
THE SUBSTANTIAL GHOST

THE night had not quite settled to its blackest when there was a movement in the brush near the cabin of Jug Snow. Two figures were meeting.

One party to the clandestine rendezvous was the tall, thin individual whom the Snows thought to be their relative from down the mountain—Fatty Irvin. The other man was the misshapen figure who traveled on the wheeled platform—Monk, the homely chemist.

"Let's get away from here—where we can talk, Johnny," Monk suggested.

"Supermalagorgeous idea," agreed Johnny, permitting himself the luxury of a big word.

Johnny, disguised as Fatty Irvin, mountaineer, had done a masterly bit of acting, not only failing at any time to spring one of his many-syllabled words, but speaking the native dialect so superbly that the Snows had been completely deceived.

That Monk and Johnny had put over the deception with ease was a tribute to their mental ability and training. Monk and Johnny—and the others of the five-group as well—were men with qualities far beyond the ordinary, men who were almost wizards when compared to the ordinary individual.

To only one man did these five bow acknowledgment as their master, and the personage was Doc Savage, muscular marvel and mental giant.

The two retired some rods into the brush, there to hold an earnest consultation.

"Doc had the right idea when he set us to work from this angle, while he worked with the Raymonds," muttered Monk. "Boy, supposin' we hadn't learned about those boxes that Jug just got!"

The bony Johnny studied Monk severely in the murk.

"An ultrapugnacious temperament nearly precipitated you into your Valhalla," he said.

"You mean I nearly got myself shot when I sailed into Jug Snow?" Monk grinned. "Did you think I was gonna let him kick me around?"

"My presence was a propitious circumstance."

"It sure was," Monk agreed, his small voice sober. "If you hadn't been there, somebody would've got shot. But I figured on you. Saw you prowling in the brush just before I jumped Jug."

The big-worded Johnny changed the subject.

"Acquisition of the assortment of warlike weapons portends no small jeopardy," he remarked thoughtfully.

"With that modern stuff, they'll massacre the Raymonds," Monk admitted. "Strange where they got it!"

"Unscrupulous individuals who supply weapons to the underworld are not extinct," Johnny reminded. "The note, tossed so inexplicably through the window of Jug Snow's domicile, conceivably bore explicit instructions about how to conduct negotiations with such a reprobative personality."

"I wish you'd change over to the American language," Monk grumbled. "That business about the notes was funny. You know what I think?"

"You have a cogitation?"

"An idea—you bet. I figure that the Squeaking Goblin tossed those two notes and the money to Jug Snow."

"A thesis possessing credibility," Johnny agreed.

"The Squeaking Goblin has some reason for wanting the Snows and the Raymonds to kill each other off," Monk continued triumphantly. "He started the feud, and has been egging it along."

"Your observation might be amended in one respect."

"Eh?"

"The Squeaking Goblin desires only the Raymonds be eliminated."

Monk thought that over, then nodded his shaven and chemically bleached head.

"Doggoned if you're not right, Johnny. The Squeaking Goblin getting these guns for the Snows, even if he did do it indirectly, shows that he wants to see the Raymonds get the little end of the stick. He wants the Raymonds killed off."

"Suppose we promulgated our conceptions upon Doc Savage," Johnny suggested.

THE two men now crept through the mountain brush, making as little noise as possible, until they came to a rocky stretch far up on the mountainside. There, after digging in the sand under a large overhang of stone, they produced a metal case which, when opened, proved to hold a portable radio telephone transmitter and receiver.

Monk put the set in operation and began calling Doc. He raised the bronze man within a few seconds. Doc was at the farm of Red McNew.

As cryptically as was possible, Monk told what he and Johnny had learned, and added the conclusions they had drawn.

"That proves what we have suspected," Doc agreed over the ether waves. "The Squeaking Goblin is fomenting the feud for some secret purpose."

"Any sign of Old Jude?" Monk asked. "These Snows don't know what has become of her."

"No trace of her," Doc replied. "I have put in most of the last two days hunting."

Monk was sober at that, for if Doc had expended two days in fruitless search, Old Jude had disappeared very thoroughly indeed.

"Where's Ham?" the homely chemist queried curiously. "Haven't seen him since we left the East."

"The Squeaking Goblin may have a radio receiving set," Doc reminded Monk. "It will be safer not to tell you where Ham is. He is doing some work that may prove valuable."

Monk asked, "What shall Johnny and I do, Doc?"

"The Snows do not suspect you?"

"Nary a suspect. You should see Johnny play hillbilly. He's almost human when he stops using them big words."

Echoing the words, there came a loud thump from the night almost beside Monk. For a fractional moment, the pleasantly ugly chemist thought Johnny had made the noise. Then there was a second thump, and a limp form rolled against Monk's ankles.

"What the—" Monk thumbed on his flashlight.

His hair all but stood on end. A cold whirlwind seemed to go down his spine.

Not six feet from him stood a macabre, towering figure clad in deerskins and a coonskin cap. Held in pale claws was a long-barreled muzzle-loader.

"The Squeakin' Goblin!" Monk howled.

The soft object against Monk's ankles was the form of Johnny. He had been smashed down senseless by a blow from the heavy muzzle-loader.

The Squeaking Goblin leveled the rifle at Monk's chest and pulled the trigger.

A CANNON might have gone off—from the sound. Flame, thundering noise and powder fumes burst from the barrel. The fire tongue seemed to reach from the muzzle to Monk's chest.

Air went from Monk's lungs with a roar. He seemed to cave in the middle, as if stepped on by some invisible monster. He tilted over backward.

But, on hitting the ground, he rolled with an agility that showed he was far from dead. In his agony, he tore at his chest where the bullet had struck. His shirt, torn open, disclosed the metallic surface of a bulletproof vest beneath.

The Squeaking Goblin made a snarling sound, inarticulate, with a quality that was hardly human. The dangling tail of the coonskin cap flapped as the figure sprang forward. The long muzzle-loader was clubbed down in a terrific blow.

Monk rolled, got clear. He came to his feet, a glowering, simian giant. A second swing of the muzzle-loader whistled over his head as he ducked.

"Here's where I clean up this Squeakin' Goblin menace!" Monk gritted, and lunged at the menace.

The homely chemist was still groggy from the blow of the bullet against his bulletproof vest, however, and the Goblin evaded him with a quick leap backward.

Monk plunged after the figure, rumbling in a noisy fashion which was in marked contrast to his usual mild tone.

The Squeaking Goblin fled into the timber. Monk pursued for a few yards, lost trace of his quarry, groped for his flashlight, and realized he had dropped it when shot at. He ran back for the light.

Consumed by curiosity, he turned the luminance upon his chest where the bullet had struck. His eyes searched for the slug. There should be some trace of it, if nothing more than a smear of lead.

There was no evidence of a bullet.

"Danged if I savvy that!" Monk mumbled. Then he ran forward, dashing his light wherever he thought his quarry might be lurking.

Monk was confident at first, but that feeling oozed speedily when he located no trace of the spectral Goblin. With more and more of a feeling akin to desperation, Monk hunted, his light leaping about with a jittery speed that seemed actually frightened.

Pausing, the homely chemist listened intently. The *whup-whup* of his own heart was the only sound. He grimaced, wet his lips and tried again. Monk's hearing was by no means dull, although not quite equalling the superhuman quality of Doc Savage's aural organs.

Monk heard nothing, strive as he might. He went forward again, then paused once more to listen.

This time he caught a faint clatter off to the left. He whirled and plunged in that direction, flashlight stabbing. In his forward movement he lunged past a large tree.

There was sound from the tree, a flutter, a thump—some one dropping out of the branches! Monk realized that, realized also that the clatter he had heard must have been a thrown hickory nut or walnut.

Then something seemed to touch off dynamite in his skull. He was tough. Going down, he weaved around. It was the Squeaking Goblin, striking with the long muzzle-loader. The sinister one clubbed again, a third time.

Monk collapsed completely, under the vague misconception that he was caught in a very black and noisy storm which was characterized by much thunder and lightning.

Chapter XVIII
THE FIERY MESSAGE

A FEW minutes less than an hour after Monk was beaten down, Doc Savage appeared in the vicinity of the spot from which Monk and Johnny had communicated by radio.

Doc had heard Monk's shout, "The Squeakin' Goblin!" and the roar of the shot—and shortly after that there had been a crashing, and the carrier wave of the other radio transmitter had died.

But, travel as he would, it had taken Doc some time to cross the rugged mountains between Red McNew's cabin and the spot where he knew, from previous communication with the pair, that Monk and Johnny had concealed their radio.

Doc found the radio. It had been smashed with a large rock. He examined the rock for fingerprints. There were none.

Johnny was not about. Neither was Monk. Doc called aloud, then listened for a long time; but he heard nothing.

He used his flashlight and read signs which told how Johnny had been struck down and how Monk had prowled in search of the assailant, himself being dropped eventually.

The giant bronze man managed to locate a trail—the tracks of the Squeaking Goblin. As before, when the enigmatic figure in deerskins had visited the Jug Snow cabin in connection with the disappearance of Old Jude, the footprints were those of moccasins or shoes—they looked more like moccasins—wrapped in fabric to disguise their size and exact conformity.

Down the mountain the trail led. There were two sets of tracks, no doubt meaning that the Squeaking Goblin had carried Monk or Johnny on one trip, making a second journey for the other.

The trail ended in a small stream which stormed over a rocky bed. The Squeaking Goblin had gone up or down, of course, but which direction proved a puzzle that even Doc's superior ingenuity and discernment failed to solve.

The speed of the stream combined with the rocky nature of the bed, had carried away and smoothed out such prints as had been made. Moreover, the flashlight beam mingled in tricky fashion with the water, casting deceptive shadows which were never still and looking, in a vague way, like tracks.

Downstream, the racing creek emptied into the larger and deeper river, while in the opposite direction, the rivulet ran very close to the Jug Snow cabin.

It was the Snows, coupled with a knowledge that he was making no headway, which moved Doc to desist in his hunt for his two men and the Squeaking Goblin.

A Snow, attracted by the flashlight, unlimbered one of the new machine guns which had come into the mountains on the pack train. The slugs clattered and hammered through the timber and drove Doc off in the direction of Red McNew's farm.

Once back at the McNew farm, Doc did not enter the farmhouse immediately, but unlimbered a radio transmitter which was concealed under the hay in the barn. He worked over the controls, setting the wavelength, then spoke into the microphone.

"Ham?" he asked.

"This is Ham, Doc," said the voice of the dapper lawyer who was the legal light of the group of five aides. "I'm in the gyro."

"Where are you, Ham?"

"About six hundred miles out of New York," Ham reported. "Flying."

The conversation was carried on with ease, despite the distance and the compactness of the apparatus, for the portable radio outfits were the product of Long Tom's designing genius.

"Have you learned anything important?" Doc questioned.

"You bet!" Ham replied over the aërial waves. "Want the details now, Doc?"

"Save them. If you go by Cincinnati, how long will that delay you?"

There was a moment while Ham calculated.

"Not over four hours," he decided.

"Then head for Cincinnati," Doc said.

After that, the bronze man gave rapid orders to his assistant far away in the night sky.

BEGINNING near the hour of midnight and occurring throughout the remainder of the dark hours, many a sleeping mountaineer was rudely awakened. The slumber-disturbing phenomenon was a great roaring, a cataclysmic cannonading which passed low over cabin roofs.

The reaction of one particular backwoodsman was repeated in scores of instances. This bearded worthy bounded off a corn husk mattress, yanked a flour sack curtain aside from a window, and poked his head outside.

"Geewhillickers, Rheuhamie!" he squawled, addressing his spouse. "C'mere and look at this damn thing!"

Rheuhamie joined him and peered at the night sky.

"Land o' goshen!" she gasped.

Strung across the night sky was a series of brilliant letters which glowed against the murky heavens. After a bit, they vanished and a fresh string of words appeared in their place. This was repeated slowly until a complete message was spelled out.

FEUD PEACE TALK
RAYMONDS AND SNOWS
SQUEAKING GOBLIN TO BE NAMED
MEET TOMORROW
TEN O'CLOCK
AT DEVIL'S DEEP

The communication from the night sky was repeated for the benefit of slow readers—and there were plenty in the mountains. Then the roaring receded slowly, the message flashing out again and again.

Possibly some of the mountaineers never did understand how the scintillating epistle came from the sky, for there were men in the hills who were not exactly posted on current events and the latest scientific developments.

But it was more likely that most of those who saw the brilliant message knew the letters were outlined with electric bulbs, these mounted on a long, flexible frame towed by an autogyro. No doubt, a number of mountaineers had seen such messages before on their rare visits to Cincinnati, or even to New York and Chicago, where that method of advertising was much used.

But the plane over the mountains was something unusual enough to arouse everyone. Some became so excited that they ran to their neighbors, for lack of anything else to do, and discussed the spectacular happening.

The spot set for tomorrow's meeting—Devil's Deep—they all knew. It was a point where the river ran narrow and deep between sheer walls of stone. At this spot, the river could not be crossed except by boat, and there was no place for a boat to land, due to the steepness of the walls. Nor was there a ford for some miles in either direction.

The river was the theoretical dividing line between Raymond and Snow territory in that vicinity. It was approximately a hundred yards in width.

No one needed to be told that the Raymonds would gather on one side of the Deep, and the Snows on the other. The old-timers could remember when this had been done, scores of years before, in another feud.

Before the day of the white man, warring Indian tribes had met on opposite sides of the Deep, according to legend, to talk peace terms.

With the embattled factions on opposite sides of the Devil's Deep, nobody was afraid of a double cross. The Deep kept them apart.

SHORTLY after dawn, the autogyro landed in Red McNew's tobacco patch, after having circled previously and dropped the long electric sign.

This had nonbreakable electric bulbs of small voltage, and was so arranged that it could spell a number of words by throwing switches, after the manner of the conventional electric sign.

Ham alighted from the gyro. He was met by scowls from Red McNew and tobacco chewing Tige Eller. Neither of these gentlemen had as yet resigned themselves to having a lowlander—and such they considered Doc Savage and his men—mingle in mountaineer affairs.

Red was also moved by the obvious interest pretty Frosta Raymond had been showing in Doc Savage.

A few moments later, Ham caught sight of Frosta herself. He was shocked at the change in the young woman. The death of her father had plainly affected her to a marked degree, for her eyes were hollow and her smile wan.

The funeral of the elder Raymond had been held the day before, and Doc had not mentioned Old Jude's strange words that, "Frosta's pappy is the Squeakin' Goblin." There was no need of increasing the young woman's worries, although the dead man had certainly not been the Squeaking Goblin.

Doc appeared.

"Good work with that sign, Ham," he said.

Ham got his sword cane from the gyro cabin. "I radioed ahead to Cincinnati after I got in touch with you last night, and found there was one of the signs at the commercial airport. It was a simple matter to arrange for its use."

"We could not have spread word for the meeting any more quickly," Doc told him.

"But why the big hurry about the meeting?" Ham queried.

Doc explained about the modern guns, the poison gas, and the masks which Jug Snow had secured and which were to be put into use at once, according to what Monk and Johnny had learned. Then Doc told of what had apparently happened to Monk and Johnny.

"The Squeaking Goblin got them, eh?" Ham said slowly.

There was a very genuine grief in the lawyer's manner as he moved back to the gyro, opened the cabin and hauled out Monk's pet pig, Habeas Corpus. Habeas had been asleep in the plane.

"Guess I've fallen heir to Habeas," he said thickly.

Ham's feeling was in stark contrast to his manner when Monk was around. No one could recall when Ham had spoken a civil word to Monk—or Monk had spoken decently to Ham, for that matter. And Ham had again and again vouchsafed a desire to turn the pig, Habeas Corpus, into breakfast bacon.

The lawyer changed the subject. "Then you've got the Squeaking Goblin spotted?" he asked hoarsely.

"Not exactly," Doc replied.

"But in the sky message you told me to flash, you said the Squeaking Goblin would be named by ten o'clock tomorrow."

"We've got to turn him up by then," Doc explained. "That is all that will stop this feud—the identification of the Squeaking Goblin, and proof that he started the feud, and why. If we wait, Jug and his Snows will kill the Raymonds off with the machine guns and poison gas."

"I see," Ham nodded, doubtfully.

THEY retired to the farmhouse, where Renny and Long Tom gave Ham a welcome that was overshadowed by the gloom which came from uncertainty over the fate of Monk and Johnny.

Attractive Frosta Raymond put a breakfast on the table, a breakfast which indicated her ability as a cook was in keeping with her ranking as a beauty.

Only when Ham had eaten did he and Doc Savage closet themselves in a remote room of the farmhouse and discuss the result of an investigation Ham had been carrying on in New York City.

"You could not find a copy of that book, *The Life and Horrible Deeds of That Adopted Moor, Black Raymond?"* Doc questioned.

"Not in New York," Ham replied. "But I found one."

No change came over Doc's metallic features, for he had schooled himself until he had the somewhat unique power of showing emotion only when he so desired.

"Where was the book?" he demanded.

"In the largest library in Paris, France," Ham said grimly. "The transatlantic telephone companies can declare an extra dividend this month on what I spent calling libraries in London, Berlin, Rome and other cities. After I located the book, I had a long synopsis of the text cabled over."

The nattily dressed lawyer drew from a money belt inside his garments a sheaf of onion skin paper. He passed this to Doc, and the bronze man read for some minutes, silently, turning the pages in quick succession, until finally he finished and glanced up.

"Frosta had the right line on Black Raymond," he said.

"Black Raymond was a bird who made himself king of a Moorish city in northern Africa, all right," Ham agreed. "From the sound of that synopsis of the book, Black Raymond was a very, very bad actor. In plain words, he was a pirate."

Doc consulted the papers. "It says that he became very wealthy."

"Worth millions," Ham agreed.

Doc studied the papers once more. Although his face did not show expression, small glowings seemed to come and go in his eyes. Moreover, his exotic trilling note, small and fantastic product of throat muscles rather than a lip-made whistle, was briefly audible, brought forth by the dawning of a great comprehension.

"Black Raymond died one hundred and four years ago, exactly," Doc continued. "And before he died—"

There was a splintering crash from the door. One panel burst open, spraying bits of wood, and let an enormous block of bone and gristle come through.

It was Renny's fist. Renny had a habit of slamming panels out of doors when he was excited.

The somber-faced engineer shoved inside, thumping, "Doc! Doc! I've got the lowdown on the Squeaking Goblin!"

Chapter XIX
SUSPECTS

DOC and Ham eyed Renny, puzzled.

"C'mon!" Renny boomed, and veered back through the door which he had smashed in his excitement.

Doc trailed him, Ham bringing up the rear. They went to the room occupied by burly Red McNew, and Renny stopped outside the door, gestured for silence, then looked in.

"Gone!" he grumbled. "Well, we can get him later."

"Something make you suspicious of Red McNew?" Doc asked.

"Suspicious!" Renny snorted. "It made me sure he is the Squeaking Goblin!"

"What did you see?"

"There's a loose board in the floor," Renny explained. "I happened to be going past the window and saw Red McNew on his knees beside the hole. What d'you think he was doing?"

"What?"

"Putting away the deerskin suit, the coonskin cap, and the long rifle used by the Squeaking Goblin!"

"Let's have a look at this," Doc suggested grimly.

They went inside, and Renny began to scrutinize the floor in search of the secret door. Finding it after a time, he lifted the plank—a long board which uncovered quite an ample space. He looked within. Disappointment overspread his face.

"Gone!" he muttered.

The cavity was empty. Sinking to a knee, Doc examined the hiding place.

"Looks as if the board was pried up only a few hours ago," he remarked. "The earth under the floor was disturbed and it has not yet dried out."

Ham eyed Renny. "Sure you didn't imagine you saw the Squeaking Goblin's stuff being handled by McNew?"

"I saw it, all right," Renny insisted.

The three men left the farmhouse. There was shrubbery nearby; tall weeds and high grass grew in profusion. It would be a simple matter for Red McNew or anyone else to come and go without being observed.

Three of McNew's farm hands loitered near the hog lot, and Doc Savage approached them.

"Seen Red McNew in the last few minutes?" he asked.

One of the hired men pointed. "Red was a-meanderin' over thot way, last I seed a' him."

Doc Savage took the direction indicated, accompanied by Renny and Ham, as well as Long Tom, who had been attracted by their grim manner. Long Tom knew the signs of trouble. Doc halted, indicated to his three aides, and spoke rapidly.

"I'll trail McNew alone," he said. "You fellows stick around and do what you can to help along that meeting of Raymonds and Snows on the banks of Devil's Deep."

Doc went on, while his three men turned back reluctantly.

Sh-h-h! We'll let you in on something. "Johnny" is not at heart the collegiate, dignified gentleman whom he pretends to be. Those four-dollar words are used by Johnny largely because they annoy his companions.

Johnny—he is William Harper Littlejohn to his learned college associates—was once the head of the natural-science research department of a famous university, hence he is no dumbbell. Few men know more about ancient peoples or their surroundings than Johnny, and he can tell you the exact formation of earth structure in nearly any portion of the globe. As an archæologist and geologist, he is second only to Doc Savage.

The big-worded Johnny loves a fight. He would rather be in a scrap than inspecting an ancient hieroglyphic with that monocle which he wears suspended by a ribbon from his lapel, and that is saying a great deal.

Johnny forgets his big words when the going gets tough.

RED MCNEW had walked boldly to the edge of the timber, his footprints showed, then he had swung sharply to the left and had started skulking through the trees.

Doc had followed the trail less than half a mile when his sharp eyes caught vague movement to the left.

The object, indistinct through the early morning fog which filled the woods, was too large to be squirrel or rabbit and too swift-moving to be a cow or other farm animal.

Sinking close to the earth, Doc raced forward.

There were dry fallen leaves on the ground, dead sticks, weeds and small shrubs, contact with any of which would make a noise. Yet there was practically no sound connected with the bronze man's advance.

Once more, Doc sighted the skulking figure, and this time saw it distinctly. He paused for a moment, flake-gold eyes fixed.

The form ahead was garbed from head to foot in beaded, fringed deerskin, and a great cap of coonskin rode the head. Hands held a rifle which was long, a muzzle-loader.

Doc went forward. He haunted bushes, kept behind tree trunks, and swung in a semicircle. Eventually, he was back of a tree which his quarry was approaching. He waited there.

Twigs snapped, weeds fluttered, as the figure in deerskins approached.

Doc crouched a little. He could hear the breathing of the other. A dead branch scraped the muzzle-loader with a metallic sound.

What ensued was simple. The bronze man merely lunged, corded fingers distended to make a quick grip.

The skulker squealed a little as the capture was made. Wildly swung blows missed; frenzied struggles proved of no avail. Quite suddenly, the prowler gave up.

Doc Savage reached up and stripped a macabre false-face mask of stiff cloth from the captive's face. It was this mask which had given the Squeaking Goblin's features their deathly aspect. It was almost as if Doc had expected to see the face which he now viewed, for he showed no surprise.

He had seized Frosta Raymond.

THE bronze man released the young woman. Nothing was said. He picked up the long muzzle-loader and inspected it intently, noting that the piece was handmade, although of rather recent construction, for the metal bore no specks of rust.

The muzzle intrigued him particularly. It flared slightly, and the sides of the flared portion were perforated with holes. The whole aspect was like that of a silencer of incorrect scientific construction.

Just what purpose the flared portion served was difficult to ascertain, although possibly it was intended as a compensator of the type used on powerful hunting rifles and military pieces, or perhaps the original designer of the weapon had tried to create a silencer—one, however, which had failed to work.

The muzzle construction undoubtedly caused the loud squeak when the weapon was fired.

Doc touched the bullet pouch affixed to Frosta Raymond's belt. It was empty, holding none of the mysterious bullets which vanished.

"What was the idea, Frosta?" Doc asked.

The young woman had stood perfectly still

throughout his examination of the gun. Her face was pale, her lips drawn.

"I will answer no questions until I talk to a lawyer!" she snapped.

"Are you the Squeaking Goblin?"

She hesitated, seemed about to answer, then said nothing.

"You can't put it over," Doc told her.

Frosta maintained a tight-lipped silence.

"You love him, don't you," Doc continued. "Isn't that why you are doing it?"

Drops of moisture appeared in the corners of the girl's eyes.

"You can't draw suspicion from Red McNew," Doc went on quietly. "That's what you are trying to do, isn't it?"

Frosta Raymond nipped perfect cupid's bow lips with small white teeth, while the moisture in her eyes gathered in drops that spilled over and glided erratically down her cheeks. Then she nodded.

"I saw Renny looking into Red's room," she said. "I knew from his manner that he was excited. He ran away—to get you, I presume, and I looked into Red's room myself. I saw—" She stopped and took hold of a trembling lower lip with her teeth.

"You saw Red and the Squeaking Goblin's clothing," Doc surmised.

The girl bowed her head. "Red left in a hurry. I did not know what to do. So I—I decided to take the garments and d-draw suspicion on myself."

"That wasn't wise," Doc said sharply.

Her lip trembled more violently. "I l-love Red."

The bronze man dropped a comforting arm over her shoulder. "You go back to the house. Give these deerskin clothes to my men. And don't worry."

The girl lifted brimming eyes. "Do you—is Red—" She could not finish.

"Try to keep your mind off it," Doc directed, and started her back toward Red McNew's farm.

The bronze man watched the young woman until she had joined Renny, Long Tom and Ham.

DOC SAVAGE resumed the trail of Red McNew. It was difficult to follow, for Red had done much twisting and turning, some of it at the most unexpected times. The burly young man with the flaming hair had crouched frequently behind forest trees and had lingered much in the lee of brush clumps.

Red apparently had been hunting something—some living creature which either had the power to do him harm, or to whom he did not want his presence revealed.

Doc continued the trail. He showed no concern, no elation or puzzlement. Red McNew might have been of no importance, the whole affair of the Squeaking Goblin one not to be greatly concerned over, if his expression was any guide.

But the bronze man's features rarely portrayed his inner feelings. Death could have been staring him in the face and he would have looked about the same, except perhaps for his eyes, which would have swirled and eddied as if tiny winds were moving the flake-gold of their depths.

Noise of a brook reached his ears, like paper being crushed briskly. Then the sound mounted to a whooping, noisily boisterous uproar that drowned out the cries of birds and the sigh of the breeze through the trees.

At the stream bank the trail vanished as it had on other occasions—by simply entering the water, after which there was no possibility of following it. Even Doc's masterful skill was baffled by the polished stone bed of the mountain stream.

He searched in vain for two hours, then turned back toward Red McNew's farm.

Chapter XX
THE GOBLIN TRAP

TEN o'clock that morning saw the clans of Raymonds and Snows assembled—one faction on the west side of Devil's Deep, the second warring group on the other bank.

Between them, the river crawled through the sheer depth of Devil's Deep, an effective barrier.

Rarely had the mountains seen such a large "gittin' together," due no doubt to the spectacular nature of the summons which had called the conclave. The autogyro and the electric sign was nearly as prominent a subject of conversation as was the Squeaking Goblin and the feud.

They came in buggies, surries, and even a few decrepit flivvers, although the mountain roads were not kind to automobiles, and not many were used. Most of the travel was by jolt wagon and horseback, or afoot.

Rifles and shotguns were profuse. Even youths of eight and nine years carried pieces longer than they themselves were. Nobody had left his gun at home for, if the peace negotiations fell through there might be a pitched battle across the narrow chasm of Devil's Deep.

One noticeable fact, however, was the lack of pistols and revolvers, very few being in evidence. The mountaineers frowned upon the use of such "short guns" as unreliable.

A few razors were tucked in the pencil pockets of bib overalls, to be employed if the "fittin' got close."

More than one eye rested wonderingly upon a crude tripod which had been erected with stout willow poles. Atop this there was a nest of three black metal horns, each pointing in a different direction. Nearby was a small glass cage in which hung a microphone.

Those mountaineers who had seen public address systems and their accompanying loudspeakers, were quick to reveal their superior knowledge and explain the purpose of the morning-glorylike array of horns.

Long Tom, aided by Tige Eller, had erected the loudspeakers. Then both had vanished and had not been seen since.

Neither were Doc, Renny, nor Ham to be seen, which was probably as well, since the presence of "furriners" would only add to the bad temper of the crowd.

Promptly on the stroke of ten, Doc Savage appeared from the edge of the timber on the Raymond side of Devil's Deep. He walked toward the loudspeakers and the glass cage which held the "mike."

So striking a figure did the mighty bronze man present that the mountaineers fell silent, staring. Later, there were a few muttered comments but they were not jocular, having rather to do with the obvious strength which the man of metal possessed and, in the case of the feminine element, with the bronze man's undeniable handsomeness.

Doc positioned himself before the caged microphone, connected to the loudspeakers, and began to talk. His voice was quiet, reproduced perfectly by the powerful amplifiers, so that all persons on both sides of the river heard clearly.

He began with what might have seemed to the mountaineers an irrelevant story, for he told them of a man named Black Raymond, who had lived more than a hundred years ago and had made himself the ruler of a Moorish city, and had garnered a fortune through the channels of piracy.

"This man Black Raymond retired to France in his later life," Doc announced in powerful tones. "He took with him his money—several millions of dollars. And before he died, he made a rather unusual arrangement in disposing of his fortune."

The mountaineers were very silent. This was money talk, and they were no different from the rest of the human race in showing much interest.

"Black Raymond arranged for a group of men to invest his money and reinvest the interest," Doc continued. "In other words, these men were simply to administer the fortune and keep it intact. When one of the group died, a successor was to be chosen. These men received excellent salaries, according to the arrangements."

The bronze man paused to let that sink in.

"Just how the legal details were managed is a story too long to tell now, but so cleverly was it handled that the trust is in existence to this day. The sum is now many times the original several millions, due to the interest accrual."

Doc paused again.

"It was Black Raymond's will that this vast sum be divided among his descendants at the end of one hundred years."

SOME seconds of shocked silence followed while this pierced the minds of the hearers, then a great rumble of excited comment went up. Here, the mountaineers realized, was a prize worth striving for. Many millions to be divided among the descendants of Black Raymond.

"The Raymond clan here in the mountains are the only descendants of Black Raymond, the Moorish pirate king of a hundred years ago," Doc continued. "Therefore, they are heirs to this fortune."

That caused another uproar. The mountaineers were a skeptical, hard-headed race, and not many of them believed what they were hearing, but it was pleasant to listen to, anyway.

"Hence, if one Raymond could kill the others off, he would be sole heir to the wealth," Doc shouted.

That caused cold silence to snap down on the assemblage.

"This story of Black Raymond was contained in a book," the bronze man went on. "The first move of a Raymond who had decided to kill the others off would be to get rid of the copies of that book, so that the authorities would have no reason to suspect that the man had known of this legacy of Black Raymond.

"Getting rid of the Raymonds would have to be done in a manner that would not arouse suspicion of the true motive. And it happened there was at hand a perfect means of doing that—the Raymond-Snow feud."

Stark quiet still gripped the crowd on both sides of Devil's Deep.

"To get the feud going, this man hit upon the idea of disguising himself as the Squeaking Goblin," Doc said distinctly and slowly. "The Squeaking Goblin is a Raymond in disguise! And he is responsible for this feud!"

BEDLAM broke at that. Snows shouted in delight, and Raymonds muttered loud rage. There was much milling about. Rifles waved above the crowd.

"All of what has just been told you can be proved," Doc said, his great voice beating down the tumult. "One of my assistants, Ham, got a synopsis of the book about Black Raymond from France. It tells how the fortune was to be invested for a hundred years, then divided among the descendants of Black Raymond. A very small amount of cabling divulged that the fortune is to be divided within a few months."

The shouting went on, but now it was becoming coherent, the calm sureness in Doc's voice having had its effect on the throng, convincing them that he was certain of himself, was telling the truth.

"Who's the Raymond thot's the Squeakin' Goblin?" men roared.

"Give us 'is name!" others bawled.

"Lynch 'im!"

"Roll 'im in pitch, then sot the pitch afire!"

"Hang 'im!"

Doc called again and again for quiet. He waved his arms, but few could see him. Moreover, it might be noted that the bronze man was very careful not to show himself outside the cage in which the microphone was enclosed.

"What's the Squeakin' Goblin's name?" mountaineers howled.

Doc waited. A close observer might have noted something of a strain on the bronze man's metallic features. It was as if he was waiting for something, something he had depended on happening and on the occurrence of which a great deal depended.

Then it came.

Wham! An object, traveling hard and fast, hit the glass of the microphone booth. The glass did not break, although the blow was fully as violent as could have been struck by a sledge.

A circular, frosty-looking patch appeared on the glass. In the center of this clung a tiny, bullet-shaped lump of some grayish substance. From the distance came an ugly, mouse-like squeak.

The glass was bulletproof, and the gray thing was the bullet fired by the Squeaking Goblin from somewhere.

This was the thing upon which Doc Savage had depended. The Squeaking Goblin would hardly stay away from the meeting on the banks of Devil's Deep, and he would hardly resist the opportunity of taking a shot at Doc, even should he suspect that the glass of the cage was of a variety resistant to bullets.

Doc watched the slug. It seemed to grow smaller, smoking slightly the while, until, in the space of a few seconds, it had vanished entirely.

That was the secret of the Squeaking Goblin's phantom bullets.

DOC sank to his knees. The cage, improvised out of the bulletproof windows from the autogyro, had protected only his head and shoulders. A bulletproof vest which he wore had taken care of the remainder of his torso.

He pitched outside and traveled through the crowd like a torpedo through a tumultuous sea, making for the spot where the Squeaking Goblin's bullet had come from. To the edge of the throng, he ploughed.

"Doc! Doc!"

It was Renny shouting. The big-fisted engineer raced through the timber as he called.

Doc flashed forward. It did not take him long to overhaul Renny.

"There!" The engineer pointed ahead. "I saw the Goblin right after he shot. The squeak got my attention!"

Doc's eyes had already flashed ahead, probing, and had located a fleeting, ghostly figure in deerskins and coonskin cap and carrying a long muzzle-loading rifle.

"He must've had more than one of the rifles!" Renny boomed.

"Right," Doc agreed. "And more than one of those masquerades, too."

They sprinted forward, making a great deal of noise, calling out at times. The uproar was so great that they could easily be followed.

Doc had stationed Renny, Long Tom and Ham about the edges of the meeting ground, and he wanted Long Tom and Ham to join the chase. The noise would guide them.

The Squeaking Goblin was running with a wild desperation, dodging frequently to keep behind the substantial shelter of trees. The course led parallel to the bank of Devil's Deep.

Renny hauled out one of the compact superma-chine pistols and juggled it, endeavoring to sight the racing target.

"No!" Doc knocked the gun down.

Renny looked puzzled, and replaced the weapon inside his clothing.

Behind them Long Tom and Ham came, gaining a little—and the fact that they did gain was proof that Doc Savage was not putting forth his full effort to catch the Squeaking Goblin. Few living men could come near equalling the giant bronze man's pace when he really sprinted.

On the opposite bank of Devil's Deep, members of the Snow clan also raced along. Occasionally they caught sight of Doc and Renny, this guiding them.

Jug took the lead among the Snows, being more agile than any of the others. Probably Jug was drawn more by curiosity than anything else, his nature being too coarse and vicious to feel indignation over the needless slaughter which the feud had provoked.

Not so the Raymonds who trailed Doc's party. Theirs was a wild desire for vengeance upon the sinister being who had started the feud in order that he might, under its cover, manipulate the death of all, or nearly all of the Raymond clan, so as to leave none, or a few, to share in the strange fortune which was the heritage from a corsair ancestor.

"Look!" Renny barked. "He's heading for the bank of Devil's Deep!"

They had been traveling downstream, and the Squeaking Goblin had veered sharply for the chasm. Here the banks were slightly less high, in places the drop being no more than thirty feet.

Gaining the brink, the Squeaking Goblin paused. Hands darted into the deerskin garments. The face of the sinister one was concealed behind one of the grisly death masks of stiff cloth.

The Squeaking Goblin produced from inside the deerskin blouse a hoodlike arrangement with gogglelike insets of glass and various mechanical attachments. This went on over the coonskin cap and was drawn snug.

With a great leap the Squeaking Goblin sailed out into the river, raised a splash in the water, and vanished beneath the surface.

Chapter XXI
THE GOBLIN'S LAST SQUEAK

DOC SAVAGE and Renny scrambled and bounded down to the point from which the spring into the river had been made. A few bubbles still came up, but that was all.

"The rifle is heavy enough to keep him down," Doc said quietly.

Renny nodded. "That thing he pulled on over his head was a compact diving hood."

"Right."

"Huh! Remember back in Maine—when he vanished by leaping off the cliff? I'll bet he just hauled his diving hood out when he got underwater and pulled it on, then blew out the water with compressed air from the little tank that must he attached to the hood."

Doc, watching the river, nodded, "No doubt. Practically every disappearance the Squeaking Goblin has made has been into water."

The bronze man now dipped a hand into a coat pocket and ladled out several metallic globules somewhat larger than bird eggs. He flicked a lever on one of these and promptly hurled it far out into the river. It sank.

There came a roar! Foam geysered; water boiled! Waves gathered themselves and rolled to the shore to slosh high up on the sheer sides of Devil's Deep. But nothing else happened.

Doc threw in another of his tiny, high-explosive grenades.

Downstream, a struggling figure appeared.

"The Goblin!" Renny howled. "He's afraid of gettin' crushed!!"

"And with good reason," Doc agreed grimly.

The Squeaking Goblin began to swim, after stripping off the ingenious diving hood and stuffing it inside the deerskin shirt. The macabre false-face was still in place, however, and the Goblin's features could not be distinguished.

Doc and Renny ran along the bank, paralleling the course of the Squeaking Goblin. They did not have to travel fast, for the skin garb of the Goblin hampered swimming.

Renny hauled out his superfirer pistol. "I can plug him with mercy bullets, Doc. Knock him out! Then we can nab him!"

"No," Doc directed.

"But why not?"

"We'll let the Goblin go, and stay right behind as long as we can," the bronze man explained. "The Goblin has some hiding place in the neighborhood—a hiding place so well concealed that I failed to locate it. Maybe we'll be led to it."

Renny holstered his machine pistol, comprehending.

So slow was their pace now that Long Tom and Ham overhauled them, and the howling mob of Raymonds drew close.

"There's going to be a lynching when they get that Goblin," Long Tom declared.

Renny eyed the bronze man. "Who's the Goblin, Doc?"

"Haven't you deduced that yet?" Doc countered.

"Holy cow! No!"

"Think back to what happened on the Maine coast!"

Renny fell to shaking his head. "I don't see through it."

"The Goblin has gotta be one of four people," Long Tom put in grimly. "It's either Red McNew, Tige Eller, Old Jude Snow—or Frosta Raymond."

"Where's Old Jude's motive?" Ham snapped, gesticulating with his sword cane. "She's not a Raymond and wouldn't come in on the Black Raymond money."

Doc Savage was keeping his eye on the swimmer below. The Goblin was stroking strongly down the middle of the stream.

"Did I tell you fellows of the startling resemblance between Old Jude and Frosta Raymond?" Doc asked.

"Uh-huh," Renny muttered. "You mean that Old Jude may be a Raymond?"

Doc did not reply. The Squeaking Goblin had veered sharply for the sheer wall of stone on the crest of which they stood.

Without an instant's hesitation, Doc ran toward

the brink and arched out into space in a dive that took him well out into the deep water, clear of the rocks which fringed the shore.

FULLY forty feet, the bronze man traveled through space before he hit the water, yet he seemed scarcely to disappear beneath the surface. Back on top, he searched for the Squeaking Goblin.

The Goblin still swam for the stone wall, obviously striving to reach a narrow ledge just above the surface.

Doc Savage stroked for that ledge. The Goblin tried to race him, but it was obvious that the bronze man possessed infinitely the greater speed.

Water had not affected the Goblin's unearthly death mask, and it showed no emotion. But the sinister one abruptly turned, seemingly under the impression that Doc was trying to catch up, and stroked madly downstream in flight.

Instead of pursuing, Doc continued straight for the ledge, gained the shelf of stone and hauled himself up on it. His flake-gold eyes roved. The wall of stone looked solid at first, then he sprang forward and shoved.

The wall of stone gave. It was a canvas curtain, cleverly painted. Doc shoved through it.

There was a chamber of moderate size beyond, formed by a natural overhang of the cliff. In this, stacked in a corner, were cases holding gas cannisters, gas masks, a machine gun, and a collapsible boat with a powerful outboard motor attached.

Had the Squeaking Goblin gained this retreat, with its weapons, there was a good chance that the sinister being might have made an escape.

But what caught Doc Savage's attention instantly was the three figures, bound and gagged, arrayed along one wall.

Monk was nearest, then the gaunt Johnny. Behind them lay Old Jude Snow. None seemed to be greatly harmed.

With efficient speed, fingers snapping cords, untying a few knots, Doc freed them. He plucked out the gags.

Monk came erect, a grotesque figure because he was still in his disguise as the deformed dummy accordion player.

Johnny, growling in an unscholarly fashion, windmilled his arms as he got erect.

Old Jude was stiff from long confinement and had to be helped erect.

Doc got details as he hauled the collapsible boat out and prepared to float it.

"Why'd the Goblin hold you?" he demanded.

"To use in case of capture," Monk grunted. "If you caught the Goblin, the idea was that you would be willing to do almost anything to find us, especially since we'd starve if you didn't locate us. The Goblin thought it might be necessary to use us to trade for his freedom."

"And why did the Goblin not kill you?" Doc asked Old Jude.

The crone shrugged. "The Goblin *would* have killed me," she mumbled. "Only I had the old book about Black Raymond, the book that told us how these here hill Raymonds was the only direct descendants of Black Raymond."

"Didn't he get the book?" Doc demanded.

Again, the aged woman shrugged. "I made the Goblin think it was in that tin box, but it wasn't. And after he up and carried me off, I warn't in no hurry to tell him whur it wur. He'd have kilt me as soon as he found out."

Doc asked one more question. "And how did you happen to get the book?"

Old Jude scowled, hesitated, then said, "Reckon as how some Snow musta stole it from a Raymond, long time back."

DOC SAVAGE had the boat in the river. Looking downstream, he could see the Squeaking Goblin, bony arms rising and digging in a rhythmic swimming stroke.

"We will not have much trouble making up lost ground," Doc declared. "Anyway, the Goblin is being watched from the brink of the Deep by my men, as well as by the Raymonds and the Snows."

They launched the boat, which bobbed and pitched on the river, for the water ran more swiftly here. Monk switched on the outboard motor, then gave the flywheel a spin. It was silenced and, starting, made little noise, but the propeller scooped water and spray out behind.

Plunging ahead, the boat overhauled the swimming Goblin.

The Goblin, twisting his grisly mask-covered face over a shoulder, saw the oncoming craft and promptly veered for the bank.

They were far enough downstream now that the shore was less steep. In a number of places it could be climbed by an individual in a hurry, for they were now near the lower end of the Devil's Deep.

The Squeaking Goblin reached the bank and began to climb.

"Darn good thing he hasn't got his squeakin' rifle," Monk grunted. "The blasted gun shoots a ball of chemical that evaporates when exposed to the air. The chemical compound is kinda like metal when the air can't get to it."

"Did you see how the chemical balls were kept from evaporating before they were discharged?" Doc asked.

"Sure. They were coated with an inflammable

paint. The paint burned off when the gun was discharged."

"Very tricky," Doc agreed grimly. "That and the masquerade as old Columbus Snow, the original feuding Squeaking Goblin, was deliberately calculated to impress the mountaineers with ideas that would not be believed in a court of law. No sheriff from the lowland country, for instance, would believe this stuff about a phantom with a muzzle-loading rifle."

Their boat slammed into the shore and they sprang out upon the rocks.

THE Squeaking Goblin was nearing the crest of the steep bank. They had landed on the Snow side of the river, and the howling of the Snows reached their ears. Evidently the Snows had sighted the Goblin.

Doc, lunging in pursuit, quickly distanced the others. He overhauled the Goblin at a surprising rate, for he was not dallying now to allow the sinister one to lead the way to the river bank retreat.

The Goblin looked back. Almost simultaneously, burly Jug Snow appeared in front of the deerskinned figure. Jug carried a rifle.

The Squeaking Goblin must have thought quickly. With the flashing agility which marked all the Goblin's movements, the form in the coonskin cap sprung upon Jug Snow. There was a brief struggle.

Jug was bested and lost his rifle. Whirling, the Goblin started to level the captured weapon at Doc Savage.

But Jug upset his plans. Undoubtedly moved more by rage than by any desire to save Doc Savage, Jug scooped up a stone and prepared to dash it against the Goblin's head.

The Goblin saw, and there was nothing to do but shoot Jug. The Goblin did that, the powder from the rifle muzzle blackening Jug's forehead, and the soft-nose bullet opening a considerable cavity through his brain.

Jug died instantly.

The Squeaking Goblin whirled, jacking at the rifle lever to get a fresh cartridge into the barrel. Doc Savage had dived to cover, however, and the Goblin began to stalk warily, seeking to discover the bronze man.

Ill fortune attended the Goblin's murder effort, for a swarm of Snow clansmen appeared over the nearest ridge, yelling, waving their guns. They saw what had happened. Halting, they opened a deliberate fire on the Goblin.

The sinister one in deerskins sought to flee, but traversed only a few yards before there was a hollow slapping of fast lead bullets into flesh.

The Goblin was knocked completely down, after which there was no movement. Yet the Snows continued to fire, their bullets kicking the body of their victim about slightly with each impact, and gradually battering it out of the shape of a human.

Doc did not advance, largely because he was not sure of the exact temper of the Snows. They might want to continue the feud.

The bronze man retreated to the river edge, where he gathered Monk and Johnny and kept them undercover, while Old Jude went forward to join the Snows and do what she could to persuade them to drop the feud.

Across the river they could see Tige Eller, Red McNew and pretty Frosta Raymond, as well as Doc's three men, Renny, Ham and Long Tom.

It was to be noticed that Ham stared anxiously until he discovered Monk, his ancient sparring mate, was safe. Then the dapper lawyer turned his back with an elaborate gesture.

Monk stood up and yelled, "Where's my pet hog?"

By way of replying to that, Ham patted his stomach and made lip-smackings which carried completely across the river.

"Ow-w-w!" Monk howled. "He's always talkin' about makin' bacon out of Habeas! If he finally has—"

From the ridge came Old Jude's voice.

"Reckon you Raymonds can come up here now if you're a mind to," she advised. "Us Snows is full up on fightin', if you-all are."

DOC studied Frosta Raymond and Red McNew for a moment before starting back to examine the body of the Squeaking Goblin.

Frosta and Red stood very close together, and they made a fine-appearing couple. There was no doubt of their love. Frosta had proven her own sentiment by trying to draw suspicion from Red.

As for Red, he had not said much, as was the way of mountain men, but Doc was student of character to a sufficient degree to tell that Red's feeling toward Frosta was on a par with the young woman's attitude toward him.

"Where have you been all morning, Red?" Doc called across the river.

"Been huntin' the Squeakin' Goblin since I found where the cuss had planted one of his outfits in my house, tryin' to throw suspicion on me," Red shouted back. "Found his trail once't, but lost it in a crick."

Monk and Johnny had already sprinted up to have a look at the face of the Squeaking Goblin. Doc followed them, his pace less swift.

There was no reason for hurry, for the reign of the Squeaking Goblin was ended and the feud was no more, its terror and violent death a thing of the past. The job was done.

Monk greeted the bronze man with a blank stare. "Durn it, Doc, how long have you known who it was?" the apish chemist asked.

"Since we left Maine," Doc told him. "The truth dawned about an hour after the fellow used his diving hood to fake his own death."

"And he must have called on you for help to get you up there where he could kill you," Monk muttered.

"He was clever," Doc pointed out. "He hoped, no doubt, to get rid of us before Frosta could get to us. And he even faked the Squeaking Goblin attacks upon himself, then pretended terror and called Tige for protection. That was to throw suspicion from himself."

Together, they looked down at the lifeless body from which someone had stripped the cloth false-face of death.

The slain man was Chelton Raymond.

Doc Savage had finished the task he had set out upon. But there would be other work for him to perform. His life was dedicated to the strange creed of helping other people out of their jams, and calls for his aid came from all over the world.

From an island of the Caribbean the next appeal would come, although Doc had no way of knowing that now. And with this summons, even preceding it, stalked mystery, stark and frightful, and a group of men who were fighting to secure such a treasure as had never yet come into the hands of mankind.

An amazing thing, out of the pages of history, was that treasure. Beside it, all the wealth of the world became small, trivial. It was a thing which men had hunted since time immemorial.

Ponce de Leon's Fountain of Youth! Thing of legend, historians had long adjudged this fountain, concluding it was a figment of American Indian imagination. But Doc Savage and his five aides were to learn differently, and, in learning, encounter terror and peril and mystery such as they had never before met.

The quest for *Fear Cay* was one hunt they were not soon to forget.

THE END

INTERMISSION by Will Murray

Exotic locales were a Doc Savage specialty. The Man of Bronze ranged from Pole to Pole and into the Far East and darkest Africa. But some of his best adventures were confined to the continental U.S. And that is the focus of this volume.

Lester Dent had just returned from a much-needed Florida vacation when he began work on a story he outlined under the curious title, "The Whistling Goblin." This was in March, 1934. It was Dent's plan to open the story in Miami, and move the action to another locale he knew well—the Ozarks. For some reason, Doc Savage editor John L. Nanovic asked for a locale change. Dent changed both, substituting Maine for Miami and the Kentucky Cumberlands for the Arkansas Ozarks.

In the process, the Whistling Goblin became the Squeaking Goblin. Kentucky with its long history of hill feuds was a logical locale for Dent to exploit. His paternal grandfather, Marquis Lafayette "Marcus" Dent, was born in Bullitt County, Kentucky. Dent's ancestors traced their roots back to pre-Revolutionary War days.

Marquis Lafayette Dent

Lester once joked, "My grandfather was a pot-washer in the Civil War, and his grandfather was a pot-washer in the Revolutionary War. I'm probably in the wrong business."

Lester Dent also had a fondness for larger than life mythic characters like Paul Bunyan and Daniel Boone, who according to legend was a Kentucky boy.

The Dent family, which traced its roots back to Ireland and Scotland, migrated from Kentucky to Ohio to Illinois, finally settling in northeast Missouri around the farming community of La Plata. Marquis Lafayette Dent fought for Missouri on the Union side. Lester's maternal grandfather, John Thomas Norfolk, also wore Union blue, but hailed from Ohio.

The Squeaking Goblin hit a snag when it landed on John Nanovic's old-fashioned rolltop desk. Despite the fact that it had been spelled out in the outline, the exact relationship between old Jude and the skull-faced marauder who was unmasked as the Squeaking Goblin collided into a Street & Smith taboo against any mention of adult topics like divorce in its magazines.

So Dent was obliged to revise portions of the story. The end result was not completely logical, so we've restored the tale to its original denouement.

Doc Savage-induced nerve problems continued to plague Lester Dent all through the 1930s. Writing a monthly novel will do that. He began summering in La Plata, the Missouri town where he was born and to which he returned when it was time to go to high school. His pioneer-stock parents, Bern and Allie, still lived there, operating the family farm.

In 1939, after a motor tour of the West which included a stopover at Pumpkin Buttes, Wyoming, where he grew up, and another in Tulsa, Oklahoma, where his writing career began, Lester and wife Norma decided to settle in La Plata permanently. Asked by a reporter what was the most interesting thing he had seen, Dent replied: "Missouri."

Dent rented a home, and began to put down roots. He needed to get away from the hectic New York lifestyle that continually frayed at his nerves. Approaching age forty, the Dents decided it was time to start raising a family.

The Show Me State began cropping up in his fiction in that year. A Gadget Man story set in La Plata called "The Minks and the Weasels" ran in *Crime Busters.* Several Docs featured Dent's birth state. *The Stone Man* included a stopover at the airport in Millard, Missouri. Just before writing *The Evil Gnome,* Dent used St. Louis for the opening chapters of *The Other World.*

The Evil Gnome is the first Doc novel to be set substantially in Missouri and in a way it's Dent's love song to the state of his birth. Portions of it are laid in the city of Kirksville, adjacent to the town of La Plata, and where in later years Dent hangered his fleet of private planes. This adventure is also the result of a new approach to plotting Doc Savage that came into existence after Dent relocated to Missouri.

Formerly, Doc plots were worked out in conference between John Nanovic and Henry W. Ralston, originator of the Doc Savage concept, in Ralston's office in the Street & Smith building. With Dent now coming to New York only once or twice a year, the new procedure called for Dent to submit a premise for evaluation. Alternately, Ralston and Nanovic might generate ideas for Dent to flesh out into an outline.

In August, Dent presented Nanovic with the following:

Lester Dent toured the Southwest during the Summer of 1932.

It has been a scientifically proven fact for some time that fish and other life forms can be frozen in ice for a considerable period, and be as lively as ever when thawed out.

Why couldn't Doc or one of his men, Monk or somebody, find a man frozen in a glacier somewhere, and the frozen man turn out to be somebody unusual—if not a prehistoric man, then one of history's leading figures, possibly one of the great conquerors of history, such as Genghis Khan (whose death is something of a historical mystery). This icy individual would proceed to give a lot of trouble, and Doc and his men, having thawed him out, would have to devote the rest of the time to catching him.

Nanovic turned down this plot possibility on the slim grounds that it resembled *The Stone Man,* and counterproposed: "...in thinking it over, Mr. Ralston doped out another one which we haven't used in Doc, and from which you'll get some ideas."

Norma and Lester Dent

Dent may or may not have bristled privately over the rejection of an imaginative springboard, but he was too diplomatic to say so. On October 4, 1939, he sent in the outline, adding: "I believe that the idea was a natural, one of the best that has come out of the mill in some time."

Dent submitted this story as "The Man Nobody Could See," a title Nanovic quickly changed to one more evocative and effective: *The Evil Gnome.* It was also firmly in the tradition Lester Dent had established with *The Sargasso Ogre* and *The Squeaking Goblin.* Actually, Nanovic took his inspiration from a chapter title he found in the outline, "The Vanishing Gnome."

Dent's penchant for titles manufactured from mythological tricksters like these harkens back to his lifelong interest in folklore. Thus Doc Savage novels like *The Gold Ogre* and *The All-White Elf* appeared often.

The inspiration may be more mundane: Dent collected old college humor magazines with pixieish titles like *Goblin, Gargoyle, Purple Cow, Sour Owl* and *Jack-O-Lantern.*

Either way, this volume features trickster villains of the type that made the original *Doc Savage Magazine* such a memorable reading experience for a generation.

During the interval between Dent submitting his original idea and Nanovic's response, Germany invaded Poland and World War II broke out. *The Evil Gnome* was the first Doc novel written as Europe was becoming engulfed in the fast-spreading conflict. Near the end of the novel, Dent's wariness over the U.S. being dragged into Europe's problems manifested itself in the form of subtle digs against touring Continental royalty and their attempts to influence America.

And once again, we have gone back to Lester Dent's original manuscript to present *The Evil Gnome* as he meant it to be enjoyed.

Will Murray is the author of over 50 novels, including eight posthumous Doc Savage collaborations with Lester Dent under the "Kenneth Robeson" byline, and 40 in the long-running Destroyer series.

His 2000 paperback Nick Fury Agent of SHIELD: Empyre *reads like a blueprint for the 9/11 terrorist attacks.*

A contributor to many anthologies, Murray has written stories featuring such classic characters as Superman, Batman, Wonder Woman, Spider-Man, Ant-Man, The Hulk, The Spider and Lee Falk's The Phantom.

Other stories have appeared in anthologies such as 100 Crooked Little Crime Stories, 100 Creepy Little Creature Stories, The Cthulhu Cycle, Miskatonic University, Disciples of Cthulhu II, The Shub-Niggurath Cycle, 365 Scary Stories, 100 Vicious Little Vampire Stories, 100 Wicked Little Witch Stories, Crafty Cat Crimes, The Yig Cycle, Weird Trails, The UFO Files, Future Crime, Rehearsals for Oblivion, Mammoth Book of Roaring 20s Whodunnits, Mammoth Book of Perfect Crimes & Impossible Mysteries, Tales of Masks and Mayhem, *and* Astounding Hero Tales.

With legendary artist Steve Ditko, he co-created Squirrel Girl, currently the most powerful character in the Marvel Universe.

For National Public Radio, he adapted the 1934 Doc Savage novel The Thousand-Headed Man *as a serial.*

As the Literary Agent for the estate of Lester Dent, Murray is dedicated to keeping the Missouri author's works in print.

A contributing editor to Starlog *magazine, Murray can be found on movie sets and locations all over the world, interviewing the cast and crews of Hollywood's latest genre films, most recently* Fantastic Four: Rise of the Silver Surfer *and* Aliens vs. Predator: Requiem. •

THE Evil GNOME

A Complete Book-length Novel by **KENNETH ROBESON**

Chapter I
THE HOT-COLD DAY

LION ELLISON got into a mess in a very simple way. The whole thing was quite innocent on her part. For all that Lion did was look for a job.

To begin with, Lion was almost broke, and she figured that practically nobody could be needing a job worse at the moment.

Secondly, Lion was a female animal trainer, so jobs in her line were scarce, the circus business having stayed in the dumps in which it had fallen. Lion was very good at her trade, but there just weren't any jobs. Cats were her specialty. She could handle any kind of cat. Burly roaring lions and striped spitting fiends of tigers got on stools when she pointed her finger at them.

If you have any idea that a female wild-animal

tamer must be a lady devil minus horns and entirely without the usual equipment of heart and soul and likes and dislikes—and nerves—which other people have, you had better get rid of the idea. They're not like that, particularly Lion Ellison.

Nor do they have to look like young witches. They can be entrancing creatures as was Lion Ellison, although admittedly not all of them are. Like a mountain flower in June. Like a strain of lilting music at dusk. Also a little like the excited scream of herald trumpets just before something great is to happen. All of that was Lion Ellison. She was a small thing. Audiences loved her, and so did circus people—and so had the head gaffer of the last show that Lion worked. The head gaffer had given her a kiss, minus permission, so immediately they had quite a clem. A clem is a fight. It was out back of the crumb castle, which is the cookhouse. The head gaffer got a black eye. Lion got the sack, for the head gaffer happened to own a good part of that particular mud-opera.

All of which explained why Lion happened to be getting off a train in Kirksville, Missouri, and looking ruefully into her purse which she found, as she had expected, contained only six dollars and some odd cents.

"Well, it can't get much worse," Lion said grimly.

This thought was an error.

Lion checked her suitcase, then walked uptown. The circus was in town. She could see that. The tack-spitters—bill-posters, called tack-spitters from their habit of spitting tacks on a magnetic hammer—had done a good job of plastering the town.

Suddenly she heard martial music and knew the parade was coming. She crowded to the curb to watch, and being a seasoned showman, she cast a speculative eye over the crowd. She could tell from the interest shown by the gillies and thistle-chins—circus lingo for the local inhabitants—that this was a good show town, and no boomer stand.

The parade came. She watched. First marched the windjammers, the band, in sartorial glory and melodic uproar. Then the bulls, the elephants. And all the gaudy rest of it. The convicts, or zebras. The big turkeys—ostriches. Two hogs—hippos—in a cage. A cage of old folks—monkeys. And another cage of zekes—hyenas, also called gravediggers. They were all there, all the great stupendous and unsurpassed wonders and marvels of the civilized and uncivilized world that make up the stock in trade of a fairly good circus. All

★ ★ ★ ★ ★ ★ ★ ★ ★ ★ ★ ★ ★ ★ ★ ★ ★ ★ ★ ★

CAST OF CHARACTERS IN "THE EVIL GNOME"

DOC SAVAGE. ***A remarkable man of perfect physique and highly developed brain who makes a profession of righting wrongs and punishing evildoers. He is one of the nation's outstanding physicians and a skilled scientist.***

RENNY. ***One of Doc's most valued assistants, an engineer of world-wide reputation and, as it happens, a whale of a guy in any kind of a fight. He tops six feet in height, and he's 200 pounds in perfect shape.***

MONK. ***Also a great rough-and-tumble fighter. But more—he's a renowned chemist. He doesn't look it, though. He's a hairy, homely man—which doesn't keep him from thinking he's a wow with the ladies. His nickname fits him better than his real name—nothing less than Andrew Blodgett Mayfair, if you please.***

HAM. ***A lawyer—and part of the cream of his profession. Brigadier General Theodore Marley Brooks—which is how his mail is addressed—looks the part, too. He's one of the half dozen best dressed men in the country. And can he fight! His favorite weapon for special occasions is a useful sword-cane, tipped with a drug which puts his opponents into a quick and harmless slumber.***

thundered past in spectacle and glory, spangles and silks not very noticeably frayed.

Lion breathed rapidly and was as excited as a little girl seeing her first parade, only with a feeling that was deeper. It was marvelous. Her eyes were moist. She hadn't realized how she had been missing it all.

She went to see about the job.

THE advertisement had appeared in a newspaper and Lion had clipped it; she now carried it with her. She just about had it memorized:

> ANIMAL TRAINER—Girl, experienced finker, no First of May, handle babies, stripes, all cats. Top pay. Apply Room 12, Voyagers Hotel, Kirksville, Missouri.

Lion Ellison considered that a divine providence had directed this advertisement specifically at her, because she was an experienced finker, which meant a circus performer, so certainly she was no First of May, which meant a newcomer to the profession. She could handle babies, which were pumas; stripes, which were tigers, and any other big cat. She also could use some of that top pay.

The Voyagers Hotel was a rather nice-looking hostelry. Room 12 proved to be on the second floor. Lion knocked.

"Goodness!" she exclaimed.

The little old man who had opened the door must have been exclaimed at a great deal by persons who were seeing him for the first time, because he smiled.

"I got used to startling people a long time ago." He stepped back. "Won't you come in?"

"I'm sorry," Lion said.

He reminded Lion of one of the "old folks"—the monkeys. He had never been very tall, and age or something had shriveled him about as much as a man could be shriveled. On second glance, Lion decided it was not age that had shrunk him. He probably was no more than forty. But he was like something out of a funny paper or a fairy tale.

He wore a tight skullcap that might have belonged to a necromancer, and a flowing robe of dark-blue velvet that might have been a bathrobe or a lounging robe, yet did not quite look like either of these. Yes, decidedly like something out of a funny paper or a fairy tale. Unusual. Something like a gnome.

Lion pulled out the ad. "I'm Lion Ellison," she said, "and I've come about this job." She took a deep breath and smiled and began selling herself.

★ ★ ★ ★ ★ ★ ★ ★ ★ ★ ★ ★ ★ ★ ★ ★ ★ ★ ★ ★

JOHNNY. *An authority on geology and archæology. Those are big words, but they're nothing to the many-syllabled tongue-twisters that William Harper Littlejohn—Johnny to you—uses in intimate conversation. He's gaunt and unhealthy-looking—a fact which has led many a thug to get the very erroneous idea that he's a pushover in a fight.*

LION ELLISON. *An animal trainer. She can make roaring lions and spitting tigers climb up on stools and like it. She can handle men, too, for she's long on looks and has what it takes.*

NEDDY ELLISON. *Lion's brother, who didn't have as much on the ball as Lion, but who wasn't lacking in skill as a circus stunter.*

ELLERY P. DIMER. *A banker who had so much money that it got him into plenty trouble.*

DAN MEEK. *A candid-camera fiend, whose hobby didn't do him so much good, either.*

BURDO BROCKMAN. *Another man with so much money that he couldn't count it—but he had more than mere money.*

ELMO HANDY ANDERSON. *A tough baby that you wouldn't like to meet in the dark—and not too often right out in the light of day.*

THE RUNT. *A small package of poison who fought humanity with most astounding weapons.*

"My father and mother were circus, and so were my brother and myself, all our lives," she explained. "I've worked with cats for several years, and I lost my last job when we had a strike and the owner of the show got ugly and closed everything down and took it to winter quarters. Here are some of the cat acts I have worked—"

"Never mind," said the wizened man who looked so much like a gnome.

Lion felt a wrenching inside her. She had the sickening thought that maybe the job had been filled.

"But—" Her words stuck.

"There's no job."

Lion felt hopelessness creeping.

"There never was a job," the shriveled little man continued. "Never a job. You see, this was all a scheme. Something I tried. I wanted to get hold of you, but I didn't know your address, and so—"

Lion blinked. "Do I get this right? You put that advertisement in the paper in order to get in touch with *me?"*

"That's exactly right."

"Hm-m-m."

"It worked, you see."

"But wouldn't it have been simpler to advertise for me by name? The way it was, you just advertised for a woman animal trainer."

The little old man smiled and shook his head. And Lion, watching him, was suddenly conscious of a strange feeling about him. She didn't exactly dislike him. But he was so strange, and he looked so unusual, and even his voice was a little weird. Creeps. That was it. He gave her the creeps.

Then Lion got a heart-tightening shock.

"It's something your brother wanted me to do," the wizened man said.

TO understand just why Lion Ellison was so heavily shocked, you have to know about her brother, Ned. Neddy Ellison was his name, and he had always been a prissy kind with milk for a brain and nothing much for a backbone. Not at all like Lion, who had sparks and electricity for a brain, and steel for a backbone. One was strong, the other weak. So it had not been good for Neddy Ellison to grow up around a circus.

There are two sides to circus business, one of them good and the other not so nice. There are the legitimate animal and aërialist acts, the things that the crowds come to see, which are good; on the other hand, there are the grifters, the lucky boys and their cappers who go after the strawberry shortcake, as the easy money is called. The right side and the wrong side of circus business. A man with a weak character sometimes has difficulty distinguishing the right from the wrong in everyday life, and in the bizarre existence of a circus where life is distorted, the distinguishing of right from wrong becomes doubly difficult.

Not that Lion believed her brother had been an outright crook. But she had always been afraid for him.

But two weeks ago, her brother had died. She hadn't been notified. She'd only seen the newspaper stories. They must not have been able to find her address, or something.

Killed when his parachute failed to open, the news items had said. It seemed that Neddy Ellison had been making jumps for a group of planes and pilots who were accompanying a circus to do skywriting and advertising, and entertain with jumps and stunts. That Neddy Ellison had nerve enough to be a 'chute jumper hadn't surprised Lion; there had never been anything wrong with the nerve of any of the circus Ellisons. His parachute hadn't opened. The headline said:

CIRCUS STUNTER KILLED

Lion stared at the little old man.

"You—you knew my brother?" she breathed.

He did not answer; he only stared at her, and there was something—it might have been in his eyes and it might not—that made a coldness go up and down Lion's back. His eyes were strangely piercing, she noted.

After moments passed and he had not spoken, Lion said, "Say, what is this, anyway?"

There was a slight movement at his mouth, a twist that was sly and quizzical, and he walked to the dresser—it was an ordinary hotel room with bed and dresser and rug and telephone stand and two chairs—and brought back a bundle. The package might have been a laundry bundle containing half a dozen shirts. It was tied with stout brown paper.

"Yours," the man said. "He wanted you to have it."

Lion put the bundle on the bed and untied the string and opened the paper.

"Oh!" she said, and her heart came up in her throat. These were her brother's personal belongings, the little intimate things which he had always prized. Lion saw neckties, a scarf, cuff links, watch chain that she had given him. She was shocked, and found herself biting her lips to keep the tears back.

With shaking fingers, she picked up a letter which she had noticed. It bore her name, but the envelope was not stamped. She took out the contents, found herself staring at what was obviously an unfinished letter:

Dear Sis:

If this letter seems incoherent, it is because I'm rapidly going mad. For hours and hours, I've

> been almost frantic. And now, finally, a solution has come. I have thought of a man who can solve this. The only man in the world, probably, who has ability to handle the matter.
>
> You remember the man whom you once told me you wished I resembled?
>
> As soon as you get this letter, I want you to take it to him.
>
> I'm going to write you the whole story. It is an incredible, horrible story. It isn't even earthly. Nothing in the Arabian Nights or any fairy story ever equaled—

It was her brother's handwriting. She was sure of that.

UNEXPECTEDLY, Lion jumped. The wizened man had touched her shoulder. "I am sorry," he said. "I must go."

Lion shook her head. "I fail to understand this."

"It is perfectly simple." The little man seemed somewhat impatient. "Those are your brother's belongings. He wanted you to have them."

"But why should you go to all that trouble to see that I got them?"

The other shrugged and glanced toward the door urgently. "I'm sorry. I must be going."

Lion decided she had changed her mind about this shriveled little ogre. She didn't like him. Furthermore, she had a feeling that if she was around him much longer, he would terrify her. She didn't like people who scared her. Suddenly she was angry at him, and she stood up.

"Now wait a minute!" she said sharply. "There's something wrong about this!"

The little old man looked at Lion, then did a strange thing. He began to laugh, and his laughing was not loud but ugly and cackling like the vocal efforts of a hyena. Involuntarily, without knowing exactly why, Lion shivered. The little man backed to the door, opened it, stepped out into the hall and closed the door.

When Lion looked out into the hall—an unpleasant kind of fascination had held her rooted in the room for a second or two—she saw no trace of the fellow. She failed to understand how he had vanished so quickly.

Lion walked out on the street carrying the bundle under her arm. It was warm. Two planes were circling in the hot sunlight several thousand feet above her head, skywriting an advertisement for the circus. She walked slowly, enmeshed in her thoughts.

She could not get rid of a feeling of ghostly unreality about her whole meeting with the wizened man, and the sensation puzzled her. She did not have a temperament inclined to become jittery without cause. She could walk past a graveyard at night and probably experience fewer qualms than the average. Yet there had been something about this meeting, a masked quality she could not define. She shivered. Creeps. It had given her the creeps.

Then Lion Ellison crossed the street. It was a warm summer day when she started across the street, but when she got to the other side she found that it had suddenly become a cold day.

Chapter II
DID I KILL?

IT happened so suddenly, and it was so unexpected, that the real significance did not dawn upon her instantly. She made an instinctive gesture to draw her coat to her throat and hunch her shoulders against the chill wind. Then she came to a wrenching stop.

Cold? But it had been warm, almost hot, a moment before!

The impossibility of it made her start to give a nervous, self-conscious laugh, but the laugh didn't quite jell. She did the natural thing, glanced at the heavens to see if a storm was blowing up. There were a few clouds, cold and gray-looking.

Lion made a grim mouth and got in front of the first pedestrian who approached. A man.

"Pardon me," she said, "but is it cold?"

"Huh?" He stared.

"I—er—just wanted to know," Lion explained.

"Do you feel sick or something?" He frowned at her. "Or is this a new kind of pickup? If it is, I don't mind telling you that I'm a deacon in my church, and not interested—"

"If you can't answer a civil question," Lion said, "would you mind just walking on?"

The pedestrian scowled, didn't know what to do.

"This is the coldest day we've had recently!" he snapped at last, and walked on with dignity.

Lion stared after him. She decided it would make her feel better if she could laugh lightly, and she did so. It didn't help much.

Nor did it help her frame of mind when it gradually dawned on her that she was ravishingly hungry. Strange. She had consumed a late and hearty breakfast, and she had no business being hungry at this time of day, and certainly not *this* hungry. She felt practically famished.

There was a drugstore nearby, and on the window a sign said, *Try Our Jumbo Sandwiches.* The combination was too much for Lion. She entered, selected a deserted booth at the back, and ordered.

She did some thinking. The bundle which contained her brother's belongings—she still had that. She placed it on the booth seat beside her. She put her purse on the table. It was a black patent-leather purse, a large one; she had learned to like large purses, for with a circus you were always traveling and you needed a place for knickknacks.

She examined her clothing. She was dressed exactly the same. Nothing seemed changed. The whole thing must be an acrobatic of her imagination. Possibly she had been worked up over finding there was no job, and receiving her brother's belongings, so that she hadn't noticed it was cold until she started across the street. And yet she distinctly remembered that it had been hot.

Deciding to repair her make-up, she opened her purse, and thus found the knife.

THE knife was such an ugly thing that she jerked her fingers back involuntarily. It had a long blade, double-edged and concave ground like a straight razor, and the hilt was very plain. A knife made for nasty work. Nor did the dry stains, dulled in color, on blade and hilt, do anything to improve the aspect of the thing.

Lion snapped her purse shut hastily and sat there. Her fingers took a drinking straw and crushed it and tore it. For now she was suddenly and unaccountably scared.

She knew—it was more than a vague feeling now—that all was not right. She did not know what it was, but something uncanny and not immediately understandable had occurred. A frosty sort of fright began creeping through her.

"Waiter," she said, "will you get me a late newspaper?"

When the paper came, she stared at it unbelievingly, finally exclaimed, "But this is impossible!"

"Eh?" The clerk was puzzled.

"Thursday—this says today is Thursday." Lion shook her head. "Isn't this Monday?"

"Thursday," the clerk corrected, and walked away.

Having bought the paper on a hunch, Lion realized that she had discovered her worst fears more than justified. Something extraordinary assuredly had happened. Her sandwich came, and in spite of the turmoil of surprise in her mind, she seized the sandwich and began wolfing it. That was another thing—being so hungry.

It was all so uncanny that Lion felt like steadying her mind by reading about wars and football games and such civilized things. She glanced over the headlines, noted among other items that the wars were still going full blast in Europe and a new neutrality debate had started in the Senate.

The principal news story on the front page was one about a murder; Lion first started to skip this because she was feminine enough to care less about a murder than a story concerning a fashion trend. But the headlines gripped her.

The governor of the State had been murdered.

The murder of a governor was sensational enough to arouse her interest. There was a huge picture on the front page; because such was her habit, Lion read the cutlines below before she looked at the picture. The cutlines said:

ACTUAL PHOTOGRAPH OF MURDERESS IN ACT

This photograph of the murder of the governor was taken by Donald Meek, 902 First Street, a candid-camera fan who happened to be passing the governor's office at the time. The photo, probably one of the most remarkable ever snapped, shows every detail of the crime during commission. The murderess is plainly recognizable, and the knife she used can be identified. The knife has not been found.

Immediately above the picture was a caption in heavy type which said:

TWO THOUSAND DOLLARS REWARD FOR THIS GIRL KILLER!

But Lion paid no attention to the reward offer. She was staring at the murderess in the picture. The murderess was herself.

IT was not easy to comprehend; in fact, she did not realize the truth at first. Not until she held the newspaper up beside the mirror that was built into the end of the booth and compared her reflected likeness with the printed one. The same. Even the frock. Hat. Shoes. Handbag. The things she wore now were identical with those in the picture.

Lion stared at the knife, then with horror tightening every fiber of her body, she snapped open her purse and compared the ugly blade therein with the depicted murder weapon. Identical.

It was very quiet in the drugstore. There were no other customers, and only two clerks were on duty, both of these standing together at the cigar counter, bending over a picture magazine. The fountain compressor motor ran, making a low whine.

Lion shuddered, closed her purse wildly. She had to make a great effort to read the murder story in the newspaper.

The printed items were lengthy, but Lion discovered they were composed mostly of a synopsis of the governor's rather spectacular career as the State's chief executive, and as a brilliant prosecuting attorney who had sent many noted criminals to prison. The truth seemed to be that little was known of the actual murder.

No one had seen the murderess enter or leave the governor's chambers. "It might well have been a ghost murder," said one portion of the story, "had it not been for the stroke of luck which brought candid photo fan Donald Meek, of 902 First

Street, to the scene with his ever-ready camera." The article stated that the camera bug, Don Meek, had made an ineffectual effort to pursue and capture the murderess, but she had escaped through a door, which she had locked.

Police had found fingerprints of the murderess on the governor's desk and on the door through which the candid cameraman had chased her. The fingerprints were reproduced on an inside page of the newspaper.

Lion pressed her fingers on the glass top of the booth table and compared the prints with those in the paper. She was no fingerprint expert, but they looked identical to her.

"I'm an accused murderess!" she thought wildly.

While she was thinking this, a policeman came into the drugstore. Obviously, he was looking for her.

Chapter III
DESPERATE WINGS EAST

THE instant she saw the policeman, Lion *knew* he had come for her, but afterward she wondered if it couldn't have been a bit of clairvoyance of her overstimulated imagination. The officer might have strolled in for a soft drink or cigarettes.

The drugstore had a back door, close at hand. Lion stood up. She had the presence of mind to behave as casually as she could, to walk slowly, until she reached the door. She was perfectly sure she was going to escape—the lights were turned off in the back of the store and it was gloomy.

Because the officer noticed her instantly, Lion knew he had come in looking for her.

"Hey, you!" he shouted.

Lion put her chin out, glued elbows to her sides, and began making speed. She hit the door, sloped through, flipped the panel shut behind her. She had no plan. Just to run.

The door opened onto a side street. No one was in sight. Lion kept going. The package of her brother's belongings handicapped her somewhat, but she decided not to drop it. An alley appeared. She veered into that.

But the cop had seen her. His excited yell came down the street, a gobbling noise. Gun sound and bullet report followed almost instantly. The lead struck something and climbed away up to the sky, screaming.

Lion's feet made a hard grinding on the alley concrete. There were no windows, only a few doors, all the latter closed. Far ahead, almost at the end of the block, a truck stood.

It was a small truck with a van body bearing the name of an electrical concern. Lion dived behind the wheel. Thank God, they had left the key. She threw the switch, stamped starter and accelerator. Lead came through, making splinters in the back and leaving a round hole and a jagged crack in the windshield.

The motor caught, gears gnashed steel teeth, and the truck went out of the alley with about the same commotion as a scared hog.

THE town had a population of around ten thousand, so Lion was not long reaching the outskirts. Luck led her onto an almost deserted road. She saw a pond, a grove of trees, and driving the truck into the trees, she left the machine.

She moved about, watching for a time and decided that no one had noticed her. On second thought, she investigated the rear of the electric company's delivery truck. There were tools, coils of wire, lengths of conduit, an old radio. There was also a long white coat, doubtless worn by the electrical service man to protect his clothing. It bore the company's name. Lion put it on—wrong side out, so that the name did not show. She left her chic hat in the truck, convinced that her rather luxuriant brown hair would be less conspicuous. That hat had stood out plainly in the murder photograph. Then she left.

The act of walking did something for which she was grateful. It cleared her mind, enabled her to get a better grasp of the situation.

Seeing the problem clearly did not make it sensible. She was wanted by the police for murder. The killing of a man of whom she had hardly heard, and certainly never met. Fantastic was a mild word for such a thing.

There was one thought she tried to keep away. When it first flashed into her mind, it was sickening enough to bring her up short.

Was it possible that during some kind of a mental lapse, she had actually committed the murder? Was she a murderer?

Most imperative of all, what could she do? How could she help herself?

An idea hit her, so she glanced about to make sure no one was in sight, then climbed through a barbed-wire fence into some brush where she was hidden from view. She opened the bundle of her brother's effects, went through the stuff, but found nothing that could be construed to explain anything. She ended the inspection with her brother's unfinished letter in her hand. Her eyes ranged the missive. And suddenly one sentence jumped out at her:

> You remember the man whom you once told me you wished I resembled?

The reference, Lion realized, would have been meaningless to anyone but herself. In fact, the reference was obviously to a long-past quarrel with her brother, during which she had explained in rather plain language just the kind of a person she had hoped he would be. She remembered the quarrel distinctly. It had come out of a clear sky while they were discussing an article they had been reading about a man named Doc Savage, a rather spectacular individual who, according to the magazine article, made a profession of aiding the oppressed, righting wrongs and punishing evildoers.

"Sounds to me like everybody was playing this Doc Savage for a sucker," Neddy Ellison had said contemptuously. "The smart guys in this world are the guys who see that they get theirs."

The remark had enraged Lion. She'd been worried about Neddy at the time; he'd been talking too much about easy money. So they had quarreled, and Lion had finally voiced the angry wish that Neddy had a few of the qualities of Doc Savage.

Lion looked at the letter in her hand.

"I don't see anything," she remarked grimly, "to prevent me from finding out whether this Doc Savage is what they cracked him up to be."

LION left the brush patch and set out in search of a telephone to contact Doc Savage.

She might be taking a foolish trip. She wondered. Her circus upbringing had given her the direct opposite of a gullible nature, so she was not inclined to believe much that she read. Yet the magazine that had carried the article about Doc Savage had been a periodical of national circulation with a vaunted reputation for accuracy. The story about Doc Savage had read as though it were exaggerated, Lion recalled. The things printed about him had sounded suspiciously like the kind of ballyhoo they used around the circus.

It was a neighborhood grocery store, not too tidy and full of the usual smells. It was located near the State Teachers College, which was probably why it had a pay telephone. College students had written feminine names and telephone numbers on the wall around the instrument. Lion got her six dollars changed into quarters, dimes and nickels. When she took down the receiver, however, she smiled grimly.

"He can't need money any worse than I do," she decided, "so I'll see if I can stick him with the bill."

To her complete astonishment, the operator eventually reported that the office of Doc Savage in New York would accept a collect call.

Lion came very close to the mouthpiece. "Put them on.... Is this Doc Savage?"

"No."

"Well, put him on," Lion requested.

"Not a chance," the voice informed her. "He's not in town."

Lion bit her lips, listened to the voice asking, "Is this something important?"

"It couldn't be much more important," Lion said grimly. "How will I get hold of this Doc Savage? Where can I find him?"

The distant listener did not seem much impressed by the imperativeness in her voice. He said, "As I see it, there are only two things you can do. You can wait and call again in the morning, or you can go ahead and tell me your troubles."

The speaker had a somewhat comical voice. It was highpitched, childlike, and sounded somewhat like a fiddle squeaking. Under other circumstances, Lion suspected she would have been amused by the voice.

"Who are you?" she asked.

"Monk," the voice explained. "The full name is Lieutenant Colonel Andrew Blodgett Mayfair. I'm one of Doc Savage's five assistants."

Lion deliberated. This was a serious matter; it was no exaggeration to say that her life was at stake. It wasn't any kind of job for assistants to be handling; Lion wanted the main guy himself.

"When did you say Doc Savage would be back?" she asked.

"In the morning," Monk explained. "And there's absolutely no way of getting in touch with him until then."

"I'll try to tough it out," Lion said, and hung up.

LION ELLISON started to leave the grocery store, stopped just inside the door, watched a car of the State police cruise slowly by. The two officers in the machine were looking at everything very intently. "Hunting me," Lion thought, and shivered.

The terror which had gripped her had become more cold and settled. At least, she could now think clearly. She had no doubt about the efficiency of the police; there was every chance that they would catch her before morning. This was not a large town, and within an hour or two they would doubtless be going over it thoroughly with a dragnet. She was almost certain to be arrested—if she remained in Missouri.

It was a time for desperate measures.

Lion made a grim mouth. "I've got it!" she said suddenly.

It was late afternoon when Lion cautiously parted dry weeds at the edge of a cornfield and studied the airport. There were two planes standing on the field, one a large and fast craft, the other a slower two-place sport craft. Lion decided on the big plane; it exactly suited her needs, pro-viding it was fueled.

There was a slight drawback to her plan in the shape of a car full of State troopers who were parked near the office.

Lion was thoughtful for a while, then she retreated. Twenty minutes later, she ran across a yard and entered a farmhouse. It was milking time; the farmer and his wife were out at the cow lot. Lion went to the telephone.

She called the airport and said, "I want to talk to the State troopers.... Hello, police? This is the girl you are hunting for the governor's murder. Do you want me to surrender? If so, will you come to a farmhouse five miles south of the airport and half a mile east of the highway?"

The cop said, "Sister, we're practically there."

Lion slipped out of the farmhouse without being observed. She heard a motor roar, saw the patrol leave the airport in rocketing haste.

It was not much trouble for Lion to reach the large plane. She lost no time. A glance showed her that the craft must have been recently refueled; the tanks were full. She worked with the starter mechanism until the motor whooped into life.

Two men ran out of the office, yelled something she could not hear. She gunned the engine, sent a cloud of dust rolling over the men. Wheel brakes released, the ship sped across the field, making a drumming sound.

Lion had once been an aviation bug, and she'd had about fifty hours of solo. That was enough. She hauled back on the wheel, took the ship off. The craft was very fast; within a few seconds, the airport range station with its radio transmitter towers was below her.

There was haze, with visibility limited to about ten miles, so a very few minutes put her out of sight.

THE State police who had taken the wild-goose chase to an imaginary farmhouse were not pleased when they found out what had happened. One of the officers had been a tractor monkey on a construction gang, and he still retained considerable ability with verbal sulphur. They said that the cows in Adair county afterward gave sour milk as a result of what he said, but this was possibly an exaggeration.

The story naturally came smoking out in the newspapers.

It must have been seven o'clock—the sun had been down less than an hour—when a wizened little man appeared at the local telegraph office. Sticking out of his pocket was the newspaper which contained the story of Lion Ellison's escape by airplane. The item referred to Lion as "the unidentified murderess."

"I would like," he said prissily, "to receive a record of all telegrams sent this afternoon."

"I'm sorry," said the manager, "but the last time I heard, we weren't showing our sent messages without a court order."

"I would show them to me if I were you," said the shriveled man.

The manager had sized up his visitor and didn't like him. There was something spooky about the fellow. The impression was not one that could be easily defined, yet it was pronounced.

"Get a court order, buddy," the manager said. "Or else quit bothering me."

The shriveled man shrugged, but there was a slyly quizzical expression on his face, a look that was half gnome and half fox. He turned and walked out through the door.

The telegraph-office manager grinned in relief.

Then he all but screamed.

Because there, suddenly and inexplicably on the counter, directly under his nose, was a heap of telegrams which were marked as sent. The afternoon's business. A moment before the business had been in the cubbyhole under the counter, with some of the messages hanging on the spindle back at the operator's desk. Now the whole thing had appeared on the counter.

"Great snakes!" the manager gulped, and leaned weakly on the counter.

At this point, the operator came to the counter, walking angrily. He leveled an arm at the business scattered out on the counter.

"Who got them messages off my spindle?" he demanded. "Hell, they haven't all been sent! Can't you see they're not marked off?"

The manager swallowed twice, nervously loosened his necktie. "Did you see that queer-looking little man who was just in here?" he asked.

"Ain't paid to look at customers," said the exasperated operator.

"If I didn't know there wasn't such a thing," muttered the manager, "I'd say that shriveled guy was one."

"One what?"

"A he-witch, I would call it," said the manager grimly.

It was possibly thirty minutes later when the long-distance operator in the telephone office had a peculiar experience. She didn't realize just how peculiar the experience was, due to the fact that she had a heavy date for a dance after she got off work, and she was giving that some pleasant thought.

She missed her pad of toll tickets, the record of long-distance calls that had been made that day. "Great grief," she thought, "Now I'll catch it."

But she found the call slips lying on the edge of a desk nearby.

It was probably fortunate for the telephone

operator's peace of mind that she did not try to figure out how the slips got there. She presumed the chief operator or someone had picked them up and left them there.

A bit later, the wizened little old man sat on one of the benches on the courthouse lawn. His gnomelike vaguely-sinister visage was pensive. He muttered under his breath, like a witch making verbal mumbo-jumbo over an evil brew. He mumbled, "So she telephoned Doc Savage. That is too bad. There was no need of them both dying, but it will have to be. Too bad."

He seemed quite matter-of-fact about it, as if death for two was already a predestined fact.

Chapter IV
THE TRAPPERS

LION ELLISON had never seen New York City before. She looked at the metropolis, all splendid in the morning sun, and thought, "My friend, you're lucky. Yes, you are." Which was a fact, because she was not in truth a very expert pilot, and she had flown twelve hundred miles or so from Missouri and hit New York City square on the nose, and she hadn't had a map.

She was wondering where to land. Locating an airport without a map would be a difficult proposition; anyway, she wasn't sure she wanted to set down on an airport—an alarm would doubtless have been broadcast for her and the plane she had purloined. She compromised by circling and flying away from the town and landing in a pasture. It wasn't as smooth a pasture as it had appeared from the air, and she left the plane standing on its nose with the undercarriage somewhat askew. She would have to pay for the damage somehow—another thorn in the brier patch.

The money she had left took her to New York, to Grand Central Station, which was the busiest spot she'd yet seen. Subways were mysteries to her; she promptly got lost in one. It was eleven o'clock before she arrived in front of the skyscraper which housed Doc Savage's headquarters.

She looked at the building which contained the Doc Savage aerie. She was impressed.

She'd read about this particular building, so she'd been prepared to be awed. But not prepared quite sufficiently. It was exactly what they'd said it was. Stupendous. Eighty-six stories it towered, not counting the dirigible mooring mast that some dreamer architect had added to the top, and which had proved about as useful as a pair of tonsils.

She walked into the place and was awed by its modernistic magnitude. The size, if nothing else, made the lobby breathtaking. There was a phalanx of elevators.

Lion went to a uniformed elevator starter, asked, "Doc Savage's office?"

"Private lift in the rear," the starter said.

Lion moved toward the back of the lobby. A private elevator in this place, she thought, must run into heavy sugar. However, the elevator was not as flambuoyant as she had expected.

The elevator, she discovered, was an automatic one. There was no operator. There were merely two buttons, one labeled "Up," the other "Down." And a small plaque over the "Up" button said, "Clark Savage, Jr.," with modest letters. Lion shrugged and gave the button a poke.

The door shut silently and the cage raised upward so swiftly that Lion had to swallow and pump at her ears with her palms to equalize the pressure. Then the cage stopped. The door, however, did not open.

Lion jumped when a voice addressed her from overhead.

"If you will remove that knife from your purse," the voice said, "you will be admitted."

LION glanced upward, saw where the voice came from—there was a small loudspeaker, hitherto unnoticed, in the cage roof. But just how the unseen speaker had known there was a knife in her handbag was a dumbfounding mystery.

"Who are you?" Lion asked uncertainly.

"Ham Brooks, an associate of Doc Savage," the voice said. "What about the knife?"

Lion said, "I'll put my purse on the floor."

She did so. At once the elevator doors opened and the young woman stepped out into a modestly decorated hallway, the walls of which were completely blank except for one door, a bronze-colored panel which was labeled, Clark Savage, Jr., in plain letters.

There was another small door at the side of the elevator, and from this a man appeared. He was a lean, thin-waisted man with good shoulders, the wide mouth of an orator, and a high forehead. Lion's eyes widened. She did not believe she had ever seen a more elegantly dressed fellow, although she had seen some fancy dressers around the circus in her time. The garb of Ham Brooks, as he had called himself, was sartorial perfection. He carried a rather innocuous-looking black cane.

Lion pointed at the elevator. "You got an X-ray on that thing or something?" she demanded. "How did you know I had the knife?"

"X-ray is right," Ham Brooks said.

"What!"

Ham said, "We take a few precautions around this place." He studied her with growing approval and Lion began to get the impression that he was susceptible to feminine charms. "Something we can do for you?" he asked.

"Doc Savage," Lion said. "I want to see him."

Ham studied her, his intent eyes searching and weighing her. Then he walked into the elevator, picked up the handbag which contained the knife. "This way," he said.

They passed through the door with the unobtrusive lettering into what seemed to be a reception room furnished with a conventional array of comfortable leather chairs, a deep rug, and two unusual items—an enormous inlaid table that must be worth a small fortune, and a huge steel safe.

And a moment later, Lion was facing Doc Savage. She knew instantly that this man was Doc Savage. She knew, too, that the magazine article which she had read long ago had not exaggerated as much as she supposed.

The Man of Bronze, the article had called Doc Savage. It was appropriate. Tropical suns had given his skin a bronzed hue that time and civilization probably would never eradicate. There were other impressive things about him—his eyes, for instance. They were strange golden eyes, like pools of flake gold always stirred by tiny winds. Powerful eyes, with something hypnotic about them.

Only when Doc Savage was close to her did Lion realize his size. He was a giant, but of such symmetrical muscularity that there was nothing abnormal about his appearance; one had to see him standing close to something to which his size could be compared to realize how big he was.

His voice was low, resonant, and gave an impression of controlled power. "You are the young woman who telephoned last night from Missouri." It was statement, not a question.

Lion asked, "How did you know that?" in a startled voice.

The bronze man's flake-gold eyes and metallic features remained inscrutable. He did not explain that his aides had made a recording of her telephone calls—as indeed they recorded all calls to the headquarters—and that he had recognized her voice. "Conjecture," he explained. "You made a fast trip to New York."

Lion said, "I stole a plane."

"We knew that."

Lion stared. "How?"

"Newspapers."

"Then I expect I had better be telling my story," Lion said grimly.

She proceeded to tell everything that had happened to her from the time she read the newspaper want ad for a woman animal trainer. She spoke haltingly at first, but more smoothly as she found her confidence in the big bronze man increasing. She spoke rapidly, pausing to think, and going back to repeat important points or to bring out incidents which she had overlooked.

Having finished, she looked levelly at Doc Savage.

"If I'm guilty of murdering the governor, I'll take my medicine," she said tensely. "I'm certain enough that I'm not guilty to take my chances. Will you help me?"

The bronze man nodded without delay. "We will," he said.

THE bronze man glanced at Ham, added, "We might listen to her story again, so that she can tell if she left anything out."

Ham nodded, and they passed through a room which seemed to be a library, containing a great array of ponderous-looking scientific tomes and entered a laboratory which Lion, although she was no scientist, could see was equipped with remarkable completeness.

From a complicated-looking contrivance, Ham removed what might have been a reel of steel wire. He placed this on another device, explaining, "Your conversation was picked up by concealed microphone and recorded on this wire with magnetism."*

Lion bent and listened to the playback, somewhat self-conscious at first, giving more attention to her voice than to what she had said. But soon she realized the purpose of letting her listen to what she had said—she began to think of things that she had left out, small items for the most part.

When the playback finished, Ham said, "As a lawyer, I have frequently found this method of stimulating the memory to be valuable. Do you recall anything important that you left out?"

Lion considered. "I barely mentioned my brother," she said. "I … er … possibly should have given you more detail about his character."

"How do you mean?" Doc Savage asked quietly.

Lion had the courage to call a spade a spade, even if the matter was as intimate as a member of her family.

"Neddy," she said, "wasn't above becoming involved with crooks."

"You have any reason to believe he was a crook himself?"

The girl's chin went up. "I don't accuse my brother. He is dead. But he was—well, he was always fascinated by the easy money and the grifters who made it around the circus."

"He was traveling with a flying circus?"

Lion nodded. "And he was killed."

"His parachute failed to open."

---

*Magnetic recording of speech upon hardened steel wire has long been feasible. There is a possibility that this will eventually replace the conventional form of recording by a needle digging a groove in wax.

"So the newspapers said," Lion admitted grimly. "I have no details. This happened only a few days ago. I wrote—I didn't have the money to go myself—for more information, but there had not been time for an answer."

Doc Savage was thoughtful, and Lion watched him. She was finding it easy to talk to him, discovering that his quiet manner made her feel better. The bronze man said, "Do you still have the package of your brother's belongings which the small, shriveled man gave you?"

"Here." Lion had retained the bundle in spite of all her troubles.

She opened it and they examined the contents.

DOC indicated the letter. "This his handwriting?"

"Absolutely." Lion made a hopeless gesture. "But what help is it? The letter doesn't tell anything, except that my brother had found out about something strange and incredible and horrible."

Doc Savage glanced at Ham Brooks, who had been sitting in on the conference, but saying nothing. Ham Brooks, in addition to being an avid pursuer of the title of best-dressed-man in the country, was also Brigadier General Theodore Marley Brooks, who had a repuation as one of the nation's leading lawyers. Ham's brain was as active as a cageful of monkeys.

"Plain as the nose on your face," Ham said.

Lion was puzzled. "What is?"

"Her brother found out something, was killed to silence him." Ham nodded approval over his own reasoning. "And Miss Ellison, here, was framed because it was feared her brother had told her what he had learned."

"But—"

Ham was enthusiastic about his theory, plunged on. "You know what my guess would be? Just this: They killed her brother, then searched his belongings and found this unfinished letter. They figured maybe it was a false start he'd made on a letter which he'd finally written and sent to Miss Ellison. So—presto! They had to get rid of Lion—Miss Ellison. There you are … Motive and everything."

Lion shook her head grimly. "No."

"Eh?"

"It isn't that simple. There's something eerie and fantastic about it. Something that—I don't know how to describe it—is ghostly and unearthly."

Ham smiled confidently, said, "Tush, tush. Your imagination, no doubt."

"Imagination—nothing!" Lion was irritated. "I tell you, that wizened little old man was like … like—something ugly out of a fairy story. I don't think he's human."

Ham opened his mouth to answer, but the telephone rang. He picked up the instrument. "Yes… You what? … Great mackerel! Hold the wire."

Ham then looked up and muttered, "Speaking of the devil—who do you think Monk just caught trying to make a sneak up here? No one else but our friend whom we were discussing—the mysterious runt."

Lion stared. "You mean—"

"None other. At least, the way Monk describes him, he's the shriveled little man who handed over your brother's belongings in Missouri."

"But how did he get here?" Lion ejaculated.

"That is what we will find out," Doc Savage said grimly. "Tell Monk to hold him."

Ham spoke into the telephone, looked up to say, "Monk says he's got him locked in a room."

Chapter V
THE MYSTERIOUS RUNT

"MONK" had come by his nickname perfectly naturally because he looked the part; it was frequently said that one would not have to meet Monk in a very dark alley to mistake him for a full-scale gorilla. He was furred over with what resembled a growth of rusty shingle nails.

Despite the fact that Monk was homely enough to frighten a goblin, he had a pleasantly entertaining personality, and men liked him. Men not only liked him, but so did women. Monk seemed to exert a fascination over the misnamed gentler sex, and the prettier the girl, the more potent Monk's charm.

Monk certainly did not look like a man who was one of the greatest living industrial chemists, but that was his ranking. As Lieutenant Colonel Andrew Blodgett Mayfair, his full name, he had an international ranking.

Doc Savage had a group of five assistants, and Monk was one of the most enthusiastic. Not that Monk had any unnatural zeal to see other people helped out of trouble and wrongs righted—but he did like excitement. As one of the Doc Savage group, he got plenty of excitement.

And likewise as a member of the Doc coterie, Monk was able to associate—and quarrel interminably—with Ham Brooks. Squabbling with Ham was Monk's hobby, to which he devoted most of his spare time.

Transcending Monk's interest in his snazzy downtown chemical laboratory, pretty girls, and bickering with Ham, was his regard for Habeas Corpus. Habeas was a pig. An Arabian hog which Monk had acquired on the Oman coast. Nature had done something peculiar to Habeas Corpus' growth glands and he probably would never get much larger than a jack-rabbit, being composed mostly of ears and legs.

Monk made a short speech to Habeas, saying, "Hog, we showed 'em. We got the bacon."

The bacon reference was to the wizened, peculiar looking little old man whom Monk had caught sneaking into the private garage which Doc Savage maintained in the skyscraper basement. From this garage, a private (it was secret, also) elevator led up to headquarters.

Monk had accosted the little man. The latter had instantly drawn a revolver, which Monk had taken away from him with great alacrity.

Monk grinned at his companion. "You figure we caught a crook?"

"Holy cow! Why else would he be sneaking in here?"

The speaker was a third member of Doc's squad of associates, Colonel John "Renny" Renwick. He had been with Monk when the capture was made.

Now Renny walked over to an instrument panel and made some adjustments with switches and knobs. The basement garage, like the entire skyscraper headquarters, was cobwebbed with burglar alarms; one of these alarms was responsible for their capture of the marauder.

Hands with which Renny made the adjustments were incredibly huge; either fist would more than fill a quart pail. Both fists obviously had been mistreated in the past. Their scarred appearance and anvillike texture lent considerable credence to Renny's favorite boast that he could knock the wooden panel out of any door with either fist.

Renny, in a rumbling voice that was like an agitated bear in a deep cave, said, "Now, listen… Isn't that our new mascot doing some yelling?"

THEY had heaved the gnomelike prisoner into a tool room just off the garage. This room, about the size of a Pullman compartment, was windowless, made of concrete reinforced with steel. It was sometimes used as a vault.

The door was a great slab of the same kind of steel that goes into the construction of battleship gun turrets.

Monk opened the door. He jerked his head back, slammed the door.

"Little runt tried to knock my brains out with his shoes," he complained.

"He mad?"

"He ain't singin' no love song."

They put their ears to the door and listened. They could hear their prisoner making rather strange sounds. Monk and Renny stared at each other.

"Sounds like a big bumblebee, don't he?" Monk ventured.

Renny said, "Holy cow! Wonder what he's doing?" and opened the door a crack. An unusual sight confronted them.

The wizened little man—he was as hideous as any frightening dwarf ever concocted by a movie director for a horror film—was standing in the middle of the room making gestures with his hands, sounds with his mouth. The hand motions were meaningless. Or were they? He seemed to be molding something in the air.

"Acts like an African witch doctor," Monk grunted.

The little man stopped and stared at them. His eyes had a blazing intensity.

He said, "You will release me at once!"

His demand was not loud, but it contained such firmness that Monk involuntarily stepped back, then caught himself and blocked the door. "No dice," Monk growled. "Doc is gonna be down here in a minute. He'll have a raft of questions."

"I will answer no questions!" snapped their remarkable captive.

"Did you ever see truth serum work?" Monk leered at him. "Doc has his private stock of the stuff. Guaranteed to make a brass monkey sing the Star-Spangled Banner."

The little man came close to them. He did not shake his fists, but the effect was the same.

"You will turn me loose, or regret it a great deal," he said in a tone that was like electric sparks.

Monk said, "Ho, ho, and a ha. You hear me laughing?"

The small man drew himself up. The intensity of his passionate rage was around him like heat. "You fools! Don't you realize that you are dealing with no mere man? That I am no ordinary mortal such as you?"

Monk and Renny discovered they were getting uncomfortable. They exchanged glances, suddenly stepped back, and slammed the steel door on their prisoner.

"I don't like that little clunk," Monk muttered.

There was a small aperture in the door for ventilating purposes. The voice of their captive, rather muffled, came through this.

"I am going to demonstrate what I mean," the little man was telling them, "by disappearing from this room."

Monk growled, "You'll what?"

"I shall vanish."

The room was in effect a vault. The threat of the little man was ridiculous. Both Monk and Renny suddenly began laughing.

"He's gonna vanish," Monk chortled.

"I heard him," Renny boomed. "Holy cow!"

Their mirth lasted some time...Then they discovered themselves looking at each other with sober faces.

Monk slammed home the big bar which secured the steel door on the outside.

"I'd like to see him disappear now," Monk said grimly.

DOC SAVAGE, Ham Brooks, and Lion Ellison arrived in the basement garage. The girl was excited, and Doc Savage outwardly emotionless. Ham was accompanied by Chemistry, his pet chimpanzee, which bore a startling resemblance to Monk. Ham had originally acquired the animal to aggravate Monk, had later become quite attached to the pet.

Monk and Ham greeted each other with no civility whatever.

Monk pointed at Ham and told Lion, "You're in some mighty lowbrow company. He comes from a long line of tramps."

Ham snapped, "Did you think that crack up by yourself?"

"Sure. Right out of my head."

"You must be," Ham said.

The pair glowered at each other.

Doc asked, "Where is the prisoner?"

Monk pointed at the steel door. "In there."

"Well, trot him out," Ham said peevishly, "and we'll see who he is and what he wanted."

Monk unbarred the steel door, opened it and stepped inside. He popped out within a split second. Coffee cups would hardly have fitted over his eyes.

"He done it!" Monk squalled.

Only Renny understood the exact significance of what Monk said. Renny roared, "Holy cow! He couldn't have!" and dived into the little room which had such solid walls of steel-reinforced concrete. The big-fisted engineer floundered around in the gloom. "Bring a flashlight," he yelled.

Ham walked into the cubicle, said, "Plenty of light comes in from the garage. There's nothing in here. Why all the fuss?"

"Nobody here—that's just it." Big-voiced Renny sounded as if he was about to strangle.

The significance of the thing dawned on Ham and the others. They stared incredulously. Ham demanded. "You mean to tell us you had the man locked in there? You're not kidding?"

Monk made gasping noises, finally managed, "I tell you the mysterious runt did just what he said he'd do—disappeared!"

Chapter VI
THE JAIL TRAIL

DOC SAVAGE owned a matter-of-fact temperament. He was not easily startled nor readily confused; he had trained himself to look deeply and with suspicion into anything that appeared supernatural, to search for an explanation. He took no stock in ghostly manifestations or magic in any form. Monk and Ham and Renny were almost as hard-headed in these matters as their bronze chief.

Monk and Renny finally got their astonishment sufficiently in hand to give a coherent explanation of what had occurred. The others listened.

Renny finished, "We caught him; we locked him in there; he said he was gonna vanish—and he did."

Monk scowled belligerently at Ham. "And don't try to tell me it didn't happen."

Lion Ellison now shook her head slowly. "There is something weird about that little man. I told you that."

"A man is a man," Monk muttered, "and one of them ain't much more weird than the next one."

Ham said, "Except that this one could vanish out of the equivalent of a bank vault."

Doc Savage moved away from the group. The bronze man had hardly spoken, and his apparent unconcern had caused Lion to glance at him once or twice. She seemed dubious about his ability; it didn't seem to her that he was even interested in the matter.

The young woman drew Ham aside and said in a low voice, "He doesn't seem very enthusiastic about this."

"Who, Doc?" Ham smiled wryly. "You don't know him yet. If you mean that he isn't excited—I don't believe I ever saw him really excited."

Lion watched the bronze man for a while. "Well, he doesn't seem to be trying to help. He's just walking around."

Without offering any explanation of what he was doing, Doc Savage left the garage. He evidently went up to the eighty-sixth floor laboratory, because he returned with a number of bottles, some empty and some containing chemicals, and an atomizer, litmus paper, and other devices which Lion didn't recognize. He entered the vaultlike room where the prisoner had staged his miracle. He squirted chemicals in the air with the atomizer, fooled around with the litmus paper, and in general—as far as Lion could see—accomplished nothing.

"It's got him fooled," she whispered to Ham.

"If he's puzzled, he isn't by himself," Ham said.

By now, Monk had taken notice of the young woman's consulation with Ham. Monk didn't approve. However, he thoroughly approved of Lion; he had decided she was about the most ravishing bit of feminity he had noticed recently. Monk ambled over.

The machine stopped very close—and three men who had been in the back seat scrambled out.

"It's my duty to warn you"—Monk jerked a thumb at Ham—"this shyster lawyer has a wife and thirteen lop-eared children, a fact he sometimes forgets to mention."

This was a black-faced lie, and not a new one. Monk had been telling the fib for years, and Ham was becoming very tired of it. He tried to find words sufficiently violent, could only make strangling noises.

Doc Savage joined them. His bronzed features were inscrutable, although his flake-gold eyes seemed more animated. "Probably we should go to Missouri," he said, "and pick up the mystery there."

LION ELLISON had discovered already that she was going to be somewhat puzzled by Doc Savage. She had expected something spectacular of the bronze man, and nothing of that nature had occurred. Or had it? His aides had captured the wizened little man, it was true.

Lion soon got a fresh dose of the awe which had overwhelmed her when she first arrived at the bronze man's headquarters. She began to realize that the establishment was more unusual than she had imagined. Doc Savage gave low-voiced orders; she overheard enough to know that he was directing the others to pack light equipment which could be carried by plane. So they were going to fly. She presumed they would take a taxi to an airport—but she got a surprise.

Because Doc Savage had enemies, and these occasionally watched the skyscraper exits and made trouble, he had arranged a unique and fast method of travel from the eighty-sixth floor establishment to the hangar where he kept his planes. This conveyance was a contraption which Monk called the "go-devil," and other things not so polite. Lion was introduced to the device. She found herself stepping into a cylindrical, bullet-shaped car which was padded, very crowded once all were inside, and which traveled in a shaftlike tube. Doc threw a lever. There was a roaring whoosh! and other phenomena.

In a circus where Lion once worked, there had been a gentleman who made his living by being shot out of a cannon into a net. He had tried to interest Lion in the projectile job, and she'd tried it out before hastily declining. Being shot out of that cannon was similar to what happened to them now.

Eventually, the bullet of a car stopped. They pulled themselves together and got out. They had gone a long distance through a tunnel.

"Some fun, eh?" Monk said. "Someday that thing is going to jump the track and land on Mars, or someplace."

Lion glanced about; her mouth and eyes became round with astonishment. She stood inside a vast building of brick-and-steel construction that looked strong enough for a fortress. There was an assortment of planes ranging from a huge streamlined thing that had speed in every line to a small bug of a ship that had no wings whatever, only windmill blades that probably whirled. All of the planes were amphibian, she noticed; they could operate from land or water. There were boats as well, lying in slips. She saw a small yacht; she stared in astonishment at a peculiar-looking submarine which was equipped with a protective framework of big steel sledlike runners. A submarine for going under the polar ice, she realized suddenly.

"Why—this is amazing!" she exclaimed.

"Doc's hangar and boathouse," Monk explained. "On the Hudson River waterfront. From the outside, looks like an ordinary brick warehouse."

Lion stared at Doc Savage. She had completely revised her opinion of the bronze man.

"All of this must cost a mint of money," she said. "Where does he get all of what it takes?"

Monk grinned. "Oh, he picks up a penny here and there."

"Maybe I'd better tell him I'm broke. I can't pay for all of this."

Monk smiled again. The source of Doc Savage's wealth was a mystery, the solution known only to the bronze man and his five associates. Doc Savage had a fabulous gold hoard deep in the unexplored mountains of a remote Central American republic—a vein of gold that was almost a mother lode, and watched over by descendants of the ancient civilization of Maya. On any seventh day, at high noon, Doc Savage had but to broadcast a few words in the Mayan tongue—a language which they had reason to believe no civilized person other than themselves understood—and the message would be picked up in the lost valley. Days later, a mule train loaded with gold would come out of the jungle. The source of wealth had come to Doc Savage as a result of an unusual adventure; the hoard was his to draw upon only as long as he used the wealth in his strange career of righting wrongs and punishing evildoers.*

"All aboard," Renny called.

They used a plane of moderate size and great speed. It taxied out through the electrically opened doors of the big warehouse-hangar, bounced across Hudson River waves for a while, then took the air.

**The Man of Bronze,* which will be reprinted in *Doc Savage* Volume 14.

THEY had flown across most of Pennsylvania when Lion gave a violent start, sprang up, hurried forward and clutched Doc Savage's shoulder.

"They'll recognize me!" she gasped. "The police. That picture. I can't go back to Missouri."

The bronze man had been flying. He glanced at the instruments, noted the altitude was above eighteen thousand, then threw a lever which connected up the robot pilot. He slid out of the pilot's seat.

"We brought along a makeup kit to take care of that," he explained.

"Disguise me?"

"Yes."

Lion shook her head. "We used makeup around the circus, so I know something about it. I doubt if you can make a disguise effective."

"We can try," the bronze man said quietly.

Twenty minutes later, Lion examined herself thoroughly in the mirror. She saw a little old lady with grayish hair, pale-blue eyes that were rather staring, discolored teeth—and wrinkles. The gray hair was the result of dye; she had expected that. The changed color of her eyes—pale-blue instead of warm-brown—was the result of colored caps of nonshatter optical glass which fitted on the eyeball; Lion had heard of invisible glasses of that character, so she was not too surprised. But the wrinkles bothered her.

Lion indicated the wrinkles. "You sure these will come out?"

"Easily."

Lion said, "They'd better!" rather fiercely. The bronze man had applied a chemical to her face; it had felt like her tongue after taking a bite of green persimmon.

The remainder of the flight was uneventful, except for speed. The pace of the plane was breath-taking. They were very high, but visibility was good, and Lion picked out Columbus, Indianapolis, Springfield, in faster order than she had believed possible. "I wouldn't have believed this," she said.

"It's not so remarkable," Monk said; then reminded her, "The regular passenger line makes it from New York to St. Louis in about six hours."

Lion watched below. She saw Hannibal, Missouri, sprawled on the banks of the Mississippi about which Mark Twain had written so much. Later she pointed, said, "There's Kirksville."

DOC SAVAGE landed, putting the plane down with hardly a jar. They taxied toward the edge of the field, where the office and the red-and-white beacon tower stood. Doc cut the motors.

A taxicab was parked near the office, the driver standing beside the machine. "Wanna cab?" the driver called.

"You bet," Monk shouted.

The driver got into the cab, rolled the machine toward them, and stopped when he was very close. Three men—they had been concealed in the back seat—scrambled out.

The three men had guns and badges that either said, "Sheriff," or "Deputy Sheriff."

"I'm sheriff of the county," one man explained. "Just take it easy while we look you over."

Other armed deputies came out of the office one after another until a round dozen had appeared. Some had revolvers; more of them carried rifles and shotguns.

"A regular army of duck hunters," Monk muttered.

"Shut up," the sheriff told him.

A man brought a fingerprint outfit. They took Lion's prints, compared them with some they had in their possession. Then the sheriff made a short speech.

"You're all under arrest," he said. "The charge is accessory after a murder, shielding a murderess, and the prosecuting attorney will figure out what else."

Chapter VII
MYSTERY MURDER

THE jail had been built a long time ago, Monk concluded after a round of his cell, during which he gave the bars of each window a thorough shaking. "Age has just toughened this place," he decided.

They had been searched and confined to the cell, and on the other side of the bars now stood the sheriff, his deputies, some city police and the prosecuting attorney. The spectators were staring at the prisoners, particularly Doc Savage, with much interest, but no sympathy.

Ham walked over, shook the heavy door indignantly and shouted, "Listen, you guys, don't you know who you've locked up?"

"Said he was Doc Savage," the sheriff answered, unimpressed.

"Doesn't that mean anything to you?" Ham yelled.

The sheriff filled his pipe and struck a match without any show of concern. "You fellows trying to tell me how important you are?"

Ham peered at him and decided it was hopeless to try to bluff the man. Ham made aimless gestures with his hands—he was at a loss without the sword cane in his fingers—and finally threw up his arms in disgust and turned to the others.

"What'll we do now?" he groaned.

"We'd better think it over," Monk said.

"Nope, let's try something you can do, too," Ham suggested.

Monk was too concerned with their plight to recognize the insult. It was as solid a jail as he had ever seen. The sheriff was not an impressionable individual, so there was small likelihood of his releasing them. The prosecuting attorney also looked as if he was ambitious.

The sheriff rapped on the cell door and made a parting announcement.

"The governor of this State was murdered, and that girl has been identified as the murderess," he explained. "You were with her. We found a make-up kit in your plane, so we know you helped disguise her. We figure that hooks you up with complicity in the crime."

"We're innocent," Renny rumbled angrily.

The sheriff snorted. "I suppose the girl is innocent, too."

"I am," Lion snapped.

The sheriff snorted again.

"You're all so innocent," he said grimly, "that they'll probably hang you."

THE sheriff returned to his office in the courthouse, put his feet on his desk, lit a cigar and engaged in some self-satisfied contemplation. He was not unaware that he had some famous prisoners in his jail, but he was determined not to be swayed by that. The law was the law, as far as he was concerned.

He did some pondering about the tip that had enabled him to make the arrest. It was a telephone tip, and the voice had impressed the sheriff as being somewhat creepy.

The sheriff now had a visitor. He was a shriveled little gentleman, very dapperly dressed, with a camera flung over his shoulder, a sheaf of copy paper in one hand and his vest pocket full of cigars and pencils.

"I'm Marty McNew from the St. Louis Daily Examiner," the visitor explained. "Understand you've arrested the girl who murdered the governor? How about it?"

"Hope so," the sheriff said.

"Heard there were some men with her?"

"Fellow named Doc Savage," the sheriff admitted. "Also three others named Ham Brooks, Monk Mayfair, and Renny Renwick."

"You going to hold them all in jail?"

"Hell, yes!" the sheriff said. "They were helping a murderess, weren't they?"

The visitor smirked. He asked a few more routine questions, presented the sheriff with cigars, and left.

The sheriff was thoughtful after the fellow left… Something familiar about that man, he thought—but I can't quite place it. He puffed at the cigar, made a blue fog of smoke, and suddenly bolted upright in his chair.

"That was the man who tipped me off that Doc Savage might show up here in a plane with the girl!" he exploded.

The thought was startling, so much so that he abruptly discarded it as too fantastic for consideration… It's my imagination, that's all, the sheriff thought…

After he had left the sheriff's office, the wizened little man entered a car and drove out into the country. The quick darkness of early winter had fallen when he stopped his car close beside a deserted farmhouse.

The car, without giving that appearance, was bodied with armor plate, had windows of thick gelatinous-collodian sandwich glass which was the nearest thing to bulletproof that science had yet developed, and the tires were filled with sponge rubber instead of air. The little man was careful not to roll the window down very far.

"How behaves the world?" he asked.

"Without understanding for the unseen man," a voice answered him from inside the rattletrap of a farmhouse.

Evidently this was a password. The little man seemed satisfied.

"They are in jail, all of them," he said. "That is unfortunate, but I do not see how it can be helped. They were fools who did not understand. They would not have listened to me."

There was brief silence inside the farmhouse, then a voice asked, "You have something further in mind?"

The little man shook his head in the darkness. He appeared sad.

"I have knowledge of a banker in Kansas City," he said. "His name is Ellery P. Dimer. You know about him, I believe."

"Yes."

"It is unfortunate about him, too," the little man said, his voice more macabre than usual. "It seems that he is going to die under strange circumstances."

Having completed this rather enigmatic conversation, the shriveled man drove away.

THE banker, Ellery P. Dimer, had been a leading citizen of Kansas City for a long time. He was noted for his charity and a benevolent understanding of the frailties of human nature. Also he had what was generally considered to be one of the widest circle of acquaintances of any man in the State. He knew everyone, had been everywhere. He owned a lusty, hail-fellow-well-met personality, which was sometimes attributed to the fact that he had once owned a circus, and for years had been in the carnival business. Even now, he was reported to have interest in several circus outfits.

But Ellery P. Dimer was a good banker.

That morning, when he dressed, he shoved an efficient-looking automatic pistol in his coat pocket. His wife noticed.

"Why are you carrying a gun, Ell?" she asked anxiously.

Dimer shrugged, grinned somewhat too expansively. "Just taking it down to one of the bank messengers. Think nothing of it, darling."

His wife was not entirely satisfied. It seemed to her that he had been worried for several days past.

Ellery Dimer drove to the bank himself, although he usually let his chauffeur perform this task. He took a roundabout route.

He went immediately to the collection department, which maintained a highly efficient group of information-getters who were called collectors by courtesy, but were more in the nature of private detectives.

"You got anything on those three men?" he asked.

He was handed three envelopes, each of which bore a name. The names were Burdo Brockman, Elmo "Handy" Anderson, and Danny Dimer.

"Are those the three?" the head of the collectors asked.

"That's them."

Banker Dimer shoved his jaw out grimly and carried the three envelopes to his private office. He opened them, studied the contents at length. Only once did he speak, and then it was a single, explosive word.

"Hideous!" he said.

Later he snapped on the interoffice communicator and summoned his bank officers, as well as the head of the collection department and three of his principal operatives. These persons assembled in the office.

"I've called you here," announced Ellery Dimer, "concerning a matter which has completely amazed and horrified me."

He frowned at them and took a deep breath.

"I am not going to beat around the bush," he said. "This thing came to my attention through my half-brother, a man by the name of Danny Dimer. I am going to tell you the whole truth, then we are going to decide—"

It was then that his throat got cut from ear to ear, the knife appeared in his chest and he began screaming.

ELLERY DIMER did not emit much of a scream. Mostly it was gurgle. And a thin horrible crimson spray flew over some of those assembled in the room. An assistant cashier fainted without making a noise.

The murder was utterly impossible.

Dimer had stood there, unharmed and speaking firmly. Then his throat was open and leaking. The knife was sticking out of his heart.

The dead man fell to the floor.

One of the collectors folded over a wastebasket and was sick. Every face in the room had drained. For moments there were no sounds but those made by the man draped over the wastebasket.

Eventually they collected their wits and called the police. And the officers were anything but receptive to the story.

The homicide officers, having listened, held a private consultation.

"The story they're telling can't be true," growled the officer, "therefore they're lying to cover up."

"Sure. One of them killed Dimer. The others are lying."

"Or they all conspired to kill him, more likely."

So all of the bank employees who had been in the room when Ellery Dimer died shortly found themselves inside Kansas City's very effective city jail. The charge was murder.

Another factor did not help. Examiners discovered a shortage of two hundred thousand dollars in the stock of cash which should have been in the vaults.

Chapter VIII
VAGUE TRAIL

THE Adair County sheriff—Kirksville, Missouri, was in Adair County—was a conscientious man. When he saw a copy of a Kansas City paper containing the story of the fantastic death of Banker Ellery P. Dimer, he went to the prosecuting attorney…

"That kind of puzzles me," he said.

"Puzzles you how?"

"Remember how this girl insists she has never been anywhere near the capitol in Jefferson City, and didn't even know the governor?"

"This Lion Ellison, you mean?"

"Yes."

"I don't see any connection."

"I just had a hunch." The sheriff picked up the paper, added, "Think I'll let 'em look at this. Might come to something."

He walked over to the jail and handed the newspaper to Doc Savage. The bronze man read the item about the banker's murder, but his metallic features did not change expression.

"Know anything about that?" the sheriff asked.

"Nothing worth repeating," Doc admitted.

"You haven't given an explanation of why you were in company of this girl," the sheriff said.

"Would it have got us out of jail?"

The sheriff grinned thinly. "Not much."

After the sheriff departed, Doc Savage passed the newspaper to the others. Renny scowled, rumbled, "Holy cow!" He stared at Doc Savage. "This helps explain why we were framed into jail."

"We were framed, undoubtedly," Doc admitted.

Monk said, "Sure we were. And my bet is that our shrunken little wart of a friend is behind it. He tipped off the cops that we would probably land here with Miss Ellison. He found out in New York that we were helping Miss Ellison, so it was natural for him to guess we would head here. So he tipped the cops off, got us locked up, and now he's going ahead with another murder."

Ham shook the newspaper violently and objected, "But this murder was impossible! Several people in the same room, all of them claiming they never saw the murder committed. It couldn't have happened."

Monk snorted.

"Listen, we had that runt locked in a room, and he vanished," the homely chemist reminded. "That couldn't have happened, either."

"To a knot-head like you, anything could happen," Ham said caustically.

Monk scowled. "It's a good thing you're locked in another cell. If I had you in here with me, I'd kick a tort and a couple of writs out of you, you shyster lawyer."

The pair exchanged bloodcurdling glares. Which was somewhat deceptive, because there had been occasions in the past where each had risked his life for the other.

Doc Savage's regular bronze features were inscrutable, but there was a foment of thought behind them. His thoughts were numerous and complicated, but they amounted to one thing, which was the simplest fact of all. They could not accomplish anything while locked in jail.

EACH of them had been consigned to a different cell, Renny getting the cubicle which was strongest, probably because his big fists looked so formidable. There was nothing extraordinary about the jail construction. It was just a good jail that was rather ancient.

Monk and Ham and Renny glanced thoughtfully at Doc Savage from time to time. They were wondering why the bronze man was remaining in jail. They did not doubt that he could escape whenever he wanted to—Monk had whispered as much to Lion Ellison, but the young woman was skeptical.

"Escape from jail whenever he wishes?" The girl shook her head dubiously. "But they searched him. They searched all of us when they locked us in here. What'll he use for a key?"

Monk looked at her and shook his own head. "You're still underestimating Doc," he assured her.

As more hours passed, it became increasingly evident to the others that Doc Savage was waiting for something. It was late that night—it was as dark outside as a bat's idea of Valhalla—when their curiosity was satisfied.

A voice arose from the street that ran along one side of the jail. The voice was that of a very tall and very thin man—in fact, this individual came nearer to being a walking skeleton than it seemed possible of any man. His clothing fit him about as gracefully as sacks draped on a framework of broom handles.

This ambling string of bones was apparently singing. However, the words he was using were not English; it was extremely unlikely that they would have been intelligible to anyone on the street. The language was Mayan—the ancient vernacular of Maya which is a lost tongue as far as modern civilization is concerned. Doc Savage and his five aides spoke the lingo, used it to communicate whenever they did not wish to be understood by others.

Monk heard the voice, gave a leap, jammed his face to the window bars.

"Johnny!" he exploded.

Lion Ellison noticed the excitement, whispered, "What is it?"

"It's old Johnny—the walking word factory," Monk explained. "In other words, William Harper Littlejohn, the eminent archaeologist and geologist and user of big words, who is one of our gang."

DOC SAVAGE went to the window, called down to Johnny in Mayan, asking, "Have any trouble?"

"What do you mean—sneaking off on a hot mystery like this without telling me?" Johnny sounded indignant.

"You were in the Painted Desert country excavating a village of the early basket-weaver era," Doc Savage said. "We didn't want to take you away from your work."

"I like to have not heard you were in jail," Johnny explained. "I flew up here as soon as I could. This is the first chance that I figured it was safe to talk to you."

"Everything set?" Doc asked.

"I've got my plane in an oatfield out east of town," Johnny said. "I've rented four cars, and they're parked in four different directions from this jail so we can get hold of one regardless of what direction we have to run."

"Good," Doc Savage said. "I was waiting on you."

The jailer came in boldly and did not notice Doc until the bronze man's fingers were about his neck.

Doc Savage moved back from the window abruptly; he had heard a small sound. The jailer walked up to the cell, muttered, "What the hell was that noise?" and finally moved away. After the man had gone, Doc passed low-voiced commands to the others.

"We'll try a break now," he said. "There was not much sense in attempting it until Johnny showed up, as it was reasonable to suppose he would."

In searching the bronze man, the sheriff had not neglected to pry up his shoe heels to make sure there were no cavities inside. But what the sheriff had failed to do was cut into, or jab an ice pick through the heel itself. Such an operation would have shown the little glass-lined vial which had been cast into the rubber when the heel was molded.

Doc unscrewed the metal cap of the vial, exposing a nib of glass which he broke off.

He walked over to the door, began to apply the liquid contents of the tiny vial to the locking bars, a drop at a time. The moment the stuff touched the metal, pronounced reaction took place. The metal seemed to turn to rust, swelling as this occurred.

Monk craned his neck to watch the operation in the pale light that came from the single bulb in the runway; the homely chemist grinned. He knew the chemical composition of the potent acid, somewhat corrosive in nature, which quickly disrupted the molecular structure of a metal.

Later Doc shoved, and the cell door came open.

THE bronze man carried only the one vial of acid; he had used all of it on the bars. Releasing the others in that fashion was out of the question.

"Monk," he suggested, "suppose you get sick."

The bronze man moved rapidly to the outer door, stepped close beside it, pressing to the brick wall. Monk got the idea and began groaning. Monk fancied himself as an actor. His groans reeked of agony and approaching death.

Big-fisted Renny boomed, "Hey, jailer! You better see what's wrong with this guy."

The jailer presumed they were all locked in cells, so he had no fears about entering the runway. He came in boldly and did not notice Doc until the bronze man's fingers were about his neck.

Doc did not choke him. He exerted pressure with fingertips on strategic nerve centers which produced quick unconsciousness. The man would be out for fifteen or twenty minutes, and eventually reviving, would have nothing more than a slight headache to show for his experience.

The fellow had the keys. Doc got them, worked with the lock until he had released his three men and Lion Ellison.

One other cell was occupied, the inmates being petty criminals, who had been picked up for local crimes. These small-time crooks had been watching with silent interest, but now one of them spoke grimly. "If this is a break—it won't stop halfway," he snarled. "Turn us loose, or we'll raise such a hell of a roar that you won't have a chance of lamming."

Doc said, "We'll have to do something about that," and walked to the cell. He unlocked the door, stepped inside.

There were blow noises, a yip or two of agony, and then quiet. The bronze man stepped out and locked the door again.

"They'll probably revive about the same time as the jailer," he said.

They had no trouble walking out of the jail. But once on the street, there was plenty of difficulty.

Came a blinding flash of light. It turned all the street white, lasted but a fraction of a second.

"Photo flash!" Monk shouted. "Somebody took a picture."

Monk's bellow flushed a photographer out of a gloomy doorway across the street. The man ran with long-legged anxiety to get away from there.

Doc Savage stopped Monk, said, "He just took a picture. Catching him will do no good."

Monk growled, "That guy was a newspaperman from a Kansas City sheet. I remember seeing him around the jail today."

They discovered Johnny. The elongated archaeologist and geologist was waving his arms to get their attention. They ran toward him.

"I'll be superamalgamated," Johnny gasped. "When that flash went off, it startled me out of ten years' growth."

THE car which Johnny had secured—he'd had a frenzied time renting four machines without attracting suspicion, he explained—was an ancient sedan which deserved a niche in the hall of fame because of the noise it made. The headlights gave just a little more illumination than candles.

Doc Savage asked, "Your plane is close to town?"

"Four or five miles."

Monk ejaculated, "Hey, we can't run away from this thing! We gotta lick it!"

"There will be enough police in that town," Doc explained, "to find us if we stayed. Furthermore, we have no clues in Kirksville."

Monk grumbled, "I don't see where we've got any clues anywhere."

"There's that murder of the banker in Kansas City," Ham reminded.

"Yeah, and Kansas City is full of cops.

Furthermore, the cops would have found any clues that had been lying around."

Johnny got behind the wheel and drove the noisy car to the highway, turned south and took the first main road left turn. The road was black-topped, and the pale headlights were almost useless.

"Holy cow!" bigfisted Renny ejaculated suddenly. "Where are we headed for, Doc?"

"You remember that picture of the governor being murdered?" Doc asked.

Lion said suddenly, violently, "I'll never forget it! Last night, all the time I was trying to sleep, I couldn't see anything else."

"It was taken by an amateur photographer named Don Meek, 902 First Street, in Jefferson City."

Ham, astonished, demanded, "Where did you get that information?"

"The newspaper that published the picture. The information was in the cutline underneath the photograph."

The old car gave a great jump, seemingly trying to swap ends, as Johnny turned into a farm field. Weeds threshed against the chassis. Johnny had wheeled his plane behind a thicket of scrub oak and maple trees which grew thickly on a spot where a house must once have stood. Leaves were gone from the maples, but frost-painted foliage was still thick upon the scrub oaks.

"Johnny," Doc said

"Yes?"

"You weren't in that flashlight picture the newspaper photographer took. There is nothing to prove that you helped us escape. And if this car is found here, they will know we left by airplane. You had better return the rented cars, and keep an eye on things. And don't let yourself be seen any more than necessary."

"Why should I keep out of sight?" Johnny asked.

"Because anyone who took the trouble to investigate could learn you were a member of our outfit," Doc reminded him.

Monk put in, "What he means is that you're about as inconspicuous as the Eiffel Tower."

Johnny sighed resignedly and remained behind. Doc put the plane into the air, lifting the ship over a hedge, and pointing it southeast to avoid the government airport at Millard, where the attendants would doubtless make note of any passing planes.

Ham stared back at the headlights of Johnny's old automobile. "I'll bet he keeps undercover—about like a Fourth of July celebration. He likes his excitement too well."

"If he'd been in that jail a couple days, he'd be careful," rumbled big-fisted Renny.

Lion Ellison came forward and put a hand on Doc Savage's arm. Excitement made her fingers bite at his arm like jaws. "Do you have truth serum that you can give this photographer? I've got to know whether he saw me—well, like the picture showed." Her voice was strained.

Monk, who had overheard her, said grimly, "We'll crack that egg without any trouble."

Ham said, "You may be counting your egg before you've caught the chicken."

Chapter IX
THE IMPOSSIBLE MURDER

OVER Jefferson City, visibility was good. They could discern the capitol building, a thing of domed magnificence like alabaster in the moonlight, with a fountain that was like a jewel before it, then the lazy silver ribbon of the Missouri River. And spread behind were the bright sparks of the city lights, with the State penitentiary a ponderous mass off to the left.

Renny pointed with a thick finger, rumbled gloomily, "That's the State lock-em-up, ain't it?"

"Think of somethin' cheerful," Monk suggested.

Doc said, "We had better avoid the airport."

This plane, which was one Johnny had taken to the Painted Desert on his archaeological expedition, was one of Doc Savage's ships, hence equipped to operate from either land or water. Doc cranked up the landing gear, swung north and dropped toward the surface of the river. There were silencers into which he cut the motor exhausts, reducing them to a sick whisper.

A little muddy water spotted the windows and dampened the metal-wing skin when he landed.

"Wonder if Johnny had standard equipment aboard?" he said.

Standard equipment included a collapsible boat, and a miniature edition of an outboard motor that had a great deal more power than its appearance indicated.

Monk rummaged for a while, announced, "Here they are."

Three quarters of an hour later, they were dragging the collapsible boat upon the baked mud bank of the river not far from the capitol. They carried the little craft to a wad of black shadow under a bush and left it there.

Doc Savage took the lead. The streets were deserted, and seemed doubly cold because they had been chilled by their ride on the river. Doc Savage moved well in the lead.

Lion touched Ham's arm and asked, "How does he know where we're going?"

"Doc? I've seen him do this so often that it doesn't surprise me any more. He probably saw a map of Jefferson City somewhere at some time."

Ham shook his head in admiration. "I think Doc puts more time in on memory development than anything else in that daily exercise routine."

"Routine?" Lion was puzzled.

"The aërialists and acrobats with a circus have to practice, don't they?"

"Of course."

"Well, every day since I've known him, Doc has expended at least two hours on what I guess you would call an exercise routine. It's an amazing thing. He has scientific methods of developing all his senses and mental abilities. As you get to know him better, you may be inclined to think he's a little inhuman—but as a matter of fact, he's an example of the degree to which a man can develop himself by concentration and persistence."

"He's an unusual man, isn't he?" Lion said softly.

"Unusual isn't half the word."

Doc Savage struck the panel and knocked it open—but

THE building was old and made of brick that an expert readily could have told had come out of the kilns before the turn of the century. It was a mongrel thing probably called an apartment house, but hardly entitled to the name. There were, as nearly as Doc and the others could tell, four apartments, the two upstairs being reached by separate wooden stairways that could have been improved with paint.

Don Meek was on the floor—dead!

Doc Savage gestured the others up the stairs; bringing up the rear, he performed two operations. At the bottom of the stairs, he sprinkled thickly a grayish powder that might have been dust. Well up the stairs, almost at the top, he scattered a different powder, this one more yellowish in hue.

Lion watched, whispered, "Where did he get—"

"Johnny had some equipment cases in the plane," Monk breathed.

"Pipe down," Ham said in a low tone. "I think Don Meek is at home. There's a light."

Don Meek had no hair on his head. He had very large white teeth, most of which he displayed in a big grin, but the grin loosened at the ends and finally collapsed as he stared at them.

"You're under arrest," Monk announced loudly. "We've got all the goods on you. The little runt confessed."

Monk liked violent actions, and he was not bashful about taking liberties with the truth.

The amateur camera fan, Don Meek, staggered back. A wintry expression of horror twisted his face.

"I—he confessed..." His voice was a gurgle.

Monk followed up, got him by the necktie and yelled, "He laid both murders onto you, the dirty double-crosser."

Don Meek was losing color; ordinarily he had a skin that was as tanned as a well-baked loaf of bread, but it had almost turned to the hue of unbaked dough. His hands made don't-know-what-to-do motions.

Monk, really convinced he was getting somewhere, bore the camera bug back to a chair, sank the man in it, and jammed their faces close together. Monk's face was an object calculated to induce considerable fright.

"Tell us the truth!" Monk roared. "That's the only way you can stop 'em from hanging you until you are dead."

Don Meek's mouth behaved like a fish out of water. Monk got him by the throat, lifted him up by pressure and choked him somewhat. "Hanging by your neck until you're dead!" Monk shrieked. "See how it feels!"

Monk figured he was doing very well. But the effect of surprise wore off, so that Don Meek got his mental feet back on solid ground. Two hot spots of color flamed in his cheeks. Suddenly he planted a hard right hook on Monk's nose.

Monk staggered back, grabbed his nose and honked and blew in pain.

"I'll tear 'im apart!" Monk squalled. "I'll liquidate him!"

"On the contrary," said Don Meek, "you'll

behave in a civil manner, or get a chair broken over your head."

DOC SAVAGE had moved to the far side of the room, where there was a door. He passed on into a dining room furnished with a dining suite that was very new and shiny. Beyond there was a kitchen, ordinary except that it contained a refrigerator so new that the interior had not yet been unpacked.

On the rear steps—they were a steep wooden tunnel sloping down in the chill blackness—the bronze man planted the two powders in the same fashion as when he had entered. The dust-colored particles on lowermost steps; the yellowish powder higher.

He went back.

"Anybody else around?" Renny demanded.

"Apparently not."

Renny jerked his thumb at Monk and Ham. "Holy cow! They're at it again."

Monk's initial attempt to bulldoze Don Meek had failed, and Ham was riding him about it.

"You missing link, you gnat among brains," Ham snarled. "We came here to ask this man some questions. And are you civil about it? No! You begin browbeating him."

"I think he's a crook," Monk said. "I still think so."

"Why?"

"You saw that picture he took in the newspapers? Well, he couldn't have took it, because Miss Ellison says she wasn't there." Having made this remark, Monk glanced triumphantly at Lion. He'd made that statement to convice her that he at least believed her.

Lion's look of gratitude was warm enough to make Monk completely forget his quarrel with Ham.

Doc Savage took over the catechism of Don Meek. The bronze man made his voice persuasive, firm without being dominating. He said, "We are investigating the murder of the governor, and the murder of a banker named Ellery Dimer, in Kansas City, and we would like to have any information you can give us."

Don Meek had completely recovered his self-possession. He stood with legs wide apart, hands on his hips.

"I don't know anything about the banker's killing," he said levelly. "I remember reading it in the newspapers. What's mysterious about it? They arrested six or seven people for the banker's murder, didn't they?"

Ham said, "The people in the room with the banker claim they did not see what killed him."

Don Meek snorted. "You believe that, I suppose? Hell, of course they saw it. They're probably all in it together."

Doc said, "We had better begin on the murder of the governor."

"Yeah?" Don Meek scowled.

"You saw it, didn't you?"

"So what?"

"There is no object in becoming hard-boiled," Doc said without emotion.

Don Meek bristled, took a step forward and leveled an arm. His voice was almost a shout. "You're not keeping me," he yelled. "I've got you pegged!"

Monk said, "I'm gonna peg you if you don't behave!"

Don Meek was not impressed. "I saw your pictures in the newspapers," he shouted. "You were arrested in Kirksville for helping the girl who murdered the governor." He swung, stabbed his arm at Lion. "And that's the girl!"

Monk said, "We're gonna have to get this cookie into a corner."

THE prisoner scowled and shook his right fist at them. "Get out of here all of you!" He did not seem in the least afraid of them. "I'm going to call the police."

Doc Savage removed a flat metal case from his coat pocket, opened it and began placing the contents on the table.

"Truth serum?" Ham asked, looking at the case.

Doc nodded.

Don Meek looked a little less certain of himself. His hands tightened and he said angrily, "You fools! You can't keep me here."

"Can't keep you—that's crazy talk." Monk glowered at him. "I personally, with one hand, could keep a dozen guys like you right here." Then the homely chemist narrowed one small eye; an idea had hit him. His face sobered.

Abruptly Monk walked to one of the doors, slammed it, and put his back against the panel.

"What's got into you?" Ham demanded.

Monk ignored Ham, looked at Renny, and said, "You remember that little runt in New York? That room? And how he got away from us?"

Renny remembered, and not pleasantly. The big-fisted engineer made a jump for the other door and turned the key in the lock. "Holy cow!" he yelled at Ham. "Look at those windows and see if they're locked on the inside!"

Ham stared at him. "You gone crazy?"

"Are the windows locked!" Renny roared.

Ham winced at the tone, looked bewildered, but went over to the window and made an examination, then said, "They're locked inside. Both of them."

Doc Savage had not contracted Renny's excitement. He knew the big-fisted engineer had remembered the fantastic escape of the wizened little man from the garage vault in their New York skyscraper headquarters. But now something happened that changed Doc's attitude.

He had caught an odor—it was an odor which was formed through reaction when two powdered chemicals were combined, even in the smallest quantities; the particular two chemicals in this case being those he had sprinkled on the stairs, front and rear. So someone had come. Some person—or thing of substance—which moved with an absence of noise that was ghastly.

"Locking the doors and windows won't help you!" Don Meek shouted. "It's too late—"

Doc Savage moved then. He put all his strength and agility into a violent lunge for the door, bowled Monk out of the way, struck the panel and knocked it open. There was a small vestibule, an outer door. He thrust that open.

It was then that Don Meek began to beat the floor with his fists. Doc heard the frantic pounding, stopped, ran back into the room.

Monk, Ham, Renny and the girl were all staring, reduced to a hypnotic silence by what they were seeing.

It was stupefying, that thing happening before their eyes. Impossible. Their minds refused to accept it.

No one moved, really, for moments, but it made no difference because, by all practical standards, Don Meek was dead, his head having been separated from his body.

Chapter X
POLICE CHASE

LION ELLISON fainted then, and went down, her body twisting as she sank so that she had turned completely around by the time she was down. She made no sound, except for the breath rushing past her lips.

Monk lunged, caught her, kept her head from striking the floor.

"She's fainted," the chemist croaked.

Renny made a gurgling sound that was all horror. His huge hands leaped out, clamped upon a chair, and he began to club at the air in the room. He struck grimly, with terrific force, always slashing out at empty air. He did not hit anything, although he covered the entire room; and finally he backed into a corner, holding the chair out in front of him like a lion tamer being menaced by an invisible beast. He had not spoken; he did not speak now.

The animal life in Don Meek's body was dead now, so that all physical movement had ceased.

Ham had been staring fixedly at Don Meek; his eyes had hardly shifted. Ham's legal training and his long practice of law had, probably excepting Doc Savage, given him a more matter-of-fact mind than any of the others. So something like this was a far greater shock to him.

Don Meek had fallen where he had been standing, the two parts of him dropping together, the head tumbling over a little to one side. The beating which his fists had given the floor had been a death throe or some kind of reflex—much as a chicken kicks after its head is pulled off.

Suddenly Ham began speaking. His voice was toneless, as if it might have been made by one of those new machines that make the tones of a voice without any of its human quality.

"There was nothing to show how it happened," he said. "We were standing here. And then, suddenly, Don Meek was falling—and his head came off."

Ham looked around with an utterly foolish grin on his face. "That's as crazy as anything, isn't it? It's silly. A man oughta laugh at it, hadn't he?"

Ham's lips peeled off his teeth. He began to titter in high falsetto.

Doc Savage took hold of Ham's arm, led him to the door, and when Ham still tittered, slapped him. Then he shoved Ham out in the hall. The dapper lawyer stood there, hands opening and closing, and got control of himself.

"Thanks," he muttered. "That thing gave me the talking willies. First time it ever happened, I think."

Doc went back into the room. He said, "Everyone be as still as possible," and moved over and fastened an ear against the wall to listen. He thought of another and better way to pick up sounds—he drew a pocketknife which he had located on Johnny's plane and brought along, opened the knife, sank the blade deep into the door casing. Then he gripped the handle with his teeth. He knew from experience that he could pick up vibrations—such as footsteps—much more readily in that fashion.

He waited for a long time, then was thoughtful. At length, he got down on all fours and began going over the floor of the room. The carpet was not new; neither was it old, and its design was made up of browns and reds and blues. Doc searched with his hands as much as his eyes.

It was his fingers which found dampness, and his handkerchief showed that the moist spot was red. Blood. The spot was perhaps two feet long, not much more than two inches wide. The cut place in the rug was about a yard from the bloodstain. It was a narrow slit, six inches in length. Doc pulled the fabric apart at the cut; there was a gash in the floor which, as nearly as he could judge, extended over half the thickness of the hardwood flooring.

Renny had come into the room and was watching. He said, "That bloodstain and the cut in the carpet mean anything to you, Doc?"

"It probably explains," Doc Savage said quietly, "why we weren't killed along with Don Meek."

DURING the next few minutes, Doc Savage did a number of things which the others failed to understand. It was not exactly clear, for instance, why he had Monk and Renny and Lion Ellison—the young woman had revived—leave the house immediately, instructing them, "When you get outside, separate. Each take a different direction. Walk two blocks, hide yourself in the darkness and wait. When you hear three sharp whistles, go to the spot where we left our boat on the river bank."

"You mean we're not to come back here?" Monk said.

"Not unless you hear yells for help," Doc said.

"You think there may be trouble?" Monk demanded.

Doc Savage did not answer—indeed, it appeared he had not heard Monk's inquiry. Monk was disappointed, but not surprised; Doc Savage had a small habit with which Monk was well acquainted, the habit of appearing not to hear a question when he did not wish to formulate an answer.

Ham soon found himself alone with Doc Savage. The dapper lawyer was still without his cane, and was lost when it was not in his hands; it was a sword cane, and he had carried it almost continuously for years. He had even had Monk concoct a chemical with which to daub the end of the sword, thus making a slight prick of the blade produce quick unconsciousness. Ham watched Doc curiously.

Ham Brooks had developed a keen brain, and he was not without analytical ability as far as reading clues was concerned. Most good lawyers are semi-detectives.

But Ham failed to see any significance whatever in a certain photograph which seemed to interest Doc Savage greatly.

They had found Don Meek's photographic dark room. It was in the attic, reached by a ladder which lowered from the ceiling of a large closet. There was the usual equipment of trays for developer, shortstop and hypo, and a good enlarger of the automatic focusing variety. There were partially used boxes of bromide papers, and jars of stock developer solution and hypo.

Don Meek's pictures were in a steel filing cabinet. There were scores of them. Doc Savage leafed through the photographs rapidly, not expending a great deal of time on any one of them. Abruptly, he began drawing pictures from the file; he spread several out for Ham's inspection.

"Recognize them?" he asked.

"No, I never saw—wait a minute!" Ham stared.

It was the wizened little man who had given Lion Ellison her brother's belongings—the strange little fellow who had been seized by Monk and Renny in New York, and who had vanished. They recognized him from the description Monk and Renny had given.

Ham studied the picture, said, "He had about as much taste in clothes as a color-blind clown."

"The fact that Don Meek had these pictures of him proved the two were friends," Doc reminded.

Doc Savage spent some time examining the pictures. Then, to Ham's astonishment, the bronze man selected one of the least interesting photos of the wizened man. The picture which Doc took didn't even show a recognizable likeness of the subject's face.

In this photograph, the little man seemed to be seated on the edge of a fountain or possibly a small ornamental fishpond. He had his chin cupped in his palm, obviously posing as a thinker. Ham gave close attention to the remainder of the picture, but he could discern nothing more interesting than an assortment of rocks, water that was distorted by reflection, and a portion of a tree or two.

This was the picture which Doc Savage took with him when they left the apartment.

THEIR departure from the apartment was about as peaceful as a riot. It began when Monk suddenly charged into the apartment. Monk was out of breath, so excited that he gobbled when he tried to talk.

"Cops!" the homely chemist managed to bark finally. "The whole neighborhood is full of cops. They're sneaking up on this place."

Ham snorted skeptically, asked, "Have you gone crazy?"

"Listen, I saw the squad cars unloading 'em," Monk said. "I tore out down the street to warn you. It was dark and they didn't see me."

"The police," Doc Savage said grimly, "would be a perfectly logical development. Let's get out of here."

They went down the stairs in rattling haste, only to have a voice shout, "Stop, you three! This is the law!"

Doc whistled three times shrilly—the signal agreed upon to send Renny and the girl back to the river.

Blinding white light pounced upon them. The police had turned on searchlights.

"Smoke bombs," Doc directed. "Fill the street with them."

Monk, Ham and Doc Savage had all loaded their pockets with the little smoke grenades, past experience having taught them that the things were useful. They began digging them out of their clothing, slipping the firing levers, and pitching them right and left in the street. The little metal globules made popping noises and sprouted fat mushrooms of smoke. The searchlight beams faded out in the sepia pall.

"We better keep hold of each other," Doc said.

They moved down the street. There was yelling, a few shots and considerable confusion… But Doc Savage and the others arrived, unharmed, on the river bank something near thirty minutes afterward.

Lion Ellison and Renny were there. The girl explained, "We were hidden, and the police didn't see us. We heard your whistle and left."

Standing on the baked-mud bank of the river, Monk made a growling noise. "Those cops were tipped off."

Renny's rumble was violent. "Holy cow! 'Course they were. Just like when we landed in Kirksville."

Chapter XI
PICTURE CLUE

LIKE a frozen bird, the plane stood on the cold river. There was a white fuzz of frost on the wings, and the river water itself was steaming in the cold. With no regrets whatever, Doc and the others quitted the unstable little collapsible boat; they folded the tiny craft, hauled it inside after them. Then, standing in the cabin, they windmilled their arms to restore circulation, and blew on their fingers.

"What burns me," Renny rumbled, "is that we're making no progress."

Without saying anything, Doc Savage produced the photograph which he had taken from Don Meek's assortment; he passed it to the girl.

"That's him." Lion's tone was strained, and her face had even become a trifle pale as she looked at the picture. Still without making comment, Doc Savage took the photograph back. He stowed it away carefully.

Ham said, "I still don't see where that picture is gonna do us any good."

Doc Savage did not volunteer any explanation. He went forward to the control cockpit and got the motors turning.

As soon as they were in the air, the bronze man began making adjustments on the radio. Watching closely, Monk perceived that Doc was shifting the transmitter to the eighty-meter amateur phone band.

Cutting in the microphone, Doc began repeating, "Calling Kansas City. Calling Bill Larner, or any twenty-meter phone in Kansas City."

Later, he signed with the call letters of Johnny's plane, and listened.

Lion looked at Monk, asked, "Who is Bill Larner?"

"Why, he's—" Monk hesitated, finally said, "He's a fellow who sometimes works for Doc Savage." Which, as Monk well knew, was a somewhat negative description of Bill Larner. But to make the girl understand all about Bill Larner would have taken a great deal of description. For instance, Monk would have had to tell her about the strange institution which Doc Savage maintained in upstate New York for the curing of criminals—a hidden place, the existence of which was unknown to the outside world.

To this remote spot, Doc Savage sent such criminals as he happened to catch; there they underwent delicate brain operations at the hands of specialists trained by the Man of Bronze, operations which wiped out all memory of the past. After this, the "patients" received a course of training calculated to fit them as useful citizens. Monk and the others frequently referred to the place as the "college."

Bill Larner was a graduate of that college; once he had been the associate of a notorious criminal, but Bill Larner himself did not know this. He only knew that he hated crime and criminals, and that Doc Savage was the symbol of his own belief.

Eventually Doc Savage got in touch with Bill Larner, who was an amateur radio bug, and asked him to investigate, then make a complete report of the murder of the banker, Ellery P. Dimer.

WHEN Bill Larner called back—it had taken him hardly more than two hours, and the plane was again at rest on the Missouri River, this time near Waverly, Missouri—he had a fairly complete preliminary report. Doc Savage listened for some time, aware that he was not receiving anything of value. Then suddenly he interrupted, "Hold it, Larner. Repeat that last item."

"Police have ascertained," said the distant voice of Bill Larner, "that just prior to his death, Banker Ellery Dimer went to the collection department of his bank, which is nothing more or less than the banks' private detective agency, and had them get all the dope they could on three people. The three were named Burdo Brockman, Elmo Handy Anderson, and Danny Dimer."

"What did the investigation show about the three?" Doc asked.

"Haven't found out."

"Continue investigating."

"Sure. Will you keep tuned in on this wavelength?"

"Each hour on the hour, whenever we can."

"Swell. Signing off."

Monk had overheard. He said thoughtfully, "Burdo Brockman, Elmo Handy Anderson, and Danny Dimer. Never heard of them before. Danny Dimer… Ellery Dimer was the banker's name. Might be some connection there. Father and son, or something."

"Are fathers in the habit of having detectives collect information on their sons?" Ham demanded.

"Suppose you explain it, then," Monk snapped.

Doc Savage had turned the controls over to Renny—all of the bronze man's associates were skilled pilots—and had moved back to the big charttable used by whoever was navigating. Switching on the light, he scrutinized the picture he had taken from unfortunate Don Meek's collection.

Ham said, "That thing still don't mean anything to me."

"Notice the pool," Doc suggested.

Ham peered. "Eh?"

"The reflection on the water."

Ham grunted excitedly, thinking he was going to see something sensational, and stared… He turned the picture to different angles, frowning.

"House," he muttered finally. "Reflection of the door of a house. Apparently a front door, because you can make out the street number of the house."

"The number is 4786."

Doc Savage's flake-gold eyes were excited in a quiet, tense way as he said, "The ugly little man looks perfectly at ease, as if he had been round that house a great deal. If we can find the house, perhaps we can locate someone who will put us on his trail."

"But just a number won't find a house for us," Ham grumbled. "It may take a long, long time to locate a house with a door that looks like that one. It's a common kind of a door, anyway."

Doc said, "Not a common street number, though.

"Eh?"

"Forty-seven eighty-six."

"So what?"

"A number like that means the house is in the forty-seventh block. How many streets in Kirksville are forty-seven blocks long?"

"Not many," Ham admitted. "Hey! Wait! How you know it's in Kirksville?"

Doc indicated the photograph. "That is a very clear picture. Don Meek might have been mixed up in something mysterious that got him murdered, but he was a wizard with a camera and dark room. Those rocks—notice their texture. Native stone is limited around Kirksville. This happens to be the best type found around there; in almost any other part of the State, a fountain pool would have been built of a better grade of stone."

Ham rubbed his jaw.

"Like all magic," he said, "it's simple once they show you how."

ASSORTED parts of the United States have received praise from time to time on their merits as the ideal spot in which to live, Florida and southern California contesting for the tops in climate, New York City with the fastest night life, New Orleans the most delectable cooking, and the Jackson Hole country of Wyoming claiming the honors for scenery.

Almost entirely overlooked is northern Missouri, particularly the section around Kirksville. And what does this district excel in? Why, it's probably the most placid and lowest-priced part of the United States in which to reside; possibly it is the most economical in the world, for it is certainly lower-priced than France before the second great war, when France was highly touted for its low-cost living.

And placid! Nothing ever happens. There are no bank robbers, no murders, no night clubs. Not even divorces, except once in a great while.

If a man wanted an utterly peaceful spot in which to seclude himself for leisure and cogitation, he could hardly do better than the section around Kirksville, Missouri. The town itself is slightly collegiate because of a State Teachers' College and an osteopathy college, but otherwise it is benevolently rural. The big night is Saturday, when the farmers all come to town. And the farmer is the most important article around there; everyone else lives off him.

William Harper Littlejohn met Doc Savage and the others when they landed. Johnny had been contacted by portable radio.

"Crepusculescence is imminently millenial," he remarked. Which was his way of saying that pretty soon it would be getting daylight.

Lion Ellison said nervously, "This radio talking you're doing—isn't there danger of being overheard? And can't they locate your transmitters with direction finders?"

Monk explained that. "Our transmitters have got tiny scramblers on them."

"Scramblers?"

"Little gadgets," the homely chemist told her, "that mix up the voices until they can't be understood, then unscramble 'em at the other end. If you'll tune in a radio broadcast receiver on the very short wave bands, such as the thirteen-meter band, you'll probably be able to pick up stuff that sounds like somebody squawking through a tin horn. That's scrambled radiophone conversation."

Johnny had brought Monk's pet pig, Habeas Corpus, and Ham's chimp Chemistry. The animals made delight noises and climbed over their respective owners, after which they took the first opportunity to get into a fight.

"I borrowed them from the Kirksville police," Johnny explained. "The police don't know it yet, however."

Doc Savage asked Johnny, "Found out anything?"

"Not a thing"—Johnny, for some reason or other, never used big words with Doc Savage—"except that there is only one street in Kirksville with a forty-seven-block number. It's named Gibbs Street."

GIBBS STREET, the outer end of it, had once been a subdivider's dream. It began downtown as did the other streets, but it extended out beyond any of them, and for the last twenty blocks there was hardly a house; in fact, the end of Gibbs Street was remote enough to be one of the local Lovers' Lanes. It was not even graveled; grass grew in it, except for a pair of ruts.

"Here it is," Monk whispered, and the words were spurts of steam past his lips.

They got down and crawled. Frost speckled their clothing and chilled their hands. The ground was frozen a little.

The house stood half out of an amazingly thick grove of trees. A house like something that was ancient and had started to creep out into the light, then changed its mind.

"Older'n the Civil War," Renny breathed.

It wasn't. But it was predepression at the least, and a virgin as far as paint was concerned. It had bulk, enormous bulk; two full stories and a garret, rooms that sprawled and meandered in all directions with the big colonial doorway as a starting point. That doorway had what everything else in the house lacked—distinction.

The door, and the pool in front of it were undoubtedly the same that had been shown in unlucky Don Meek's photograph.

It was getting daylight. Off in the distance a dog was barking, and roosters were crowing at a farmhouse somewhere.

Doc said, "It won't hurt to watch the back door. I'll do that."

He crawled away from the others. The weeds had not been cut all that summer; they were high enough to conceal him.

There was one thing noticeable when you got very close to the house—the thing wasn't really as dilapidated as it looked from a distance. And it was inhabited; there was a path from the rear door in which no weeds whatever grew, an indication the path had been used all that summer.

Renny beat on the front door. Thunder like that could only come from the engineer's big fists. After the clamor, there was silence—

The large, benign gentleman who came out of the back door was in a hurry.

Doc Savage stood up and said, "Good morning."

The man stopped, growled, "What in the devil is this?"

Doc Savage made a mental note. This benign old fellow was scared. He had nerve. But he was nevertheless scared.

"We are looking for—ah—the proprietor," Doc explained.

"That's me—Burdo Brockman."

BURDO BROCKMAN announced his name with a crochety abruptness, as if it was supposed to mean something. And Doc got the feeling the name should carry weight... He searched in his memory, knowing the name was familiar, but failing immediately to recall it. His own failure to pull the correct recollection out of his memory cells was vaguely irritating; he had spent countless hours training his mind in an effort to make it an efficient filing cabinet. Grope as he would, he couldn't think why Burdo Brockman's name should mean something...

An ample man was this Burdo Brockman. He was like a big bulldog, somewhat old and of pickled disposition. His hair was white and as tousled as freshly picked cotton; his whiskers were reddish and hadn't been cut for a week or more. He had clear eyes. His clothes were old, slouchy, had been very expensive when he bought them.

Monk came ambling around the house muttering, "Doc, we can't raise—" He halted and stared.

"This is Burdo Brockman," Doc explained.

"Burdo—" Monk grinned suddenly. "Ain't this somethin'! Burdo Brockman is one of the guys that bank was havin' investigated."

Burdo Brockman interrupted sharply, "Say, say, what goes on here, anyhow?"

"Did you know Ellery P. Dimer?" Doc asked.

"Who's he?"

"A banker who was murdered in Kansas City under—well—odd circumstances, to say the least."

"I never," said Burdo Brockman, "knew him."

"You knew he had been murdered, though?"

"I think," said Brockman, "that we had better do some talking."

Monk said, "Yeah. We can talk about why you went sneaking out of the back door when we turned up."

They entered the house. Doc Savage watched closely when Burdo Brockman met Lion Ellison, but if the sturdy old gentleman had ever seen the young woman before, he was actor enough to conceal it. Lion glanced at Doc, shook her head slightly; Brockman was a stranger to her.

Brockman abruptly pointed a finger at Doc. "I think I know who you are—the fellow they call the Man of Bronze. Clark Savage, Jr. Am I right?"

Monk said, "That's right. And the rest of us are his assistants. Now—why were you taking a sneak?"

Ham punched Monk, said, "Listen, you homely wart hog, suppose you keep your bassoon out of it this time. You had no luck with Don Meek."

Brockman made a grunting noise. "Don Meek—I believe I know him." He frowned at them. "Amateur photographer, isn't he?"

"He was."

"Eh?"

"He's dead, too." Monk scowled. "Under, like Doc said, circumstances that were—odd."

Brockman suddenly sat down and took his face in both hands… When he looked up at them, there was something intense in his eyes. He said, "You better tell me about these murders."

Doc Savage described, in a steady voice that had no noticeable emotion, the weird death of Don Meek. He slighted no details in telling how Meek had been murdered before their eyes. The bronze man's account of the affair acquired drama from the complete calmness of the recital to such a degree that the others were holding the edges of their teeth together by the time he had finished.

"That photograph," Brockman said hoarsely. "Have you got that?"

Doc handed him the picture. Brockman took it, stared at it, holding it assorted distances from his eyes, then shook his head.

"My glasses," he apologized. "Have to get them. This desk here."

He went to the desk. From there, it was only one long jump to the door. He made it.

Chapter XII
THE SUDDEN ASHES

MONK emitted a roar and made for the door like a torpedo. But he had underestimated the strength of the seasoned wood of which the door was constructed. He bounced back, sprawled on the floor, dazed.

Ham took one window. Renny took another. They were outside, and the room was full of the jangling of breaking glass.

Lion cried, "I saw a flashlight!" and ran for the spot where she had seen it.

Doc Savage did nothing very drastic; he merely stood and listened. His sense of hearing was acute. He caught a faint thump of a noise, got down and put his ear against the floor.

He decided that Burdo Brockman, instead of rushing wildly out of the house, had gone into the basement.

Monk got up off the floor, full of rage, and yelled to see whether he was hurt. The yell was satisfactory. Monk hit the door again. This time, he broke it down. He galloped around through various parts of the house and finally howled, "The place is empty. He got away."

Doc went to the back door, stood there. He heard a grating sound, decided it was Brockman opening one of the basement windows to crawl out.

The bronze man wondered how Brockman expected to escape from the house. He got the answer to that almost at once, when he heard a whine that was quickly stifled. A dog. Brockman had a dog in the basement; apparently he was lifting the animal out of the window.

Doc distinctly heard Brockman growl, "Go get it, boy!" After that, there was a slight thud some distance from the house. The man had thrown a stick and sent his dog after it.

Renny and Ham saw the dog. It was a large, dark animal, and in the foggy murk preceding dawn, they thought it was Brockman.

"There he goes!" Ham roared.

They set out after the dog. Monk and Johnny and Lion joined them. The dog got scared, fled. They chased it.

"Heck, it's a pooch!" Monk barked, halting.

They raced back to the house, and Ham yelled, "Watch it, Doc! This was only a dog."

There was no answer. They searched, cautiously at first, then with growing consternation. For there was no trace of Burdo Brockman, nor of Doc Savage.

"What a pack of dopes we turned out to be!" Lion Ellison complained. "Chasing a dog!"

Monk pointed at Ham, said, "There's the head dope. He saw the dog."

"At least I had my eyes open," Ham said angrily. "I wasn't butting doors like a goat."

"Maybe," said Johnny, "an ultraconsummate indagation is in gradatim."

Lion asked, "Does he use those words all the time?"

"Worse ones," Monk admitted. "I'll translate: He thinks a complete search of this place is in order."

THE old house was furnished, they discovered, to fit a man's idea of complete luxury. There was nothing frilly or fancy, no article that would break easily. Nor were many of the articles cheap.

"Fellow had money," Ham remarked.

"And he liked to take it easy," Renny agreed.

The kitchen was well stocked with food, and there was canned stuff in the cellar. But nowhere was there anything to give them a line on Burdo Brockman. The desk was empty, except for a litter of old Kirksville daily papers, pen and ink, and some stationery.

Johnny stared at the stationery.

"I'll be superamalgamated," the big-worded archaeologist and geologist remarked.

"Huh." Renny came over and stared. "Holy cow!"

The stationery was printed:

RAJAH HUNTING LODGE,
SIMLA, INDIA.

Monk remarked, "Funny kind of stationery for a farmer in Missouri to have."

"This Brockman wasn't any farmer, I'm betting," Ham said. He prowled through more drawers in the desk. "Hey, look! More photographs!"

They fell upon the pictures eagerly, giving them a thorough inspection. They were hunting pictures. Burdo Brockman was in all of them. In some, he was standing upon a dead elephant, holding a rifle. In others, he crouched beside a slain tiger, with the rifle. In fact, all of the pictures had the same theme—Burdo Brockman and a rifle and a slain big-game animal.

It was big-worded Johnny who eyed the pictures and snorted.

"What's wrong?" Monk asked.

Johnny explained, not using big words. "You fellows know that I'm a geologist, and that as a geologist I have some knowledge of what India really looks like, not only the rock formations, but the vegetation as well."

"What are you trying to say?"

"That I would know a real Indian jungle if I saw one," Johnny said with dignity.

"Isn't this one real?"

"Phony."

"You mean—"

"I mean," said Johnny firmly, "that the jungle in these pictures was probably never any nearer India than some New York photographer's studio."

Monk grabbed the prints, eyed them closely. His knowledge of chemistry extended to photographic printing papers; once he had worked several weeks developing a high-speed bromide projection paper of high contrast for press use.

"This is a bromide paper," Monk said, "and it is American paper—not English, as you'd expect to find used in India."

"The animals in the photographs looked stuffed, now that you start thinking about it," Lion Ellison said. "I've worked with real animals enough to know a stuffed one when I see it."

"The pictures are phonies," Ham announced flatly.

"Which proves what?" Monk asked.

Renny consulted his wrist watch, grunted and made for the door.

"Where you going?" Monk demanded.

"You remember Bill Larner in Kansas City?" Renny reminded. "He is going to call us by radio every hour on the hour. It's that time now."

THEY had driven from the spot where they had left the plane in one of the cars which Johnny had rented, and in the machine was Johnny's portable shortwave radio outfit. The apparatus—it was as compact as a suitcase, including batteries—had been developed by the fifth member of Doc Savage's group of assistants, Major Thomas J. "Long Tom" Roberts, the electrical wizard, who was not with them this time. Long Tom was in England, working on some kind of a super-detector for submarines.

Bill Larner was enthused; they could tell from his voice that he had accomplished something.

"You remember those three men the murdered banker was having investigated—the men named Burdo Brockman, Elmo Handy Anderson and Danny Dimer?" Bill Larner asked.

"Sure. You got anything?"

"Well, I got some dope—say, this isn't Doc. Who is it?"

"Renny Renwick."

"Oh, hello, Renny. I should have recognized your voice; better work on this receiver of mine, hadn't I? Hi! Well, I got the dope that the bank-collection department turned up on Burdo Brockman."

Renny said, "Swell. Brockman is the one we're most interested in right now."

"Brockman is a rich New Yorker," the distant radio voice advised. "Owns factories and corporations and things. Richer than chocolate cake, but not very well known because he doesn't seem to be much of a society guy. Kind of the retiring type. Right now, he's in India, big-game hunting."

"He is like hell in India," Renny rumbled.

"This report said he was."

"The report is wrong."

"Well, I wouldn't know, would I?"

Renny asked, "What else you got on Brockman?"

"Nothing. Nothing on the others, either. I only got the report on Brockman this time. Could only cop one envelope when I went down to the bank to get a story, claiming I was a newspaper reporter. I'm going to make another trip and try to cop a second envelope. Think I can only get one at a time. This one was on Brockman. Next time,

I'll get one on Elmo Handy Anderson or Danny Dimer."

"Thanks, Bill," Renny said warmly.

"Oh, that's all right," said Bill Larner. "Doc Savage has done a lot for me, hasn't he?"

After the radio was switched off, Monk looked at Renny and grinned and said, "Bill Larner only knows about half of what Doc has done for him."

The reference was to the fact that Bill Larner, as a graduate of Doc's criminal-curing "college," had no idea that he had once been a bloodthirsty crook of a type he had been taught to hate while in the institution.

Bill Larner merely thought he was a man who had suffered the loss of his memory in an accident, and had been educated in Doc Savage's institution as an act of kindness on the bronze man's part.

Monk and Ham wandered off together.

THE separation from the others precipitated Monk and Ham into an experience that came near standing their hair permanently on end, but that was not their intention. The reasons for their getting together were probably twofold. First, each wanted to get the other out of the company of attractive Lion Ellison. Second, they were in a state of mind over the vanishing of both Burdo Brockman and Doc Savage, and they wanted to soothe their feelings by indulging in a good, satisfying quarrel.

They wandered around behind the house and came upon a path.

"I think we should follow this path and see where it goes," Ham said.

"I don't," Monk growled.

So they followed the path.

"Listen, you homely gosson," Ham said grimly, "I want you to stop rolling your eyes at that girl. I'll admit you seem to make some kind of headway with her, but it must be because she takes pity on such a combination of hairy size and gnat intellect. You lay off, see."

"You lay off her!" Monk growled. "I don't want her fallin' for some oily talk and a two hundred dollar suit of clothes."

"I'm not trying to make love to her!" Ham snapped. "I've known a lot of girls, and not one of them ever fell for me."

"You sure pick out intelligent girls, don't you?"

It took a moment for it to dawn on Ham that he had been insulted.

"I won't say what I think!" he snarled.

"If you said what you think, you'd be speechless."

Ham was trying to think up some suitable comeback when he discovered a bulk in the trees ahead. He quickened his pace and then snorted.

"A strawstack," Ham said.

"Yeah." Monk was thoughtful. He advanced, shoved an arm deep into the strawstack, then looked knowingly at Ham. "I feel boards," he explained.

"What?" Ham explored. "Say, there's a building of some kind inside there."

"Sh-h-h."

They listened, caught no sound. Monk backed away a few yards and gave his attention to the frost-whitened ground.

"Hey, look here." The homely chemist pointed. "Tracks."

Undeniably there were footprints, and they led around to the back and ended against the strawstack.

"Must be a door there," Monk whispered. "Stand back where you'll be safe, and I'll try it."

"I'll try the door," Ham corrected. "You get back."

The solicitude they were showing for each other's safety apparently struck neither as being an incongruous contrast to their attentions, wordlessly expressed a few moments earlier, of tearing each other limb from limb.

It was then that the event occurred.

The strawstack was in flames before their eyes. Not only in flames—practically burned to the ground. They had been looking at an innocent-appearing strawstack which they knew wasn't innocent. Now it was blazing, practically consumed.

Monk and Ham did what was perfectly natural under the circumstances—they got up and ran.

Chapter XIII
THE UNEXPECTED PRISONER

IT is an accepted fact in psychology that the human mind is largely a creature of habit and the product of experience, which is probably another way of saying that a man will believe only what he has learned to be possible. That a man will accept only what experience has taught him is usual, is borne out by credibility that small children place in fairy tales; after a man grows older, and fails to encounter either fairy or miracle, he concludes neither exists.

Monk must have been thinking somewhat along that line, judging from his remark after he stopped running.

"If this stuff keeps on happening, I may get to believe it," he said.

Ham said hoarsely, "Did you see what I saw?"

"The strawstack turned to flames and ashes in front of our eyes?"

"I didn't see it turn—it just suddenly was flames and ashes."

"On second thought—I don't believe it."

"Neither do I. Let's go back and look."

They went back through the woods and stood staring. There was no doubt about there having been a strawstack, and there was less doubt about it being in the advanced stages of burning down.

Renny, Johnny and Lion Ellison came dashing up, panting and wide-eyed with curiosity.

"We were in the house," Renny puffed. "Didn't see the fire at first, I reckon."

Monk pointed at the flames and asked in a hollow voice, "Do you see a fire now?"

Renny peered at him doubtfully, finally turned to Ham and asked, "Has Monk got hit on the head again?"

"Getting hit on the head never hurts him," Ham said soberly. "I guess you see that fire, all right."

"What kind of crazy talk is this? Of course we see a fire. Looks like it was a strawstack. Why'd you set it on fire?"

"Us set it on fire?" Ham gaped at him.

"Well, didn't you set that fire?"

"That fire," Monk said, "just suddenly was."

Monk and Ham circled the flames dubiously. The heat of it was intense against their faces; the smoke from it made them cough. There was no doubt about its reality, although they were having difficulty accepting the concrete existence of anything about this strawstack.

Additionally, it became increasingly evident that there had been some kind of a structure inside the strawstack. But the nature of the thing they would not be likely to learn, they concluded, because it developed that they were not going to be able to remain in the vicinity until the ashes cooled sufficiently for them to make an investigation.

A man ambled out of the trees. They had never seen the man before, and he had no distinguishing feature except that he wore overalls and was cross-eyed.

"Gee whizz!" He stared, his crossed eyes very wide. "Lot of dry leaves this time of year! Figure I better call the fire department. Don't want no forest fire."

"Sure," Monk said gloomily. "Call the army and navy if you want to."

The cross-eyed man—they presumed he was a native who had seen the smoke—galloped away. He had been gone four or five minutes when Monk gave a nerve-shattered jump.

"BLAZES!" Monk exploded. "He went after firemen. We can't stay here. We'll get arrested!"

Being a fugitive from the law, particularly on a charge of complicity in murder, was a new experience for Monk; he had momentarily overlooked existence of the fact.

They dashed for their car and lived through several sweating minutes before they loaded themselves and the two pets in the machine and got safely clear of the vicinity. The fire apparatus—it was a small chemical truck—passed them, and it was trailed closely by a car containing two State-highway patrolmen, which did nothing for the peace of their nerves.

"I'm sorry about all this," Lion Ellison said glumly. "It's my fault, involving you in such a mess."

"That's all right," Renny told her kindly.

"I don't care—I feel bad about it," Lion said. "If I hadn't gone to you for help after being accused of murdering the governor, you wouldn't be fugitives from the law."

"This kind of thing is our business," Renny reminded her.

Johnny said sourly, using small words, "And sometimes strikes me that a darn poor business it is, too."

The car was a sedan, neither large nor new, but fairly comfortable riding. They were traveling a side road that was dirt, but it had been dragged and was smooth. Around them were barbed-wire and hedge fences, open fields, not many barns or houses.

"It wouldn't be so bad," Ham complained, "if it made any sense. Miss Ellison here was framed for the murder of the governor. A banker in Kansas City was murdered in a way that looks impossible. Then a photographer was killed the same way. I ask you—does that make sense or hook up together?"

"The death of the photographer makes sense, all right," Renny rumbled. "He was killed because we were about to give him truth serum and get some facts."

"All right—take Burdo Brockman; where does he come in?"

"How would I know?"

"Humph."

"He ain't in India," Renny said meaningly.

"You know what I think?" Ham asked thoughtfully. "I think those letterheads of a hunting lodge in India, and those phony pictures of Burdo Brockman standing with animals he had shot were part of a system Brockman was using to make people think he was in India."

"Could be, at that," Renny admitted. "Brockman could write a letter about the hunting he was doing, writing like he was in India, and enclose a fake picture. Then he could mail the letter to somebody in India, who would remail it to the United States."

"Which would mean," Lion Ellison interrupted, "that Burdo Brockman is a crook."

The homely Monk had been unusually thoughtful and silent; usually he was a noisy fellow who used his tongue as if it was tied in the middle and loose at both ends. He came out of his muse suddenly and poked Ham.

"I just remembered somethin'," he said. "You recall when we was standin' at the strawstack? Well, the next thing we knew, it was about burned down. But when we saw that, we were sittin' down. We should've been standin', shouldn't we? We had been standin'."

"Well?"

"Maybe that means somethin', huh?"

"You figure it out," Ham said sourly.

The car rolled along, turned onto a red shale road that was rough. Johnny drove, keeping a close watch on the road. The others were silent. All of them were worried.

When a calm voice spoke to them from a spot near their feet, Monk all but jumped out of the car.

THEY had in the excitement over-looked the portable radio, which reposed on the rear floor boards. The receiver portion of the machine had been left switched on and turned to the wavelength which the bronze man's group usually employed for communication. "Calling Monk or Renny or one of the others," the voice said. "Hello, some of you."

Monk snapped on the transmitter, grabbed up the microphone and waited for tubes to warm.

"Doc!" he exploded. "Where on earth are you?"

It was undoubtedly Doc Savage's words, but he did not answer the question. Instead he said, "You might tune in on the State-police radio station at Macon."

"Why?"

"Tune in, and you'll see. Then come back to this frequency."

Monk shifted the receiving frequency to the police bank immediately below the broadcast wavelengths, and fished with the tuning knob until he had a loud signal and a voice saying:

"—height over six feet. Very large man. Particularly huge fists. Sad-looking face. This man may be dangerous. Use care."

Monk looked at Renny, said, "Sounds like he means you."

"These four men and the girl," continued the radio announcer, "were last seen at a burning strawstack near Kirksville about twenty minutes ago. There appears to have been some kind of building inside the strawstack, so it is believed this was the hideout of the gang, and that it burned."

Monk snorted. "So now our hideout burned!"

The State-police radio man finished, "These persons will probably be riding in a 1935 model Superior sedan, black color. License Missouri 007-936."

"That's this car!" Monk roared. He stared at the others.

"You know what I think?"

"Same as the rest of us, probably," Ham said grimly. "That cross-eyed fellow who turned up at the strawstack fire wasn't as innocent as we figured. He recognized us, got the license of this car, and turned it over to the police."

Monk nodded, muttered, "We better see what Doc says about this," shifted the wavelength back to their accustomed frequency, and picked up the transmitter mike. "Doc, the law is wise to us," he said. "What'd we better do?"

"You want to help me collar Burdo Brockman?" Doc asked.

"Great blazes! You find him?"

"I trailed him," the bronze man admitted, "to a spot several miles south, on a small lake." Doc described the location of the lake accurately.

"We'll be there pronto," Monk said.

"Be careful of the police. They are looking for that car."

Johnny leaned back to say, "Yes, but they don't know I rented four cars—or I hope they don't."

IT was a small lake surrounded by trees and with a railroad close by; seen from the road, the water was like a glint of steel. Renny guided the car—they had exchanged another machine for the one in which they had been riding—off the highway on to a byroad some distance from the lake, and hidden from it by the thick trees.

Doc Savage came out of thick scrub-oak brush. Dry, brilliant fallen leaves lay thick on the ground, but his big bronze form moved with very little noise.

Monk alighted from the car and threw out his chest. "Like to see that fellow give me the slip again," he growled.

They moved through brush, stooping and twisting to evade branches, stepping high and carefully to lessen the rustle of leaves.

Abruptly there was a lane. A car stood there, a big touring car with a wooden box built on the back so that the vehicle resembled a makeshift delivery truck.

Doc said, "This is Brockman's machine. He kept it in a shed in the woods some distance from where that strawstack burned."

"Kept it in a shed, eh?" Monk frowned. "Looks as if he was fixed for a quick getaway."

"The man was badly worried before we got there." Doc opened the big box constructed on the rear of the coupé. "I managed to get in here without being noticed. So following him was no trick. Look."

Doc indicated a collection of stuff that might have been found in the car of any man who liked outdoor life—a fishing rod, tackle box and some camping equipment that included a cook kit. All of the stuff was worn; the cooking pots were black.

"Fingerprints!" Ham grunted, and seized upon a sooty pot lid.

"Exactly," Doc said. "Brockman left some fingerprints on the steering wheel, and we had better compare them to be sure."

The prints were the same; they determined this easily, for they were clear prints, and all of Doc's men knew something about the science of fingerprinting.

"Boy, his hands were dirty." Monk ran a finger along the wheel's rim. "Soot. Hey, this is soot!"

"So what?" Ham said.

"Well, that strawstack burned," Monk reminded him. "And Burdo Brockman has sooty hands. Kind of a coincidence, don't you think?"

"What do you make of it?"

"All I make of any of this," Monk said gloomily, "is that my head is beginning to ache."

Doc Savage said, "Brockman should be down by the lake."

A CABIN stood on the shore, built out partially over the water. It was a rambling shack of a thing, made of boards that had badly needed paint for five years or so.

Daylight had come, but clouds were piled up in the eastern sky to make a dark rampart in front of the sun. It was gloomy. Fog covered the lake surface to a depth of fifteen or twenty feet, very thick and dark fog that was like a layer of newly shorn, unwashed wool.

"A hideout," Monk surmised.

"Scatter," Doc suggested in a low voice, "and watch all sides of the place."

Lion Ellison moved away, took concealment behind a tree from which she could watch the west side of the shack. But she did not give her attention to the house immediately; instead, she kept her eyes on Doc Savage… She was remembering how she had been somewhat skeptical of the bronze man's ability at first. He was much different than she had thought. He was a man of amazing ability; just how remarkable he was she had only begun to realize. Or hadn't she felt this way earlier?

He disappeared while she watched him, merging with the shadows in some skillful fashion; later she suspected that he was moving in the fog close to the lake's edge, but she was not sure.

Doc Savage reached the cabin. The lake fog swirled around him, clammy and as cold as frost. He listened for a while, and decided there was one man moving inside. He advanced slowly. The ground underfoot was soggy, and covered with a frozen crust that broke with a faintly audible crushing underfoot.

Then the dog came. It was a big dog, and it came fast, making one "woof!" noise before it tried to take Doc by the leg. He moved fast, diving and getting the animal by both ears, holding its jaws away, which would have settled the thing had not two more dogs arrived. The first dog had looked big and fierce, but these two must be his pop and mom. Doc heard them coming, saw them bulking big in the fog.

Both dogs hit him together, and he was upset. The animals were big and well trained. They took hold of him, and their teeth hurt.

The noise the dogs made was loud enough to be heard fully a mile away.

A man crashed the cabin door open and bounded out on the porch with a repeating shotgun.

JUST how Doc Savage had managed to follow his peculiar occupation and still remain alive as long as he had was a point that was puzzling to persons not intimate with the bronze man. To those who knew Doc, it was not a mystery, but a source of wonder. The reason was very careful planning. Forethought against every emergency, and advance preparation.

Typical sample of his precaution was the assortment of small grenades which were packed in flat metal cases and used by himself and supplied to his aides. These bombs were tiny and of great variety.

The grenade—it was not very much larger than a commie marble—which he crushed between his fingers was made of thin-walled glass and contained a combination of chemicals which had been concocted to frighten almost all animals. The principle of their concoction was simple. All animals have some odor which frightens them—bear smell, for instance, being terrifying to most breeds of dogs. Doc had duplicated the odor with chemicals, added those frightening to other common animals—he had even added an acid typical of a deadly, stinging sea growth which was the thing most feared by sharks—and the result was the little grenade which he now broke.

The dogs let loose, growled in fright and backed away.

On the porch, the man peered downward. The porch was high; he was trying to see what was below in the fog. He had unsafetied the shotgun, held it ready.

"What's wrong?" a voice called from inside the cabin.

"Dunno. Maybe the dogs caught a coon, or somethin'." The man with the shotgun strained his eyes. Abruptly he growled, "Hell! I'll take a shot or two and scare the thing away." He lifted the shotgun.

Doc Savage threw another grenade. This one was high explosive. He planted it against one corner of the cabin and there was an ear-splitting moment when the cabin corner came apart and the porch ceiling jumped up, gave a big flap as if it was trying to be a wing, then fell back.

The shotgun wielder got up from where he'd been toppled, made noises like a big frightened hog and went into the cabin.

Men inside the cabin got organized quickly, for almost instantly shotguns began going off with cannon violence.

Doc retreated. He had a great deal of respect for a shotgun.

From behind a tree, he called out sharply in the Mayan tongue. "Do not try to use gas. The wind."

A chill breeze was blowing from across the lake. It would sweep gas back upon them if they released the stuff.

On the higher ground, among the trees, there was less fog. Monk, doubling low and zigzagging, joined Doc and demanded, "How many guys in there? Did you see anybody when you trailed Brockman here?"

"Brockman walked straight into the cabin and closed the door. He had a gun in his hand when he entered. I got the idea there were four or five men in the cabin, maybe more."

At this point, there was a commotion at the cabin. Angry shouting. Shots.

Renny's voice bellowed, "They had a prisoner!! He's gettin' away!"

Doc had seen the man. He seemed to have both ankles bound. A rope dangled from one wrist. He was hopping, falling down, heaving up, hopping again. He had a shotgun.

The man came out of the fog some distance from the cabin, miraculously unhit by shotgun fire, and toppled behind a tree.

Monk barked, "I'll see who he is," and raced toward the man.

Suddenly Monk was squalling in rage, and heading for the most convenient tree.

The prisoner they had just seen escape from the cabin had thrown down on Monk with his shotgun and peppered the homely chemist.

Monk got behind a tree, scratched the spots where the shot had gone in, and said many loud words that he could never have taken to Sunday school.

Renny boomed, "Hey, you—" at the hobbled man with the shotgun, but let it go at that when the man sent a charge of shot that knocked bark off the tree which sheltered the big-fisted engineer.

There was some more shooting. But none of it from the cabin. A minute or two must have passed.

Doc Savage was moving warily, approaching the man with the bound ankles and the shotgun. He could see the man distinctly, could have winged him, except that he had no gun. For a long time, Doc had made it a practice not to carry a gun, feeling that the possession of one would lead him to put too much dependence on the weapon in an emergency—he had seen how helpless professional gunmen became when disarmed.

The man with the shotgun began staring at the cabin. Something seemed to dawn on him. He turned wildly in the direction of Doc's men.

"Hey!" he yelled. "Maybe I've made a mistake!"

Monk said, "You sure did!" and added some choice sulphur-coated words.

"I'm Burdo Brockman!" the man shouted.

Chapter XIV
BURDO BROCKMAN, CRIMINAL

HAM called softly to Doc, "He sure ain't the Burdo Brockman we followed down here from Kirksville."

The new Burdo Brockman had not decided they were friends; he held his shotgun warily. "Who are you?" he demanded.

Ham called, "Doc Savage's party."

The new Brockman's groan was audible to all of them. He threw down his shotgun.

"Come here," he wailed. "I've made a terrible mistake." He stared hopelessly at them while they ran to his side and sank in the shelter of a tree clump.

"I broke away from them," the man said. "When the shooting started, I figured they had fallen out among themselves. I got my hands loose, grabbed a shotgun, clubbed a man over the head and jumped out of a window."

He was a long-legged, long-armed man who had a short body. His face was somewhat red, his nose was slightly on the beak side, and he had a mouth that was wide, grim, lipless. He was the kind of man who gave the impression of always going around looking grim and forbidding. You looked at him and instinctively knew that he worried over details.

He pointed toward the cabin. "While I was shooting at you," he said, "they got away."

Monk stared at the cabin. "How do you know they got away?"

"You don't hear them, do you?" The new Brockman shook his head gloomily. "They had three canoes on the back porch. All they had to do was drop them in the water, get in, and paddle away."

Johnny growled, "I'll be superamalgamated!" He dashed forward, holding his arms up before his eyes as he ran. He did not fear the shotgun pellets, except in his face, because he wore a light undergarment of alloy chain mesh that was impervious to ordinary bullets.

He was almost to the cabin door when Doc Savage caught him and stopped him. "Use our heads," the bronze man warned.

Johnny understood. He ran around to the lake edge, stood there listening. The bronze man was beside him. Johnny whispered, "Hear anything?"

Doc nodded. He said, "They are heading straight across." Then he spun, called, "Ham, you and Renny are fast on your feet. Go north around the lake and try to head them off."

"Where'll you be?" Renny demanded. "We don't want to be jumping on you by mistake."

"Swimming."

Renny looked at the water. There was a fringe of ice like glass along the edges. He said, "Br-r-r!" and ran away with Ham.

Getting into the water was like entering a bath of sharp needles. The bronze man's routine of exercises—the regular daily two-hour period which he devoted to scientifically developing his physical and mental faculties—had conditioned his body to intense shock; nevertheless, he had to keep his teeth clamped tightly to prevent them from rattling.

He swam a fast crawl, arms coming up and lunging out ahead with machine regularity, a long line of swirling water and foam trailing out behind.

When he came out on a muddy shore, it was close to three beached canoes. Paddles had been flung down carelessly beside the craft. He listened.

A motor car was leaving the vicinity, traveling fast.

Enough frost still remained on the grass to show footprints. Doc followed the tracks of the men who had been in the canoes, a trail that led him to an old cowshed. From there, tire tracks led to the road.

Ham and Renny arrived, puffing, clothing muddy.

"They got away," Doc said quietly.

THEY walked back to the canoes, paddled across to the cabin, and Johnny met them. Johnny looked shocked, and was perspiring slightly in spite of the cold.

"It's luck-lucky you stopped me from charging into that cabin," he muttered, using small words.

"What ails you?" Renny peered at him. "You look as if somebody had taken the lid off and let you see the works."

Johnny beckoned, and walked to the cabin. He leaned in through a window from which the glass had been broken, pointed. "Just suppose I had opened that door."

He meant dynamite. There was almost a case of it. On top of the dynamite had been scattered a box of caps. A heavy crowbar was propped against the door where a slight shock would dislodge it, causing the heavy bar of steel to fall on the caps. The shock would doubtless have detonated the caps; the dynamite in turn would have exploded. It was an ingenious quick job of fashioning a death trap.

Renny said hoarsely, "We better fix that thing before it takes a notion to go off by itself." He clambered in through the window.

Doc Savage and Ham searched the cabin rapidly. They found evidence that a number of men had used the place for some time. Judging from the stock of food on hand, they had intended to use it for a considerable period.

In a table drawer, they found a number of bills. They were made out to Elmo Anderson.

"Elmo Anderson." Ham rubbed his jaw thoughtfully. "This hitches together, Doc. One of the three men the murdered banker was having investigated was named Elmo Handy Anderson."

Monk and Lion Ellison entered the cabin, accompanied by the new Burdo Brockman. They had freed the man's ankles, although the bit of rope still dangled from his right wrist.

Doc said quietly, "So *you* are Burdo Brockman?"

"Yes." The man moved his gaze from Doc to the faces of the others. He must have seen disbelief. He seemed embarrassed. "I don't blame you," he said. "It is a fantastic thing."

"You don't blame us for what?" Ham asked.

"For not believing me."

"You haven't told us anything yet."

Monk said, "He told me and Miss Ellison his story." The chemist glanced at the long-legged, sour-looking man. "Maybe you better tell it again."

The man took a deep breath and seemed to recite his whole story without coming up for air. "I am Burdo Brockman," he said, "and this is a fact you can ascertain by consulting my lawyers, my brokers or any of my business associates in New York City. I am—ah—well, I own a few factories and things. Three weeks ago, I was seized by four men I had never seen before, put in a plane, and brought here. They've been keeping me here since. I do not know why. I do not know who the men are." He scowled darkly. "It is all a confounded mystery to me."

DOC SAVAGE made no comment; instead, he walked through the cabin, making another quick search, after which he joined the others and voiced a warning. "There was a great deal of shooting here," he reminded them. "Someone is sure to come to investigate."

"Yeah, and the cops will probably get tipped off again," Monk muttered.

They went back to their car. There were seven of them now, including the man they had rescued, a well-packed load for the machine.

The car rolled in silence. The sun had climbed above the bank of clouds and was pouring cold white light over the khaki-colored cornfields and the brilliant foliage of such trees as had not yet lost their leaves. The car had no heater; it was cold enough in the machine that they could see their breath. The windows and shield soon fogged so that Doc, who was driving, had to keep rubbing the glass with a palm.

The new Brockman spoke suddenly. "I think I am supposed to be in India."

"Eh?" Monk stared at him.

"That's the trick they worked," he explained. "I saw some stationery with the name of a hunting lodge in India on it. I think they were using it to write letters to my folks in New York."

Monk said, "But that picture—" and Doc kicked him on the shin. "Ouch!" Monk finished.

"What did you say about pictures?" the long-armed man asked.

Monk could think fast.

"Why, we got a picture of a little wizened guy," he said. "I wonder if you know who he is?"

They passed the picture of the mysterious runt, as Monk had taken to calling him, back to their passenger, and he examined the print. He pursed his lips, sucked at a tooth, scratched his chin with a fingernail. "No."

"No what?" Monk asked.

"Never saw him before." The man looked up. "Is he involved in this?"

"That little runt," Monk said grimly, "is involved in something, all right. Maybe he is the something. He reminds me of the guy who popped up when they rubbed the lamp in that Aladdin story. To tell the truth, we don't know—"

Doc Savage interrupted quietly, asking. "Mr. Brockman, have you ever heard of a man named Danny Dimer?"

"Never," said the man promptly.

"Or a banker named Ellery P. Dimer?"

"No."

Monk had been watching Doc Savage curiously out of the corner of one small, quizzical eye. It had occurred to Monk that he had better keep still and let Doc conduct this conversation.

Doc said, "Mr. Brockman, do you know a man named Elmo Handy Anderson?"

Their passenger reacted to that. He gave a jump, sat up very straight.

"Why, that's my old handyman," he said. "Handy worked for me for years. He's a short, small man. Or haven't you met him?"

Ham, who also rode in the front seat, opened his mouth and got as far as, "We haven't"—before Monk stopped him with an elbow jab in the ribs.

Doc said. "That doesn't quite answer his description. By the way, did you know the cabin we just left was occupied by Handy Anderson?"

"What?" The man looked stark.

"Apparently it was. There were grocery bills made out to that name in the place."

The other frowned. "Handy Anderson isn't short or small. I told you that because I—hah, hah—was testing you. Handy is an elderly fellow with white hair that is always tangled, and he'll remind you of a bulldog more than anything else."

Monk leaned over to Doc and whispered excitedly, "That guy he just described is the first Burdo Brockman we met. The one at Kirksville, where the strawstack burned."

Doc turned around to look levelly at the man in the back seat. "Testing us, you say?"

"I—I'm sorry." The man grimaced. "This is all very mysterious and confusing."

Doc said, "Have you any idea why the man whom you have just described as Handy Anderson should be masquerading as Burdo Brockman?"

The long-armed man leaned back in the rear seat. "I'm dumbfounded," he said.

MONK was completely confused—Ham, Renny, Johnny and Lion Ellison were in the same boat with him—and he could not have suggested their next move. They would, of course, have to avoid the police and arrest, for once they were in jail there was little chance of Doc's influence getting them out, even on bail. The charge was murder—murder of the State's governor. That Doc had contrived an escape from the Kirksville jail did not mean a jail could not be constructed strong enough to hold him. Monk was confident there were quite a few bastiles which could hold the bronze man.

Monk could see nothing that they could do now except try to keep out of jail.

He suspected Doc had more tangible ideas. The bronze man had turned off the highway and was taking dirt roads north and west heading in the general direction of the spot where they had left the plane.

Certainly there was nothing in Doc's movements to enlighten Monk after they reached the field where they had left their plane. The ship still stood there. Several farmers were walking around the big streamlined craft, but there were no police in evidence.

Doc drove past without stopping, continued until he came to an abandoned farmhouse. It was not difficult, in this part of Missouri, to find abandoned farms. Monk opened a barbed-wire gate, and Doc drove through tall dead weeds to the barn and ran the car inside.

"Machine will be out of sight here," he explained.

"It occurs to me," Renny rumbled, "that our plane is going to get some attention. A strange ship abandoned in a pasture several miles from town is certain to arouse comment."

"Well, I'll be superamalgamated!" Johnny exploded. "Once the police come, they'll investigate and find out the plane is registered in Doc's name."

"Which will make it too bad," Renny agreed.

Doc Savage volunteered no comment. He walked to the farmhouse, which was in fair condition. After working on the lock with a piece of wire, he got inside. He looked around and registered satisfaction.

"This will do," he said. "Mr. Brockman and myself can stay here while the rest of you go and get those fellows."

"Go get what fellows?" Renny blurted.

Doc brought his hand to his mouth and made a sound that was apparently clearing his throat. Actually, the noise was a few Mayan words, the equivalent of, "Don't give this away."

Renny blinked, understood, and said, "Oh, sure. I get you."

"Take the car," Doc continued. "Leave the plane where it is. Mr. Brockman and myself may need it for an escape."

"Right," Renny agreed.

"You will have plenty of time," Doc explained. "They do not suspect that we have the least idea what it is all about. Certainly they won't dream that we have a great deal of dope on them—enough to seize many of them."

The bronze man smiled. He was aware that the long-armed Brockman was staring at him in droop-jawed amazement.

"They don't know we've solved the mystery of those killings and the rest of the stuff they've pulled," Doc added. "So get going, fellows. Bring them in."

Renny asked, "You mean all of us? Monk, Ham, Johnny and myself? Everybody?"

"Yes."

Amazed curiosity got the best of long-limbed Brockman. He clutched Doc's arm, demanded, "What on earth does this mean?"

"It means," Doc said, "that we've solved this mystery. And now we're going to lay our hands on most of the men really responsible for these murders."

Chapter XV
A TRICK PAYS OFF

MONK, Ham, Renny and Johnny had one thing in common—they were not mind readers. Hence they had no idea what Doc was talking about, and they were as surprised as anybody, but they had the judgment to make their astonishment look as much as possible like eager enthusiasm. Lion Ellison was probably less amazed; she had seen just enough of the bronze man's remarkable ability to be willing to expect anything.

"All right, Doc," Monk said. "We're off. Wish us luck."

Doc nodded. "We'll all need luck."

Renny and the others walked to the barn and climbed into the car. They were silent—there didn't seem to be anything to say. The sedan rolled through the tall weeds to the dirt road, bumped over the grader rut and turned left.

Monk said, "That was one of the most unexpected things I've seen Doc do."

Renny, Ham and Johnny wrestled silently—and vainly—with their thoughts.

Lion Ellison said, "What are we supposed to do?"

"What we usually do in a case like this," Monk told her, "is stick around and keep an ear cocked at the shortwave radio. Guess we'll do that."

They drove on down the road.

Back in the abandoned farmhouse, Doc Savage went through the motions of making himself comfortable. The place was bare. Going out to the barn, the bronze man came back with an armload of dry timothy which he had collected from the loft; he heaped this in a corner. "Do for a bed," he explained.

The long-armed, long-legged Brockman stared at him in astonishment. "We going to be here that long?"

"It will take time."

The other seemed to be in the grip of complete astonishment. He went through the usual puzzle motions—scratching his jaw, rubbing his head and screwing his face around in thinking shapes. Finally he muttered, "You have solved the whole mystery?"

"Practically."

"What is back of it?"

Instead of answering the query, Doc Savage seemed not to hear. He leaned back, half closed his flake-gold eyes, and after a moment indulged in what appeared to be philosophy. "You know, it has often occurred to me to wonder whether the human race might not be fundamentally evil. Otherwise, why should social behavior apparently be controlled by fear?" The bronze man's flake-gold eyes rested on the other. "You do not understand what I mean, do you? Take this situation, for example. The thing could have been a great boon to mankind, but due to the evil texture of certain minds, it is going to be anything but a boon, unless we can stop it."

"What you're saying doesn't make sense to me."

"You'll understand when my associates come back with the prisoners."

The bronze man got up, moved to the door and stood there for a while.

"Hungry?" he asked.

"Not very."

"I am." Doc stared off into the distance. "There is a farmhouse across the field three-quarters of a mile or so. It might be a good idea to go over there and buy a chicken or something we can cook. Want to go along?"

"I—hm-m-m—guess not. I'm kind of tired."

"Be with you soon."

The bronze man moved away from the house and was soon lost from sight in a cornfield.

The man who had said he was Burdo Brockman stood in the door staring after Doc. Nothing on his face was pleasant.

"This plays hell with our plans," he growled.

THE man who had said he was Burdo Brockman forced himself to remain where he was until Doc Savage had been out of sight for some moments. By that time, impatience had got a little perspiration out on his body. Finally, deciding it was safe, he lunged off the rickety old porch, galloped through the weeds, hurdled the barbed-wire fence and took out down the road. His haste-frenzied feet knocked up little dust puffs.

The plane—Johnny's ship, which Doc's party had been using—stood in the pasture, a great glinting metallic insect in the morning sun.

Several curiosity viewers—they were neighborhood farmers—were examining the plane or loafing about discussing crops and prices. A wagon and two cars had stopped on the dirt road.

The long-armed man studied the scene carefully.

"No cops," he grunted aloud. He seemed very relieved.

The man straightened his clothing, brushed off the weeds and walked out boldly. He approached the plane.

"Hi-yah," he said to the farmers.

"Howdy," they greeted, and stared at him curiously.

"My plane." The man gestured at the ship carelessly. "Broke a little gadget in the engine last night and had to land. Been to town and got it." He spoke airily and with excellent convincingness. The farmers seemed unconcerned, not even greatly interested in the machine. As a matter of fact, planes were not unusual to any of them, and they were standing around visiting, not gaping in awe at the aircraft.

The man climbed up on the wing and unsnapped a port in the streamlined cowling that gave access to the vitals of one engine. He fumbled therein for a while, making a pretense of repairs, but actually being careful to touch nothing.

Later, when he went to the plane door, he found it locked. He swore under his breath, then demonstrated that he was quick-witted.

He fumbled in his pocket, pretending to look for a key.

"Hell! I've lost my key," he said loudly. "Guess I'll have to force the door."

He got in easier than he had expected. One hard wrench snapped the door open. He clambered inside, scrambled forward to the controls.

The practiced manner in which the man fingered the controls showed he knew flying, but apparently he lacked experience with this type of ship. He expended several moments familiarizing himself with the instruments. All the time, he kept throwing sharp glances over the vicinity. But the farmers did not seem interested.

He tried the starters. They growled briefly, then motors coughed blue smoke and noise. Later, the plane took the air in a manner that caused the man to breathe, "Sweet!" under his breath. As soon as he was lined out on a course, he began using the two-way radio.

THE little radio transmitter had a frequency-marked dial, so that setting it to a definite wavelength was a simple matter. The man moved down into the shortband past twenty megacycles where a little power was sufficient for transmission over tremendous distance, then disconnected the "scrambler" attachment.

The man began calling, not using any call letters, which was a violation of Department of Commerce law. As long as he was operating a portable, there was little chance of a radio inspector with a direction-finder locating the transmitter.

The man consulted his wrist watch, noted that it was exactly eleven o'clock; he began at the figure one and lettered the alphabet around the dial—he started A, B, C, and so on—until he reached the figure eleven, which proved to be the letter K. This was the key to a code, it developed, because he began speaking into the microphone words that began with the letter K. He gave them in a rambling fashion, as they entered his mind.

His calling went something like, "Knee, knack, kidnap, kid, keg, keep, kaffir, kick—"

After he had called for a while, he signed off by simply saying. "Come in."

His first call got no response, so he scowled and tried again. He kept it up for almost thirty minutes, and twice during that interval rage so overcame him that he pounded the empty seat beside him in fury.

"All right," a voice out of the ether said finally.

The man recognized the voice. He snarled, "Where the hell have you been?"

"Keep your shirt on," the voice advised. "We just went out for lunch."

"I told you, damn you, to keep that radio on," the man yelled.

"What are you squalling about? I just talked to the boys who were in that cabin on the lake, and they got away in fine shape. So everything goes smooth."

The man in the plane swore violently.

"I've been trying to get hold of you to tell you that Doc Savage's men are on their way to pick some of you up," he shouted.

"Pick who up?"

"I don't know which ones. But Doc Savage has found out a lot more than we thought he had."

The distant man was inclined to be skeptical and critical. He said, "What's the matter with *you?* Did they find out you weren't what you pretended to be?"

"They never suspected me."

"Then why didn't you kill Doc Savage? That was why you jumped out of the cabin, pretending to be a prisoner, wasn't it?"

"I didn't have a chance," the man explained sourly. "They were all together until the last, and then Doc Savage pulled out after a chicken before I could get a chance at him."

"Weren't scared, were you?"

The man in the plane swore violently. "The fact that we're both mixed up in this thing doesn't give you any right to be impertinent. If you know what's good for you, you'll keep a civil tongue."

"O.K.," the other said soothingly. "I didn't mean anything by it. What have you got on your mind?"

"Get the men together. Assemble at headquarters. I'll join you."

"This must be serious," the other said in an impressed voice.

"It is."

THE man picked up a double-tracked railroad and followed it until he reached the outskirts of Kansas City. He swung over to the river and trailed it around until the flat expanse of the municipal airport was discernible—then he changed his mind about landing.

"No use taking chances," he muttered.

It had occurred to him that Doc Savage might have reached a telephone at Kirksville and in some fashion have spread an alarm for the plane.

He set down on the river itself, cranking up the landing gear and handling the plane gingerly, for he had never manipulated a seaplane before. He sent the ship against the bank with jarring force; the hull slid far up on the mud.

The man bounded out, lost no time about leaving the spot.

Almost immediately, an apparently solid section in the wing of the plane heaved up, and Doc Savage clambered out of the recess that was exposed. The thick streamlined wing had been equipped with that recess specifically for stowaway purposes, such tricky devices being a part of the bronze man's stock in trade.

Doc's usually expressionless face showed pleasure. It had worked very nicely: The sending of his men away on a trumped-up mission of seizing their enemies—that had frightened the man who said he was Brockman into taking flight. The departure of Doc, ostensibly to get a chicken for lunch, had given the man his chance to flee. Watching the fellow, Doc had known immediately that he was heading for the plane. He had gotten there first; there had been barely time to explain to the farmers that they must act as if they hadn't seen him get into the plane. Probably the farmers hadn't understood; but what they had comprehended were the ten-dollar bills he had distributed to pay them for their trouble. Yes, it had worked very nicely so far.

Doc got on the shortwave radio, put it on his usual wavelength, and said, "Monk?"

"Yes?" Monk's voice said.

"The action in this thing is swinging to Kansas City," Doc said swiftly. "Burdo Brockman lived in Kirksville—that's why the thing started around there. But now they're moving in on Kansas City. You and the others had better get down here."

"May take us some time. We'll have to drive down in the car. Might have some cop trouble."

"Do your best."

"Right. Where'll we meet?"

Doc explained where the plane lay. "However, I will take one of the small radio outfits with me and try to contact you en route."

The radio which the bronze man carried away from the plane was a compact little outfit of the "transceiver" type, not much more bulky than a good-sized folding camera, very efficient to horizon distance. It had a carrying strap.

It was snowing; the ground was white, flakes were whizzing through the air like particles of glass.

Going up the river bank, he carefully stepped in the tracks of the long-armed man—a forethought, in case the man should come back.

There was brush at the top. Doc moved rapidly. There was a busy street off to the south, and the quarry had made for that. When Doc located the fellow, he had just reached the boulevard and was waiting beside a sign that said, "Bus Stop." He was beating his arms in the cold.

The bronze man had a trained muscular ability that made him very fast on his feet—but his speed was remarkable only when in competition with another human; against a bus, he did not think much of his chances.

So he veered left, ran, and managed to find a taxicab—it was his idea to board the bus before it stopped for the long-armed man, if he had to—and followed his quarry through the storm without difficulty. The man got out in the downtown district, not far from Seventh and Grand.

Chapter XVI
PENTHOUSE STORY

IT was one of Kansas City's largest buildings; even in New York City, it would have been rated a skyscraper. There was a bank of eight elevators, all operating, any one of which a visitor might take.

Doc decided to use caution about trailing his quarry, soon was glad that he did so.

Since the day was rapidly turning into a blizzard, they were using the revolving doors. Sidewalks were crowded. Doc was close to the man—thirty feet or so back—when the fellow entered the revolving door, and all set with what resembled a small rubber ball in his hands.

He threw the ball; it struck in the compartment of the rotating door with the man near his feet. It burst, as it was designed to do, and released a small spray of chemical that splashed on the fellow's shoes and trousers cuffs.

The man glanced down, but the rubber container, having collapsed, resembled a pencil eraser; he shrugged, went on.

Entering an elevator, he said, "Hello, Joe," to the operator. "If you see anybody acting suspicious, or anyone asks about me or any of the others, you know what to do."

"Sure," the operator agreed. "Tip you off."

Doc Savage got some of that from the sidewalk outside, but it was a little far away—and the door glass distorted vision—for effective lip reading.

The long-armed man was looking directly at Doc just before the elevator went up, but there was no sign of recognition.

It was fortunate, Doc reflected, that he had used a tube of darkening stain on his face and hands, and turned his coat inside out. The coat was lined so that it reversed a different color and cut. Also he had changed the color of his eyes by using the little tinted glass optical caps such as he had employed in disguising Lion Ellison much earlier. He had done this in the taxi.

He walked into the warm lobby of the building and watched the indicator over the elevator. The first stop the cage made was on the sixteenth floor. That helped.

Doc took another cage, rode to the sixteenth, got out and produced a sealed metal canister which looked like a talcum-powder can, and in fact was labeled as such.

He sprinkled powder on the floor in front of the door of the elevator which the long-armed man had taken. Nothing happened, so he took the stairs to the next floor.

He repeated the operation until he reached the topmost floor, and still nothing happened.

Doc leaned against the wall, disgusted and puzzled. The acid which had been in the rubber container was very potent—its vapor, present in unbelievably minute quantities, would cause the normally bluish powder to turn red.

The acid on the man's shoes would leave vapor wherever he walked for a while, and the vapor was heavier than air so that it remained close to the floor… But it hadn't worked.

While Doc was pondering, a rising elevator went past. Something strange about that, because this was supposed to be the top floor.

There was a stairway and a steel door that he had presumed led up to the elevator-machinery housing on the roof.

The door was locked. He started to pick the lock, then became cautious.

He detached a small gadget of wires and tubes which had been affixed inside the lid of the radio. A wire ran from this, and he plugged it into a jack on the radio which utilized only the receiving amplifier. He ran the gadget around the edges of the locked door.

The door was wired with a burglar alarm—one of the most effective types which utilized a circuit continuously charged with a small current which would be broken the moment the door was opened. The gadget had registered presence of the tiny electrical field surrounding the alarm wires.

THERE was a frost-glazed window at the end of the corridor. Doc opened it, and biting cold wind and cutting snow particles whipped his face. He studied the brick wall, the ornamental coping, with no enthusiasm whatever.

He climbed out and began going up, closing the window behind him. There were hand holds—cracks between the stones into which he could wedge fingertips—and ordinarily climbing would not have been treacherous, if one discounted the fact that to slip was death, and the half-inch width of the fingertip supports.

The cold wind pounded his clothing against his body; it pushed at him, and made a doglike whining around the carved facets of the ornamental coping above. There was ice in some of the cracks where his fingertips had to grip; at first, when his fingers were warm, it was easy to tell when they were resting on ice, but soon the cold and strain made it nerve-shatteringly difficult. Destiny would allow him only one slip. Automobile horns in the street below sounded far away.

At length he swung over the coping and lay there on a narrow tarred ledge; he had only to get up and clamber over a low wall onto the roof. He was safe now. He looked down. It was too cold a day for people to be idly lifting their faces into the wind and looking up; apparently nobody had noticed him.

There was a penthouse atop the skyscraper.

Some of the trees in the penthouse garden were stunted evergreens; the others were scrawny and naked of leaves. There were flower and plant boxes, the stringy contents looking as dead as bits of binder twine. The snow had drifted over everything.

Doc moved carefully, using a hand to wipe out traces of his footprints as best he could.

He did not try to enter the penthouse, feeling that opening a window or door would send a chill betraying draft racing through the place. He found a niche, an angle between two walls, where the snow was deep and a window was convenient.

And now he made use of another accessory of the radio, this one a contrivance no longer than an overcoat button. It was a microphone, equipped with a suction cup which would hold it to a window-pane; wires ran to a small plug which fitted the receiver amplifier jack on the radio. It was an ultra-sensitive eavesdropping device.

Doc Savage attached the contrivance very cautiously to a windowpane—he selected a window which he judged from the proximity of a fireplace was a den or living room—and quickly settled into the deep snow. He used his hands to fill his tracks, then covered himself with snow as best he could.

Within a few minutes, the howling wind would obliterate traces of his coming.

FOR a long time in the room, they talked about race horses and racetracks and gambling joints.

They panned some gambler they all knew, lambasting him as a crook and a welsher.

When the talk swung to circus life, Doc sharpened his interest. After a while, he had catalogued at least part of the men as to profession—flying circus. Evidently they belonged to a group of daredevils who traveled with planes, furnishing advertising and thrills for a more ordinary type of circus.

There was a circus background in the mystery somewhere, Doc knew. Lion Ellison's brother had been a flying-circus employee, and Lion herself had belonged to the circus. The circus thread even extended to Ellery P. Dimer, the murdered banker; he'd had a financial and personal interest in various circuses and carnivals, Doc recalled from a newspaper account of the man's life which he'd read.

The gang was assembling in the room. That accounted for the idle waiting. From time to time a new arrival appeared.

But at last an authoritative voice spoke out. "All right, guys. We're pressed for time. The bunch hasn't arrived from Kirksville yet, but we won't wait on them."

Doc recognized the voice. It belonged to the long-armed man he had trailed here, the fellow who had said he was Burdo Brockman.

There was a brief wait while the men lighted cigars or got liquor and settled themselves to wait.

"We've been working in separate groups," said the pseudo Burdo Brockman. "Some of you may not know everything that's been done. Part of you went to New York with Danny Dimer after the girl. Some of you were in Jefferson City. Others were here in Kansas City. And of course the boys from Kirksville haven't shown up yet."

The man cleared his throat noisily.

"We'll have kind of a roundup of the situation," he said. "But first, I want to make damn sure everything is safe. Some of you go out and look around the terraces."

"Hell, nobody could get up here from the outside."

"They could use ladders—the kind that firemen use, with hooks on the end."

Several men left the room in obedience to the command. The microphone pickup was very sensitive; Doc could hear the men howl when they stepped out into the biting cold. His unaided ears picked up the grinding of their footsteps as they walked around the terrace.

At least two men walked directly past Doc, while he remained tense, ready to explode out of the snowdrift the instant their footsteps stopped. But the men continued on.

They assembled inside again, and a man reported, "Nothin' out there but the cold."

"Here's a roundup of the situation," the false Brockman announced. "When we started this, it looked perfect. Brockman didn't suspect a thing. It looked like everything was getting off to a smooth start, until that damned Neddy Ellison had to go pure on us. Neddy, the young sap, had been working in Danny Dimer's flying circus for quite a while, and Danny thought he was O.K. We needed O.K. guys, so we rung this Neddy Ellison in. As soon as he found out there were to be killings, Neddy turned sanctimonious on us. We had to croak him, and Dimer did that by fixing Neddy's parachute."

The speaker stopped to swear impressively. "That fixed that," he said, "except for one thing.

After Neddy Ellison's parachute split and he hit the ground, he took about fifteen minutes dying. He talked. Nobody but Dimer heard him talk, so that didn't do any harm—but we learned something that put us in a hell of a spot. Neddy Ellison made a dying statement that he'd wrote his sister the whole story."

THE least thing that could be said about Doc Savage's listening was that it was interested. He had been enlightened on several points. There had been nothing in the previous development to plainly show how Lion Ellison had happened to become involved in the mystery, although the bronze man had surmised that something of this sort must have occurred.

"It then became necessary," continued the speaker inside the penthouse, "to put Lion Ellison where she couldn't do any harm. Some of the boys were squeamish about killing a girl, so we decided to frame her. We didn't know her address; we just knew she lived in St. Louis. And we knew she was a circus performer. So we advertised for a circus performer that fitted her description, and sure enough, she turned up."

The man suddenly began laughing.

"You know how the framing was done," he reminded.

Then the speaker's joy died a rather cold death in his throat. "The damned police didn't arrest the girl in the Kirksville drugstore after we tipped them off," he said. "And she stole a plane and struck out for New York to get to Doc Savage, the little devil." He swore violently. "So our troubles commenced."

"Where is Brockman now?" a man asked.

"Oh, he got suspicious and rushed down to that cabin of mine on the lake, and I had to grab him. The boys coming down from Kirksville are bringing him. Don't worry about Brockman."

"The guy to worry about is Doc Savage, eh?"

"He's been lucky so far, damn his hide! His men grabbed Dimer in New York, and Dimer figured he was lucky to even get away. We tipped off the police, had Doc Savage put in jail when he came to Kirksville, but he got out."

"I've heard a lot about that bronze guy," another man volunteered. "He's supposed to be the correct person to stay away from."

"He moves fast," growled the long-armed man who had masqueraded as Brockman. "He turned up in Jefferson City, and grabbed Don Meek. He was about to use truth serum on Meek, which would have been too bad for us. Fortunately, some of the boys were around there, and they took care of the situation although they had to kill Meek. They would have killed Doc Savage too, except one of them was using a meat cleaver from the kitchen, and the blade broke off, which left them without a weapon. They had no other weapon they were willing to tackle Doc Savage with, so they beat it without finishing him. You dopes! You realize what an opportunity you passed up?

"Listen, we did the best we could," a man growled. "The damn meat cleaver broke. I told you how long we had to work. There was no time."

The leader said, "Tsk, tsk!" angrily. "You let Doc Savage and his men get away; and they came back to Kirksville and found Burdo Brockman. Brockman was suspicious. Brockman burned his laboratory so they couldn't find what was in it—"

"So Brockman burned the laboratory!" a man ejaculated.

"Sure. Brockman didn't want the truth to get out. He was scared, and worried."

"Was that when Brockman got wise that you had stolen the thing?"

"He was sure then. Before, he had just suspected."

"The way I understand the rest of it," someone added, "you joined Doc Savage with the idea of getting rid of him yourself. What happened to that scheme?"

The man who put this query was the fellow who had just been criticized for the failure in Jefferson City.

The leader did not relish the criticism. He swore. "There was no chance to carry out my plans. But I found out the bronze guy was sending his gang to grab part of our outfit. I put a stop to that, didn't I?"

"Let's stop this bickering," interposed a fellow who had not taken previous part in the conversation. "What comes next?"

"Plans."

Chapter XVII
THE PRINCE

DOC SAVAGE disconnected the eavesdropping microphone from the radio amplifier, and put the radio in regular operation. He held the microphone very close to his lips, so that his voice was no louder than a whisper, inaudible outside the snowdrift. It was a little difficult to work under the snow, but efficiency of the shortwave radio should not be hampered a great deal. The height of the skyscraper roof should improve operation of the set.

"Monk," Doc said.

The homely chemist's response over the radio was almost instantaneous. "Yeah, Doc."

"How near are you to Kansas City?"

"We ain't near it—we're in it."

"How come?"

"We got a lucky break. Got to a town named Brookfield, saw a plane on a little airport there and rented it off the guy. We landed it on the edge of Kansas City, and we just rented a car from one of those Drive-It-Yourself places. What's up?"

Doc Savage told him what was up. The bronze man spoke rapidly, concisely, giving explicit directions and full details where he thought full details were necessary. Monk heard him through without comment.

But Doc's directions were surprising to Monk and the others, because Doc heard Renny's astounded, "Holy cow!" in the background of the other microphone.

"You understand fully?" Doc asked.

"I think so."

"What about Ham?" Doc inquired.

"R'aring to go," Ham advised.

The bronze man switched off the radio, reconnected the sensitive eavesdropping device. He listened. The room was so quiet that he had a fleeting suspicion that the apparatus was not functioning; there was a sound of someone clearing his throat.

"How long will it take those guys to get down from Kirksville?" the fellow asked.

"Not more than another half hour," said a voice.

Doc Savage recognized that voice—not directly, but from the description which had been given him both by Lion Ellison and Monk and Ham.

It was the small, wizened man. The mysterious runt, Monk had called him. The little fellow who had vanished under such fantastic circumstances in the basement garage of the bronze man's New York headquarters.

Doc continued listening, but there was a silence that struck him—unfortunately, he did not realize this until it was too late—as being peculiar. He turned over suddenly, dug a hole in the snow, and put an ear against the cold tiling of the terrace floor. But that was too late also.

There were seven or eight men, and they all landed on the snowdrift at once, driving clutching hands into the snow.

DOC tried to evade them, keeping under the snow. He kept the radio apparatus in his hand. But a man got hold of each of his legs.

"Don't kill 'im!" a voice yelled.

After the shout, Doc Savage stopped trying to keep undercover. He came to his feet, deliberately used the radio as a club—and struck. The little radio was tough, downed two men, and Doc kept on using it violently as a club, his idea being to mangle the apparatus as completely as possible, so that they would not recognize it as a radio. When the radio was broken, he dropped it and they trampled on it some.

The bronze man kept on fighting, not with his full ability, but enough to make it look good. Sufficient to keep them from realizing he was shamming.

He was beaten down, held arm and leg, and carried into the penthouse, to a room that was long and rather shoddily furnished, but warm from a blaze leaping in a fireplace at one end.

Nearly a dozen men were present. Doc studied them, decided most of them were strangers to him, and none of them important other than they fell into the general classification of the enemy. There were two exceptions.

The wizened little man stood there, an unlovely grin on his strange and rather mystical face.

"Danny Dimer," Doc Savage said dryly. "You operate a flying circus which does advertising and stunts for the common garden or three-ring variety of circus."

Dimer showed his teeth. "If I could have gotten to you in New York, I would have been spared this meeting."

"You might have, at that," Doc agreed. "Not knowing your mysterious method of murder, I would have been lucky to escape."

Dimer said, "So you've figured everything out?"

"Not everything."

"He hasn't," interrupted the long-armed man, "figured out how he's going to get out of this mess."

Doc studied the long-armed man. "You are Elmo Handy Anderson."

"So you figured I wasn't Brockman?"

"Yes. You were Brockman's assistant. Brockman is a scientist and inventor. When he perfected the thing you wanted, you stole it from him."

Handy Anderson scowled. "How'd you figure that?"

"Brockman was worried when we found him in Kirksville," Doc said. "He already suspected you. He escaped from us and went to your cabin—probably to confront you with the truth."

Handy Anderson's anger showed how close to truth the guessing must have come. He got up swearing, yelling, "Half of you guys scatter! Get out and find how many guys this bronze devil brought with him."

"I was alone."

Anderson scowled at Doc. "I'll bet."

"I stowed away in the plane." Doc explained the exact location of the plane on the Missouri River.

Anderson was unconvinced. "Look this place over," he ordered. "Give those elevator operators hell. They're getting a hundred a week not to let something like this happen."

At this point, another man entered. He had a bundle of newspapers under an arm. He stopped and stared at Doc in astonishment.

"Well, well—snap out of it!" Anderson rapped impatiently. "What do the newspapers say?"

The man handed over the newspapers.

"The schedule of the prince has been decided upon," he said. "He will register at a hotel, attend a banquet, and be at the Automobile Show."

Anderson said, "That's good. Just so we know where he'll be."

A man looked puzzled and asked, "Is this prince—"

"He's the next victim in an instantaneous murder," Anderson said grimly.

DOC SAVAGE craned his neck, got a look at the newspaper and identified the prince referred to. He could have made an accurate guess, anyway. Front pages of late had been devoted almost entirely to that prince.

Doc didn't approve of the prince's visit. The prince himself was probably a nice-enough guy; at least, he was patriotic enough to be making this American tour.

He was Prince Axel Gustav something-or-other of a neutral nation in war-torn Europe, a little dab of a country that was about to be gobbled up by the wolves. Prince Axel was making a "good will" tour of the United States. That shouldn't have fooled anybody for a minute, really. What Prince Axel Gustav something-or-other was doing was capitalizing on the well-known fact that the Yankee public is generally a pushover for the royalty racket. The Rumanians had worked it back in the 1920s, the English had worked it in 1939, and now Axel was trying it.

Putting it over, too. The newspapers and newsreels were giving him a lot of notice. True, as the royal purple went, he was small fry. But he was a nice, photogenic kind of a guy with a big grin and a good brand of English that was almost Yankee. His publicity men had dug up some gags for Prince Axel to use, so he was a wow.

The real idea, of course, was to dupe your Uncle Sam and make him the goat by getting him to intervene in the coming crisis in which Axel's country was fairly certain, unless Uncle interfered, to get gobbled up.

The fact that Prince Axel's country had been manufacturing cannon and guns and shells by the shipload and selling them to the enemy of the nation that was about to do the gobbling—well, that might have had something to do with it. But Axel was careful not to mention it.

Doc Savage watched Handy Anderson and Danny Dimer.

The pair were looking at each other, and getting excited while they were doing it. They were like two cats visioning a mental mouse, and licking their chops.

A man picked up the newspaper, examined it, said, "It says here the police have nothing new on the murder of Banker Ellery P. Dimer."

Danny Dimer swore cheerfully. "That banker was my half brother, and a fool. He had a name of being a right guy in the circus business, so I figured he would be glad to finance us on this scheme. Hell—he knew too much before I found out he wouldn't touch it. So we had to put him away."

Danny Dimer said, "Nice combination, too. We had to kill him, but he was also prominent enough to give us the kind of a front-page murder we wanted."

"Like the governor, eh?" said the man with the newspaper.

It was Handy Anderson who swore this time. "That damned governor got me a stretch in the penitentiary while he was prosecuting attorney. That was years ago, before he got to be governor. I swore I'd pay him off."

A man was tying Doc Savage's ankles, doing a slow but painstaking job, while two more stood by with sawed-off shotguns leveled.

The bronze man fitted together what he had been hearing. Murder of the governor, murder of Banker Dimer—those crimes had been for a double motive. In the banker's case: silencing and publicity. In the governor's instance: revenge and publicity… Publicity!

They had been killing, it appeared, for publicity —which was a motive as incredible and hideous as the murders themselves.

THE behavior of Anderson and Dimer was peculiar. The two were staring at each other again, and smirking with increasing pleasure. At last, Anderson burst out in cackling mirth.

"Ten million," he chortled.

"Should be that much," Dimer agreed, and rubbed his hands together.

"We may be able to raise the ante."

"We can try."

Doc Savage watched them. He had guessed at a great deal about this affair; much of the surmising had proven correct. But one thing still puzzled him—the motive behind it.

Dimer got up and walked around the room excitedly, his evil little face warped with greed. "The killing of this prince should be enough for us to move into Europe," he said. "The thing will get worldwide publicity. It alone may be enough to fix things so we can make the deal."

Anderson nodded.

"First, we'll go to Washington," he said, "and approach the diplomats of nations on both sides in the war. We'll put our proposition before them, and make the deal with the highest bidder."

Dimer kept pacing. "Swell, swell."

"I think we can get more than ten," Anderson continued. "Why, hell, if we walk in and kill off the leaders and main guys on one side of the war, that'll end the thing, won't it? The other side should pay up—well—hell, the ceiling is the limit."

The man tying Doc Savage said, "This bronze guy is listening to you."

"Fat lot of good it'll do him," Dimer said.

Anderson suddenly leveled an arm at Doc and roared gleefully, "We'll knock him off like the prince. Make some more good publicity for our system."

Doc Savage was grimly silent. He understood the rest of it now. Murder to advertise! That was what they had been doing. A governor, a prominent banker, had been killed to publicize an unusual and incredible method of murder.

And once this murder method was built up, once the world was convinced these men had an incredible and unfailing way of inflicting death, they were going to approach one side of the warring coalition in Europe and try to get themselves hired to kill the leaders of the other side!

The bronze man must have looked utterly amazed, because Danny Dimer laughed at him.

"Something new under the sun, eh?" Dimer said.

The part of the gang that had been in Kirksville arrived a moment later. Burdo Brockman was with them, a prisoner. They were disheveled; two of them were slightly cut about the face and hands.

"What happened?" Anderson asked sharply.

"Ah, dammit, we had an automobile accident," a man explained. "Some lamebrain ran into us. Crossbow, here, got banged over the head by the guy who ran into us. An ambulance came and got Crossbow and started off with him to a hospital, but Crossbow got out again."

The man referred to as "Crossbow" was the cross-eyed fellow who had appeared at the burning strawstack near Kirksville, the man whom Monk and the others had mistaken for a local citizen.

Crossbow was excited. He had something else on his mind.

"I didn't tell you guys," he barked, "but coming up here, I saw those four Doc Savage helpers and the girl."

Dimer made gurgling noises, howled, "Where?"

"In front. Watching this building."

"Can we grab them?" Dimer yelled.

Crossbow wore a bandage over one eye, but his other orb glittered with enthusiasm.

"I don't see why not," he said.

Chapter XVIII
TROUBLE FOR HAM

DIMER howled, charged out of the penthouse, and was trailed by all the gang but four. This quartet, armed with shotguns, remained behind with Anderson to guard Doc Savage and Burdo Brockman.

Brockman was slammed down on the floor beside the bronze man.

Brockman said, "I made one hell of a mistake. In Kirksville, I should have told you the whole story. Instead, I thought I could settle it all myself."

"You already suspected Anderson, here, had stolen the stuff?" Doc asked.

"Yes." Brockman nodded. "I went after him, thinking I would get it back. I didn't know he had a gang."

Brockman was bound hand and foot. Doc's wrists were also tied by now. He tested the lines, but not even his strength would budge them.

Brockman groaned. "I've always been a fool. Like to go off by myself and work in my experimental lab." He glanced at Doc ruefully. "Being rich gets to be a devil of a bore. I've been slipping away. Rigged it so my family would think I was in India, big-game hunting. Love my family, and all that. But they bore me. Kids are grown. My wife gone all the time chasing around in society." He groaned again. "But everything would have been all right if Handy Anderson hadn't been a crook."

He fell silent and scowled gloomily.

The gang which had gone after Doc's men—it seemed impossible that they could have accomplished their purpose so soon—returned, howling gleefully over their success.

Monk, Renny, Johnny and Lion Ellison were marched in, hands above their heads.

Monk glanced at Doc, said sadly, "The crooks! They sneaked up on us. Couldn't have managed it if it hadn't been so cold. Heater in our car must have had us dopey, or something."

Anderson scowled. "Where's the other one?"

Dimer looked uneasy. "The fancy-dressing one, you mean? Ham Brooks, or whatever his name is. He wasn't with them."

Anderson came over and slugged Monk demanding, "Where is this Ham?"

"I don't know," Monk said angrily.

The cross-eyed man, Crossbow, stood back and smirked and looked proud of himself.

"Remember, it was me that got 'em caught," he reminded.

"We won't forget that," Dimer told him. He wheeled to Anderson, said, "We're fools to let 'em stay alive. Thing to do is get rid of them now."

Anderson nodded quickly. "You bet."

"What about having their dead bodies appear all of a sudden in—well—how would the police station strike you?"

Anderson licked his lips. "O.K."

Dimer said, "I'll get the stuff. Rest of you wait here."

He went out of the room.

Doc Savage said, "It seems to be now or never."

The man called Crossbow sidled around until he was clear of the others and facing them. He had picked up a sawed-off shotgun. He lifted this weapon, swept the group with its menace.

"Everything better be slow motion," he said.

Crossbow, it seemed, was Ham.

THE silence felt as if it was ready to split.

Burdo Brockman broke it, asking, "But how did this man—"

Monk said, "Ham took the place of the real Crossbow. We staged that automobile accident they mentioned. A friend of Doc's named Bill Larner helped us. Doc gave us the idea over the radio. Seems he had noticed Crossbow and Ham were the same build. Only difference was Crossbow's crossed eyes. So we fixed that with a bandage."

Doc said, "Throw me a knife, Ham."

The knife landed at the bronze man's feet. He got it, cut himself free and heaved erect. He loosened Monk and the others.

"I will go after Dimer," the bronze man said.

Dimer had gone into another part of the penthouse, Doc surmised. The bronze man moved in that direction, walking lightly and using his ears.

He found Dimer on his knees in front of a large and obviously new steel safe. The man had opened the safe, and had taken a cardboard box therefrom, placed it on the floor in front of him and was removing cotton packing carefully.

Doc went silently for him.

The thing might have ended there, except for the yell and the blasting reports of a repeating shotgun that came from the room where Doc had left the others.

Dimer whirled, saw Doc, clawed a gun out of his clothing. He was like a scared dog; he went over on his back, arms and legs flying about, as he tried to get the gun in action. Doc fell on him. Dimer had luck, and kicked the bronze man in the face. It hurt. Pain blinded Doc momentarily. Dimer fired. Missed. Doc got hold of the gun arm and there was a dull breaking sound and Dimer began shrieking in agony. The shrieking stopped when Doc stroked the man's jaw with a fist.

Doc leaped up, hesitated. There was plenty of fight noise from the other part of the penthouse, but no more shooting.

Turning to the safe, the bronze man searched.

There were about two dozen gas masks of an ingenious type. They were of rubber so thin that it was transparent, and they pulled entirely over the head. The respirator portion of the masks was a chemical filter not much larger than a pocket watch. As masks, they were probably more ingenious than efficient; but at least they would function for five or ten minutes.

The gas masks had another ingenious feature. They folded into little packets which were mounted on adhesive tape, so that they could be stuck to the skin anywhere under the clothing, preferably in a spot where they were not likely to be found in a search.

The second item in the safe was the score or more of cardboard boxes. Each of these—Doc guessed that, after opening two—held a goodsized bottle of particularly villainous-looking liquid.

Doc put on one of the masks.

He took a bottle of the liquid and went back to the fight.

EVIDENTLY Monk and the others had collected all the shotguns but one and thrown them out of the window before the fight started, only to have the last man endeavor to make a break when they sought to disarm him. That accounted for the absence of firearms in the fray.

It was a complete battle. Chairs, pictures, table legs, vases and other knicknacks were in the air. Renny was in a corner, flailing furiously with his enormous fists. Ham was down. A man was choking Lion Ellison, but not very successfully, for she had her thumbs in his eyes. Johnny had wrapped his elongated self around two opponents.

Doc uncorked the bottle and threw the entire contents out into the air of the room.

Results were almost instantaneous, and peculiar.

Monk had torn himself free of an opponent, knocked the man down. Monk remained with his fist cocked.

As if through uncanny magic, all action ceased. Johnny kept his long arms and legs wrapped around his two foes, and they made no effort to free themselves. The girl and her assailant froze exactly as they were.

No one, friend or foe, seemed to have the least realization of what was going on, or have any emotion left, neither hate nor rage nor fear.

Doc Savage watched curiously. The effects, he decided, were about as he had thought they would be. But his guessing had been only of a general nature.

It was the perfect anaesthetic. That much, he knew. Science had sought this thing for generations, and doctors had hinted it would be one of the great contributions of all time.

The perfect anaesthetic. Odorless, colorless, producing an instant state of insensibility, with no sensation whatever. No pain, no nausea afterward—not even a consciousness that the patient had entered an anaesthetized condition.

A gas which doctors could use with such smooth effects that the patients would not even know when they had been gassed.

A boon to surgery. And a sinister weapon in the hands of crooks.

Doc walked over to Johnny, said loudly, "Let them go! Take your hands off them."

Johnny made a very slight move toward releasing the two men whom he had been fighting.

"Let them go," Doc repeated loudly, and this time he took hold of Johnny's arms and untwined them from their victims.

Johnny obeyed the command, very slowly, and without anything approaching mental understanding. He did not know what was happening, would not remember afterward, so that this interval would be a complete blank in his mind.

But the period of Johnny's unconsciousness would be more than a blank. It would be a gap of which he was not aware. Awakening, he would not realize he had been gassed, would have no suspicion that he had stood for minutes with no awareness of what went on about him or what happened to him. The anaesthetic was undoubtedly odorless and colorless; its effects seized upon the victim instantaneously, without even the sensations of becoming sleepy.

This stuff accounted for the weird murders. It explained how the wizened little man—Danny Dimer—had escaped from the basement garage vault in the New York skyscraper—he had simply had some of the anaesthetic concealed on his person where Monk and Renny had failed to find it when they searched. Dimer had ejected some of the anaesthetic from the vault, possibly through the ventilator in the door so that Monk and Renny had been gassed. The vault door had not been locked at the time, and Dimer had experienced no trouble in walking out.

This gas accounted for all the mysterious murders.

In the case of Banker Ellery P. Dimer—and the photographer Don Meek, for that matter—the anaesthetic had simply been used to stop the mental processes of a roomful of people while the murderer, wearing a gas mask, walked in and committed the crime.

The ideal anaesthetic, undeniably.

Doc opened the windows wide, letting the cold wind roar inside; carrying hard particles of snow, and sweeping the gas out of the place.

He got ropes, tied the prisoners. Then he waited… He had no idea how long the effects of the gas lasted. Only a few moments, probably, unless the stuff was administered repeatedly, in which case the victim probably could be kept under its effects for days. Lion Ellison had been certain she had been out for at least two days—and it was fairly certain they had kept her under the effects of the anaesthetic long enough to take her to Jefferson City, where the governor was murdered, and the anaesthetized girl placed in posed photographs, so that she could be framed with the murder. Evidently it was then that her fingerprints had been planted, and the knife placed in her purse, as well. Later, she had been taken back to Kirksville and permitted to revive in the same spot where they had gassed her.

Monk seemed a little confused when he awakened.

He peered at the man he had hit just as the anaesthetic got him. The man was now tied hand and foot. Monk looked at his own fist.

"When I hit 'em," he muttered, "I sure wrap 'em up.

PRINCE AXEL GUSTAV something-or-other went back to Europe and his country wasn't invaded because the American government sent some very threatening notes, so Axel's tour landed under the heading of a great success.

But long before that happened, Doc Savage's unique criminal curing "college" in upstate New York got a fresh batch of patients which included Dimer and Anderson and their associates.

And Burdo Brockman had made a decision. "I can change their anaesthetic formula," he said. "I can do it. I'll use one different chemical, and that will give it an odor and anybody who takes the stuff will certainly know they've been gassed. We'll destroy all the present gas."

"You won't make as much money out of it," Renny reminded him.

Burdo Brockman grinned. "What the hell—I've got plenty of money."

And there was another development—Ham had made an unpleasant discovery.

One frosty morning, Ham came tearing into the New York headquarters. He glared at Monk. "You lop-eared missing link," he shouted.

"Me?" Monk looked innocent.

Ham turned purple and whirled on the others. "You know what?" he yelled. "Monk stole some of that anaesthetic before it was destroyed. And he's using it on me. Tonight I was making a speech to a group of eminent lawyers. And all of a sudden I was standing on the platform in nothing but my shirt tail." He shook his fist under the homley Monk's nose. "And I know who was responsible!"

"Have you ever heard of Lydia Pinkham?" Monk asked mildly.

"Why?"

"You remind me somewhat," said Monk, "of one of her pills."

Big-fisted Renny sighed deeply. "Things seem to be back to normal," he said.

THE END

PULPSMITH by Will Murray

Lester Dent (1904-1959) was an accidental writer. He had been a horse wrangler, cowboy, sheepherder, trapper, oilfield pipeline roustabout, stenographer and telegrapher before embarking upon his true career. Dent was punching a Mux Telegraph-typewriter on the "Hoot Owl" trick in the *Tulsa World*'s wire room when the writing bug first bit him:

> One afternoon I went in the office early, about 2 o'clock, and there was one of the other operators at his typewriter. I knew he never came to work early and I said, "What are you doing here?" And he said, "I'm writing a story." I laughed and laughed—I just laughed a rib out! Gosh, that was funny to me! And then he flashed a check for $450 he'd just got for a story, and I said, "My God, how long has this been going on?" Then I grabbed a sheet of paper and started writing a story too—
>
> I wrote 13 of them, and three of them were books. Everybody thought I was crazy. A writer, you know, he's just a sort of crackpot. All my friends just laughed. And my wife would get some of my love scenes and read them out loud to me, and just laugh and laugh and laugh—
>
> And then, by golly, one day here's a check for $250, and I just took it over to the bulletin board and stuck it up with a thumbtack for everyone to see. They all looked at it—and before the end of the week, they were all taking lessons from me on how to be a writer.

The pulp magazine powerhouse Street & Smith took Dent's first professional story. "Pirate Cay" appeared in *Top-Notch Magazine,* September 1929. Other sales followed. Evenings and weekends and holidays, Dent pounded his typewriter with a seemingly inexhaustible energy. Not everything he wrote sold, but most stories did.

Lester Dent had become a professional writer. With characteristically irreverent humor, he boasted that he had "suddenly discovered it was an easy racket for any nitwit who wants an easy living."

Dent had only been selling a few months when the Stock Market crashed in October of 1929. The pulp boom spawned by the Roaring Twenties was over. Rates collapsed. Magazines folded. Rejection slips piled up. Street & Smith stopped buying his stories.

Times were bleak. It was hard sledding for the tyro pulpster.

"This writing is an etheric racket, especially when you're on the outside," Dent recounted. "Nothing is quite as sickening as getting story after story back and wondering 'why?' It takes things out of you. It sort of curls you up. There is nothing concrete to grasp and go to work against. You cannot stand back and look at your completed work as a carpenter can examine the house he is constructing, strangely enough. And when one editor says the figurative roof of your story is too flat, and the next says it is not flat enough, you begin to think yourself dizzy."

One day in 1930 he finished an air-action yarn entitled "Hell Hop." Dent showed it to a colleague, who suggested that he burn it. Instead, Dent mailed it to Dell's *Sky Riders.*

Editor Richard Martinsen accepted the story and offered Dent a job in New York City as a Dell contract writer.

"But I thought he was nuts," Dent admitted. "I'm still not sure—"

Moving to New York, Lester learned to write fiction according to pulp formulas. He once claimed he pounded out his earliest tales "through brute strength and awkwardness," but over time he applied himself seriously to the craft of writing. He developed his Pulp Paper Masterplot, a blueprint for writing action yarns in all genres.

Dent summarized this blueprint in a talk:

> In the first line, walk your hero in, then reach in a pail of grief and take a good handful and swat him with it. He squares off and fights back. For the second part, pile on more grief, and bring in some struggle and physical conflict. For the third part, do the same thing some more. For the fourth part, do the same thing some more, until he doesn't have a chance—
>
> Now you've reached the place where, in the old melodramas, the hero is tied in a shack on a hill, and around the track the train is coming—Whoo! Whoo! Whoo!
>
> Then the hero has got to extricate himself through his own ingenuity—it can't be by an act of God. Don't have lightning strike the shack for instance. He's got to do it himself.

When it was published in *The 1936 Writer's Year Book* the Masterplot brought in sacks of mail from beginners seasoned and veterans alike, all of whom praised it for helping them sell more pulp stories.

"And that," Lester later complained, "was the most awful thing I ever did. I got 780 letters from fellows who said they tried my formula and sold their first story—and that was building up a hell of a lot of competition for myself!"

While the Dell experience also ran afoul of the economic realities of the Great Depression, soon Street & Smith reached out to Lester Dent to help realize their new pulp superman, Doc Savage.

"I didn't realize how many people wanted to be supermen," Dent later confessed. "It's more clear to me now. A man comes in from driving a taxi all day to find his wife threatening to throw him out on his ear for not bringing home more tips to turn over to her. Naturally, he wants to be a Superman. Or a barber who had to vegetate in his shop all day, don't you reckon he yearns for a chance to go out and re-order the life of whole continents? Doc is the what-I-would-like-to-be dream of everybody, including me.

"But I really enjoy doing Doc, superman tripe though it is. I like scientific gadgets, and so Doc used them. He invented new ones, several of which were actually perfected by scientists and put in use. I like adventure and Doc is an adventurer. Doc is a big man and so am I—6 feet 2 and 215 pounds."

The glamour wore off soon enough. In 1934, Dent told an aspiring writer:

> From the outside looking in, writing has glamorous promise as a career. Inside looking out, it becomes another job, something to hack away at day after day. It would be deceit indeed to claim that the business of grinding out blood and thunder has no attractions, for otherwise I would not be in it. I like it. I am making more than I ever made at anything else. I live, eat and sleep pulp fiction.
>
> On the other hand, I work harder at it than I ever worked at anything else. There have been times when I wondered if I would ever make another dollar writing, and when I looked with avidity at … ditch diggers. They, at least, weren't getting gray trying to think up new ways to kill people on paper.

Doc Savage's sheer popularity inspired many imitators, but none possessed the spark of near genius with which Lester Dent imbued the character's adventures. Dent always scoffed at such praise. And he refused to take himself seriously.

Billy G. Smith was a young Missouri Doc fan when Dent visited La Plata in 1936:

> Mr. Dent was asked to address the high school on "How to Write Fiction Novels." I could scarcely contain myself! The secrets of how to write Doc Savage stories! I was about to be disillusioned!
>
> His formula for adventure yarns, and here I think I can recall his exact words, was "give your hero plenty of grief. When the reader thinks the sun is about to shine, hit your hero with another bucketful of trouble."

Fellow pulp writer Mort Weisinger once related: "Lester Dent, alias Doc Savage, says that the secret of filling up the entire issue of his magazine is 'to get someone in a tight predicament and then let Doc Savage, the hero, do his stuff.'"

John Yauk, a Missouri teenager who spent a week on Dent's boat off Florida in 1936, recalled:

> He wrote so damn much I never could figure out where all the words came from. A prolific writer, you know.
>
> One time I asked him, "Where do you get all of your ideas for all these weird stories that you write?"
>
> "Well, it's just a cultivated sort of a thing. There's nothing inspired about it. You just start making up things." First, he'd make up a situation, you know. There's a man on top New York's Empire State Building, we'll say. And you go on thinking from there. How did he get up there? Well, he landed in a balloon. What was the balloon doing up there? Well, the balloon was this. You just go on from there. And finally you wind up with a story.

Dent sometimes reduced the Doc Savage formula to the simplistic need to embroil the Man of Bronze in "a hellofafix."

Dent's writing schedule was to rise at 11 AMand work until 4 PM. During this break, he read the newspapers, took a walk or a napped for an hour. The evening stint would last to 3 or 4 AM. This was a five day a week routine.

He once produced 32,000 words in a single day on his dictaphone; 24,000 on a typewriter. An entire 45,000 word Dent pulp novel was created in a night, a day and part of a night—a total of 45,000 words.

A nervous writer, Dent invariably wrote with a pipe clenched tightly in his teeth. He did not smoke it. He chewed. Dent habitually chewed through a stem a day, and he was perpetually searching for the strongest pipe stems he could find. Although he bought them by the gross, he never found one tough enough to resist his teeth.

Dent had another habit. As he pounded the typewriter keys, he stomped the floor with one foot, as if rhythmically working a treadle. Over years of this, the 215-pound writer actually pounded a hole in the pine floorboards of his Missouri writing den.

Is it any wonder that Lester once told his wife never to ask about what went on behind the closed door of his writing room?

Like The Shadow's Walter Gibson, he learned to quit work in the middle of a sentence. This made it easier to pick up the writing flow again.

Dent had one other idiosyncrasy. Mrs. Dent recalled a pulp editor telling her that he would never send a Dent story back for revision. Lester would instead submit a fresh story in its place. He hated revising.

When a new *Doc Savage* editor asked him to write Doc Savage more realistically, emphasizing an atmosphere of fear, Dent replied: "Fear is a mood. I do Doc best—it's easier to keep from going nuts, too—when I gallop through it as if on a picnic, a mood which makes it hard to get fearsome, but makes swell entertainment."

A fiercely ambitious man, Dent often insisted that his writing career was primarily motivated by greed.

Asked by a reporter if he had any unrealized literary ambitions, Dent growled: "One million of them, all made of silver, called dollars, and in banks, preferably several banks."

At one point, Dent took on a pen name for the purpose of selling his rejects to downriver markets—H. O. Cash. The "H" stood for "Hard."

"The sole purpose of fiction, as I see it," he once wrote, "is to put something into the pocket of the fellow who writes it. As a secondary, but rather necessary evil, it must variously amuse, entertain, horrify, instruct, or sicken whoever pays out his hard, round dollars for the privilege of reading it."

Lester Dent in Jefferson City, MO.

Knowing that Dent had only one compelling interest, "to garner in the silvery sheaves," one of his Tulsa cronies suggested that Lester set his sights higher than the easy money of the pulps, adding, "But dern you, you want to confuse literature with banking!"

Tongue firmly in cheek, Dent once counseled aspiring pulp writers on how to break into the field:

> If you're under-sexed and inhibited, start with confession stories. If you're two-fisted and like to bust around, try adventure.
>
> Read the magazine you're going to write for. Get it and read it for years back, and find out just what it uses. Then get a copy that is just out, and pick out the story in it you like best, and write one exactly like it. Just change it enough so you don't get caught. Change the names, and change the place, but don't change it any more than you have to—
>
> Sell one story and you're set for life. Don't get excited and try to do a different one. When you've found one that will sell, just keep on writing it and selling it.
>
> Don't worry about titles. You can get get titles out of Shakespeare. Any page of Shakespeare will give you a dozen titles. But concentrate on plot: never have your hero do anything that you wouldn't like to do yourself.
>
> The way to get ideas to be a writer, is to steal everything in sight. There is no such thing as inspiration.

Dent planned to stay in the pulps for only six years, then move on to the slick magazines, which paid better. Although he wrote dozens, he actually sold only two slick stories late in his career. But he was proudest of his Oscar Sail stories, which appeared in *Black Mask* during the waning days of Joseph T. Shaw's legendary editorial stint:

> My tenure with Cap Shaw was short. I sold him, I think, only three pieces. Then he gave up the helmsmanship of *Black Mask* over a policy dispute, which, I am convinced, is what kept me from becoming a fine writer. Had I been exposed to the man's cunning hand for another year or two, I could not have missed. Cap did try to work with me and guide me after he left *Black Mask,* and became an agent. But in those days I was fiesty and greedy, and also Joe no longer had the money-apple to dangle in front of me—a sale to *Black Mask*. Instead I wrote reams of saleable crap which became my pattern, and gradually there slipped away that bit of power with words that Shaw had started awakening in me.

The continued popularity of Doc Savage almost 50 years after the passing of Lester Dent shows how very wrong a writer can be about his own work. •